# The Fifth Commandment

By

Don Bozeman

# The Weiss Saga

**Honor thy father and thy mother that thy days may be long upon the land that the Lord thy God giveth thee**

*Exodus: 20: 12*

To the Fallen of Ploesti

   To you who fly on forever I send that part of me which cannot be separated and is bound to you for all time. I send to you those of our hopes and dreams that never quite came true, the joyous laughter and showery tears of our boyhood, the marvelous mysteries of our adolescence, the glorious strength and tragic illusions of our young manhood, all these that were and perhaps would have been, I leave in your care, out there in the Blue.


   John Riley Kane, Colonel, U.S.A.F. (Ret) – Medal of Honor Recipient

# **<u>Dedication</u>**

To those American heroes who flew
into the hell

of Ploesti on August 1, 1943

# Prologue

David Weiss sat in the shade at the far end of his picnic table. It was early morning, but the sun was already beating down. A large sycamore that he had planted twenty years ago, when he and Ruth moved back to Maryland, offered shade to that corner of the garden. He glanced up at the sound of a creaking gate, its rusty hinges announcing the arrival of Ben Jacobs the neighborhood mailman. David welcomed the interruption. He had been attacking the weeds in his garden since seven-thirty, after finishing his coffee and putting down the *Baltimore Sun.* Beads of sweat still dripped off his face, making soft splats as they hit the newspaper.

"How you doin' this mornin' Colonel? It looks like we're in for another scorcher today."

\*\*\*\*

Ben had been their mail carrier since David and Ruth moved to Frederick in 1975. After 35 years, three wars, and untold diplomatic postings, Colonel David Benjamin Weiss had earned his retirement. They settled here in western Maryland to be near his family in Baltimore and hers in Silver Spring. They liked the open countryside and the unimpeded views of the

Catoctin Mountains to the west. They chose the spacious, two-story cottage on Rockwell Avenue for its location and the expansive, hedge enclosed garden. It was a comfortable walk to the small park nearby where they could feed the ducks on Culler Lake. David had taken a position at nearby Hood College where he taught political and military science and Ruth, who earned two degrees in nursing during David's frequent postings in Washington, became a lecturer there.

Now, ravenous beltway-bandits, feeding the insatiable appetite of the federal government, had exploded up the I-270 corridor, engulfing one small village after another. Now with the children scattered to the four winds, he and Ruth had considered moving. They certainly didn't need the large house anymore. But the twenty plus years they lived there had created a bond that he could not bring himself to sever—this was their home, they would not leave it.

****

"It sure does, Ben. It seems like we haven't had any rain in a blue moon. We're bound to get some thunderstorms soon, what with all this heat and humidity. You know Maryland summers. You got anything for me today?"

"The usual, Colonel, some catalogs and some junk mail."

Ben thumbed through the stack of mail in his hand.

"It looks like there's a letter from your brother's wife down in Florida. How's she doing since Bernie died?"

"You know Ben, we're all getting along in years. Bernie was ten years older than me and Murray. We were a late surprise to our parents. I pray Marie will be all right, but I fear Bernie's death may be too much for her."

David's words trailed off as his thoughts harkened back to a time when they were all so young, and strong and full of life; a time when all their hopes and dreams ran before them, a time when they felt limitless and indestructible. That was so long ago yet it seemed as close and as real as yesterday. He looked up as Ben dropped the stack of mail on the table and began to walk away.

"Sorry Ben, I kinda got lost there for a second, thinking about Bernie and Marie and Murray and a time when life was simpler; when we were all so innocent."

"I sho' do understand Colonel. I catch myself doing that a lot more myself lately. Well, the next time you write to Marie tell her I asked about her. You take care of yourself and don't go gittin' no heat stroke out here in this broilin' sun."

"Thank you, Ben. I know Marie will appreciate that. And thanks for bringing the mail in. You take care out there."

David watched as Ben adjusted the leather straps on his bag and pulled a red bandana from his pocket. He pushed the garden gate open, wiping the perspiration from his face as he trudged up the sidewalk.

"Yeah, it's going to be another scorcher in western Maryland today," David said to himself.

He stood to move further into the shade as the sun encroached on his corner. He dropped the other mail on the table while holding Marie's letter up to the sun. Her quaintly precise script acknowledged the sender well before he read the return address. She and Bernie had been so faithful during the time when he was missing and when they didn't know whether he was dead or alive. All the War Department telegram had said was ... "missing in action over enemy territory."

As he sat down, he slid a nail under the flap of the envelope and removed the contents. A single sheet of yellowed, onionskin stationery fluttered to the table. Glancing down he could see the letter was in another hand and obviously written a long time ago. Puzzled, he returned to Marie's letter.

*"Dear David,*

*I was sorting through Bernie's correspondence, trying to get things in some kind of order, when I ran across this letter from Murray. I had completely forgotten about it, but since it concerns you I thought you might want to have it—something to pass on to your children and grandchildren. They'll be as proud of you as we were. It doesn't seem possible that fifty years have come and gone since then."*

The remainder of the letter was a thinly veiled attempt on Marie's part to mask her loneliness and the great void in her life created by Bernie's death. She closed with her usual invitation for him to visit her in Florida.

David leaned his elbows on the table as he reflected on the old days growing up in Baltimore's ethnic neighborhoods. Now, gone forever are the close-knit, multi-generational families that made East Baltimore their home then. Families like his, which had migrated to the more affluent suburbs, struggled to maintain their old ways. Time, ambition, progress had relegated that life to fading photo albums and the failing memories of a dying generation. David took a long drink from his glass of water and picked up the tattered yellow letter. He recognized the faded handwriting of his twin brother Murray. It was dated October 10, 1943.

*Dear Bernie,*

*I wanted to let you know as soon as possible that David is all right. He was evacuated from Yugoslavia with a group of other downed airmen. Ever since he was shot down he's been moving around with a band of Yugoslav partisans. The army arranged to have a C-60 troop plane fly in under cover of darkness and whisk those boys right out of there. As fate would have it, they brought him back here to our base in Bari, Italy. The first I knew he was safe was when I heard a page over the PA system— "Flight Officer Weiss, you have a visitor." Man, was I surprised. I walked into the orderly room and there stood David. You'll be relieved to know that he is hale and hearty and not much worse off physically from his ordeal. I'm letting you know first so you can break the news to Mama. I know how worried she's been, not knowing if she'd ever see David again. Call her as soon as you get this. I know she'll be as relieved as I was to know that David is okay.*

*Love,*

*Murray*

David's tears traced rivulets of white through the grime on his face. Memories he had suppressed for so long, memories buried under the layers of the intervening years, came rushing back—memories of college, courtship, marriage, children, careers, the death of his parents, and now Bernie. The letter opened the floodgates. His resolve, so carefully preserved over the years, began to crumble. The stoic and unyielding warrior surrendered to the images that came rushing to the surface. He had not even known of the letter's existence until this very moment.

He had tried to avoid dwelling too much on the past. There were too many bitter memories. Now, this letter, appearing like some yellowed apparition, beckoned him back, forcing him to revisit those critical moments in his life, those transforming events that sent him careening down paths often not of his own choosing, rendering him an observer of his own unfolding destiny. He could almost sense Bernie and his parents sitting there across the table, urging him to tell his story—their story. To tell it so that those who follow will know and recognize what he had done—what they all had done; and what an incredible story it was! How a skinny little Jewish kid named David Weiss from the rough streets of Baltimore, and a pretty, Irish redhead, were caught up in history's greatest struggle. He knew now that he had to give voice to that clash of good versus evil that he and Ruth had witnessed. It would give him, in some small way, an opportunity to honor the debt he owed to his family, his people, and to America. A chance also to stand for all those who had abandoned everything to come to America; a chance to honor all those they left behind.

Ruth, her vivid red hair now streaked with gray, came out to sit with him. She saw the tears and the letter. She picked it up and began to read. When she finished, her own tears mingled in the dust with David's.

"Oh, David," she said, "what a journey. So many don't recognize that the awful horror didn't end with Hitler's death in that Berlin bunker. What came after is too incredible for anyone who was not there to believe. The emotions of the time were too raw and the outrage too present to give voice to them. Now I think it's time for the world to know the entire, unbelievable story."

# BOOK ONE

## The Golden Door

# 1

# Crossing Over

It was raw and bitterly cold as the S.S. Wilhelm rounded Sparrows Point and took a northwesterly heading up the Patapsco River into Baltimore. The full force of the ice-flecked wind was directly in the passenger's faces, its crystalline needles stinging their eyes. They stood at the rail, unfazed, ignoring their discomfort, straining for that first glimpse of their new home. Soon, Fort Mc Henry loomed on the horizon, a dramatic beacon to the weary pilgrims arriving in Baltimore after weeks at sea. Suddenly, the enormous flag, with its red, white and blue symbolism fluttered into view. Whipped by the strong gusts of wind, it was as much a talisman to these exhausted travelers as the lady on Bedloe's Island in New York harbor. Emma Lazarus' **golden door** awaited them all.

The Wilhelm eased to port and slowed her engines as she entered the harbor. She submitted to the embrace of the harbor tugs chugging out to greet her, to gently nudge her into the Locust Point docks. As the giant ship edged sideways into her berth, eyes along the rail strained for familiar faces in the crowd on the dock, searching for loved ones not seen for years. Still others tried to resurrect mental images of once familiar faces, whose features were dimmed by space and time—images that had been sacrificed to the stark immediacy of survival in the *shtetls* of Eastern Europe. Still others along that rail faced the unknown alone. No familiar face would welcome them ashore. They were bolstered only by a deep inner faith and their unshakable belief in a righteous God. It had been a long and arduous twenty days since the Wilhelm pulled away from the dock in Bremen, Germany. Twelve hundred souls, gathered from the far corners of Eastern Europe, boarded her there. The passengers, mostly Jews, were fleeing the small villages and larger cities wedged in between Russia and Poland known as the "Pale of Settlement." The "Pale" was a region where most Jews were relegated during the many re-settlements and *pogroms* carried out by Czarist Russian regimes. From Vilna, Riga, Minsk and Kiev they came. It was 1910 and the Cossacks were again rampaging across the western regions of the Czarist Empire. From the Baltic to Odessa, and from Lodz to Rostov, a palpable fear filled the land. The entire "Pale" was in upheaval. The Cossacks, with the tacit approval of the Czar, were carrying out yet another in an unending cycle of *pogroms* against the Jews. Life for the persecuted was an unyielding succession of gray days and dark nights, filled with a relentless struggle for survival. The refugees ascending the Wilhelm's gangway in Bremen were just the latest in a swelling tide, joining the ranks of thousands of other immigrants flowing to America. They would add to a rapidly increasing Jewish population—one which stood at 3000 in 1810 but had risen to over 300,000 by 1910.

Jacob and Leah Weissgarten held back from the crush at the rail, not that they were any less anxious than the others for a glimpse of their new home. Leah was eight months pregnant and had been violently ill during the crossing. The ship's doctor had feared that she might lose the child. So the Weisses, of all the passengers that day, gave a special thanks to God for their safe delivery to their new home.

Still, with all the excitement of seeing America for the first time, there was an undercurrent of dread among the passengers. Most spoke little English. Russian was their official language in Belarus, however Yiddish was the *lingua franca* of their Jewish culture. Jacob and Leah had been studying English for the entire year prior to leaving Borisov, Belarus. Still, they were not comfortable with their grasp of the new language. That only served to increase Jacob's mounting anxiety and compounded his fears about finding work in Baltimore. He didn't want to impose on Leah's brother Seth and his wife Rachel any longer than necessary. For Jacob Weiss these last few minutes before the gangplank clanged into place were a jumble of bright anticipation and dark foreboding.

All the Weissgarten's worldly possessions lay several decks below, in the two small trunks they were allowed. Everything else was left behind in Borisov. The price of passage for more than two pieces of luggage was well beyond their means. Jacob told his oldest brother Levi to take what belongings they couldn't pack and to distribute it among his and Leah's brothers and sisters.

Jacob was informed only three weeks prior to their scheduled departure that embarkation had been moved up by ten days. The accelerated schedule turned out to be a blessing in disguise. It would get them to Baltimore ten days earlier, in case the baby came sooner, and it would also cut short the long, sad procession of farewells for the couple, especially for Rachel. Knowing that she was leaving her mother and sister was emotionally overwhelming. It pained her to think that neither would be present for the birth of her first child. They would not be there to help her or to share in the age-old traditions of their faith. The choice to leave Borisov for Baltimore was the hardest decision either had ever made, but it was a choice they had to make, not only for themselves but for their unborn child.

Leah's brother Seth Epstein and his wife Rachel had reached that same conclusion for their family three years earlier. Now they were jostling among the crowds on the dock, straining to make out the faces of Leah and Jacob in the throng scrambling down the gangplank. They were held back from the disembarkation area by a tall picket fence, topped by barbed wire. They could see the stream of humanity flowing off the ship but could not distinguish Jacob or Leah among the throng. Still, it was sufficient to know they were up there and would soon come through the gates to their life in a new world. It was comforting to know they were among that mass of people making their way through customs. The Weissgartens had arrived safely in Baltimore now, and that was all that mattered. These would be the first members of their family that they had seen in three years. Seth had sponsored the Weissgartens and obtained their visas for them. It would now fall to Jacob to sponsor other family members; to keep the chain unbroken.

Jacob was only twenty-five years old but had already apprenticed to a tailor near Minsk for five years, as Seth had done before him. Seth had been sponsored by a distant relative, Moses Isaac Berman, a men's clothier with a small shop on North Front Street. Baltimore had emerged as a hub for clothing manufacture and tailors were in great demand. Seth was convinced that Mr. Berman would have a place for Jacob.

Had Jacob understood the vast network of support awaiting him, he would have been less anxious. Over the past sixty years the Jewish community in Baltimore had created an extensive network of support institutions to assist the newly arriving émigrés. There were hospitals and hostels, orphanages, schools and banks with money available to assist those willing to start their own business. Moses Berman himself was the recipient of such a loan, one he had repaid years earlier. Unmatched by any other émigré ethnic group, the Jews were obsessed with "making it" in America. 5000 years of history taught the Jewish community that they could only rely on their own, so that meant building a bridge of opportunity for their newly arrived brethren.

****

That realization and feeling of community did not mean that all arriving Jews were created equal. There was a definite pecking order within the Jewish society of Baltimore. The old German families who began arriving in the early 1800s were nestled securely at the top of the social ladder. Most of those families had long since moved out of East Baltimore for the more affluent neighborhoods to the north and west of the city. Hard on their heels, fresh boatloads of Russian and Middle European Jews flooded into East Baltimore, assuming their position at the bottom of the social ladder. It was into this flux that Jacob and Leah Weissgarten would begin their life in America.

****

As the Wilhelm transited the Chesapeake from Norfolk to Baltimore, the passengers underwent the necessary preliminary medical examinations and quarantine. However, further examinations and lengthy customs interrogations awaited at Locust Point. The cavernous structure, housing immigration and customs offices, was erected with the cooperation of the North

German Lloyd shipping line, owners of the S.S. Wilhelm, whose return voyage to Bremen would exchange the 1,200 passengers with a cargo of tobacco and lumber, commodities in great demand in an expanding European economy.

When the exhausting process was finally over, the weary couple made their way to the baggage claim area where Jacob quickly retrieved the two trunks. He had been unwilling to part with any of his meager funds for a porter, so he dragged the trunks over to the exit and shoved them through, knowing that Seth would be on the other side to help him. Leah, shivering from the late afternoon chill, drew her heavy cotton shawl more tightly around her shoulders and followed Jacob through the exit.

# 2

# Arrival

To Leah, at that moment, no angel's face could have shone more brightly than Rachel's. There she was alongside Seth with two-year old Simon hiding shyly behind his father's legs. Rachel cradled a young baby in her arms, trying unsuccessfully to shield it from the howling winds. Ignoring her own bulging abdomen Leah ran to Rachel and embraced her while tears of joy streamed down her cheeks and mingled with the rain dampening the baby's blanket.

"Rachel, Rachel, I've never been so happy to see anyone in my life," Leah sobbed. "It seems like an eternity since we boarded the ship in Bremen. I was so sick on the crossing that I thought I might lose my baby. Thank God you and Seth are here."

"Leah, it's been so long since I've seen you or any of our family," Rachel said as she held the sobbing Leah at arm's length. "Let me just look at you. You have the bloom of motherhood on your face. Thank God you're all right."

The greeting between Seth and Jacob was a bit more subdued, as befitted two proper Jewish *mensches*. A hearty handshake followed by a clap on the back sufficed as the male counterparts of the women's tears and hugs.

"It's really good to see you Seth," Jacob said. "I hate to think what coming to America would be like if we didn't have someone here that we knew. I can't tell you how much we appreciate your obtaining visas for us and sponsoring us."

"It's the least we could do, Jacob. It means so much to Rachel and me to have you here, especially Rachel. She's been so busy with two babies she hasn't been able to make a lot of new friends."

Then Seth's tone turned more somber.

"Tell me Jacob, how are things back home?"

"They're not good. Every day there's a new tax or a new license requirement and as soon as those are met the government thinks of something else to make life more difficult. When we left there was a new *pogrom* underway. No one in your family or ours had been hurt so far, but it's only a matter of time. And, the Cossacks keep stirring up trouble in the villages. Most of the gentiles will no longer associate with Jews for fear of reprisals. It's not good."

"We'll have time to catch up on all this after we get back to the apartment," Seth said. "Meantime, we need to get the women and children out of the cold."

Seth hurried away to fetch the dray Mr. Berman had loaned him. The babbling voices of Leah and Rachel receded into the distance, drowned out by the howling winds and the din of the docks. In minutes he returned. He and Jacob hoisted the trunks onto the bed of the dray. They helped the women and Simon onto the makeshift benches while they climbed onto the seat behind the steaming flanks of the two horses.

Seth headed west from the dock as they left the immigration center. He followed the contours of the harbor until they were abreast of the steamship piers along Light Street. Ships linking Baltimore to the eastern shore of the Chesapeake and beyond were flying the flags of many famous lines: Baltimore and Philadelphia Steamboat, Potomac and Rappahannock Rivers, Baltimore Steam Packet Company — names and places completely foreign to these strangers from Belarus — and a world away in space and time.

Seth swung north along Light Street making his way carefully through the crowds streaming away from the docks. Light Street had been broadened into a major commercial thoroughfare following the devastating 1904 fire that destroyed 1,500 buildings and threw more than 35,000 people out of work. A few "horseless carriages" were parked in the median separating the north and south lanes. Both electric streetcar and rail tracks were set into the cobblestones of Light Street, combining for a teeth-shattering passage for wagons and carriages and their steel rimmed wheels. The crowds seemed more subdued here as the exhilaration of the docks gave way to the anxieties that lay ahead.

Their route of travel was accompanied by a wide assortment of conveyances carrying the disgorged passengers away from the docks; some to their new homes in Baltimore, yet others to the train station and far-flung destinations elsewhere across the sprawling continent.

Within minutes they felt the gradual incline as they crossed Pratt Street and the roadway began to rise toward the Baltimore heights. Almost immediately, Seth turned east onto Lombard Street. In a few blocks the street passed over Jones Falls, a fetid canal that drained the wastes of central Baltimore into the harbor. All manner of human waste floated under the bridge, the noxious odors wafting up to an already stifling stench at street level. Three blocks further Seth reined the horses to a stop in front of a three-story tenement.

The building boasted a brick façade with businesses on the ground floor and walk-up tenements above. There were shops of every description arrayed up and down Lombard; butchers, grocers, delicatessens, bakeries, tailors, haberdasheries, and cobblers; any establishment required to sustain Jewish life in Baltimore was found in that five-block area.

"We're on the third floor," Seth said. "I guess we'll have to lug these trunks up the two flights, Jacob. Shouldn't be a big problem. Rachel and I had to do it three years ago when we moved in."

The Weissgartens stared in amazement at the hectic street scene as it repeated itself up and down Lombard in both directions. The Epstein's apartment building was smack-dab in the middle of Baltimore's Jewish life. The signs above each storefront were in both English and Yiddish with a little Polish and Russian thrown in for good measure. The frenzied atmosphere was so alien to the quiet streets in Borisov that they sat staring in wide-eyed astonishment. It certainly didn't match the image they had invented in their minds. The vision of an Eden overflowing with milk and honey quickly evaporated. The horrible stench, a foul mix of horse manure, dried chicken blood, rotting vegetables and other unidentifiable smells, was overpowering.

"Seth does it always smell like this?" Leah asked. "It's just awful."

"I'm afraid it's something you'll just have to get used to, Leah, at least for a while. If it's like this in winter you can imagine what summer is like. It's not quite as bad up on the third floor. I pray that with Jacob's added income we'll soon be able to move further west to York or maybe Hanover Street. It's mostly residential over there and not quite so stinky. I'm doing pretty well at Berman's and I've been able to put away a few savings.

"I know it's all a little overwhelming right now, but the opportunities you'll have here are so much greater than you had back home. In a little while, with hard work and God's blessing, all this will fade away like a bad dream. That's why this neighborhood is called "the dream factory." There are Jews on the north side who were living in these same tenements ten years ago. Those people now live in mansions on Eutaw Place, belong to private clubs, and have chauffeured limousines. They are mostly the German Jews, but that's no reason to think that we can't make it too. They didn't have any more when they came here than we do."

"Come on," Jacob said as he jumped down from the wagon, "it's too cold out here for the children. We'll have plenty of time to talk after we get upstairs."

This world of tumult and smell surrounding them was disappointing for Jacob, but he knew that Seth was right. America, so far removed from the terror that was gripping Belarus, held such promise for freedom and opportunity that all this was a small price to pay.

The small walk-up flat on the third floor was in the back of the building. Even with the windows open, the smell from the back alleyway was not quite so overpowering. The apartment stared across at its dreary twin that was also swathed in soot and grime and with the same ramshackle wooden stairs leading down to the alley below. Clotheslines, laden with the day's laundry, already frozen in place, zigzagged back and forth across the alley. They swayed in the wind with their rusty pulleys and hinges complaining noisily at each gust of wind. The accompanying squeals and clanks echoed down the alleyway as dark forms darted in and out among the garbage cans below as yet another species was enjoying the bounty of the New World.

The men carried the trunks into the dimly lit parlor. Jacob's eyes slowly adjusted as the Spartan surroundings took shape. A hallway off the parlor led to the back of the building. The kitchen, dining area, laundry and bathroom were to the right. Across the hall were the two sleeping rooms. The arrival of the Weissgarten family meant that Simon would have to move back in with his parents and the young baby. Simon was too young to understand or be upset by the upheaval.

The men struggled to move the two trunks down the narrow hallway to the first bedroom, which was windowless. Any ventilation had to come from the lone window at the end of the hall. The room was furnished sparingly with a bed, a dresser, two night stands and a boxy armoire. Seth walked to the middle of the room where a single light bulb hung, suspended by a pair of green, twisted wires that disappeared into a white ceramic insulator on the ceiling. He pulled on the dangling chain and light flooded the room. This was Jacob's first experience with electricity. He was awestruck as he shielded his eyes from the glare. Seth saw the astonished look in Jacob's eyes.

"If you think this is something, wait until you get down to Berman's," Seth said. "Why, they even have sewing machines powered by electricity. And, speaking of sewing machines, were you able to bring yours?"

Jacob took a key from his vest pocket and opened the larger trunk. The heavy hasp fell away as he turned the key, striking the trunk with a loud thud. He lifted the insert and rummaged through the jumble of clothes beneath. With a grunt, he pulled the head of a treadle powered Singer sewing machine from the tangled mass.

"I would have needed another trunk to bring the base. I couldn't afford it. Do you think I'll be able to find one here?"

"It shouldn't be a problem. I'd be surprised if Mr. Berman doesn't have one at the shop. If not, there's a drummer who comes by every week. I'm sure he'll be able to find one for you." It was nearing sundown and today was *Ereth Shabbat*. Seth pulled his watch from his vest pocket. "It's less than twenty minutes until sunset.

"We'd better join the women for supper."

"I know you must be starved by now," Rachel said as she bent over to remove a roasting pan from the oven. "I left this brisket on to cook when we left for the dock. I remember it was your favorite meal back home Jacob. I hope you enjoy it."

Rachel had placed two white *Shabbat* candles and the *Kiddush* cup in their proper places on the table, which was covered by her best white tablecloth. She placed a white lace kerchief on her head and lit the candles then placed her hands over her eyes while she recited the *Shabbat* blessing.

"*Barukh atah adonai eloheinu melech haolam asher kid-shanu be-mitsvotav vetzivanu lehadik ner shel Shabbat*"

("Blessed are you Lord our God, King of the Universe who has sanctified our lives through His commandments, commanding us to kindle the Sabbath lights")

Seth then raised the *Kiddush* cup and recited the familiar blessing of the wine.

"*Baruch ata adonai eloheinu melech haolam, borei pri hagafen*"

("*Blessed are you Ruler of the Universe, who created the fruit of the vine*")

In silence they performed the ritual washing of the hands and the blessing of the bread. Seth retrieved a small book from the shelf. The front was embossed with a *menorah* and the back with a crown and a *Torah*.

"This is your first meal in a new home, in a new land. We have honored the traditions of our people, therefore, I think it is appropriate that we give special thanks to God for your safe deliverance."

With that he bade them to hold hands as he read from the book of prayers.

"We will render thanks to Thee, O Eternal, our God! For having caused our ancestry to inherit a land, desirable, goodly, and ample, and for having brought us forth; O Eternal, our God! From the land of Egypt, and delivered us from the house of bondage, and for Thy covenant that Thou hast sealed in our flesh, and for Thy law that Thou hast taught us, and for Thy statutes that Thou hast made known unto us, and for the life, grace, and mercy that Thou hast graciously bestowed upon us, and for the enjoyment of the food wherewith Thou feedest and sustaineth us constantly every day, at all times and at all hours. And for all these things, O Eternal, our God! Do we render thanks unto Thee."

For the Weissgartens, no meal they ever had could compare with this, their first feast of *Shabbat* in their new home — in America.

"Jacob, let me see your papers from customs immigration. You'll need those when we go to see Mr. Berman on Monday."

David rustled through his coat pockets and produced the entry papers.

"Here, I didn't get a chance to read them at the docks."

Jacob took one look at the entrance visa and gasped.

"Seth, they've misspelled your names!"

"What? That can't be. I spelled it out for the agent."

"Well, they have. This has happened to several men I know at the shop. The agents get overwhelmed and just write down what they think they hear."

"How did they spell it?" Jacob asked in astonishment.

"It just says Weiss. They completely dropped the - garten."

"What should we do? I'll go back down there and get it changed."

"I don't think you should do that," Seth said. "Others have tried and in all the confusion some have even been denied entry."

"Then what can I do?"

"I know it may seem harsh, but if I were you I'd leave it alone. Just accept that your last name is now Weiss. With that name on your documents, everything else you sign will have to match."

*"Oy Vey!"* Jacob swore, "I've been in America for one hour and already I have a new name. Leah, what do you say?"

"Seth knows better than we do, Jacob. I don't mind. Weiss is a lot easier to write and spell."

Jacob looked crestfallen. Then he looked up and smiled.

"Well then Mrs. Weiss. Welcome to America."

# 3

# Acceptance

The rain and wind had slackened overnight, and the walk to *B'nai Israel* under the cold winter sun was chilling but invigorating. Little Simon ran ahead, anxious to see his friends at synagogue, his little puffs of breath rising into the frosty air. *B'nai Israel* was on Lloyd Street in east Baltimore. By tradition Orthodox Jews walked to synagogue on *Shabbat,* requiring that their homes be located nearby. Many other neighborhoods had sprung up in east Baltimore as the tide of immigrant Jews flowed in. Within a mile radius of *B'nai Israel* were four other temples serving the religious needs of the Jewish community: *Adath B'nai Israel, Mikro Kidesh, Aitz Chaim and Beth Jacob.*

*B'nai Israel* was known as the "*Russhchki Shul*" since its congregants were mostly middle European Jews drawn from the immediate neighborhood. All middle European Jews were re-ferred to as Russians regardless of their country of origin. *B'nai Israel* served both as a religious and social hub for this disparate community of Jews. The synagogue was a refuge from the con-stant struggle to fulfill their dreams and to assimilate into the local culture. It was a sanctuary into which they retreated on *Shabbat*, sealing out the noises, the pressures, and the smells of an alien land. It became an exultation of what used to be — and what could never be again. Few regretted their decision to abandon their homeland and come to America, and, if asked, few would return. For most, however, there was an occasional yet powerful urge to embrace the old and the familiar, a com-munal need to breathe in the essence of their memories and then to breathe them out onto the embers of their dreams — to rekindle the hope that brought them to this faraway land.

The Weisses were warmly received into this diverse mix. They quickly became active participants in the ongoing develop-ment of the Jewish traditions of a young, brash, thriving Balti-more. Future generations would come to venerate their contri-butions to the perpetuation of Jewish culture and tradition, just as their generation, descendants of the *Diaspora* did still labor-ing and suffering in "The Pale."

Jacob awoke early on Monday morning. He crossed qui-etly to the bath area, closed the hallway door and turned on the light, taking care not to wake Leah and the Epsteins. Seth would be rising shortly, for at 7:30 he was to take Jacob to meet Moses Isaac Berman. Almost all the tailor shops began work at eight and closed at six. Jacob was edgy, nervous about the interview and whether he would be hired.

Indoor plumbing had not made its way to the tenements of east Baltimore in 1910. The combination bathroom and laundry consisted of a wash stand with a pitcher and basin, two large galvanized wash tubs, and a small curtained alcove containing a chamber pot. Chamber pots were emptied each morning and evening into special barrels in the alley. This distasteful chore usually fell to the eldest son. The city provided "honey wagons" that came around twice weekly to cart off the malodorous containers.

Cold water was piped into the room and heated on a kerosene stove for the kitchen and the bath. On Fridays the laundry tubs were filled with noisy children getting scrubbed for *Shabbat*. Mondays they were filled with the week's laundry. The women of the household picked a discreet time when all the males were gone to perform their own *toilettes*. Most men, finances permitting, took their weekly scrubbing at one of the many neighborhood Turkish baths.

Jacob's hands shook as he stropped his straight razor and began to shave. He held his head back to tighten the skin on his neck and drew the razor down. A trickle of blood appeared just above his Adam's apple. He reached for a cloth and wet it in the wash basin. He held it to the cut. His shoulders drooped as he thought about the impression he was going to make on Mr. Berman. He hoped the bleeding would stop and that he could hide the cut with his shirt collar. He opened the small cabinet above the wash stand, looking for some paper to press on the wound. He took a small sheet that appeared to be tobacco rolling paper and tore off a corner. He held it to his neck for a few seconds until it adhered, and no fresh blood appeared.

Jacob brought his clothes into the bathroom the night before. He slipped on his shirt and added another piece of paper between the starched collar of his shirt and his neck. He knotted his black tie then slipped on his pants. When he was satisfied that the bleeding was stopped he put on his vest. He left the coat hanging until after breakfast. Light began to filter into the window on the alley and Jacob could hear Rachel stirring as she rose to prepare breakfast. He hurriedly left the bathroom to give her privacy. Leah was emerging from their bedroom when he crossed the hall.

"Good morning, Jacob," she said. "You must have gotten up awfully early."

"Yes, I couldn't sleep. So much depends on today. Leah, I don't know if I'm ready."

"Oh Jacob, you shouldn't worry so. No one in Borisov could hold a candle to you as a tailor. Mr. Berman will be happy to have you in his shop. Just you wait and see. Now come on and help me and Rachel with breakfast. It'll take your mind off the day."

"Thank you, Leah. I should know with you in my corner everything will be all right."

The shop was two blocks east of Seth's building. Mr. Berman was waiting inside the front door when Jacob arrived.

"Mr. Berman, this is Jacob Weiss. He and his wife Leah just arrived on the Wilhelm Friday. Leah is my sister. I told you about Jacob's work in Belarus. I'm sure he will make a great addition to your staff here."

"Good morning Jacob, welcome to America. It's the greatest country in the world. I've been here twenty years and I love it more each day. She's been very good to me. I trust you had an uneventful crossing?"

"Thank you, Mr. Berman. Well, it was a little rough at times. Leah is expecting, and she got pretty sick, but she's all right now. We're both so glad to be here. I'm sure you know what's going on back home. It's a very bad time."

"Yes, I come from Minsk. I get letters every week from my family. I'm trying to get them out, but it's a very slow process. When is the child due?"

"In about a month we think."

"That's an awful lot to have on your plate all at once. Let's see what I can do to help. Come into my office."

Moses Berman's office was a jumble of desks, cutting tables, piece goods and mannequins. He took a bolt of cloth off a chair and pulled it up to his desk.

"Have a seat young man and tell me about yourself."

Jacob hesitated as he cleared his throat. He wished he had some water.

"I'm twenty-five years old and I have apprenticed with Solomon Weinstein near Pinsk for the past five years. He had put me in charge of five other men and we were considered among the best tailors in that area.

"Both my parents and my six brothers and sisters are still in Borisov. I finished six years of school and was enrolled at *Yeshiva* until I began my apprenticeship. I can read and write and I go to *shul* every week, I don't drink or smoke and I'm very reliable. I missed only two days of work in the five years I was with Mr. Weinstein."

"Very good young man, Seth has told me all this, but I wanted to hear it from you, not that I doubted him at all. Seth is one of my finest employees and I trust his judgment. If he vouches for you, that's good enough for me. The most important thing is how well and how fast you can sew. We represent several men's stores in the area. They bring their measurements to us and they specify the material. From that we build them the best suit around. That's what you'll have to do to work here.

"Now, I have a proposition for you. I want you to take my measurements and that bolt of cloth that was on the chair and turn it into a suit for me by the end of the day. If you do a good job and you finish on time, you have a job. Do you have a sewing machine, son?"

"Yes sir, but it's only the head. I couldn't bring the base on the ship. No room. It's at Seth's house."

"Go get it and come straight back. I'm sure we have a base somewhere around here that will work. Hurry, you're on the clock."

Jacob bolted out the door and raced back to the apartment. He told Leah what was happening and ran out with his sewing machine. He was back in the Berman shop in ten minutes flat. Berman had produced a new base for his Singer. Within minutes they had the head attached and the treadle belted to it and Jacob was in business.

"Follow me." Berman said.

He led Jacob to an adjoining room which was used for fittings and began to undress.

"Okay, young man, let's begin. I'm all yours."

Jacob picked up a tape measure from the cutting table and began. He measured Berman's neck, his waist, his inseams, his arm lengths, his chest, and any other measurement he thought he might need, diligently recording them on a pad.

"I think that's everything, Mr. Berman. I'll get right to it. I should be ready for the first fitting after lunch."

"Good luck, son. I'll be in my office if you need me."

"Thank you, Mr. Berman. Thank you for the opportunity."

"You're welcome Jacob. Show me what you've got."

"I will, sir. I hope you'll be pleased."

Jacob flipped the bolt of gray flannel cloth onto the cutting table, selected the proper patterns, and began to mark the cloth for cutting. He double checked his measurements against the pattern and marked the cloth with a sliver of chalk. By noon he had the three pieces assembled with pins and asked Mr. Berman to come in for the first fitting. Seth made a few adjustments and took the suit back to his machine. He sewed the pants first since they were easier for him to judge his progress. At one, he had Mr. Berman try the pants. They were a perfect fit. He took them back to finish the cuffs. By two he had fitted the vest and started sewing it as well. He chose a black lining material and had the vest completed before three. He needed to make a slight change under the arms that took only fifteen minutes. Now would come the real test, getting the coat done right. He had a little over two hours left and he was beginning to sweat. He reached for the shears to trim a seam. His eyes were on the coat, and he knocked the shears onto the floor. The noise brought Mr. Berman hurrying in.

"Is everything all right, Jacob?

"Yes, sir. I'm just a little nervous and I knocked the scissors off the table, but I still think I'll be finished by five o'clock."

"Good. I'll let you get back to it then"

The clock in Mr. Berman's office struck five as Jacob clipped the last threads from the coat's seams. He breathed a sigh of relief when the door opened, and Mr. Berman came in.

"Is it ready?"

"Yes, sir, I just finished. If you'll slip on the pants and vest, I'm ready with the coat."

The shop owner took off his shoes and slipped on the pants and vest. He fastened the four buttons on the vest and turned as Jacob held the coat for him. He stepped back into his shoes and faced the full-length mirror on the wall. He adjusted the coat and turned to see how it fit in back.

"Jacob, I've made many suits and I've had many suits made for me, but I don't think I've ever had one that looks this good on me. That's saying a lot when you consider my girth. Portly sizes are more difficult and you've really pulled it off. Welcome to Berman's."

Jacob slumped back into his chair. He was at a loss for words. Finally, he found his voice.

"I don't know what to say. I've been in Baltimore for three days and I already have a job. It's like a dream. One that I hope I don't wake up from."

Mr. Berman went to the door into the shop and called Seth.

"Epstein, get in here," he yelled.

Seth almost fell over getting out of his chair as he rushed to the office.

"Yes, sir, what's wrong?" he said ashen faced.

"What's wrong is absolutely nothing. Do you see this suit I'm wearing? Your brother-in-law did this today. He's an amazing tailor. I have to thank you for bringing him to me. Now, you boys go home and celebrate with your families. Then get back here at eight in the morning and make those machines sing."

He was smiling broadly as he ushered them out the door.

Jacob ran up the street in a state of disbelief. Seth struggled to keep up with him. Jacob bounded up the two flights of stairs yelling at the top of his lungs.

"Leah, Leah, I got the job, I got the job!"

Leah heard the shouting and ran to meet him. She reached for the knob as the door flung open. He grabbed Leah and swept her off her feet, whirling around the room. He sat her down and kissed her.

"Leah, I can't believe it. Mr. Berman said I made the best suit he's ever worn. He gave me the job right away. I start work tomorrow."

The words poured out in a torrent. He couldn't wait to share his great fortune with the love of his life. Rachel came running from the kitchen just as Seth made it to the top of the stairs. She was drying her hands on her apron and grabbed Jacob. She hugged him tightly.

"Oh, Jacob! That's wonderful! I'm so proud for you."

"It's going to be great having you work at Berman's with me," Seth said. "This calls for a celebration."

He ran into the kitchen and took down a green bottle from a cabinet.

"When Rachel and I were on the ship coming over we met a man who was coming to Washington as a diplomat from Poland. He knew we were recently married and kind of took us under his wing. He was returning from Krakow where his son was just married. I think he saw something of his son in me. During supper the last night of the trip he came down to our level and gave me this bottle of *schnapps* as a parting gift. He said, 'If I can ever help you, just look me up at the Polish embassy in Washington.'"

Seth popped the cork with a flourish and poured four small glasses for them, raising his in salute.

"*L'chaim,* Jacob, and *Mazel Tov!*"

# 4

# Rebirth

Jacob settled easily into a regular routine at Berman's. He was up every morning at six, had a quick breakfast, and was out the door with Seth by seven-thirty for work. Some days the wives brought their lunches to work while on others they would hurry home for a quick bite with the family. On rare occasions the boys would join some of the other tailors at Sussman and Lev's deli for a celebration. Sussman and Lev indisputably made the best corned-beef-on-rye sandwich south of Brooklyn.

At home, Leah was becoming more uncomfortable by the day. She left most of the chores to Rachel. Six weeks to the day after reaching Baltimore, Leah experienced an unsettling sensation. She quietly left bed and hurried to the bathroom. She felt a warm surge of fluid down her leg spilling onto the tiled floor. She felt vast relief. Her time had come. She called to Rachel.

Dr. Milo Sussman came by later that morning to gauge Leah's progress. Most babies born in east Baltimore, especially to poor immigrants, were born at home with a midwife in attendance. A few others were fortunate enough to afford a doctor's care. Dr. Sussman had attended the births of both Epstein children, Simon and Natalie. Natalie's birth had been uneventful, but Simon as the first born, had a difficult arrival. He created two long, difficult days of labor for Rachel. Two agonizing days that now, once filtered through the gauze of time, seemed golden. Once she held the small, pink bundle to her breast, an instinct older than time and newer than tomorrow, began to work its miracle anew on Rachel Epstein.

By four in the afternoon it was clear that Leah's baby could wait no longer. The contractions began to cascade over one another. Rachel sent Jacob to summon Dr. Sussman and began preparing the hot water and towels he would need to attend her. The doctor arrived in time to coax Leah through her last few contractions. Suddenly, the room was filled with the piercing cry of young Bernard Daniel Weiss — American citizen. Leah lay back on the bed exhausted, glistening with the exertion and radiant with joy. Now the Weisses were a real family.

Jacob was allowed back into the room after Dr. Sussman severed the umbilical cord and the baby was given its first bath. The smell of birth was still in the room, a smell both ancient and eternal, a sacred scent anointing a new life.

Jacob took the tiny bundle from the doctor and walked over to the light. He gazed down into the small, pink, helpless face.

"Welcome to the world Bernard Daniel Weiss. Welcome to America."

He walked back over to the bed and placed the baby on Leah's bosom.

"Dear Leah, look. Look at our beautiful new son. If I live to be a hundred, this moment will live with me. Thank you."

He bent to her, kissing her firmly on the lips then left the room. He dabbed at his eyes with his shirt sleeve as he went through the door. The effort to hide his emotions was futile. He couldn't fool Leah. She smiled knowingly, proud of Jacob's tenderness and love. They were just two of the qualities that would make him such a great father.

Leah quickly regained her strength as the ensuing days flashed by. Bernie flourished. Soon it would be eight days and time for the *bris,* the ritual circumcision performed on all Jewish sons. The *bris* commemorates the seven days of creation of the physical world. On the eighth day, by tradition, the child transcends from the physical to the spiritual world. The covenant between God and man is sealed on that day.

Rabbi Kantor from B'nai Israel was a practiced *mohel,* with rabbinical training to perform the *bris*. He was asked to celebrate this tradition for little Bernie. Seth, Rachel, the Bermans and a few of Jacobs co-workers were invited to participate in the sacred ceremony. As the godfather, Seth held Bernard for the circumcision.

"And what shall we call this child of God?" Rabbi Kantor asked.

"He is to be called Bernard Daniel in honor of my grand-father who died fighting the Cossacks before I was born."

Among the Ashkenazi Jews of Europe, it was traditional to name newborns for deceased ancestors.

The guests were asked to join the family in the social hall afterward. Rachel and Leah had draped a table with white cloths and had placed lighted candles among the plates of sandwiches and sweetmeats.

"Welcome to you all." Rabbi Kantor said, "Especially to this newest member of the tribe, and our Hebrew family. May he grow in stature and in the grace of Jehovah, our God."

Bernie was sleeping quietly in Leah's arms, having recovered from the pain of the circumcision. He remained oblivious to the celebration in his honor going on around him. It was just as well, for this was only the first of many traditional rituals he would pass through on his way to manhood — and It was the only one he would be allowed to sleep through.

The arrival of Bernard brought profound changes to the Epstein/Weiss household. Two babies in the same apartment lent new meaning to the word havoc. The clothesline across the alley was in constant motion.  Between diapers and work clothes, interspersed with bloomers and blouses, the laundry got a major workout.  And the kitchen was in constant flux with two families preparing, cooking and serving meals for three children under the age of two plus the four adults.

The women shared the duties of the house and the rearing of the children. When one was cooking the other was usually doing laundry or cleaning. When either showed the frustrations of the day the other would quickly sweep up the charges and take them for a stroll in the fresh air or a romp in the park for Simon. The tumult gradually settled into a pattern, assuming a rhythm that accommodated their life at home. It was a pattern not unlike the life they had known in Belarus where extended families lived together for the same reasons.

The lives of Jacob and Seth settled into a similar pattern, one accommodating that at home. Their work shifts started at eight and ended at six, Sunday through Thursday and until noon on Friday when everyone went home to prepare for Shabbat. The seemingly strenuous schedule was actually a reprieve from Jacob's old job in Pinsk where he often put in twelve to fourteen-hour days. Saturday afternoon following Temple was their jealously guarded time for family activities. A special monthly treat was the trip to Handler's creamery on Lloyd Street for a dish of the world's best ice cream. They always found the fountain staffed by non-Jewish employees since the Handlers could not work on *Shabbat*. That fact did nothing to diminish the indescribable taste of the fifty different flavors prepared by the Handler family and left for their patrons.

# 5

## Settling In

The days and weeks stretched into months. Young Natalie and Bernard added even more chaos as they began to crawl and walk. Every trinket, whatnot and tchotchke to be placed out of reach of their probing hands. Both families prospered, but it quickly became evident that Jacob's skills as a tailor far surpassed that of the other workers, and even Seth. His talent and his way with the customers set him apart. At the end of his third year, Berman called Jacob into his office. Jacob couldn't imagine what he may have done wrong to merit such a summons.

"Jake, you've been here for three years now and your work is beyond reproach. We've reached a point where I can no longer supervise all the workers. We now have sixty tailors. I want you to take responsibility for twenty of them. You will decide their work assignments and will supervise them. You have a great way with our customers, so I want you to help me with that side of the business as well. I'll be taking you with me on sales trips, so you can get a better feel for what's required."

The company had expanded beyond tailored suits, made to order for each client, and were now offering high-end, ready-to-wear clothing for a few upscale men's stores in the Washington and Baltimore area. A casual inspection of the leaders of both houses of Congress would reveal several members attired in Berman's finest. The same was true for the captains of industry as well.

Jacob was dumbfounded. He had no idea such a surprise announcement was in the offing. He was at a loss of words. He finally was able to gather himself enough to speak.

"I don't know what to say, Mr. Berman. It's hard to believe that you would choose me for this promotion. I've only been here three years. Why, Seth and some of the others have been here for five or more."

"Don't sell yourself short young man. You have a natural talent for this business and for leadership. That's been obvious to me since the first day. Now, are you going to take the position or not?"

"Yes, sir, thank you. I promise you I will work very hard to justify your faith in me. Leah will faint when I tell her."

"When she wakes up, she'll be very happy to know that you will also receive a twenty-five percent raise. Come with me. I'm going to make the announcement on the shop floor."

Seth hardly spoke on the walk home that evening. It was apparent that he was shocked by the announcement. He had secretly been hoping for such a position, and he was keenly disappointed. One saving grace in the change was that Seth didn't report to Jacob. Still, it was a galling disappointment, and Seth tried to rationalize the decision. He knew that Jacob merited the promotion based on his work but that did little to diminish his feeling of betrayal — both by Mr. Berman and Jacob.

"Seth," Jacob said, breaking the awkward silence, "I want you to know that I had no idea Mr. Berman was going to promote me. I even argued that you were more qualified than me due to your time here and your fine work, but he would not listen. He basically said that if I didn't do this it would limit my future. I'm sorry if you are upset, but please don't blame me."

"I know it's not your fault Jake, but it still hurts. I know I can't blame you, but it'll take a while to get used to."

They climbed the stairs in silence not knowing how to break the news to Leah and Rachel. What should have been a grand celebration for Jacob, was now cloaked in the darkness of Seth's despair.

The wives sensed that something was wrong as the men entered the room silently. Leah and Rachel looked at each other and began speaking in chorus.

"What's wrong?" Rachel said.

"What has happened?" Leah chimed in.

"Come and sit down," Jacob said, steeling himself for what was coming.

"There have been some changes at the shop that affect all of us. I have been offered a promotion to supervisor over some of the other men and also to help Mr. Berman with sales. I knew this decision would upset some of the men, especially Seth, and I tried to turn it down. Mr. Berman basically said I must take it or my career in his shop would be over. So, I said yes. I know how upsetting this is to Seth and the others, but I didn't know what else to do."

Rachel was the first to speak.

"Is that all? With your long faces I thought someone had died or something. I think that's great news. Sure, we can understand Seth's disappointment, but we also know his turn will come. He's a good worker and there'll be other openings at the shop. Look, this just means we'll be able to move sooner, into a better neighborhood."

"You're right of course," Seth said. "I have no reason to rain on Jake's parade. We are both the same honest, decent, family men we were when we left here this morning. That hasn't changed with anything that happened today, so congratulations, Jake. You deserve this."

"I think it's wonderful," Leah added. "Rachel and I have been talking about out living arrangements and how nice it would be to afford our own homes. Jacob's added income will help that dream come true even faster. We've always known this arrangement was temporary until Jacob could get established. Now that our financial situation is improving, Rachel and I think it's time to think about that move to the west side we've always talked about. We've both been able to put aside some money. We think we may be able to afford the rent in those new houses on Hanover, just west of Howard Street. Several have been completed recently and Rachel and I walked over there to check them out. They would be perfect for our growing families and they're still within walking distance of B'nai Israel and Berman's.

"While we were looking at the property with their sales agent, he told us that we may qualify with the Hebrew Free Loan Society to actually buy them. He also said they were helping to finance new businesses for Jewish immigrants who meet the requirements."

Rachel, who had been nodding furiously in support of Leah's conclusions, could contain herself no longer.

"Jacob, you know how you and Seth have dreamed of starting your own business. Well, why can't we start planning for that now? The Hebrew Society will help you develop plans, secure property, find suppliers and anything else you may need. And, with the reputations you've both established at Berman's, I know you won't have any trouble attracting customers."

The men were stunned by the emotional outpouring of their wives. The previous gloom surrounding the announcement was drowned in their passionate appeal. They were caught off guard and took time to catch their breath.

"You know," Jacob said, "as painful as this has been it could be a hidden blessing. Leah, you and Rachel have reminded us of the dreams we all had when we came here. Along the way we've kind of forgotten them as we got wrapped up in our day-to-day lives. I don't know if Seth and I would have revived them on our own without your kick-in-the-pants. We needed something to shake us up. I think you are right. We are capable of doing this, of starting our own company. Seth and I both have the skills and talent to pull this off, and with the two of you behind us there's no way we can fail. What do you say, Seth?"

"It will take a while to pull everything together, but I agree that we are capable of doing this. We'll need to get our finances in order and make the move to Hanover, then see how long it'll take to secure the financing for a business. I suspect it'll take a year or more.

"The only sad thing will be leaving Berman's. He's been so good to us. It'll feel like we are betraying him."

"He'll understand, Seth," Jacob said. "He had to make this same decision when he started his business. I think he'll be happy for us."

The next year flew by. When not at work or at Temple, their waking hours were consumed with planning for the new business. They made arrangements for the loans to purchase the Hanover Street homes and they moved into the side-by-side row houses with their wrought iron enclosed, whitewashed stoops. The new neighborhood was bustling with the activity of other young families that were moving up to the next rung of the ladder. The cries of small children with their games of stickball and hopscotch filled the street. It was June 1914 and the distant rumblings of an impending war rolled across Europe. The letters from Borisov were tinged with fear and uncertainty but also with the innate optimism of a people used to upheaval and danger.

In May, Jacob and Seth told Mr. Berman of their plans. He expressed disappointment that he was going to lose two of his most valuable employees, but as Seth had predicted, he congratulated them and wished them well. He asked them to stay on for another three months while he made arrangements to replace them. When the three months had passed, they had leased a building, equipped it with sewing machines, hired five employees, ordered inventory and lined up their first prospective customers. Contacts Jake had made in his sales role at Berman's proved critical. His reputation among the area's retail establishments quickly translated into orders. "Epstein and Weiss, Fine Men's Clothiers" was open for business.

"Epstein and Weiss" added five new customers in their first year of business, including the prestigious Hecht's chain and Hutzlers in downtown Baltimore. Their net income of $3,300 was triple what their salaries would have been at Berman's, but they had to plow most of the profits back into the business. They took on five more tailors and hired a full-time salesman. They were back to their fifteen-hour days, but they didn't mind. They were now working for themselves and they could see the appreciating rewards for their efforts.

Seth gravitated toward the management of the shop floor where his skills were apparent; Jacob handled the front office, sales, marketing and finance. Both wives pitched in to help with bookkeeping and other chores. None of them seemed to mind the extra hours needed to get the business off the ground because their efforts were supporting the dream. Five years on and the gulf between their life in Borisov and their life in Baltimore continued to widen in more ways than miles or time could measure.

Epstein and Weiss flourished under the skillful management of its owners. They were constantly scouring the Baltimore community of clothing manufacturers for the best and brightest workers. They instituted novel strategies that made the firm more attractive than their competitors. They helped the men with their insurance and finances, making it possible for many to buy their own homes. They made sure that their children had access to the best medical care and education. They saw to it that the wives got the best prenatal care available and offered them assistance during the first three months after birth. Worker turnover at Epstein and Weiss was almost nonexistent. All these benefits, while adding to the business' costs, resulted in much improved efficiency, lower personnel costs and higher profits which allowed the company to acquire several of their struggling competitors. They also resulted in improved quality, which allowed Jacob to add customers from Atlanta to New York including Rich's and Macy's.

Despite the heavy reinvestment in their business, Jacob and Weiss were able to withdraw more of the profits for their own benefit. They bought better cars, better furnishings for their homes and better clothes for their wives and children. The sent their children to the best *Yeshivas* to assure them a firm foundation in Judaism. They were able to be more generous with their synagogue and the other institutions that had helped them along the way. They fulfilled their promise and sponsored ten Jewish families to Baltimore, keeping the chain unbroken. Life was good to the Epsteins and the Weisses.

# 6

# New Life

1922 was a pivotal year in the lives of Jacob and Leah Weiss. In the twelve short years following their arrival on the docks of Baltimore they had moved from the teeming streets of east Baltimore to their own home on the west side; they had partnered with Leah's brother Seth to start their own business; and now, they were embarking on the next stage of the immigrant Jewish dream — they were planning a move to their new home on Linden Avenue in the Lake Drive neighborhood.

Linden Avenue was northwest of Eutaw Place, the neighborhood of choice for the upwardly mobile German Jews that came before them. The new house was within walking distance of Druid Hill Park, the epicenter of the affluent Jewish community of Baltimore and home to many of the German Jews whose wealth did not merit a home on Eutaw Place. It was also a community that welcomed and embraced the newly affluent "Russians" who could afford the stylish houses gracing the tree-lined boulevards.

Shortly after Jacob announced that he had purchased the new house, the second momentous event of 1922 occurred — Leah discovered that she was pregnant for the second time. The couple had consulted with many specialists over the past few years to determine why Leah had not conceived again. All the doctors were in agreement that there were no physiological reasons and concluded that perhaps the traumatic experiences Leah had endured during her first pregnancy had somehow affected her ability to conceive. The Weisses had accepted that Bernie wouldn't have any brothers or sisters. It was a great disappointment to them, especially Jacob, who wanted a big boisterous family like he grew up with in Borisov.

The December Leah discovered she was pregnant again was cold and overcast, eerily reminiscent of the one twelve years earlier when they first arrived in Baltimore. Leah arose earlier than usual that day to prepare for Jacob's workday and to get Bernie off to school. She kept secret her mid-morning appointment with a staff obstetrician at Sinai Hospital. She had been experiencing problems with her menstrual periods and had actually skipped a couple. She saw Dr. Sussman who recommended she see Dr. Jeremy Katz, a renowned fertility specialist and head of obstetrics at Sinai. Several of her friends used Dr. Katz and had nothing but praise for him. Leah needed to resolve all the nagging questions that had plagued her for the past few weeks, and she didn't want to alarm Jacob.

Leah ascended the marble steps leading to Mt. Sinai's entrance promptly at 9:45 am. She passed between the massive Corinthian columns guarding the entrance to the hospital that were the dominant feature of the block-square structure. The columns were a bequest from the Hess family. A popular guessing game among the ladies was how many pairs of shoes they had to sell to pay for them.

Dr. Katz's offices were on the third floor of the office wing that stretched down a long corridor off the elevator lobby. The doctor was just coming off early morning rounds in the maternity wing and Leah was his first office appointment. He held the door open for her to enter.

"Mrs. Weiss, I assume?"

"Yes, you must be Dr. Katz."

"Yes, I understand that you've consulted with Dr. Sussman and he recommended that you see me," he said as he ushered her into his consulting room. He handed her a gown. "You can change into this in the bathroom."

"I'm sure you've learned from the reports from Dr. Sussman that Jacob and I have one child, Bernard, who is twelve. I was pregnant when we arrived in Baltimore, and he was born a few weeks later. We've wanted more children, but it just hasn't happened. Other doctors have concluded that something may have happened during Bernie's birth that prevents me from becoming pregnant. My periods have been fairly normal until recently. They have become irregular and I missed the last two entirely. "

"Have you noticed any other changes in your health recently, any tenderness in your breasts, any changes in your weight, any emotional changes or any significant changes in your physical activities that may have caused stress to your body?"

"I have noticed some tenderness," Leah said as she leaned forward. She wrinkled her brow, adding, "and I've caught myself snapping at Bernie over minor things. I just attributed that to winter cabin fever. Do you think there might be any significance?"

"I'm not sure Mrs. Weiss. Let me ask a few more questions about your family history and then we'll go into the examining room to see if we can resolve this little mystery of yours."

Leah lay on the examining table, her feet in the stirrups, wondering if all women hated this experience as much as she did. It was embarrassing enough to have to discuss these subjects with a man, albeit a doctor, but having to submit to the physical probing was the most humiliating experience she could imagine. She rationalized the need for it and she could even admit to its significance in detecting disease and problem pregnancies, however, none of those reasons could overcome the revulsion she felt at having to endure the process.

"Mrs. Weiss," the doctor said, peering across the draped sheets, I have to agree with Dr.  Sussman's findings. I can't find any medical reason for your inability to become pregnant. Quite to the contrary, everything appears to be in fine working order. Let me run a few more tests on your blood and urine and on the swab specimens I took. Those should help me to rule out most of the more common problems. I should have those back from the lab in a couple of weeks at which time we'll call to schedule another appointment."

~ 56 ~

Leah heard the phone ringing as she came back from seeing Bernie off to school, though at his age he was beginning to chafe at her zealous attention. Reluctantly, she had to agree that he was now capable of catching the bus alone.

"Hello, this is Mrs. Weiss."

"Mrs. Weiss, this is Dr. Katz' receptionist. Will you hold a moment, please; Dr. Katz wants to speak to you."

Leah could hear a muffled conversation in the background and then Dr. Katz' familiar voice came on.

"Mrs. Weiss, this is Dr. Katz. As I expected, none of the tests indicated anything wrong. On the contrary, they proved that everything is right. Mrs. Weiss, you are pregnant. It seems we all overlooked the obvious. Congratulations, you should expect to deliver around the first of August. I'll make a full report to Dr. Sussman so that he can follow up with you as necessary. I assume he'll be attending you during your pregnancy? Give him my best when you see him."

Leah clutched at the back of a kitchen chair as the black and white tiles on the floor began to spin. She plopped into the chair with a loud thump. She couldn't possibly have heard him right.

"Will you repeat that Doctor? I'm sure I must have misunderstood you. Did you really say I am pregnant?"

"Why, yes, Mrs. Weiss, that's what I said. I'm sorry if I startled you. I thought you might have suspected as much yourself. Perhaps I should have been a bit more tactful. Are you all right?"

"I think so," Leah stammered. "It's just so unexpected. It took me by complete surprise. You're sure your tests are accurate?"

"Yes, ma'am, these tests have been proved extremely accurate. You are definitely pregnant. I don't see any reason why you shouldn't have a normal, uneventful term. You're healthy and you're only thirty-seven, still of normal child-bearing age. Let me know if I can help you. As I said, I'll' give a complete report to Dr. Sussman, and I'll check back with him in a couple of weeks."

"Thank you, Dr. Katz. I'm sorry if I over-reacted. I just had no idea I could become pregnant. Don't get me wrong, I'm very excited. My husband and I had hoped for a very large family. As you may know, we both come from large families in the old country and had hoped for one of our own. We have many relatives here now that we were able to sponsor. Having them here has given us a large, extended family, but adding to our own will be even more rewarding. Jacob will be so happy with the news. He'd like a whole houseful of kids. Thank you so much, and I'm sure we'll speak again in the next few months."

Leah eased the phone back into its cradle while trying to grasp the enormity of what she had just heard. She had so many unanswered questions.

"How would she break the news to Jacob and how will he react?"

"How will Bernie feel about a new baby in the house?"

"How will this affect their plans to move to the house on Linden?"

Suddenly everything in their lives would change. So many things they had planned had to be reconsidered in light of this unexpected blessing. What about Bernie's new school, and decorating the new house, and her commitments to the Jewish charities, and other causes she had assumed. These would become less important as she prepared to welcome a new life into the family. Seth and Rachel will be very happy for us, she mused. Their brood of eight will now have another cousin to play with, and It won't be as awkward at family gatherings where well-intentioned and compassionate remarks always carried a hint of pity. Yes indeed, the Weiss family was in for many changes.

The tempo around the Weiss household visibly increased over the next few months. Jacob was concerned for Leah's health and decided to hire a maid to help around the house. The maid, Esther, was the eighteen-year old daughter of Max and Emma Sarofsky, distant cousins who had been sponsored by the Weisses in 1917. She proved to be a splendid worker and her family welcomed the additional income.  By the end of the school year in May, the revised plans for the Linden Avenue house were completed. The second-floor addition off the master bedroom was expanded to house a nursery for the new baby. Bernie was anxiously preparing for his first summer camp near Frederick and his first extended separation from his family. Leah was almost totally preoccupied with preparations for the baby. She worried about how Bernie would handle being separated from home for two weeks. Jacob shuttled back and forth between home, work and the Linden Avenue work site. Nothing had gone right since he gave the changes to the contractor. The completion date was moved back from July to September. It was looking more certain than ever that the move from Hanover to Linden would include four Weisses, not three. Leah's pregnancy appeared much further along at seven months than had Bernie's. Discomfort inhibited her ability to do the many things she had planned. With two months to go, Dr. Sussman asked Dr. Katz to see Leah again. He had some concerns. There was nothing in particular. He said he would just feel better if Dr. Katz could examine her once more. Leah made the appointment and asked Jacob if he would drop her by Sinai on his way to work. She could take a taxi home.

"Don't worry, Jacob, I'm sure everything is all right," Leah said as she leaned across to kiss him before exiting the car. "I'll see you at supper. Her pace up the steps was markedly slower than during her first visit. She struggled to balance herself and she clutched the handrail. She made her way slowly to the elevator, up to the office wing, and was breathing heavily when she entered the doctor's office. Dr Katz entered from the opposite door as the nurse was escorting Leah to the examining room.

"Mrs. Weiss, while you change into the gown I'll take a minute to review Dr. Sussman's notes. I'll be right with you."

He disappeared into his private office, absorbed with the report in his hand. When he returned Leah was already on the examining table, once again resigned to the indignities of more probing. Dr. Katz rolled a stool closer to the table.

"Mrs. Weiss, is it true that there were several multiple births in both your families? According to Dr. Sussman two of your grandparents had twins."

"Yes, as I told Dr. Sussman, I remember my parents talking about them. One set of the twins died shortly after birth, and I never knew them. Do you think that has anything to do with my situation?"

Leah remembered that many children died in infancy in the old country. Was it possible she had inherited some dangerous trait and brought it to Baltimore with her?

"Before we begin the exam, there are a couple of things I'd like to check."

He moved around the table to retrieve something from an upper shelf. It was an odd-looking stethoscope with a double bell He said it was a new development by one of his associates on the staff at Sinai.

"Dr. Rappaport asked me to try this for a while to see if it makes a difference. The large bell is for regular exams and the smaller one is extra sensitive for picking up fetal heartbeats. It is much more sensitive and amplifies the sound. He placed the small bell on Leah's bulging abdomen, closed his eyes and listened intently. After a few seconds he slid the bell to another spot and repeated the process. He smiled wryly.

"Mrs. Weiss, I think I've solved your mystery. You are going to have twins."

Leah had been resting on her elbows as she observed the doctor. She fell back with an audible gasp. First, she couldn't get pregnant at all, and now, all of a sudden, she was having twins. It was too much to take in all at once. She rose to her elbows again, staring at Dr. Katz.

"Are you sure?"

"Yes, there are two distinct heartbeats. I couldn't hear them with the old scope but they are loud and clear with the new one. Would you like to listen?"

He removed the stethoscope from his ears and placed it on Leah's. He slowly moved the bell to the places where he had heard the heartbeats. He watched as Leah's eyes widened in astonishment. There was no denying the two distinct beats — she was having twins. All she could think of was the look on Jacob's face when she told him. He will be speechless. Then he will be overjoyed. Tonight was going to be interesting.

"Doctor, you obviously saw something in Dr. Sussman's report that led you to suspect twins?"

"Yes. First it was the weight gain compared to Bernie. Secondly, it was your history of twins in both families. There appears to be a recessive hereditary gene pattern with twins. In many cases, with multiple birth families, the gene skips a generation, which made you a prime candidate for its reappearance. This shouldn't complicate your remaining few weeks. However, I recommend that you limit any strenuous activities and stay reasonably close to home. Otherwise, carry on as usual, and, as I said before I'll keep in touch with Dr. Sussman. I'll ask him to give me a call when you go into the hospital and I'll be available should he need me."

The taxi ride home was a blur. The shimmering heat rising from the hot July streets created mirages that seemed perfect accompaniments to her bewilderment. Through their contorted reflections she re-experienced that first ride home from Sinai. Leah's mind was abuzz with a thousand thoughts. What further changes would this latest development bring? Will the added expense impact our plans? Will we still be able to afford the life we have planned on Linden Avenue? She knew that she and Jacob had overcome much larger obstacles than this on their journey thus far, and they would cope with this one as well.

Esther had just finished putting supper on the table when Jacob came through the door. She normally would leave for home at this point but Leah placed a hand on her arm and asked her to stay a while. Then she called Jacob and Bernie to join them in the dining room.

"I have some news from Dr. Katz which affects all of us, including Esther. As you know, I have asked Esther to continue with us after we move. She has been such a blessing to me for these past few months. I don't know if I could have managed without her. She has agreed to help with the new baby, in addition to her other duties. Well, now she will be helping me with two new babies. Dr. Katz has determined that I am carrying twins."

Jacob's face filled with a flood of emotions; surprise, joy, anxiety, fear, concern, love. Six months ago he had been resigned to life with a single child household. Now, out of the blue, he was to have three.

"Did the doctor find anything wrong otherwise? Are you all right?" Jacob asked excitedly.

"Yes, my beloved, I am very healthy. I just have to be careful over the next few weeks. Otherwise, I can carry on as usual. The doctor recommended that I stay close to home and to keep a bag packed. He said twins have a habit of being unpredictable. It's safer to be prepared."

Jacob came around the table to embrace his wife. He had tears in his eyes.

"I know this comes as a shock to you Leah, but I want you to know that it makes me very happy. I don't want you to be concerned about anything but delivering two healthy babies. The business is doing well and this won't change anything as far as finances are concerned."

He turned to look at Esther.

"In fact, I was thinking of asking Esther to move in with us here and then move to Linden with us. This makes that all the more reasonable. With the plan changes made in December, we added another room upstairs next to the nursery. That'll be perfect for Esther, and she won't have to make the long trek back to east Baltimore every day."

A smile danced at the corners of Esther's mouth. She had secretly wanted to ask if she could live in. Five younger siblings in a three-bedroom tenement flat was making life difficult for the eighteen-year old.

"That would be wonderful Mr. Weiss. I have always secretly wanted to study nursing, and this will help get me there sooner. I have already talked to the Hebrew Benevolent Society and they will help with tuition and moving in will allow me to save even more. I thought it would take me five years to save enough, but this may cut that to four or even three. I've talked about this with Mrs. Weiss and she and I agree that my sister Naomi will be ready to take my place when I leave. This will be a big help to my family. You know how hard life can be in the tenements, and I know I can help Bernie and the twins more if I live in."

"Well, it's settled then," Jacob said. "There'll be a ten-percent increase in your wages and I'll set up a separate account for you to save toward your education. For every dollar you deposit, I'll add fifty cents. You have been such a blessing to Leah and Bernie. I'm sure you will be for the twins as well."

Leah's eyes welled with tears as Jacob wrapped her in a warm embrace.

"Now that that's settled, let's eat. I'm starving. Esther, join us and let's have a special bottle of wine to celebrate this amazing day."

# 7

# New Arrival

It was even hotter early on the morning of July 15, 1922 when Leah's water broke, and she felt the beginning of contractions. She was a couple of weeks early according to Dr. Katz' projections, but she was not surprised. The small signs had been present all week, and she had warned Jacob and Esther to be prepared.

"Jacob, I think you should wake Esther. It's time. Contractions have begun, and we'll need to leave for Mt. Sinai soon."

Jacob bolted out of bed and hurriedly dressed. He ran down the hall to Esther's room to discover that she was already up. Dr. Sussman had decided that Leah should go to Mt. Sinai for the delivery, just in case there were any problems.

"Esther, Leah's labor has started. We'll be leaving soon. Will you take care of Bernie till I can get back? It may be a long day."

"Certainly, you just go on. I'll take care of everything here."

"Thank you, Esther; it's a good thing you're here. It may be a long day. I'll call you later to let you know when to expect me back."

"Don't you worry about a thing. Bernie and I will have a great day. You just take care of Mrs. Weiss. We'll be waiting to welcome the twins when you bring them home."

Jacob grabbed the packed bag and helped Leah to the car.

The granite façade of the hospital was a now familiar sight to Leah. Jacob drove past the columned front and turned the corner. He stopped at the side entrance to the maternity ward, jumped out, and came around to help Leah from the car just as an attendant arrived with a wheel chair.

"Good morning and welcome to the Mt. Sinai Maternity Hospital. I'll take the lady upstairs while you park the car, sir. There's a special lot for family members at the end of the block. You'll see the sign."

The attendant turned to wheel Leah up the ramp.

"We'll be on the fifth floor when you come up," he yelled.

Jacob parked and locked his black Packard in the special lot and ran back to the hospital. When he reached the nurse's station, he was told that Leah had been admitted to room 577. She would remain there until her contractions were less than four minutes apart, signaling a move to the delivery room. Since Leah was expecting twins, Dr. Katz had requested additional staff to stand by. Jacob was allowed to stay with Leah until she was moved to the delivery room. He pulled his watch from his vest as the nurse came in to wheel Leah out. It was only seven-thirty. The next few hours would be more trying and dangerous than anyone could have ever imagined.

"I'm on my way," Dr. Katz replied to the call from the floor nurse.

He sat his coffee cup on the kitchen counter.

"Go ahead and move her to the delivery room and notify Dr. Sussman. I should be there in about fifteen minutes."

The nurse said that Leah had begun to hemorrhage.

"If it gets worse we may need blood transfusions. She has several relatives in the area. Get their names from Mr. Weiss and contact as many as you can. Ask them to come in for compatibility typing and try not to alarm Mr. Weiss. Tell him it's just a precautionary measure. Also, have Doctors Perry and Liebenthal notified and make sure they are available at the hospital in case we need them. Oh, and you'd better notify my office staff. We may need to reschedule some appointments for today."

He kissed his wife good-bye, grabbed his raincoat, and headed for the door.

"It may be a long day honey, so don't make any plans for the evening. Mrs. Weiss is going into labor and it looks like there may be complications. I'm supposed to pick Julius up from

Hebrew school this afternoon, but I may not get back in time. Can you take care of that for me? Thanks. I'll see you tonight."

He bolted out the door and headed to Mt. Sinai.

Perry and Liebenthal were the finest of a new breed of specialists produced by the hematology program at Johns Hopkins University. Scientists had unlocked many of the mysteries associated with blood in the previous decade. It was now possible to collect and preserve blood for several days. The donor and recipient were no longer required to be in the same place to effect a transfusion. Blood could now be combined with anti-coagulants and stored in refrigerated sterile glass jars for several days.

Dr. Sussman was already on site when Dr. Katz arrived. He was with Jacob, trying to reassure him that Leah was in the finest hands and everything would be all right.

"Good morning, Mr. Weiss. I see Dr. Sussman is already filling you in on the situation. I don't believe the slight hemorrhaging your wife is experiencing is serious; however, I've taken the precaution of screening some potential donors just in case. We have two of the foremost experts in blood pathology here at Sinai and I've asked them to be on standby. Dr. Sussman, if you're ready, we can join Mrs. Weiss in the delivery room. Mr. Weiss we'll keep you informed of our progress."

The two doctors hurried down the corridor and disappeared through the swinging doors of the maternity ward, leaving Jacob to his own thoughts and concerns.

By ten it was obvious to the delivery team that things were not going well. The contractions were less than a minute apart and the hemorrhaging had increased, and the first baby had not moved into the proper position for delivery. Dr. Katz looked up from his position at the foot of the delivery table obviously concerned.

"Ladies and gentlemen, the degree of dilation we can see and the position of the fetuses is inconsistent with her contractions. I believe the placenta has slipped and is obstructing the cervical opening. I have observed this condition twice before, but never with a multiple birth. Dr. Sussman, I think we need to consider having at least four pints of blood available. She has already lost at least a pint, and if my diagnosis is correct she will lose quite a bit more. I'm going to perform a Caesarian section. Dr. Perry has been alerted and I believe he has at least three donors prepped. If you'll call him and get the ball rolling, I'm going to try to confirm my diagnosis. Nurse, what are her vital signs?"

The head nurse was standing at the opposite end of the table alongside the anesthesiologist. She squeezed the bulb a couple of times and waited for the column of mercury to stabilize.

"Her blood pressure is 95 over 65, her pulse rate is 93 and her temperature is 99.2." Mrs. Appleby said.

"All the readings have deteriorated in the last few minutes."

"That settles it then. Prepare her for surgery and call in the rest of the standby surgical team. Begin an intravenous saline drip."

His words set off an explosion of activity in the room. To the untrained eye it may have seemed chaotic; however, each team in the room and those streaming through the swinging doors were trained and practiced for just such an emergency situation. Nursing assistants wheeled in carts of sterile implements, positioning them for easy access by the surgical assistants. Other carts contained materials to help stanch the hemorrhaging. Two teams of neo-natal specialists stood by to receive the newborns. Within five minutes of his order, every-thing was in readiness for Dr. Katz to begin the surgery. He saw Dr. Perry enter the room with the first pint of blood.

"Okay, let's see if we can deliver two healthy babies here. Mrs. Appleby, please call out her vital signs to me every two minutes. We don't want to bring these two babies into the world without a healthy mother to care for them now do we? Everybody keep on your toes. We're in some uncharted waters here, so let's get this right."

Leah's abdomen was already shaved and sterilized. Dr. Katz made a few quick measurements and marked the incision limits. He asked for the scalpel and made a ten-inch incision through the skin and abdominal muscles, exposing the mem-branes surrounding the fetuses. The assistant on the opposite side worked feverishly to stem the blood flow and clear the area around the incision. Dr. Katz made a second incision through the membrane of the uterus, exposing the placenta. When the area was cleared, he made one final incision through the placenta, then stood back while the remaining amniotic fluids were ab-sorbed and removed. He could now see the exposed head of the first baby. He reached in with forceps to gently lift and pull the baby forward so that he could grasp the infant and remove it from the mother's womb.

"It looks like we have a healthy baby boy here. "

He handed the first baby to a neo-natal team and re-turned to his work, motioning for the nurse to wipe perspiration from his forehead. He returned his attention to Leah and the second baby. This one was not going to be so easy. It was in a lateral position and had not fully descended. He had to manipu-late the baby into a head down position before it could be delivered. He had already determined it to be another boy, probably identical twins.

"Doctor, her pressure is dropping fast," Mrs. Appleby said. "It's down to 85 over 55 now."

"Okay, I'm going to make the incision wider. I'm going in to get this young man."

He added two inches to the cut and reached his hand into the cavity to grasp the child by the head and pull him down into the light. He handed the second baby to the other neo-natal team then returned his attention to Leah. She was ashen and bleeding profusely. The placenta was attached so close to the cervix that the entire passage was blocked, preventing any possibility of a normal birth. He was amazed that Leah had made it this far without worse complications.

"Dr. Perry, start that third pint of blood and see if we can get two more pints on standby. She's going to lose a lot more before we can get this thing stopped."

Blood was pouring from the placenta. Katz severed the placenta's attachment to the uterine wall and quickly stitched up the wound. Blood pooled in the bottom of the uterus. As soon as the assistant cleared it he could see blood flowing from around the cervical opening. He reached across for the cauterizing electrodes and told Dr. Weintraub to turn on the machine. Dr. Katz leaned in and placed the electrodes on the bleeding wound. The smell of burning flesh permeated the operating theater. He continued to apply the electrodes until he was satisfied that all the bleeding was stopped.

"How's she doing now, Mrs. Appleby?"

The nurse squeezed the bulb again.

"She seems to be stabilizing, doctor."

"Her respiration is better," added the anesthesiologist.

"Do you think she needs more blood?"

"Probably," Dr. Katz said. "What do you think, Perry?"

"She's certainly lost a lot, and I imagine there'll be some residual bleeding for a while. I think she should have one more pint, just to be safe, and I'm going to line up another couple of donors to be on standby."

"Good. I concur. Dr. Sussman, will you see if you can arrange that? Dr. Weintraub, will you close here? I think she'll be out of the woods by the time you finish, and the transfusion is complete. I want to keep her here for an hour after that. Will everyone please stand by until then? We'll move her to recovery if there are no more complications.

"I'm going to go over and check on the babies. I want to be sure they weren't damaged by the process. There are sometimes other problems when the placenta implants that near the cervix. They looked healthy, but I want to be certain before I report to Mr. Weiss. Dr. Sussman, after you check on those donors, will you please join me. I'd like you to be there when we talk to Mr. Weiss."

Dr. Katz stood to remove his bloody scrubs before going to clean up and change into a clean set of whites. He left the OR in the very capable hands of Dr. Gerald Weintraub.

By the time he had changed and dropped by the nursery to check on the twins, Dr. Sussman was already in the waiting room with Jacob. Jacob's hands were shaking as he tried to remove a cigarette from a pack of Camels. The flash of the match as he attempted to light it revealed beads of sweat. He had received periodic reports during the surgery, but none hinted at the seriousness of Leah's condition.

"Mr. Weiss," Dr. Sussman began, "I can report that your wife and twin boys are doing well. I won't lie to you though. It was touch-and-go there for a while. You have the remarkable knowledge and skills of Dr. Katz here for pulling Leah through. I don't know another OB/GYN in Baltimore who would have recognized her condition as quickly as he did, nor one who could have responded so quickly to the situation. She'll be transferred to the recovery room as soon as we're sure she's completely stabilized. She'll be in recovery for twenty-four hours before transferring back to her room. When she's settled in you can go in to see her. In the meantime, you might want to join me in the nursery to say hello to your two new sons. Dr. Katz has already checked with the pediatricians and they say both boys are perfectly healthy. Being twins of course their body weight is a little less than a single birth, but in a few weeks, they'll catch up with those other babies in there. Leah will probably need to stay in the hospital for a couple of weeks to let the surgery heal and to regain her strength. We'll keep the twins here as well for their feeding and to bond with Leah. "

"I appreciate those kind remarks, Dr. Sussman," Dr. Katz said, "but I'm sure many others on the staff here could have performed as well as I did. By the way, we all owe a great debt to your cousin Esther and her family. Their blood donations literally saved her life. I'm sure you'll want to express your appreciation to them and please pass along ours as well. It was a very selfless act on their part and one not everybody would make."

Jacob tried to absorb the torrent of words. He heard the most important ones; Leah and the twins were going to be all right. Bernard was not going to lose his mother. Those two boys behind the glass across the hall were going home, hale and hearty. He understood better now Leah's state-of-mind for the past few months. While he had his work and the new house to occupy him, Leah had been immersed in running the household, supervising Bernie, preparing for the twins, planning for the new home and being attentive to his needs. Meantime, he selfishly attended to his own interests. That had to change. At that moment he vowed to himself that he would change. He would cherish his family more and not be afraid to show his emotions. God had given him so much. He had spared Leah and given him two healthy new sons. He had built a prosperous business. It was time for him to recognize his good fortune and to give back more.

"Dr. Katz, words can't express how grateful I am to you for bringing Leah through and safely delivering my two sons. I don't know what I would do if I lost Leah. It's at times like this when we realize what's really important to us. If you don't mind I'd like to see my wife now. I need to tell her how much I love her."

"You bet. As soon as she's settled in the recovery room I'll have someone call you. Meantime, go and enjoy your sons. I have a feeling that they're going to be something very special. Dr. Sussman I'll catch up with you later. Thanks for your help in there."

Dr. Katz hurried off to the OR for one last check on Leah before heading for home. It had indeed been a long day.


Leah lay as still as possible in her hospital bed. Even the slightest movement was unbearable. She avoided moving all night. She drifted in and out of a fitful sleep induced by several pain pills. Her disjointed dreams were of both Bernie and Jacob in various stages of danger. She tried in vain to climb from the abyss she was in to help them but kept falling back into a dark

~ 74 ~

hole. Her silent screams went unheeded. She roused sufficiently to recognize that the ghostly vision before her was not part of her dream. It was Jacob leaning over her to wipe her face with a cool cloth. He had been there all night despite the staff's urging that he go home and get some rest himself. He left her side only twice during the long night, once to go to the bathroom and once to visit the nursery to gaze besotted at the two small helpless babies beyond the glass; Murray with his thumb in his mouth and David with his mouth agape in an unheard scream. This was while the nurses came to express milk from Leah's swelling breasts. The twins with their incessant demands showed no mercy for their ailing mother. It would be another forty-eight hours before she could stand the pain of nursing them. When that time came, she couldn't fully take pleasure in their closeness for the pain.

It was the end of the first week before she could leave her bed to sit quietly in the sun-dappled solarium in the center of the ward. The solarium was the inspiration of Mrs. Hess who remembered with horror the harsh surroundings accompanying the births of her children, which occurred in a less enlightened place and time.

By the end of the second week most of the pain had subsided and the twins were visibly thriving. Dr. Katz dropped by as the Weisses were packing to leave the hospital.

"I heard you were going home today and I wanted to look in on you one last time before you leave. I've spoken to Dr. Sussman and Dr. Weintraub and they both report that despite your ordeal you are recuperating nicely. I stopped by to see the twins on the way here. They are growing like weeds. I can't tell you how pleased I am with your progress.

"Dr. Weintraub says he discussed with you the extent of the surgery we had to perform to stop the hemorrhaging. I'm afraid the damage will not allow you to have any more children. I'm sorry, but it was unavoidable if we were to save your life. But, on a lighter note, I imagine the twins will keep you so busy for the next few years you won't have a lot of time to worry about that.

"I wish you the very best of everything and please give me a report from time to time on their progress. As I said before, I expect great things from those young men."

"Thank you, Dr. Katz," Leah said. "I owe you my life and the lives of David and Murray. Jacob and I will be eternally grateful for what you did. If there's any way we can ever help you, all you have to do is pick up the phone."

"By the way, we delayed the *bris* until I could leave the hospital. We've scheduled it next Saturday at our home. Rabbi Kantor from B'nai Israel will perform the ceremony. We'd consider it a great honor if you and your wife can attend."

"Thank you. I'll check with Deborah and if we're free it would be an honor to attend. I'll get back to you on that. Until then, good-bye and God bless you."

Dr. Katz shook Jacob's hand and left. The same attendant that brought Leah to Room 577 two weeks ago was waiting in the corridor as Dr. Katz exited. Jacob, Leah, David and Murray Weiss were going home.

# 8

# Transitions

"Dr. Katz, it looks like your work is done here," the porter said. "I'm gonna take these folks down to their car while the nurses fetch the babies. I know they'll be glad to get home after all the trials and tribulations they's been through."

Leah settled gingerly into the wheel chair, still mindful of the painful incision. Jacob held the door for their exit then hurried ahead to retrieve the Packard from the parking lot. He circled the building one last time through the now painfully familiar streets. He looked forward to getting home and trying to settle back into a normal routine. He had hardly spoken to Seth for two weeks and had virtually abandoned Bernie to Esther's capable care. He had no idea what progress was made on Linden Avenue. On second thought, with twin babies in the house things may never get back to normal again. And certainly, his vow to be more emotionally involved with his family and his business would require a new "normalcy."

Esther was standing in the driveway, all aflutter, as Jacob rolled to a stop. She opened the rear door for Leah who was trying to cope with the two squirming babies.

"Welcome home, Leah. Bernie and I have been up since six, making sure everything was ready for you. He's so excited to see his new brothers he can hardly stand it. I asked him to wait inside until we can get you settled. I know you must still be in a lot of pain and don't need any extra jostling. You can see him there in the kitchen window. They wouldn't let him visit you in the hospital for fear of infecting you or the twins."

The words poured out in a torrent, betraying Esther's own ill-concealed excitement as she took the twins in her arms and started up the steps. Jacob took his wife by the arm to assist her into the house.

"Welcome home darling. It's certainly a different place than the one you left two weeks ago. With you and the twins home and healthy I couldn't be happier. Thank you.

"Now, I want you to take it easy until you get your strength back. If Esther needs some help for a while we can bring someone in. I don't want you going up and down the stairs a lot. That was a pretty serious operation you had.

"I went by the Linden house on the way over this morning. I think we'll be able to move in about three months. I want you to be completely rested and well when that day comes."

Leah leaned against Jacob as she negotiated the steps to the kitchen. The joy of being back in her own surroundings with her family gave her a renewed conviction that she could endure anything now. Little could she have imagined just six short months ago all the staggering changes that were coming her way. Now they would end with the family and home she dared not even dream of ten years ago.

The next few weeks flew by. With the help of the Epsteins and Sarofskys, the *bris* was a huge success. Doctors Katz and Sussman were there, as were many close friends from B'nai Israel. Others from Jacob and Seth's business world also came. The ceremony was solemn yet joyful, with Rabbi Kantor striking just the right balance between tradition and celebration. David and Murray Weiss took their place as full members of the tribe. Everyone was conscious of how special these two little lives were and how perilously close they had come to losing them and their mother.

Jacob was immersed in catching up with the business and satisfying himself that the renovations on Linden Avenue were going according to the latest architectural revisions, all the while trying to maintain his vow to make more time for his expanded family.

Leah slowly regained her strength. Day by day she was able to shoulder more of the burden of caring for the twins, while at the same time reestablishing her role in the planning and directing of her household. Late in the evening, when the children were all down and Esther had retired to her room, the Weisses spent their time planning for the impending move. More than just a physical relocation, the move from Hanover to Linden would mark a spiritual and cultural transition for the entire family.

When Esther was not engaged with the twins, she still had to attend to the cooking and the household chores. Her sister Naomi came three days a week to help and Esther spent time tutoring her in the fine points of running the Weiss home. The little time left found her late at night poring over chemistry, biology and anatomy texts. She was preparing for the exams she would ultimately take for the Hopkins nursing school. More times than not, she awoke to the five o'clock alarm with a textbook resting on her chest and the reading lamp still burning. She was happily pursuing her dream.

Bernie was fascinated with the twins. Leah and Esther found that satisfying the curiosity of a precocious twelve-year old boy was almost impossible. Every afternoon, when Bernie finished his homework, he was allowed to help with the boys. Leah often found him sitting by their cribs, staring in rapt wonder as they slept. He was captivated by their antics and wondered aloud why they did this or that particular thing. There was little surprise, when Bernard Daniel Weiss grew up to become a world-renowned pediatrician, author of several books on child development and a professor at Johns Hopkins University — nor that he was in great demand on the lecture circuit.

The new house was finally ready in late September. All the packing was complete, the movers alerted, and anticipation honed to a keen edge. Everyone was exhausted at the moving preparations and the preceding ten weeks of bedlam. Jacob and Leah prayed that the tempo of their life would settle down once the move was complete. In some ways it would. In others it definitely would not.

The leaves of the trees along Linden Avenue were tinged with the first hues of autumn as the moving vans pulled up to the new house. Neighborhood children breezed by on their bicycles or clustered at the periphery of the yard as each formed his own opinion of the Weiss family and the impact it might have on their particular neighborhood routine. The Hyatts were the previous residents. They had moved further out to a new development off Reistertown Road near Pimlico Racetrack. The children had already absorbed the departure of the Hyatts, cataloguing their youthful sadness at their departure under *"life's uncontrollable changes."* With the resilience given only to the very young, they had begun preparing to welcome the new kids on the block.

Bernie was a particularly welcome addition to the mix on the street for he helped to balance a huge gender disparity. One made even worse by the departure of the Hyatt boys. In the twenty houses on that block of Linden there were fourteen girls and with Bernie's arrival there were only eight boys. David and Murray were too young to count.

Directly across the street lived the Sternberg family with eleven-year old Isaac, six-year old Pearl and one-year old Joseph. Next door to the right were the Tomlinsons. They were a very large family that had lived in the Druid Hills neighborhood since the turn of the century. Several of the older children had moved on to college and careers. Only sixteen-year old Josephine and nine-year old Thomas still lived at home. Thomas, like David and Murray, had been a late surprise to Nancy and Tom Sr., but he was loved the more for it. On the Weiss' left lived the Kahns. Edith was the oldest at thirteen. Sidney, who would forever hate his name, was ten. Isaac, Tom, Sid and Bernie forged a bond that would last a lifetime — not withstanding that Tom's family was Presbyterian. He was one of the few *goys* accepted into the neighborhood gang.

With Bernie's quick acceptance into the gang, Leah and Esther bent their efforts toward settling in. The bright and airy nursery, located upstairs next to the master bedroom, made life much easier. Esther's room was at the other end of the upstairs gallery, tucked under the eaves, with its own small sitting room and a window with views of Druid Hills Park. As the late October leaves began to fall she discovered that her view included a small corner of Druid Lake. In the few quiet, reflective moments that she snatched from her busy routine, she would sit by her window and watch the children stream in and out of the park. She was the happiest she had ever been. She was able to visit her family on her Wednesday afternoons off and on *Shabbat*. Bernie occasionally begged to go with her and Leah obliged him more often than not. It was a short walk from the house to Lower Park Heights Avenue where they could catch the Number 5 or Number 33 streetcar to downtown Baltimore. Bernie loved visiting the Sarofsky family. Any deprivation the family may have felt was lost on Bernie. He reveled in the lusty give-and-take of the boisterous clan as they gathered to celebrate the ancient traditions that had always bound wandering Jews together. He returned each time brimming with wild tales from the Sarofskys.

The twins rapidly fulfilled the prophecies of the doctors. By their second birthday they were as strong and healthy as any of the dozens of young boys tearing around the green expanses of Druid Hills Park on a sunny *Shabbat* afternoon. When Bernie was not off with Esther on such days, he could be found shepherding the two little human dynamos, attempting, and failing, to keep them out of trouble. The twins were impish hellions, polar opposites to their serious and studious brother, and they were hell-bent on making his life miserable. If they weren't harassing the ducks and chasing them into the lake, they were disappearing into the woods. Bernie often came home covered with poison ivy after his frequent forays into the forest after them. Miraculously, the twins appeared to be immune to all of nature's torments. Nonetheless, through it all, Bernie loved and protected his wards as he mentored them through their introduction to life on Linden Avenue.

# 9

# Growing Up

The World War that raged across Europe in the years just prior to the birth of the Weiss twins brought the upheaval and displacement of tens of thousands of ethnic Jews. The massive suffering produced by the tumult unleashed a wave of immigrants who were fleeing from the fighting to their east and the persecution to their west.

From 1916 through 1919 Belarus – the Pale – was occupied at different times by Germans, Poles, Russians and Ukrainians. It mattered little to the Jews of the region who their masters were, for they all displayed varying degrees of cruelty, indifference and contempt for a population still reeling from the Cossack pogroms. Starvation, forced labor and conscription were the order of the day. Over a million Jews fled, were killed or were exiled during the period.

The remnants of Jacob Weiss' family finally gave up and left Borisov for sanctuary in Romania. War and politics had thwarted Jacob's efforts to move them to the United States. As a final desperate measure, he had turned to the Polish count that befriended Seth many years before. During the brief period that Poland held sway over the territory Jacob persuaded Count Pulaski to funnel money through the embassies in Warsaw and Washington to influence the right people. Documents were finally issued allowing 17 members of the Weiss family in Borisov to board a train in Minsk to carry them unmolested to the small oil town of Ploesti, Romania. Cousins who had fled during the pogrom that took the life of Bernard Daniel Weiss' grandfather and namesake greeted them at the train station.

Ploesti, Romania became the center of petroleum development south of the Carpathian Mountains earlier in the century and would play an even more decisive role in the Second World War as a source of fuel for Hitler's war machine. The Weiss family members who fled earlier and those fleeing the aftermath of the First World War found lucrative employment in the refineries.

Simultaneously, as the economy of the roaring twenties flourished in America, many more of the displaced survivors from Europe made their way to America's shores. Among them were many members of the Weiss and Epstein families that had been scattered along the Carpathian divide. Jacob sponsored as many as he was allowed and gave many of them employment in his own factories. For others he found employment in the many tailor shops and retail stores of east Baltimore. His greatest disappointment was that he couldn't convince his oldest brother Levi to give up his job at a Ploesti refinery and bring his family over. Levi worked for a British oil company and had risen to a post of prominence. He was reluctant to give it up for an uncertain future in Baltimore. After all, many Jews worked in the refineries and were treated with respect by the local population. The Romanians were much more tolerant of the Jews than were the people of the other Balkan states. When David and Murray turned three they had over forty relatives in the Baltimore area. All of them were in various states of assimilation into the Jewish community of their new home and attended synagogues in east and south Baltimore.

Jacob had long ago decided that it made no sense to travel back to York Street to attend *B'nai Israel*. In 1925 he and Leah had moved their membership to *Chizuk Amuno* at the corner of Eutaw Place and Chauncey Avenue. It was close enough for the family to walk, even though Jacob no longer practiced the strict orthodoxy of his parents. He had secretly wanted to worship at *Oheb Shalom,* a striking temple of neo-Moorish design, located further down Eutaw Place. The most dominant feature of that temple was its soaring dome directly over the *bema* and its sacred t*orahs,* where sunlight poured in from the glass ceiling. However, despite his wealth, Jacob did not feel comfortable mingling with the mostly German Jewish congregants. They maintained a strong prejudice against the Russians, regardless of their position in society.

The German Jews lived in the splendid apartment houses lining Eutaw Place and the other streets surrounding *Oheb Shalom*. The well-appointed buildings in their grand conceit stared at each other across the manicured esplanade of Eutaw Place: the Emersonian, Temple Gardens, the Marlborough, The Riviera. The cream of Baltimore's German Jewish society lived in cosseted splendor behind the ornate facades and secured lobbies of these monuments to their *"nouveau riche"* status.

"Leah, we have to make arrangements for Bernie's *bar mitzvah* soon," Jacob said.

It was already June and Bernie's thirteenth birthday was fast approaching. *Bar mitzvah* is the Jewish rite that ushers the males of the tribe into manhood. It is a solemn occasion requiring the celebrant to memorize several passages from the *Torah* and to answer questions from the rabbi. The celebration is also marked by much partying and the bestowal of many gifts on the young celebrant.

So it was that Daniel Bernard Weiss found himself on the *bema* at *Chizuk Amuno* reciting scriptures and answering questions, surrounded by friends old-and-new and family old-and-new. The two-year old twins sat wriggling and squirming alongside their parents on the first pew. They were sorely trying Bernie's powers of concentration. He summoned up all his reserve and fixed his eyes on the stained-glass figure of the angel Gabriel above the balcony, while he recited the designated passages from the *torah* that he had been memorizing for the past three months. He stepped down from the *bema* to the powerful embrace of his father.

"Welcome to the tribe my son," he said.

The reception following the *bar mitzvah* was held at the prestigious and exclusive Phoenix Club at 1505 Eutaw Place near *Temple Oheb Shalom*. Max Hochschild, a member of that bastion of German Jewish society, and a close friend of Jacob Weiss, had made the arrangements for the catering hall to host the celebration. It would take ten more years, following a seismic upheaval in Baltimore's German Jewish society, before Jacob himself was invited to join the Phoenix Club.

Life took on a pleasant routine following Bernie's *bar mitzvah*. With the move completed and the family settled in on Linden, Jacob was free to focus his attention on the business and the expansion of Epstein and Weiss. Mindful of his promise, he was always home for dinner and did not allow himself to be consumed by business affairs as before. When on the road he faithfully called home each night and spoke to all four members of his family. It was on one such occasion away when Jacob was inspired to think about buying a vacation home on the Eastern Shore of Maryland. The area was referred to by its inhabitants as "down shore."

Jacob was on a trip to Norfolk for a clothier's convention. He took the "President Warfield," one of many packet steamers plying the Chesapeake waters. This wouldn't be Jacob's only experience with the Warfield. A second encounter was to occur in 1946 and figure prominently in the post-war history of Baltimore.

As they sailed past the city of Tolchester, a traveling companion made an off-hand remark that a friend of his owned a beachfront cottage there and was thinking of selling it. Many years ago, the Weisses had visited friends in the Kent County village and remarked how nice it would be to have a place there. It was just a dream then. Now, the growing specter of polio had many families looking for ways out of town during the infectious summers. He considered the idea that he could bring the family over when school let out and they could stay all summer. "The Tred Avon" carried passengers from the inner harbor to the eastern shore twice a day, so getting back and forth to work wouldn't be a problem for him.

"Leah, I was just talking to Morris Hess on the way down here," Jacob said. He had just checked in and was sitting on the edge of his bed.

"Do you remember the gray, shingled, cottage in Tolchester, next to the Hamburger's shore home? Morris tells me it's for sale. I remember when we talked about someday having a place on the shore. With all the polio that's rampant in the summer I think we should consider getting you and the kids out of town. Besides, I think it would be a good investment and I could catch the steamer down on Thursdays and spend long weekends with you. What do you think?"

Leah had never heard Jacob bubble with such excitement.

"Do you think we can really afford it? We've spent so much on the new house and the hospital expenses were astronomical. Don't get me wrong, I think it would be great, but I just don't want us to get overextended."

"I understand and your right to be cautious, but the proceeds from our old house plus what we had saved allowed me to buy the new house with no mortgage and the proceeds from our "Workmen's" policy paid all the hospital bills. The business is growing, and Seth and I have squirreled away a big nut for any inevitable downturn. So, if finances are your only worry, let's do it. Don't tell the kids until we have a deed in hand. I want to surprise them. Bernie will love the beach and the twins can work off all their excess energy. I'll be back in two days and I'll talk to the owner, Mr. Safire, and see if we can strike a deal. Good night my love. Kiss the kids for me."

Jacob bounded down the stairs to join Morris Hess for dinner. He hadn't been excited like this in a long time.

# 10

## Despair

The decade of the 1920's was drawing to a close and everyone in Baltimore was talking about the obscene profits being amassed on Wall Street. Bernie Weiss enrolled as a student at Johns Hopkins Medical School. Esther Sarofsky graduated from nursing school in the spring, and Naomi had already become the glue that held the Weiss family together. The twins moved on to P.S. 61, a scant three blocks from home, carrying their reputation for mischief-making with them. Teachers at their new school could only stand and shake their heads in amazement that these terrors were Bernie Weiss' brothers. All in all, life was very good on Linden Avenue.

That all changed on October 29, 1929 when Bernard was well into his second year at Hopkins, Esther Sarofsky became a nurse in the maternity ward at Mt. Sinai, and David and Murray Weiss were constantly challenging the staff of P.S. 61—and Wall Street experienced a financial meltdown.

"Jacob, did you see this in the Sun," Leah asked as he came in from work.

"What is it? More bad news."

"It's Ethel Rosen's brother, he works for J.P. Morgan in New York. He lost everything in the crash. He was found on the sidewalk outside their offices. He apparently jumped to his death. I haven't summoned the courage to call Ethel yet, but I must do it."

"I don't know a family in Baltimore with relatives on Wall Street that hasn't been affected by this", Jacob said. "I don't know why they couldn't see this coming. With all the rampant speculation going on, it was bound to happen. It's tulip bulb mania all over again. Thank God Seth and I didn't get ourselves overextended. We're losing some business and may have to cut back, but we'll be all right."

The Great Depression spawned on that fateful October day, swallowed-up the roaring twenties with its dissolute jazz age and plunged the nation into a decade of despair. It took a worldwide cataclysm, a magnificent invalid, and a resilient nation tested by fire, to pull the nation out of its most desperate crisis since 1865. For years the "dust bowl," the westerly migration it precipitated, unrelenting joblessness and soup lines became the common themes of the era, and *"Brother Can You Spare a Dime"* became its theme song.

Baltimore was less affected by the pandemonium that was unfolding in Philadelphia, New York and Boston. Those financial centers were devastated. Baltimore had established a broader industrial base and its leaders, from their more remote vantage point, were leery of the stock market and its oily hucksters. Many, like Jacob and Seth, were first generation immigrants who had risked too much to bet it on the stocks of companies they didn't know or understand. The city suffered its own setbacks, for sure, but they were manageable and there were no bodies falling from tall buildings.

The hardships were relative. Everyone shares the pain when 20% of its men are unemployed and the demand for goods and services drops. That was especially true for deferrable items, such as suits and other apparel.

Epstein and Weiss at its peak employed 350 people in five locations around the city. They found it necessary to consolidate into three of their factories and reduce the workforce to 200. They chose the facilities that were surrounded by the newer immigrants, the ones who worked for the lowest wages.

"Jacob, I'm sure I'm getting an ulcer, Seth said one morning when another agonizing decision was before them. "I don't think I can face another employee and tell them there's no more work. It's gnawing a hole in my gut."

"I know how you feel. I haven't been able to get a full night's sleep since this whole thing started."

To cushion the blow, they worked hand-in-hand with the Jewish Benevolent Society and other relief agencies. Furthermore, over a twenty-year period, Epstein and Weis had adopted a philosophy unheard of at the time. They had created a reserve fund that was available to help their laid-off employees. Many firms with less foresight went under and had to shutter their operations. By 1935 the company was making enough progress to begin rehiring, and those grateful former employees came back in droves. Business thrived, and the profits were used to acquire other failed firms. The good fortune was occurring just in time. The world was once again moving inexorably toward war and their seven factories and 1,000 employees were to be enlisted to do their part. Events unfolding in Europe were casting a dark shadow over the entire civilized world. Hitler had extorted the Sudetenland from Neville Chamberlain and Goebbels had unleashed Kristallnacht on the Jewry of Germany and Austria.

Each new atrocity by Hitler and his cronies in the *"Third Reich"* sent nervous ripples through the Jewish community of Baltimore. Every religious and social gathering was abuzz with the latest news. Jewish organizations both locally and nationally were mobilized to pressure FDR to intercede on the part of the oppressed, especially the Jews, who were receiving the brunt of Hitler's demented fury. More clandestine efforts were underway to assist in the rescue of the persecuted all across Europe. While maintaining an outward mantle of neutrality, America was gearing up to provide armaments to both England and Russia to confront Hitler's war machine. Despite the strident cries of the isolationists to stay out of the war, the handwriting was on the wall. Sooner or later America would be drawn into the battle.

Rumors of war and of ethnic persecution in far-off lands were not pressing matters for eleven-year-old boys growing up in Baltimore. Especially if you knew that all the other neighborhood boys were down at Mannheimer's Pharmacy playing the pinball machines and you were forbidden to join them.

"Mama we're going down to the "Y" for a swim," Murray shouted to his mother as he and David bolted out the back door. "We'll be back by five."

Leah didn't have time to respond before the two were tearing around the corner. She could never get used to the riotous behavior of the twins. Bernie had been such a joy. She couldn't recall a single incident when he required even a mild rebuke. Even now, in his second year of medical school he was at the top of his class and involved in a multitude of campus activities. Murray and David, on the other hand, were into so much mischief that their obvious academic skills were overshadowed by the terrible comportment marks on their report cards. She and Jacob had experienced more trips to the principal's anteroom at P.S. 61 than they could count. No level of cajoling or threatening seemed to matter. They finally became resigned to the fact that this was their reality. The twins were not bad boys; they were just highly spirited and intent on wringing every ounce of joy out of life. They were not malicious, and their antics never caused anyone harm. They were just David and Murray; boisterous, trying, frustrating and pure delights.

Vacations "down-the-shore" quickly became a rite of summer. One that was keenly anticipated as the days of spring lengthened and the end of school approached. Bernie had experienced only a few vacations in Tolchester before leaving for Johns Hopkins. As he began his internships, his days at the beach were few. He stole away as often as possible to join the twins cavorting in the water and traipsing through the woods.

Summers on the Chesapeake were a welcome respite from the pressures of life in Baltimore. Leah and Jacob were both heavily involved in the synagogue's efforts to reclaim Jewish lives from Hitler's killing machine. Endless campaigns for financial support and pleas for political intervention poured into their small synagogue. They responded with their time, their talent and their means as best they could and together with thousands like them, they made a difference.

# 11

## Mount Airy

It was the spring of 1937, when the twins found out that Stanley and Burt Kahn were going to summer camp near Frederick, Maryland. The camp was scheduled for three weeks prior to the opening of the cottage in Tolchester. Many Jewish families sent their children away to summer camps in the Poconos, the Catskills and other mountain retreats for most of the summer. Those who had "shore homes" sent theirs away for shorter periods.

"Mama," David said at dinner that night, "the Kahn boys are going to camp at Mount Airy as soon as school is out. Can Me and Murray go? We'll be back in time for the shore."

"It's Murray and I, and you'll have to wait until Jacob gets home from New York. Camp costs a lot and I don't know if we can afford it. Bernie's school expenses have gone up and things are a little tighter."

Jacob returned the next day. He was besieged immediately by the twins asking for permission to go to Mount Airy.

"Let me think about it," Jacob said. "I'll let you know tomorrow."

The twins were down for breakfast early, anxious to hear Jacob's decision. Jacob came down a few minutes later. He adjusted his suspenders and took the copy of the *Sun* from the hall table, reading the headlines as he crossed to the dining room.

"Okay boys, here's the deal. If I let you go to Mount Airy you must promise to do all the yard work and maintenance at the Tolchester house for the entire summer. I checked on what it cost me last year, and it just about equates to the fees for camp. If you fail to live up to this commitment, you'll be sent home immediately. Do we have a deal?"

David looked at Murray and Murray looked at David. Both broke into big grins.

"Yes, sir," they said simultaneously.

As school wound down in late May, the neighborhood was abuzz with preparations for camp; clothing was bought, labels were sewn in, camping gear was assembled, insect repellents, suntan oil and calamine lotion were stockpiled, all in readiness for the great adventure.

Promptly at eight a.m. on June 6 the twins clambered aboard a bus in the parking lot at P.S. 61, along with 40 other revelers from the surrounding Jewish neighborhoods. They were setting sail for summer camp and two weeks of freedom from their parents and a chance to discover another world. It would prove to be a life altering experience for David and Murray.

The bus headed west, picking up State Route 140 through Reistertown. Busy city streets quickly gave way to fields of ripening tobacco and corn. Within an hour they were winding up a steep, one-lane, gravel road through dense forests of oak and maple. The trees on either side of the narrowing road began to brush against the bus when suddenly they burst from the forest into a large clearing containing several athletic fields. To the left was a tin-roofed gymnasium, its sides open to the elements. Soccer fields and archery ranges ran down the hill to the right toward the woods. The road ended at a large administration building. Tennis courts and a pool flanked the building. Narrow paths ran up and down the hill toward the cabins to the north and toward a lake to the south. The entire camp sat at the top of one of the highest hills in the Catoctin range, overlooking Thurmont to the east and the Blue Ridge to the west.

The bus wheezed to a stop amid clouds of dust and screaming kids. The bus door swung open and the Linden avenue gang piled off to the whoops and shouts of the earlier arrivals. Two other buses rolled up behind them and began disgorging their boisterous cargo. Camp counselors, in their distinctive blue and white uniforms emblazoned with camp logos, herded the noisy troop back up the hill to the gymnasium. When the rowdy group of 150 boys was seated in the bleachers, a piercing whistle silenced the excited crowd.

"My name is Dave Kaufman. I am the head counselor here at Mount Airy. You may consider me God. Everything you eat, sleep, breathe or do for the next two weeks will be done in accordance with the rules of Mount Airy. Each of you is being handed a list of those rules by my assistant counselors. The assistant counselors are to be considered only slightly lower than God. You are to obey their orders at all times. If you do not, you will be brought to my office for discipline. You do not want to be brought to my office for discipline. You do not want to come to my office for any reason.

"Read the rules. Memorize them. There are only 12. Scan down the list to number 12. *"No member of the camp is to leave the campground at any time."* Simple and straightforward. Camp Louise for girls is located down the road beyond the lake. All contact between the boy's camp and the girl's camp will take place on Friday during athletic competitions and during sanctioned social events on Sundays. The other rules are self-explanatory. There is one other unwritten rule. You will each write to your parents twice a week. Your counselor will check you off as you retrieve your stamped envelopes from the post office. I do not want any parent calling to say they have not heard from their child. Understood??

"Tomorrow's activities are posted at each cabin. Read them. Your cabin numbers and your counselor's names are posted on the boards at the rear of the gym. Find your cabin number, reclaim your gear, and report to your cabins. Your counselor will have further instructions for you there. Lunch is in the dining hall next to the cabins at twelve o'clock sharp. See you there."

Dave Kaufman turned on his heel and marched out to stunned silence. No one had warned them that this was a boot camp. They had learned much in a short period of time. There was a lot more to learn in the next fourteen days. The trek to their cabins took them three hundred yards up a steep embankment. Everyone was panting and gasping for breath when they dropped their gear on the cabin porches.

The "gang of four" from Linden Avenue was allowed to stick together in Aspen Cabin along with ten other Baltimore teens. Nathan Snyder, a twenty-two-year-old medical student from George Washington University was the Aspen counselor. He assigned the boys to their bunks and lockers, showed them where the latrines were and handed them their first week's work assignments. Murray and David, along with Sid and two other boys were assigned to latrine duty. They were responsible for cleaning the toilets, showers and sinks after each meal and assuring a constant supply of soap, toilet paper and paper towels.

"Reveille is at six each morning. Breakfast begins at six-thirty. Dorms will be vacated by eight. There will be three activity sessions each morning and three more in the afternoon. Yours will be posted on the cabin bulletin board each evening before lights out sounds. Supper is at six. There's a free hour from five to six. After supper there will be special presentations in the amphitheater until nine. Friday evenings and Saturday morning, we observe *Shabbat*. Saturday afternoon after synagogue is free time. Write your letters. Sunday is for hiking, boating, swimming, etc. Boys and girls are allowed supervised mingling on Sunday afternoons but not in the dorms. Any questions? Okay then, let's get washed up and get some chow."

Nate moved around the dorm greeting the campers individually and giving each a name tag. He then showed them how to pack their lockers and gave them a tour of the bathrooms and the assembly room used for study, writing and meetings.

Following their orientation, Nate shepherded his dazed flock to the dining room for their first meal at Mount Airy.

Equally traumatized campers were straggling in from the other cabins. They joined the 16 counselors and the 10 other camp personnel for their first official meal of this camp session. Each cabin was assigned a separate table; Ash, Aspen, Beech and so on with Yew bringing up the rear in accordance with the arborist's alphabet. The campers were called in cabin alphabetical order to the food line. The fourteen boys from Aspen filed through while the counselor received his food from a different line. The boys were convinced it was because the cooks had laced their food with saltpeter. Everyone was served within twenty minutes and the mess hall was empty thirty minutes later. The twenty years of operating Mount Airy had fostered a great deal of efficiency in all camp operations. The bracing mountaintop air was a welcome change from the heat and humidity of Baltimore. The brisk wind and chilled air was invigorating, and all the boys were ready to burn off their excess energy in physical activity. Mornings were dedicated to activities in and around the cabin area. Afternoons were taken up with athletic competitions. Fridays always found the boys splashing in the camp pool. There was an hour of water games followed by an hour of competitive racing. These Friday afternoon sessions often included coed competitors from Camp Louise.

# 12

# Ruth

David checked the swim-racing schedule and saw he was competing against Ruth Braddock in the 200-yard freestyle. Mount Airy had not yet followed Camp Louise's lead in allowing non-Jewish friends of campers to attend. Ruth was invited by her close friend Natalie Perlman, also from Silver Spring.

David stood at the edge of the pool, waiting for his competitor to appear. He was not expecting to see a five-foot-eight, copper-haired Amazon with soul-piercing green eyes who would have been right at home in the Irish Games but who stuck out like a sore thumb at Mount Airy. She took her place, glancing over at her competitor as she flashed a dazzling Gaelic smile. David stood mesmerized as the starter gun sounded. Ruth was a good two yards ahead by the time he entered the water and she maintained that lead at the turn. Despite his best effort, David was unable to make up those yards by the finish line.

He climbed out of the pool, not quite sure what had just happened. He only knew that her tossed-hair, ear-to-ear grin, and sparkling laugh were both captivating and infuriating at the same time. He couldn't take his eyes off her. Feeling his stare, she blushed and turned to join her teammates.

David retreated to the shadows of the pool house to lick his wounds. The structure offered a vantage from which he could observe the stunning, red-haired, water sprite without being seen by her. He remained there for the remainder of the hour, alternately feeling humiliation and fascination. He had never felt about a girl as he did about Ruth. Sure, there were adolescent flirtations and a more serious crush on Baila Graber in *Yeshiva,* but nothing had ever affected him like this.

At that moment David Weiss knew, in some unplumbed depth of his soul, that someday he would marry Ruth Braddock; even though marriage was a subject that had never entered his mind — especially marriage to a Gentile. He thought of all the objections his parents would raise, especially their deep conservative belief that marriage within the faith was a given. He decided he would face each objection as it arose, but in this moment, in this epiphany, he was undaunted. The conviction he felt was unshakable.

Long after the last swimmer had departed David sat alone in the dusk, sorting through the events of the afternoon.

He accepted that he had crossed a great divide in his life and that nothing would ever be the same again. He glanced up at the clock and jumped to his feet. He was due back at Aspen an hour ago.

"Where have you been?" Murray said. "Nate is out scouring the compound for you. He's getting ready to send out a search party. You'd better get the PA announcer to call him before all hell breaks loose."

David ran down the hill to admin where he had Nate paged. He arrived back at Aspen to face his irate counselor.

"Mr. Weiss, you'd better have a damned good excuse for all the uproar you've caused."

"I'm sorry Dave. I fell asleep in the pool house and didn't recognize what time it was."

David had never knowingly lied in his life, but he didn't want this flap to get in the way of his plans.

"Okay, David. I'll let you off this time, but this means another week of latrine duty. Now, get cleaned up and get ready for the *Shabbat* supper."

No activities, save mandatory synagogue attendance, were scheduled for Saturday. David spent his free time searching the bulletin boards trying to find out whether Ruth Braddock would be at Mount Airy on Sunday. The last board he checked, located in the pool house, showed coed competition in swimming, water polo and fencing on Sunday afternoon. Ruth's name appeared on the fencing schedule at three.

David slept fitfully that night. He was up before anyone in the cabin. He dressed and slipped quietly from Aspen. He wandered around the complex, still trying to absorb the events of the previous day — and his reaction to them. A night's sleep had not changed the way he felt. If anything, his attraction to Ruth had only intensified. He went back to Aspen and joined the others for lunch before again wandering about while willing the hands on the clock to spin faster. Three o'clock finally arrived. He strode down to the gymnasium where he spotted Ruth as she watched a teammate parry her opponent's thrust then touch her epée to his padded vest.

"Touché," she declared as another red-faced boy slinked away in defeat at the hands of a mere girl.

"Ruth, my name is David Weiss," he announced in a tremulous voice at least two octaves higher than normal.

"Yes, I recognize you from yesterday in the 200 meters. I wanted to speak to you afterwards, but you were gone. I'm sorry if I embarrassed you. I know the start was messed up. I don't know if I would have beaten you otherwise."

"That's what I wanted to talk to you about. If I go back to Baltimore and tell them I was beaten by a girl, I'll be razzed out of town. So, how about a rematch? There's still time this after-noon."

"You do know that I was state champion in the 200 at the Annapolis meet last spring?"

"Uh-oh, someone forgot to let me in on that little detail. Oh well, the offer still stands. If I go down in flames at least I'll have a good excuse."

"Okay, if it means that much to you. I'll get my swimsuit and meet you at the pool in an hour."

Word of the rematch spread like wildfire. When Ruth re-turned, the stands around the pool were filling rapidly—with both boys and girls. Murray and the Linden gang were on the top bench eagerly awaiting David's further humiliation at the hands of a girl. There were even betting pools between the various cabins.

What had begun as a sophomoric stunt to meet Ruth was quickly turning into a personal nightmare. David had lain in his bunk wondering how he got himself into such a pickle and what he would do if he lost again.

"Not only will I be a laughingstock, but she likely won't have anything more to do with me afterwards," he thought.

Reluctantly, he rolled off his bunk with a sigh of resignation and got his trunks from the locker.

Ruth was already warming up when David arrived to catcalls from his buddies. He jumped into the water and swam a lap then he climbed out of the pool and approached Ruth. She had that same impish grin from yesterday's defeat.

"Hello, David. You ready to do this?"

"Yeah, I guess so. Look, I'm sorry to cause such a circus. I didn't mean for this to get so out of hand."

"Don't worry about it. It'll all blow over in a day or two no matter the outcome. You ready?"

The two antagonists stepped onto the starting blocks as the swim-coach counselor walked up.

"Okay you guys. Two hundred meters, down and back twice."

He stepped back and put the whistle to his mouth, did a one-two-three with his fingers, and blew the whistle. The two bodies knifed into the water together and when they surfaced

Ruth had a slight lead. When they made the flip her lead had extended to three feet. Panic showed on David's face as he attempted to close the distance. At the turn for lap two he was still two feet behind. He had made up one of those when they turned for the final leg. He summoned every ounce of strength in him and tore through the water. He could see they were neck-and-neck ten yards out and felt sure he would prevail. He turned when his fingers touched to see how far ahead he was. He was dumbfounded when he looked over to see that beguiling grin staring back at him again.

"Dead heat!" the referee said. "Well done both of you. Is that it, or do you want to go again?"

David stood on the side of the pool, doubled over and gasping for breath.

"I submit," he said as he bowed in Ruth's direction. "I know when I've met my match."

He reflected on the double meaning of his comment and smiled; for he had truly met his match. The spectators piled down from the stands to surround the two and offer their congratulations before everyone began to drift away. Within minutes Ruth and David were alone, toweling themselves off. They had recovered enough to utter short bursts of speech. Ruth went first.

"That was fun. We'll have to do it again sometime," she said with a wink.

"No thank you. That's enough embarrassment for a lifetime. I really think you let up a little at the end. Thanks."

"You'll never know, will you? And it doesn't matter."

"Say, would you join me for an ice cream soda to celebrate?" David said. "You'll be going back to camp shortly and I may not see you again. I'd like to know more about you. Please."

"I guess it won't hurt. Sure. Let's go."

They walked over to the ice cream parlor near admin and took two vacant stools.

"What would you like," David said. "I'll get it. It's the least I can do."

"How about a chocolate malted with an extra scoop?"

"You got it," he said as he signaled to the soda jerk.

They were half-way through their sodas before either spoke.

"Ruth, I know we'll be going home next week and I don't know anything about you, and I'd really like to. So tell me, 'Who is Ruth Braddock'?"

"Well, I'm a sixteen-year-old student at Silver Spring High School. My mother teaches fifth grade at Chevy Chase and my father works for the State Department. They are both second generation Irish. I have an older brother, Brian and a younger brother, Rory. I like sports and no, I don't have a regular boyfriend. Now what about you?"

"Well, I'm definitely not Irish," he said laughing. "My parents emigrated from Russia. My father has a clothing business and my mother is a homemaker. As you know, I have a twin brother, Murray. I also have a brother, Bernard, who is 12 years older. Murray and I were kind of unexpected. We live in Baltimore and I'll be a sophomore at Cardozo High in September. And, like you, I have no steady girlfriend."

"What would your parents say if they knew you were having ice cream with an Irish Catholic girl?" Ruth asked.

The question caught David by surprise. He hadn't given a thought to her religious background. He just knew he wanted to be with her.

"Oh, my mother wouldn't say a word. My dad might raise an eyebrow. I have many non-Jewish friends at school. There's never been a problem. What about your parents?"

"The same. Mom wouldn't think anything about it. She's pretty liberal. With my dad, I don't know. We've never discussed the subject. I suspect he'd be more concerned who the Jew was more than the fact of his Jewishness."

"I'd like to see you again before we go home," David said as he finished his malt. "There's a lot more I'd like to know about you. I understand that there will be some rowing events next Friday. Do you think we can meet by the lake and take a canoe out?"

Ruth hesitated as she took one final sip of her malt. She knew the territory they were about to enter was a potential minefield. She liked David, but their religious and racial divide was sure to become an issue if they moved beyond a summer friendship. However, she had never shied away from going where her heart led her, and she was not going to start now.

"I don't see why not, David. I'll see you by the lake at noon," she said.

She rose from her stool to leave, leaned over, and gave him the slightest peck on the cheek in passing.

David sat and watched her walk away. No act of tenderness in his life had ever affected him like that — and no malt would ever again taste so good. There was no longer a shred of doubt in his mind that one day he would marry this girl. He floated back to Aspen on a cloud.

"Where have you been?" Murray asked. "The race was over an hour ago. You've almost missed supper. Come on. Get dressed and get ready for another razzing in the chow hall."

"Murray, I had a soda with Ruth Braddock — the girl I raced today. I really like her. We're taking a canoe out Friday before the boat races. I just have to see her again before we leave on Saturday."

Murray was silent. He turned and rested his crossed arms on their bunk. After a minute he spoke.

"David, have you thought this through? If this goes beyond Mount Airy you know there will be trouble. Mama won't make too much fuss, but you know Papa will raise hell. He won't stand for you going outside the faith. His roots go back to the Temple in Borisov. His parents were Orthodox and even though he's mellowed some he still clings to the old ways. Be careful. You'll be letting yourself in for a lot of pain."

"I know Murray, but I really do like her. I've never felt like this about a girl before. If it gets serious I'll just have to deal with it—and face Papa."

"Okay, but don't say I didn't warn you."

# 13

# Hooked

David steered the canoe away from the pier and headed across Lake Louise. There was a small cove on the shore near the girl's camp that was screened from the lake by a spit of trees. He beached the canoe and held Ruth's hand as she stepped ashore. She took the small picnic basket she had prepared and followed David to a grassy glade that had been hollowed out by a herd of deer. She took a blanket from the basket and spread it on the grass.

"I was afraid you wouldn't show up this morning," David said. "I'm glad you did. I didn't want to go home without having a chance to talk to you."

"I'll confess that I had second thoughts about it—as much for you as for me. I know how difficult it will be for both of us if this relationship goes any further, but especially for you. Catholics can be very defensive of their religious beliefs, and I've seen some bad outcomes among my friends who have crossed over. I don't want that to happen to us."

"I know. Murray and I had a long talk last night, and he said the same thing. But, if it's to be, it's to be. I don't think anyone should have to live their lives just to conform to someone else's beliefs and traditions. Besides, the best I recall, we both believe in the same God."

"That's true, but the Jews and the Catholics arrived at those beliefs along very different paths. There are some in my church who still hate the Jews because they crucified Jesus. They are a very small minority, but they are very vocal."

"So, what do we do about it?" David said.

"Let's just let nature take its course. If we decide to keep seeing each other then we'll have to face those things as they arise. Like the old adage says; cross that bridge when you come to it. "

"Sounds good to me," he said, changing the subject. "What do you have in the basket?"

"Well, there are some egg-salad sandwiches and a thermos of iced tea. And, if you're good, there are a couple of chocolate chip cookies."

"Great. I worked up a real appetite rowing across the lake."

Ruth unwrapped the sandwiches, handed one to David and took out two paper cups. She poured the tea. They sat in silence as they ate their lunch, each absorbed in thoughts of the future and where it might lead them. David was first to break the silence.

"I realize we are still very young and have many years ahead of us before we have to make any big decisions about life, but I also know that I want to continue seeing you. I'm willing to face my parents and take the consequences of that. How about you?"

"Yes, I am, but I think we have to wade into the water and not dive in all at once. I'll talk to my mother first and test the waters, no pun intended. If I can get her on our side, then it'll be a lot easier with Dad."

"That's a good idea. My mother will be a lot more sympathetic than my father, too. Tell you what. I'll talk to her when I get back and I'll call you later in the week. Maybe by then you'll have spoken to your mother and we can see how things stand."

"Great. Now let's finish our lunch and get on with that conversation you were so eager to have."

Two hours later, they knew as much intimate detail about each other as was possible for two teenagers — their fears, hopes, dreams, aspirations, desires: every emotion accessible to young people of their limited maturity — all revealed, explored, cherished and stored away in those special repositories of the heart and spirit that are reserved exclusively for young lovers. Relatives, friends, family, community, school: all were explored — all the minutiae associated with growing up

Jewish and Catholic in depression era Baltimore and Washington.

The afternoon shadows began to stretch across the glade. Yet David and Ruth had not nearly exhausted the seemingly endless list of topics that arose and then tumbled over each other in their eagerness to share themselves. Reluctantly, it was time to go. Time to return to the world they left behind just a few short hours ago: a world that was now gone forever. They would return to a new world that each would view through the melded prism of their kindred spirits, their thoughts and actions persuaded by their experience that Friday afternoon, on a lake, in a meadow, lost in each other's eyes. They parted at the boat ramp but not before David mustered the courage to kiss Ruth tenderly on the lips. A kiss that she welcomed and returned.

"I will call you and I will find a way to see you again this summer." he said.

"I know you will, David. Despite the reservations I had, I had a wonderful time. I cannot imagine a more perfect place than that quiet spot on the lake for our first meaningful talk. I've never told anyone many of the things I told you today. I don't know what that says about me, but it must mean that I felt so comfortable with you that I could say anything and not be afraid of the consequences. Thank you. I'll be waiting for your call."

She disappeared beyond the trees on the lake path back to Camp Louise. David remained transfixed, standing on the little dock, savoring every moment of the most wonderful day of his life.

"The future be damned. I'm going to marry that girl."

# 14

# Home and Hell

Murray shook David's shoulder as the bus turned into the dusty schoolyard at P.S. 61.

"Hey, you haven't spoken a word since we left Mount Airy. I've never seen you sleep with your eyes open like that. What's the matter with you? You've been acting really weird lately and you completely disappeared Friday. Wouldn't even tell me where you were. This doesn't have anything to do with that little redhead from D.C. does it?"

David looked up, startled that they were already back in Baltimore. His every thought for the past hour was about Ruth. There was already a dull ache in his stomach that could not be ascribed to any known medical condition.

"No, and besides, she lives in Silver Spring, not D.C."

David slipped back into his reverie as the bus clattered to a stop and all the kids started grabbing their bags. How was it going to appear to the gang if he had gone all squishy about some girl? He punched Murray on the arm and bolted off the bus.

"Last one home is a rotten egg," he said as he scooped up his backpack and raced off, taunting the other gang members as he ran

David had always been the fastest kid on the block. Today was no different. He burst into the kitchen a full block ahead of the other guys.

"Hey Mom, we're home. What do we have to eat?"

Leah came down the stairs just in time to see the screen door fly open and David disappear into the kitchen before she could say a word. When she caught up to him, Murray had arrived and dropped his bag, joining the chorus for food.

"Didn't they feed you anything at Mount Airy? One might think you haven't eaten for the past two weeks. There's some roast chicken and mashed potatoes left over from supper last night. Naomi made some lemonade before she left. It's in the fridge too. You boys go get cleaned up while I put the food out then I want to hear all about your experience at camp."

"Ma, you're not going to believe this," Murray said as he hurried back to the kitchen ahead of David. "Old David has a girlfriend. She's a redhead from Silver Spring. They met when David raced her in swimming. She beat him. Now he's wandering around in a fog all the time. He's so lovesick it makes me want to puke."

"Mind your language. That's no way to talk. Besides, how did you meet girls at Mount Airy? I thought it was only for boys."

"It is Mama, but Camp Louise for girls is less than a mile away across a lake. They let the girls come over on Fridays and sometimes on Sunday afternoon. You should have seen David. He's been mooning over her for a week. You'd think he had the flu or something. Why, old blabbermouth didn't say ten words on the bus ride home. He looked like he was asleep with his eyes open. I've never seen him act this way before."

By now David had returned to catch the remnants of Murray's tale.

"Mama, don't you listen to him. Him and Isaac and Sid have been riding me all week and I'm sick of it. He's making a mountain out of a molehill. Tell him to lay off."

Murray was having too much fun at his brother's expense to let it go.

"Mama, he spent all day yesterday out on Lake Louise in a canoe with her. I can't believe he's gone so mushy on us."

"Murray, that's enough. I think David is perfectly capable of speaking for himself. Is it true David that you met an interesting young lady at Mount Airy?" Leah said, continuing to give Murray that 'don't say another word' look.

"Yes ma'am, but I don't know why Murray's making such a big deal out of it. Her name is Ruth Braddock and she lives in Silver Spring. Her dad works for the State Department and her mother teaches school. Turns out we have a lot in common and she's fun to talk to. It's better than wasting my time trying to talk to these idiots anyway."

Leah stopped in mid-stride at the refrigerator door, her face a frozen mask.

"Braddock doesn't sound like a Jewish name, David."

"That's because it's not, Mama."

"What is she then, if not Jewish?"

"She's a Catholic. Her grandparents came over from Ireland during the potato famine there."

"Do you think it's wise to be seeing a non-Jewish girl considering our strong Jewish faith? Jacob will be very upset. I know he's not as staunchly religious as his parents were, but he still draws the line at certain things. And going outside the faith is one of them. How serious is this thing with, what's her name, Ruth?"

"All I know is I like her a lot. We talked about our religions and decided that if our seeing each other became a problem we'd just have to work it out."

"This is not something your father will want to "work out" as you say. You'd better get ready for a real fight when he gets home."

"What about you Mama. How do you feel?"

"You know I must support Jacob no matter what. He comes first. You'll just have to talk to him. Don't get your hopes up. He's very set in his ways about some things and this is one of them. Now, tell me some more about this girl who seems to have stolen your heart."

David spent the next half-hour trying to explain to his mother what he saw in Ruth Braddock that he hadn't found in all the Jewish girls he knew: why he was attracted to this *"shiksa."*

"She sounds like a very nice girl from a nice family, David, but I'm afraid that won't be enough to satisfy Jacob," Leah said. "If you can convince him then I won't stand in your way, but that's going to be very difficult. We'll just have to wait and see."

David paced nervously on the front porch, awaiting his father's return from a meeting at the synagogue. He wanted to catch him before he went into the house so that he could tell him about Ruth without the rest of the family around. Shortly after five Jacob's big, black Packard pulled into the driveway.

"David, I see you're back from camp. How was it? You managed to get a good tan I see."

"It was fine Papa. Before you go inside I wanted to talk to you about something."

"What is it son? Did something happen at Mount Airy?"

"No sir. Not in that sense. But, yes something did happen that I need to talk to you about."

"What is it?"

"I met this girl there. She was at the girl's camp across Lake Louise from ours. I like her very much and we spent a lot of time together, talking about our lives and all. It turns out that we have an awful lot in common and she's just a neat person."

"So, why's that a problem. Boys and girls have been doing that for thousands of years."

"The problem is she's not a Jew."

Jacob looked as if he had been hit in the forehead by a poll axe. He stared at David with a stunned look. It seemed an eternity before he spoke.

"Then what is she?" Jacob asked, trying to maintain a calmness that he didn't feel.

"Her name is Ruth Braddock and she's a Catholic from Silver Spring. Her father, Sandy, works for the State Department and her mother teaches school. Her ancestors came over during the potato famine in Ireland. She's a really nice girl Papa, and I like her very much," David spouted in a torrent of words believing his passion might somehow transform his father. It didn't.

"David, you must know how I feel about maintaining our faith. For over five-thousand years the non-Jewish world has been trying to make the Jews go away. First it was the pharaohs of Egypt, then King Nebuchadnezzar, then came Caesar and Torquemada's Spanish Inquisition. Now it's a little tin-pot Austrian named Adolph Hitler. So far none of them have succeeded. Do you know why? It's because we wouldn't let them. Through all those years and all those tribulations we stuck together as a people. No matter where we were driven and no matter what the trials, we maintained the purity of our race. Being Jews was all we had and the only way to continue to be Jews was to marry within the faith. We are a matriarchal society. Our Jewishness is handed down from mother to child. If the mother is not a Jew, the child is not a Jew. If you were to marry Ruth Braddock, your children, my grandchildren, would not be Jews. We've come too far and suffered too much for me to allow that to happen. You may not continue seeing this girl, period."

Jacob went inside, leaving David to digest his lesson in Jewish history and ponder why Ruth Braddock could not be a part of his life.

# 15

# Tolchester

As promised, David phoned Ruth on Wednesday to relay the bad news. Jacob Weiss was adamant that their relationship had to end. Despite much pleading and appealing to Jacob's sense of fair play, he would not budge. Faith and family trumped adolescent infatuations, for that was how his father saw their relationship — mere adolescent infatuation.

"What about your parents? How did they take the news?" David asked.

"As I expected, Mom was a little surprised but not too upset. She said, 'Ruth, you are a mature young woman and I will trust your judgment in this matter. Just don't do anything foolish and let me know what's going on.' Dad, on the other hand, was a little more vocal about it. After a few well-chosen words about how complicated this could make my life, he agreed to withhold judgment until he had a chance to meet you. I think he feels like your dad, that it's an infatuation that will pass with time. I believe he will come around, given enough time and familiarity. He deals with many more complex situations in his work and has developed a broader feeling for what's right and wrong in human relationships. It seems to me that our major hurdle will be your father. I don't know how to handle that."

"So far I don't either. He seems so doggedly determined that no Jew should go outside the faith. We're going down to our summer place in Tolchester on the eastern shore this weekend. I hope I'll have a chance to try to convince him there where things aren't so hectic."

"I didn't know you had a place in Tolchester. What a coincidence. My Uncle Jimmy has a small cabin down there, too. When will you get there? How long will you stay?"

"We're going down on Saturday and open the place up. Bernie is taking a week off from his internship in Salisbury to come over with his girlfriend. He'll stay until the following Monday. Papa's going to stay until Tuesday before he catches the ferry back to Baltimore. He'll be gone on a business trip for several days after that. I plan to pester him till then. Maybe he'll just give up and say it's okay."

"Good luck with that. Give me a call when you get to Tolchester and let me know how things are going. Take care, David. I miss you. Hope to see you soon. Bye."

Leah answered the doorbell expecting to see the delivery boy from Stansell's grocery with her food order. It was Thursday of their first week down shore, and the boys were eating her out of house and home. Instead, she was surprised to see a strikingly beautiful, green-eyed, red-haired, young woman standing on the porch. She knew instantly from David's lively description that this had to be Ruth Braddock.

"You have to be Ruth." She said. "David's description of you doesn't do you justice. You are so beautiful. Please come in."

Thank you," Ruth said, blushing from ear-to-ear.

She had not expected such a warm greeting from Leah Weiss. She instantly liked the woman. Leah didn't fit any of the preconceived, stereotypical, notions of Jewish mothers that Ruth carried around in her head. The woman opening the door was trim, pretty, well dressed, well-coiffed with an upswept hairdo and displaying the warmest of smiles. Leah epitomized for Ruth what she wanted David's mother to be.

"I've heard so much about you from David. Welcome. Come on in. What are you doing in Tolchester? It's a long way from Silver Spring."

"David probably neglected to tell you that my Uncle Jimmy has a cabin here as well. It's only a few blocks away. My mother and I came down for a few days since she's on summer recess from school. I thought I'd surprise David and just show up. I hope you don't mind?"

Ruth followed Leah through the house to a broad veranda stretching across the back of the house with a view across the marsh to the bay. Leah motioned for her to take a seat on the rattan glider at one end of the porch. It was nestled under the rampant growth of a wisteria vine, its tendrils encircling the porch columns and its clusters of purple blossoms hanging like grapes.

"Of course not, my dear, may I get you some tea or lemonade? You must be thirsty after your walk over here."

"Thank you, Mrs. Weiss that would be very nice. Lemonade please."

Ruth glanced around, hoping to catch a glimpse of David in the backyard.

"He's down at the beach," Leah said. "He and Murray and some of the neighborhood boys from Baltimore are swimming. You probably met Stan and Burt at camp. The other young man is Joel Sternberg. Why don't you go down and surprise David while I get your lemonade? Then we can sit down and get acquainted."

When Leah returned with the lemonade, Ruth and David were trudging through the sand that separated the cottages from the beach.

"Mama I'm sorry I forgot to tell you about Ruth's Uncle Jimmy and his cottage. It just slipped my mind. Ruth had mentioned coming down this summer, but I didn't know it would be so soon. "

Leah saw through the covering 'little white lie' for what it was and refrained from embarrassing him in front of Ruth.

"That's okay David, I'm just glad for the chance to meet Ruth. I have some lemonade and cookies for you. I need to check on something in the kitchen. I'll be back in a few minutes and

Ruth and I can spend some time together," forewarning David to make himself scarce.

"I know we talked about you coming down," David said after Leah left, "but I didn't know you would be able to make it so soon. I'm glad you are here. How long will you stay?"

"Well, Mom is off for her summer break and I kind of pressured her into asking Uncle Jimmy if we could have his cottage for a week. He said, 'Sure, I won't be using it until late July,' so here we are. Mom, Mike and Gabe are back at the cottage getting everything unpacked. I couldn't wait, so I took off down here."

"I'm sure glad you did. I haven't been able to get you off my mind since we left camp. You won't believe the grief I've been getting from the guys — and from Papa. Mama has been more supportive. She seems to understand what I'm going through."

"It's different for boys than for girls," Ruth said. "Girls are expected to fall in love and go gaga over boys. But guys are scared to death of what their friends will think and the effect it may have on their membership in the gang. They don't want to be thought of as soft and it's scary to think they won't be one of the boys anymore. It's a rite-of-passage all boys seem to go through. I've seen it with Gabe. Eventually, when you realize it's an experience shared by all young boys, it becomes less threatening. You find that you can have a girlfriend and still be one of the boys. Women instinctively understand this so there's never any great mystery with them. That's why your mother is so understanding. "

"What am I so understanding about?" Leah smilingly asked as she returned from the kitchen.

"I was explaining to David why he's getting so much ribbing from his friends," Ruth said, "and why it won't matter for long. I also told him that he needs to go back down to the beach and finish the volleyball game. It was tied when we left."

"I can take a hint," David replied. "All right you two. Don't talk about me when I'm gone," although he knew he would be the main topic of their conversation. "We'll be back for supper soon Ma, why don't you ask Ruth to join us?"

"Can you my dear? We'd love to have you."

"Thank you, but I told Mom I'd be back to help with setting up the house. Maybe I can come back later in the week."

"You certainly can, and I'd love to meet your mother. Maybe we can get all the men out of the house and have it to ourselves. Meanwhile I want to hear all about you," Leah said as she refilled Ruth's glass.

Ruth spent the next hour filling in all the blanks left out by David while Leah regaled Ruth with tales about David that he would never divulge on his own; stories that would mortify him if he knew. Finally, Leah broached the subject that had been hanging like a pall over the afternoon's conversations.

"Ruth, you must know that David's father does not approve of your relationship, and I must admit I had my own concerns before having met you. Now they seem much less important. I don't know if you'll ever be able to persuade Jacob. I can only tell you that I will help in any way that I can, but in the long run, I must support my husband."

"I understand that, and I truly appreciate your honesty. I don't know for certain where this is headed, but I do know that I like David very much and I hope something can be worked out.

Maybe if you can talk about this with my mom it will help. I hope so."

"So do I," Leah said as Ruth walked down the front steps. "Call me if you and Elaine can drop by for lunch later. I want to meet her and see if we can sort out this dilemma you and David have presented to us."

She smiled and waved goodbye, knowing full well that their problems had just begun.

The week flew by with Ruth and David either swinging on the veranda or walking on the beach each afternoon. Elaine Braddock agreed to lunch on Monday and Leah bustled about making certain the house was picked up and tidy and that she had the proper ingredients for Irish soda bread and shepherd's pie. The fateful hour arrived when Ruth and Elaine Braddock arrived for lunch at *"Shorebird"* the fanciful name that Jacob had given to his idyll by the sea.

"Welcome to our home," Leah greeted Elaine. "I've been looking forward to meeting you. Ruth and I have gotten to know each other very well during the past week and she's told me a lot about her family so it's good to finally meet you."

"Thank you, Mrs. Weiss. It's good to meet you too. Ruth's been carrying on like a magpie the past few days."

"Please call me Leah and I'll call you Elaine. There's nothing formal about us. Come on in. Lunch is almost ready, and I've sent the boys off so we can have time to ourselves to get acquainted."

Leah led the Braddock women through the house to the small table she had set on the back veranda. There was a cool breeze coming off the Chesapeake. They could hear the raucous shouts of the boys at play on the beach.

"What a lovely home you have here," Elaine said. "My brother's place is a bit more modest, but anything on the shore in the summer is good and we appreciate the opportunity to come over here. It's already sweltering in Silver Spring."

"Yes, we were very lucky to hear of "Shorebird's" availability and to buy it. Homes over here get snapped up as fast as they come on the market. Why don't you and Ruth have a seat and I'll get lunch on the table."

"This looks delicious," Elaine said as Leah sat the steaming pie down on its trivet. "I haven't had shepherd's pie and soda bread in ages. How thoughtful of you."

"Well, they are pretty much staples around here too. There must be some historical link between the Irish and the Jews that accounts for that."

Without meaning to, Leah had steered the conversation to the subject that was uppermost on the minds of all three women at the table. Now that the genie was out of the bottle there was nothing to do but discuss it.

"Ruth has told me that you have taken a wait-and-see attitude about the difference in our family's religions. I appreciate that. It's basically the same conclusion I have reached. I know these two are mature enough to know that sorting all this out won't be easy and I trust them to behave responsibly in the process. How does Mr. Braddock feel about it?"

"Sandy is a bit more of the old school than I am," Elaine said. "His initial reaction was negative. His Irish Catholic roots kicked in and his first response was negative, but after a few days of reflection he came around to my point-of-view. We have raised our children to be independent thinkers and now that we've experienced that with Ruth it would be hypocritical of us to change. So, we both are willing to let the two of them work this out in a sober and responsible way. I understand Mr. Weiss is strongly opposed to the relationship."

"I'm afraid that's true. You must understand that Jacob comes from a long line of Orthodox Jews, including several rabbis. He's changed a lot in the 25 years we've been in America, but it's still difficult for him to turn loose of the old ways. He's mellowed quite a bit and we attend a reformed synagogue now where such ideas are more acceptable, but the old values run deep. Jacob sees marriage outside the faith as denying 5,000 years of Jewish heritage. He believes we have survived as a race and religion through all that time by staying true to our biblical teachings. He sees other cultures that have been assimilated by their conquerors and then lost all touch with their heritage. He doesn't want that to happen to the Jews."

"I think that's admirable, however our generation represents the past and Ruth and David's generation represents the future. If the events occurring in Europe today are any indication we're going to need our best and brightest to make decisions about that future. If their relationship continues it is my fervent hope that Mr. Weiss will not make it difficult for them."

"I pray so too. Now, enough of that serious talk, let's have our lunch."

The balance of the afternoon passed in contented conversations with much laughter and merriment. Religious differences aside, a more congenial atmosphere could not be imagined. Leah and Elaine parted with rekindled hope that their differences as families could be bridged and that their children could find the happiness they sought.

The Braddock women returned to Silver Spring and Jacob Weiss returned to Tolchester. Much had changed in the hearts and minds of everyone that week with the exception of

Jacob Weiss. When told of the visit by Ruth and Elaine Braddock to "Shorebird" Jacob let it be known in no uncertain terms that he disapproved and demanded of Leah that it not happen again. The rest of that summer in Tolchester took on a somber mood that would not lift no matter the trying.

By the time "Shorebird" was shuttered for the winter, the Braddocks had returned to Uncle Jimmy's cottage twice, however it was during times when Jacob was down shore for long weekends. Leah was afraid to invite Elaine based on Jacob's unbending opposition to their children seeing each other. David found it necessary to slip out in the evening to meet Ruth on the beach. They were both miserable and despaired of ever being free to pursue a normal relationship, but neither was willing to give up on their hopes for a future together. They believed and prayed that they would find a way.

David was morose and withdrawn on the ride back to Baltimore. What had begun as a luminous vacation on the Chesapeake had turned into a series of clandestine meetings under cover of darkness. This was not how he envisioned his summer when he stepped down from that bus at P.S. 61 after spending a glorious week at Mount Airy with Ruth. He had to find a way to convince his father that seeing her would not threaten his family's Jewish religious foundations. Every tactic he had used thus far had met with the same determined refusal from Jacob to allow him to continue seeing Ruth.

David and Murray turned seventeen during their stay down shore at Tolchester, that summer of 1937. In three weeks they would begin their junior year in high school and neither had committed to a career choice after graduation. Leah kept dropping broad hints that they should follow Bernard into medicine or, barring that, study law. So far neither had risen to the bait.

Meanwhile, Jacob was encouraging them to follow a course of study in business, so they could join Epstein and Weiss when they finished school. Murray had indicated an interest, but David was not so inclined. Eager to give his own views a decided advantage he asked the boys to spend their last days before school as interns at the factory.

"Papa, I really don't think I'm cut out to be in the "rag trade," David said at the end of the three weeks he spent on the floor. "I know how much you enjoy your work and I appreciate the life it has given us, but I just don't think it's for me. Murray seems to like it though. Maybe he'll be the one to carry on for you. I hope you're not disappointed with me. I'm still leaning toward medicine or the law. I still have a couple of years to decide. I think that's what Mama wants me to do. She's so proud of Bernie. Her eyes light up every time someone mentions his name. She has become the typical Jewish mother. *My son the doctor.*"

"Of course I'm not disappointed in you, David. I want you to do whatever will make you happy. It would be great to have both you and Murray in the business, but it will continue regardless. I'm pretty sure a couple of your Uncle Seth's boys plan to join us. In any case, Epstein and Weiss will remain in our families for a long time to come. You know, we've had offers to sell the company, or to take it public, but Seth and I will not do that. We don't want to expose ourselves and our families to another 1929. The company is a legacy for both our families and we want to see it remain that way for generations to come. So, you are free to go where your heart leads you and with my blessings. All I ask is that you work hard, be honorable and make us proud of you. We have been so blessed by this great country, ever since Leah and I came over to join Seth and Rachel in 1910. We've gone from penniless migrants to successful merchants. We've worked very hard to achieve the American dream. We are proud to call ourselves Americans and to have the opportunity to give back to this wonderful community, this nation and our people. As long as you uphold and honor those values, it won't matter what vocation you choose. I just ask you to do it well and with integrity and to always remember the great debt we owe to America."

Jacob's eyes brimmed with tears and his voice choked with emotion, surprising David. He had never seen his father cry and was taken aback at the tears and the strong outpouring of emotion. Jacob's evident allegiance to his new home displayed a love that could be fully appreciated only by someone who had stared into the abyss of despair and escaped it. At that moment David realized that his legacy from his father would consist of much more than the fruits of Jacob's labor. His true legacy would be his continuation of his father's good works and thereby honoring his debt to America. David could not know then what a high price he must pay to keep that promise alive.

# 16

# War Clouds

The Weiss twins began their junior year of high school as war clouds gathered over Europe. The long, dark night of the depression maintained its unyielding grip on the country. Terrible stories of the Nazi treatment of Jews and other minority groups made their way to Jewish enclaves around the world, including Baltimore, Maryland, USA. Leah, already heavily involved in efforts to assist the Jewish relief groups in Baltimore, became even more involved. She went almost daily to the offices of the Jewish Relief Agency. Letters and notes furtively passed from the overrun territories painted a picture of such horrifying magnitude that few dared lend credence to them. Through the smoke and fire of the Nazi blitzkrieg ominous names began to appear: Goebbels, Himmler, Hess, Goering, and Eichmann. It would be nearly a decade later before the fog of war lifted sufficiently to expose the extent of the grotesque inhumanity of this cabal of Hitler's henchmen. Broadcasters and writers were just beginning to hint at what would become known as *The Holocaust, a* dark blight on humanity that can never be erased. Walter Winchell's Sunday night broadcasts were mandatory listening in millions of American homes, yet his vehemently anti-Semitic boss, William Randolph Hearst, would not allow him to mention the Nazi atrocities on the air.

Refugees who were able to escape the German dragnets made their way to the neutral territories of Switzerland, Spain and Portugal. To obtain travel documents, many had to forfeit all their possessions. A few were able to sew diamonds into their hems and hide gold in hollowed out shoe heels. These treasures determined whether many would be allowed to board trains or ships to Zurich, Madrid or Lisbon in order to escape the encroaching inferno, or whether they wound up in Dachau, Auschwitz, Buchenwald or one of dozens of other Nazi slaughter houses. Hundreds of these refugees ultimately made their way to Baltimore and into the life of Leah Weiss. Through her efforts at the Jewish Relief Agency she sought to bring hope and sanity to the lives of their displaced families. Stories told by them chilled her blood, kindling dire fears for the safety of her own family in Belarus.

An international conference held in Evian, France sought to find a solution to the growing crisis. It failed to provide any refuge or relief for the swelling tide of displaced persons. All Jewish documents were now being stamped with a large "J" as Britain and France acquiesced to the increasing demands of

Hitler. Germany annexed the Sudetenland in western Czechoslovakia while expelling thousands of Jews into Poland.

Herschel Grysnszpan's family was among those shipped to Poland. Herschel, himself a refugee, was hiding in his uncle's garret in Paris. Acting out of his profound frustration at his inability to emigrate to Palestine, and in a misguided effort to avenge his parents, Herschel walked into the German embassy in Paris and shot Foreign Service Officer Ernst van Rath. Van Rath died two days later from the two bullet wounds in his stomach.

The day that van Rath died, November 9, 1938, Herman Goering unleashed *Kristallnacht* across all German controlled territories. The pogrom that followed witnessed the wanton killing of many Jews and the destruction of most Jewish businesses. Goering justified the actions by stating that Grynszpan's act established *"the collective responsibility of all Jews."* That would become the catchphrase used to justify the atrocities committed on that *"night of broken glass"* as well as all subsequent actions by the Nazis in implementing *"the final solution"* for the Jews. From that day forward the fate of six million European Jews was sealed.

The Jewish Times lay on the Weiss' kitchen table, its headlines screaming, "Kristallnacht kills thousands of Jews across Germany." The follow-on stories described the brutality unleashed across the Third Reich: hundreds of synagogues burned and vandalized, thousands of Jews herded onto trucks and trains for transport to concentration camps, Jewish owned businesses looted and destroyed. The complete impact of that tragic orgy of evil would only be known years later. The entire world would come to realize the terrible darkness that fell across the face of all humankind that dark night. German society had fallen under the spell of a mustachioed, charismatic, little

Austrian corporal named Adolph Hitler. The world was being driven, relentlessly, into a nightmare of unimaginable proportions.

"Jacob I'm terribly worried about the folks back home," Leah said, gesturing toward the newspaper. "Just look at those headlines. Terrible things are happening all over Europe and the world is just ignoring them. Hitler is a madman. He's using the Jews as an excuse to overrun other countries. Austria and Czechoslovakia are already gone. The German armies are massed on the borders of Poland and Hungary. All we get from France and England is lip service and appeasement. I tell you he's not going to quit until he rules all of Europe. And, he's going to kill every Jew along the way. The Jews are becoming the scapegoats for his evil ambitions and there's no one to stop him. History is once again repeating itself. Our own government has just swept it under the rug and the isolationists and moneygrubbers with interests in Germany are tying Roosevelt's hands. They say it's not our problem and we should leave it to the Europeans to sort out. Well it's going to be our problem, I can tell you that. Some of the stories I hear from the refugees will make your hair curl and your blood run cold. It's the "Spanish Inquisition" all over again, but the bottom line is still the same — dead and displaced Jews. Just a different set of characters with a different set of excuses. Jacob, we have to do something! I know we're helping those who make it to Baltimore, but there are thousands, hundreds of thousands, who are trapped in Europe, including many of our own relatives."

Jacob was stunned at Leah's outpouring of alarm. He had been following the news as well and knew that things were getting worse for the Jews in Germany. However, his preoccupation with the business and other civic activities had dulled his awareness. Leah was on the front lines of the relief effort and emotionally caught up in the looming terror.

"Leah is it really that bad. I know things are not going well but do you really believe the Germans will kill all the Jews. Why, many of the leading citizens and contributors to German culture are Jews. Why would Hitler want to get rid of their contributions?"

"Do you think all those killed during *Kristallnacht* weren't contributing to their culture? It seems to make no difference to the Nazis. It's the Egyptians, the Babylonians, the Romans and the Spanish all over again. Jews contributed well beyond what their numbers would suggest to all those cultures, but that didn't stop their rulers from persecuting them and driving them out. Jews are convenient targets for whipping up fear and hate among the masses."

"I understand how upset you are, Leah. I will try to become more involved and see what I can do to help."

"Thanks Jacob. That means a lot to me. I didn't mean to unload all my worries on you. I know you have a lot on your mind. I just want you to understand I'll be spending a lot of time on this."

By now the fourth daughter of the Sarofsky clan was living in the Weiss garret. Deborah was sixteen and took a keen interest in the twin's life. She knew that they were spending time with their mother at the Jewish Relief Agency and were caught up in the near-panic developing around the refugee problem. She kept the home fires burning and was anxious each evening to hear the latest news. The Sarofskys had left behind many relatives in Pinsk.

# 17

## Leah's Cause

The twins were born the same year that Henrietta Szold moved from New York to Palestine. She was sixty years old. As the oldest daughter of the rabbi at Baltimore's Temple Oheb Shalom, and a prominent figure in Baltimorean Jewry, she was deeply involved in the growing crisis concerning Jewish refugees in Nazi Germany. In 1903 Henrietta had founded the Russian Night School on Lombard Street in East Baltimore. The school quickly expanded to serve the entire eastern European immigrant population. Most had only rudimentary skills in English. By the time Leah Weiss enrolled in the Russian School in 1911

Henrietta Szold had moved on to study at the Jewish Theological Seminary in New York, however Szold's spirit lived on in the school and was passed on from class to class. She returned often to Baltimore and spoke to each new generation of students. The seeds sown in the Russian School continued to bear fruit years after they fell to the ground.

Henrietta's legendary status in Baltimore achieved even more eminence when she moved to New York. She traveled to Palestine as part of her studies and became involved in the Hadassah Study Circle, a Zionist Women's Organization. Her energetic leadership led to the founding of the Women's Zionist Organization in New York, the first Zionist organization chartered just for women. The original goals of the group were to improve the health conditions in Palestine. The group later changed its name to Hadassah (Esther) and became the largest Zionist organization in the world.

One of the seeds planted by Ms. Szold in a 1911 visit to the Russian School lay dormant until 1938 when it blossomed forth in the person of Leah Weiss. Long occupied with her duties as wife and mother, she had served only sporadically on various boards and committees. The rising threat in Europe coincided with her new found domestic freedom and kindled in Leah a passion that would become a lifelong calling.

Henrietta Szold became the head of *Youth Aliyah in Palestine* in 1933. The *Aliyah (going up to Israel)* sprang from the need to fight the growing anti-Semitism in Germany under Hitler. When the Nazi curtain fell across Europe in 1940, after Hitler's push into Germany's neighboring states made no more rescues possible, the *Aliyah* had spirited over 11,000 Jewish children out of Europe to Palestine. Many of these children later became leaders and heroes during Israel's fight for statehood and a Jewish homeland. 11,000 rescues represented an amazing feat, until one considers that more than one million Jewish children's lives were snuffed out during the *Holocaust*.

Now, in 1938, Leah Weiss was being summoned by her old friend in Palestine to help her rescue the Jewish children of Europe from certain death. The little Russian School had come full circle. Leah threw herself wholeheartedly into fundraising and recruiting for the *Aliyah* cause. She dragooned her husband and the twins into the effort as well. David and Murray who had lived on the periphery of the unfolding Holocaust were thrust headlong into the effort to salvage an entire generation of their European kinsmen. Their witness to the violence against the Jews of Europe changed forever their view of the world and their perception of their own Jewish identity. They emerged from their mother's crusade committed to the Zionist call for a Jewish homeland and to the vow of "*never again*."

Word still trickled out to the Weisses from Romania and Belarus about the worsening conditions as Hitler moved inexorably eastward. In late 1939 Hitler's Gestapo murdered several Polish inmates at the Sachsenhausen concentration camp, dressed them in Polish military uniforms, and then displayed them to a group of international reporters as invaders of the German homeland. This fabricated invasion of Germany served as a pretext for Hitler to invade Poland on September 1, 1939 – – World War II had begun. Britain, France, Australia, India and New Zealand immediately declared war on Germany. Meanwhile, Hitler, having plotted with Joseph Stalin in a non-aggression pact in early August, proceeded to slice Poland into a Russian occupied east and a German occupied west. Warsaw surrendered by the end of September, and the Poles long winter of suffering began. The mistreatment of the Jews in Poland began to migrate eastward, and fear was rampant in the Pale. Those who had the means to escape did. Those who didn't prepared for the worst.

Romania was still free of German domination, but the distant rumblings from across the Transylvanian Alps were unmistakable. The German army in southern Czechoslovakia was now linked with Poland. It was only a matter of time before the unquenchable thirst of Hitler's war machine would descend on the oil fields of Romania. In WWI Kaiser Wilhelm had seized the wells around Ploesti, Romania, and there was no doubt Hitler would do the same.

French and English engineers working in the Ploesti refineries were ordered to draw up plans for their destruction in the event of a German invasion, but Hitler's luck held. German intelligence captured one of the last convoys out of occupied Paris. It contained classified records describing how and when the French engineers should destroy the Ploesti fields. That evening Ion Antonescu's operatives moved through the streets of Ploesti arresting 35 engineers and officials of the oil companies who were whisked away to torture chambers. Their coerced confessions prohibited the sabotage. The next day, Antonescu was made foreign minister. He immediately complied with all of Hitler's demands and became his puppet ruler in Romania.

Jacob's brother Levi Weiss and his family toiled on in the refineries, oblivious to the storm gathering across the mountains to the north. The lives of the Jewish workers in Ploesti still carried a facade of respectability and acceptance. Their skills were critical to the smooth flow of oil and no one in Romania was going to interfere. That all changed dramatically, when the storm rolled over the Alps and down the Transylvanian plain.


The school year flew by as David continued to plead with his father to allow him to see Ruth. Jacob remained resolutely opposed. Leah attempted to mediate the quarrel, but she could do only so much. Thankfully, her work at the agency occupied her thoughts and kept her from dwelling too much on the family strife.

"Mama, if I go down to see Ruth will you tell Papa?" David asked late one afternoon in the winter of 1938.

It took Leah by surprise. She was unaware of the many secret calls he had been making to Ruth from the payphone at Mannheimer's drug store with money he saved up from his chores.

"I wasn't aware you two were still in contact," Ruth said with a calmness she didn't feel.

"I've been saving my money and calling her from the drug store."

"How long has this been going on?"

"I call her every two weeks and she calls me at the drug store every two weeks also."

"David you know I cannot go against your father's wishes . . . but if you went into D.C. to pick something up for me, I guess I wouldn't know about any detours you might take."

"Thanks, Ma. I promise you I will not abuse the privilege. Her mother invited me to come and said she'd love to see you as well."

"I'd love to see Elaine too, but I dare not deceive your father. He won't be back from New York until Sunday, so you'd best pick up my new dress at Bloomingdales on Saturday. You'd better call Ruth and let her know you're coming – and you can use our phone."

"Thanks again Ma. You've made my day."

Ruth was waiting at the door when David arrived on Saturday morning. She gave him a quick peck and ushered him into the kitchen where her mother was finishing her coffee.

"Sandy is working today," she said, "but he knew you were coming. It's all right with him."

"Thanks. I wouldn't want to get off on the wrong foot with him."

"How's Leah? I have meant to call but I wasn't sure I should."

"She'd love to hear from you. My father is traveling a lot and aside from her work at the agency she doesn't get out much."

"What agency?"

"She goes almost every day to the offices of the Jewish Relief Agency in Baltimore. They're coordinating all the relief efforts for the displaced Jews in Europe. She's also heavily involved in what's called *Aliyah* which is a separate group working to get Jewish children out of Germany. *Youth Aliyah* is headed in Palestine by Henrietta Szold who came from Baltimore. My mother first met her in school after she and Papa came over. She moved to Palestine the year Murray and I were born."

"I've heard of them from Sandy," Elaine said. "We still have many friends in Europe from Sandy's postings there with the State Department. I just can't fathom what's happening in Germany. Hitler seems to be taking all of Europe down a bad road. There are a few Jewish families in particular that we were friends with and I would like to know what's happening to them. Do you think Leah can make some inquiries?"

"I'm sure she can. Better yet, why don't you and Ruth come up to Baltimore and meet the people at the agency? I know they'll be glad to help you. Murray and I work there a couple of times a week."

"I'll try to find a day when we both can come. I'll let you know. Now, let me make myself scarce so you and Ruth can catch up. See you later before you leave."

Ruth and David spent two hours catching up on all the little things that didn't make it into their abbreviated phone conversations.

"I made the swim team again this year," Ruth said. "I was elected captain. We'll be going back to Annapolis in April for the state championships. Maybe you can come over to see us."

"Just let me know the dates, and I'll be there," David said. "By the way, I made first string on the football team as a tight end and I'm going to play baseball this spring."

"Listen to us," Ruth said. "You'd think we were a couple of full-time jocks."

"Yeah, we're afraid to recognize the 600-pound gorilla in the room. Ma's trying to get Dad to loosen up a bit, but it's very slow going. I know he'd feel different if he met you and your family, but he just won't relent."

"All we can do is to keep on trying. Maybe if Mom and I come up to Baltimore he'll agree to meet us at the agency."

"Hey, that's a good idea. He drops by on occasion. I'll make sure he's there when you come up. He can't help but love you as much as I do."

It was the first time either of them had let the "L" word slip out. David realized immediately that he may have overstepped his bounds.

"I'm sorry. That just came out. I know we haven't known each other long enough to be saying that. But, now that it's out in the open you might as well know that's how I feel.'

"It's all right David. I don't think there's any secret that when we left camp that we both felt that way. Certainly not after the time we spent together in Tolchester. We'll both be 18 and seniors in high school soon and I believe we're mature enough to know our own feelings, regardless of what others may think."

David leaned across the table and kissed Ruth full on the lips. It was the first real, honest-to-goodness, kiss in all their time together.

"That was nice. I guess this means we are "steadies" now," she said using the current high schooler term for commitment.

"I guess so," David blushed. "As far as I'm concerned, we've been "steadies" since that first time I saw you on the side of the Mount Airy pool, and we'll always be "steadies" no matter what my father thinks. Sooner or later, I'm going to win that battle — one way or the other."

David made the obligatory pick-up at Bloomingdales and headed back to Baltimore with a spring in his step and a firm belief that he could make things turn out the way he wanted them to.

With each wave of *Aliyah* children pouring into the *kibbutz* of Palestine, the stories of atrocity and privation became more chilling. Frightened, emaciated, and alone, they were a living testament to the unspeakable crimes being committed by Hitler's death squads. With accelerating speed the Jewish community coalesced around the urgent call of Henrietta Szold and *Youth Alliyah*. They began to make a difference. Money to buy forged travel documents and to bribe corrupt officials was funneled into offices across Europe and the lives of the children were being bought like so much chattel. Even though the numbers were pitifully small, each life saved was precious and each a monument to the tenacity and love of the Jewish people.

Elaine and Ruth finally got to Baltimore in late March and met Leah at the JRA. It was a joyous reunion. True to David's word, Jacob came by in mid-afternoon and was trapped into meeting the women. He was gracious and hospitable to them but remained aloof and cool. He realized he had been set up and the look he gave to David expressed his resentment.

"Elaine," Jacob said after a few minutes of small talk, "why don't you and I go into the canteen for a cup of coffee."

The tone of his invitation established that it was to be a private conversation. Ruth and David eyed each other nervously. Leah blanched.

"Elaine, I know Leah and David conspired to get me over here to meet you today," Jacob said as he sat down and stirred his coffee, "and I know they had the best of intentions. But, I'm sure David has told you how I feel. It has nothing to do with you and Ruth. I'm sure you are fine, decent, upstanding, law-abiding and God-fearing people. It has only to do with my beliefs and about the sanctity of the Jewish family. My people have been under attack by so many for so long that we are in a constant state of vigilance. This group of people here," Jacob said as he swept his arm around the office, "is testament to that fact. They are trying to fight the latest manifestation of the age's old, on-going, persecution of my people. Every Jew who marries outside the faith diminishes our strength and brings us one step closer to annihilation, and that's why I am opposed to this relation-ship."

"Mr. Weiss, I can understand that. My people have had some pretty bad experiences with the British as well. I know that doesn't compare to what you are talking about but it gives me some appreciation.

"Look, I didn't ask for this to happen either. To use your words, it's an age-old inclination for young people to fall in love. If Ruth and David do truly love each other, I believe we should try to find some accommodation for that. After all, they're going to be 18 soon and we won't be able to tell them what to do. Don't you think it would be better if we all looked for a way to make this work rather than categorically saying no and drive them away? I don't know what the future may hold for them, but I certainly know I want to be a part of it, and I think you do too."

"Elaine, we're a matriarchal society. If the mother is Jew-ish, then the children are Jewish. Ruth is Catholic. What will my grandchildren be?"

"Don't you think you should ask David and Ruth that question? Is it a foregone conclusion that they will follow either religion — or none?"

"You know, I hadn't looked at it that way. Maybe you're right. Why don't you and Ruth come over to the house for dinner tonight and let's talk it out? Can you do that?"

"I don't see why not. I'll have to call Sandy and tell him he's on his own for dinner. He won't mind, it'll let him listen to the Orioles undistrubed."

"Great. We'd better tell those three out there that we're making plans for them."

"Mr. Weiss," Elaine started to say when Jacob interrupted her.

"Please call me Jacob. If we're going to be this intimately involved, Mr. Weiss is a little too formal."

"Okay then. What I started to say was that the main reason I came here today was to see if the JRA or *Aliyah* could help us locate some friends in Germany. There were two Jewish families in Berlin that Sandy and I were close to when he was stationed at the embassy there. We've tried to contact them but haven't gotten any word back so far. When David told me about what Leah is doing here I thought she may be able to help us."

"Wow," Jacob said. "I'm sorry I jumped down your throat like I did. I just made the assumption that this was all about David and Ruth. I feel a little sheepish now. Please forgive me."

"Don't worry about it," Elaine said. "At least it got the subject out in the open so we can talk about it. That's the first step to solving any problem — first define the problem and then talk about it. Now let's go back out there and see if Leah can help us."

After putting the wheels in motion to locate the Moshe Ginsberg and Joseph Abrams families in Berlin, the Weisses and Braddocks headed to dinner. Leah called Deborah Sarofsky to alert her that there would be two more at the table that evening.

"Ruth, why don't you ride with me," Jacob said. "We've got a lot of catching up to do. I am afraid I haven't let David tell me much about you. Let's see if we can't remedy that situation on the way home."

Ruth and David looked at each other in stunned amazement. Neither could make sense of what might have gone on in that break room in the last fifteen minutes. They only knew that whatever it was it seemed good. Sitting down together over dinner was certainly better than the icy impasse they had lived through for the past several months.

Ruth was anxious as she closed the heavy door on Jacob's Packard. She didn't know what to expect on the ride back to his house. She wanted to say something but didn't know how to begin.

"I know you must be concerned about this, Ruth, being trapped in a car with me for half an hour," Jacob said. "Please don't be. I know how strongly David feels about you. That tells me all I need to know of your character. David and I have always had a strong bond and I know I can rely on his judgment and I also know I can trust him. This is the only time we've ever seriously disagreed on anything. For him to take me on as strongly as he has, tells me a lot about your relationship. I'm sure he's explained to you why I am opposed to it. As I told Elaine back there it has nothing to do with you, your family or your values. It has everything to do with our faith and my beliefs."

"Yes, sir he has told me everything. He explained about the Jewish religion and the role of the woman in the family and I respect that," Ruth said.

"The Jewish community around the world has witnessed its numbers decline over the past few decades. Much of that decline is because of intermarriage with gentiles and a falling away from our beliefs. If enough of us don't defend the old ways, more and more will fall away. Now we're seeing the rise of anti-Semitism in Germany and other countries. Jews are dying under Hitler's *pogroms* by the thousands. I despair for the continued existence of Judaism."

"David has been telling me about what's happening over there, and my father gets all these reports at the State Department. I grew up with the Ginsberg children in Berlin and it breaks my heart to think they may have come to harm. That's why we're trying to find them and see if there's anything we can do. Dad has tried through his government channels with no success. Maybe the JRA has people who can help."

"I assure you, if anyone can find them it's the people on the ground in Germany with *Aliyah* that can. A group called by its Hebrew name *Bricha* has been operating throughout Europe for years. It was established by the Jewish leadership in Palestine for just this purpose. They are allied with the *Aliyah* representatives across the area to facilitate the rescue of all Jews but especially children. I bet you'll know something in a week."

"That would be wonderful," Ruth said.

"Now let's get down to brass tacks about you and David. Are you two really serious?"

"Yes sir. I think so. I like David very much. I've not dated very many boys. Most of them turn out to be brainless or are interested in only one thing. I am not ready for that in my life. David is not like that. He's serious, intelligent, and thoughtful – – all the qualities a girl could ever expect. We seem to have a real understanding of each other's needs and ambitions that goes beyond the normal teenage crushes. We can talk to each other about anything and know the other will respect us. I don't know if what we have will get to the level of marriage, but it's something we've talked about."

"If it did get to that level, what have you two discussed about kids and religion?"

"We have discussed that. We basically said we'd cross that bridge if and when we came to it. I guess we're about to cross that bridge."

"Yeah, strange how life kind of does that to you sometimes. Look, I know that at some point soon we won't be able to stop you from doing whatever you want to do. I just hope that, before that time comes, we can all come to some mutual understanding that will satisfy everyone concerned. But for me, you need to understand that my bottom line is that I want my grandchildren to be Jewish," Jacob said as they pulled into the driveway on Linden Avenue. The two other cars were already there.

Leah, Elaine, David and Murray were seated in the parlor. Deborah was passing around some snacks and lemonade. Murray and Elaine were getting to know each other.

"I can't get over how identical you and David are, Murray," Elaine said. "If one of you came in without the other I don't know if I could tell which was which."

"I'll let you in on a little secret," David said as he held out his right arm. "I have a small mole in the crease of my elbow. Murray doesn't. Sometimes when I wake up in the morning I check that mole to be sure I'm me."

Murray punched David while the others burst out laughing.

"What's so funny?" Jacob said as he hung his jacket on the hall tree.

"Oh, David was just telling that old story about the mole," Murray said. "He does that every time he has a new audience. It's starting to get old for me."

"I think it's hilarious," Elaine said. "I'll certainly never forget it."

The conversation bounced around the room among the two families gathered there but never landed on the one subject everyone was thinking about. Apparently, that was waiting for the dinner table. As if on cue, Deborah announced that dinner was served.

"David," Jacob said as he ladled a spoonful of mashed potatoes onto his plate, "Ruth and I had a stimulating conversation on the ride home and I can tell you she's every bit as sharp as you said she was. She certainly held her own. "

"Yes," Ruth said "and I discovered that your Dad isn't as scary as I thought he might be."

"That's because you're not his daughter." David said with a chuckle, "He can be pretty scary to me and Murray."

"Aw, c'mon David," Jacob responded, "you know you and Murray get away with murder around here. If you want to see scary, just go over to your Uncle Seth's house. Every time Seth says jump to his boys they say, "how high."

"Oh, it's not that bad," Leah said. "You both can be pretty strict. You can also be pushovers. I think Ruth may have found your soft spot."

"Whatever, she can stand her ground as well as anyone I've met. I like that. A little gumption is a good thing," Jacob said.

"The taboo subject came up during our ride and neither of us felt threatened by the other. I made my stance clear and

Ruth gave me some thoughts to chew on. She said that she and David have talked about it but came to no strong conclusions. They've agreed it's something they will decide if and when the time comes.

"Elaine also made some good points this afternoon. How do we know which religion Ruth and David might choose if they got married, or if they'd choose any religion? We, as parents may have our own hopes and aspirations for our children but in the end, they must choose for themselves. We all know that I want my grandchildren to be reared Jewish. Some may think that very selfish, but I don't. As I've explained, my race is threatened with annihilation and I need to do everything I can to see that that doesn't happen. Assuring that future generations continue the Jewish tradition is one way to do that."

"What would that mean for Ruth?" Elaine asked. "What choices would she have to make?"

"Well, as I explained, we are a matriarchal culture and the religion is handed down from mother to child. If the mother is Jewish, there's no problem. If she's not, I see four options. The mother can convert to Judaism. Or, she can agree that the children will be raised Jewish without converting. Thirdly, they can choose no religion and the children can make their own determination when they come of age. The last option would be for the children to be raised in the religion of the mother. You all know my position. Let me hear what you think."

"Naturally, as a Catholic, I would like my grandchildren to be raised Catholic," Elaine said. "But, that's not my decision to make. It's for Ruth and David should they get married. I would accept whatever they decided and I'm pretty sure Sandy will as well."

"What about you Ruth?" Jacob asked.

"It's a decision that will take much thought and prayer. It will also take a lot of study on my part. I've known many Jewish kids in Europe and here, but I've never gotten into religious discussions with them. It just never came up. It will also depend on how strongly David may feel about any of the options. I certainly wouldn't go into a marriage knowing we had a basic disagreement about such a major aspect of our lives. So my answer is, 'I can't answer that question now'.

"Fair enough," Jacob said. "How about you David? How do you feel?"

"Pretty much like Ruth said. It's too big a decision to enter into lightly. I'll need time to figure out what's best for the two of us and at the same time try to meet your expectations. Look, it's another eighteen months or so before we finish high school. Nothing's going to happen before then, so all I ask is to let Ruth and me continue to see each other and give us time to work this out. As she said, there's no guarantee that we'll get to that point, but we certainly won't if we can't talk to each other — and to all of you — in the process."

"That certainly makes sense to me," Leah said. "I know that everyone involved in this discussion is a sensible and mature individual. Let's give these kids the time necessary to come to their own conclusion as to what's right."

"Thank you, Leah," Elaine said. "I totally agree."

"Furthermore," Leah said, "why don't the two of you come back to the JRA next week? We should have some answers for you by then, and it's a great place for Ruth to begin her education in all things Jewish. Maybe, David should plan on spending some time with Ruth at the Catholic Relief Agency in D.C. He could use some educating too."

"I can see when I'm outnumbered," Jacob said, his arms raised in mock surrender. "I yield. We'll reconvene this discussion in a few months. I look forward to finding out what everyone has learned by then — myself included. And, I look forward to meeting Sandy. Based on the family sampling I've seen today he must be a pretty great guy."

"He is," Ruth said, "he is."

The Braddock women returned to Baltimore and the JRA on Wednesday. The *Aliyah* workers in Germany found that the Ginsberg family had fled to Amsterdam after being harassed by the Gestapo. They were trying to get visas to come to the United States, So far they were unsuccessful. The Abrams family had left Berlin and no one could confirm where they had gone. One rumor had it they were transported to the camp at Buchenwald. Another said they had made it to Palestine.

"Thank God the Ginsbergs made it safely to Holland," Elaine said, "and I pray that the Abrams are in Palestine and not Buchenwald. I shudder to think of those beautiful children suffering and maybe dying there at the hands of the Nazis. It breaks my heart. The Abrams were the warmest and kindest friends you could ever ask for. I'm going to see if Sandy can help get the Ginsberg's papers to come here. I'm afraid they won't be safe there if Hitler invades the Low Countries.

"Leah, is there any way to confirm whether the Abrams got to Palestine or not?" Ruth asked.

"We've contacted all the agencies in Jerusalem and they are searching the roles of recent immigrants. If they are there, someone will find them."

David and Ruth stole as many private moments as possible during her visits to Baltimore. She and Elaine volunteered their services to the JRA and came as often as possible on Saturdays to help.


As spring rolled into summer and their junior year was complete, Ruth came more often. She traveled with David and the *Aliyah* teams to synagogues and schools across the area to drum up support from other youth groups. Their relationship matured beyond youthful infatuation into a deeper and more respectful appreciation of each other and their differing beliefs. These early steps into adulthood and the harsh realities they saw unfolding in the world beyond their sheltered childhood had a sobering effect upon them. David especially began to see his duty as a Jew to look beyond his insular life. He saw an obligation to fight a modern tyrant who was trying to destroy his people just as Nebuchadnezzar had tried 2500 years before when he destroyed Solomon's temple and scattered the descendants of Abraham to the four corners of the earth. The same blood that coursed through the veins of those who died defending the Temple still flowed through his. Their trumpet call to sacrifice echoed still. David Weiss would not refuse the call.

# 18

# Leaving the Nest

Their senior year flew by in a blur. Ruth and David were involved in so many extracurricular activities, as well as with the war relief agencies, that there was little time for much else. They saw each other often at these events but less so informally due to the crush of time and the distance between them.

"David, can you drive down next Saturday," Ruth pleaded.

Jacob had bought both boys old Ford jalopies for their birthdays and David had driven down to Silver Spring a few times. It was now mid-April, and everyone was busy with preparations for graduation at the end of May.

"Mom is going to be at a conference in Annapolis and Dad's away again somewhere in Europe. He can't say where, but I think its Russia. I thought we could talk more about our plans for college. I'm still not totally certain, but I think I'll go into nursing. I've been accepted into George Washington University and they have a great nursing school."

"That sounds great Ruth. Dad still wants me in the business, but I've told him no. I'm looking at med school. I've been accepted at Johns Hopkins and at Georgetown. I'm really torn. Bernie went to Hopkins and he got a great education. He's about finished with his residency at Duke University and plans to move back to Baltimore. Murray has already decided on the business school at the University of Maryland. But if you're going to be in D.C. that makes Georgetown sound even better, although Papa doesn't necessarily like it because it's a Jesuit school. I kidded him that it might help me learn more about Catholicism like we discussed last summer. He just gave me one of his stern looks."

"Tell you what," Ruth said. "Just hold those thoughts until Saturday. We have to be very sensible about this whole thing. These are decisions that need to be made on a practical basis and not just because we want to be near each other."

"You're right as always. At least one of us is practical. Unless something comes up I'll see you Saturday around noon. Maybe Elaine can leave us some of that famous pecan pie she makes."

"I'll ask her. Take care. I'll see you then."

David rolled up to Ruth's house just before noon on Saturday. He had already retrieved Leah's purchases at Bloomingdales. There were no cars in the driveway, suggesting that Elaine had left for Annapolis and obviously Sandy was still away. Ruth heard the car drive up and was waiting at the door.

"Hi, David," she said. "I was beginning to think you weren't coming."

"Sorry. I decided to pick up Mom's things first, so I wouldn't feel rushed to get back."

"Okay, I guess I'll buy that feeble excuse," she said mockingly. "Just don't let it happen again. Come on in and we'll have some of that pie. Better hurry before Brian and Rory finish it. Mom told them to leave it for us but they didn't pay any attention to her, as usual."

"That may be a good thing," David said. "Ever since football season ended I've been putting on weight. I need to cut back a bit."

"Well I think you look just fine. Besides, when you go off to school you won't get all this fine home cooking. That'll knock a few pounds off."

They settled at the kitchen table for their pie and coffee. David could hear footsteps upstairs as Ruth's brothers moved around. He looked across the table as she took a bite of pie.

"You know you're even more beautiful than when I first met you."

"What a nice thing to say, David. But, you do realize you can have another piece of pie without the compliments."

"I mean it, Ruth. I can't stand it when we don't see each other for such long periods of time. That's the reason I wanted to go to Georgetown. I had a knock-down-drag-out with my dad over this. He's adamant that I go to Johns Hopkins. His explanation is that all the support he's given them with Bernie's studies gives us an inside edge, whatever that means. He also says it's closer to home and I'll be able to commute for a couple of years. We both know his real reason. He wants to keeps us as far apart as possible. Well, I don't care what shenanigans he pulls, he's not going to come between me and you."

"Oh, David," Ruth said as the tears came. "I was looking forward to us having more time together too. Oh well. Anyway, I hear the first years of nursing school and pre-med are really hard. We have to make sure that school and studies come first. Maybe in a strange way this makes sense. There'll be plenty of time later to catch up on anything we might miss out on."

"I know you're right, but I don't know if I'm strong enough to resist. Maybe I'll just go to Georgetown anyway. I can get a scholarship and work my way through."

"Don't even go there. I can see it's going to be up to me to keep you on the straight and narrow. We'll work it out some way. Four years will fly by and then I'll be a nurse. We'll get married and I'll support you through med school. Let's don't let this spoil the rest of our summer."

They spent the remainder of the afternoon talking about plans for the upcoming graduation ceremonies. Ruth's was a week before David's, and both he and Leah had accepted invitations. Jacob was invited but he still stubbornly resisted becoming entangled in their relationship until the subject of religion was settled. Elaine and Ruth were scheduled to attend the twin's graduation; however, the unpredictable nature of Sandy's travels made it impossible for him to commit. The best he could do was promise to come if he was in town.

The Silver Spring graduation took place in the football stadium. The 1200 graduates and several thousand friends and relatives nearly filled the stands on one side of the field. Two invocations were pronounced, one by a priest and one by a rabbi, in recognition of the predominant religious compositions of the town. Ruth, as the salutatorian of her class, gave a brief talk on duty and responsibility. The major address was given by Maryland Senator Millard Tydings. His speech touched on the same points that Ruth and the valedictorian had stressed. He then asked for the prayers and support of all of the citizens of Maryland for President Roosevelt and the members of Congress as they faced the difficult decisions being forced on them by the growing crisis in Europe. The senator closed his address and the benediction was said by the president of the Youth Fellowship Club at the school. The graduates and attendees began to file out of the stadium.

"My mother has already gone with yours to the house," David said to Ruth as he met her at the door to the gym where she had changed. "They were kind enough to give us a little time alone."

"Well, it may have not been all kindness. I had asked Mom to let you drive me home. I know we'll be seeing each other next week at your graduation, but I wanted to steal a few more minutes alone with you. It's going to be a long summer preparing for college and I don't know how much time we'll have alone. I've landed a part time job at a nursing home. I don't know what my hours will be or how much time I'll have off. By the way, Mom and Dad have asked me to commute to school, at least for the first year, to save on expenses."

"Well to complicate things a bit further, Murray and I are going to help out at the factory three days a week. Papa says it'll

~ 162 ~

offset some of the college expenses for us. I don't think it will make that much difference, I just think he wants to spend some time with us before we start college. Despite that gruff exterior he can be pretty sentimental at times. I think he remembers how it was before they left Russia and he wants to make sure his family doesn't miss out on the things his people lost."

Ruth's family and guests were in full celebration mode when they got home. Aunts, uncles and cousins crowded the kitchen and dining room where Elaine had prepared a smorgasbord of goodies and drinks for the party. Leah was seated in the living room beside an elderly man. She was trying desperately to balance a plate on her knee while holding a drink in the other hand.

"David, come and meet Ruth's great-uncle Seamus. He was just telling me about life in Ireland where he grew up. His parents, Ruth's great-grandparents, survived the potato famine of the 1850's and then came to America around 1870. He says they settled in Boston at first and then Ruth's grandfather moved his family to Maryland. Most of their relatives are still in Boston and New York."

"Aye, that they are," Seamus said with a thick brogue. "It's great to see how far Sandy has come what with his big government job and all. Elaine's a lovely colleen and Ruthie here's the spittin' image of me grandmother. "

"Come on Uncle Seamus, you're embarrassing me."

"Nay, Lassie, it's all true. She's a fine one David. Better take good care of her or I may have to get the clan after you," Seamus said with a wink.

Blarney was being served in large portions along with the tea and sandwiches. The party broke up around five and Leah bid her goodbyes.

~ 163 ~

"I was hoping Sandy would make it back in time," Elaine said. "I'm sorry he missed the ceremony and the party. Thankfully, many of the Boston and New York crowd are staying on a few days. I'm certain he'll be back in time to see them."

"It was a wonderful day, Elaine," Leah said. "Give my best to Sandy. I hope he'll be able to make the twins graduation next week."

"So do I. He's missed out on so much because of the war in Europe. Senator Tydings was right to ask for our prayers. Things don't look good over there and I'm afraid we may get dragged into it."

"Oh, I pray not," Leah said, "so many of our young men are of fighting age. I can't bear the thought of Bernie or the twins having to go off to war. I don't know if I could stand it."

David pecked Ruth on the cheek, embraced Elaine, and opened the door for his mother.

"See you next week," he said as he closed the door.


Through Jacob's business connections Leah was able to reserve the social hall at Temple *Oheb Shalom* for the twin's post-graduation party. Stan, Burt and Joe, three of the neighborhood seniors had been asked to join the celebration. The hall at *Chizuk Amuno* could accommodate no more than 75 while the *Oheb Shalom* room could handle up to 300. Even though Jacob had been extended an invitation to join *Temple Oheb Shalom*, he had declined. The boy's entire religious childhood was built around their old synagogue and Jacob felt it unfair to sever those relationships just to satisfy his own ego. Prestige could not triumph over family, friends and familiarity. So, their membership remained where their hearts were.

The social hall at *Temple Oheb Shalom* was filled to over-flowing. Four main tables had been arranged for the four seniors. Each was piled high with food, drink and brightly wrapped presents. Guests wandered from table to table to assess the offerings and to greet the other families. David and Murray were kept busy stuffing envelopes full of money into their pockets.

Ruth and Elaine were there. They were welcomed warmly by Leah. Jacob was courteous and civil to the Braddocks, but after a few minutes he wandered off to greet Weiss relatives from New York. The obvious chill was not lost on either Elaine or Leah.

"I'm sorry Elaine. He just won't let go. I don't know if he'll ever relent unless he gets his way."

"It's all right Leah. I understand how he feels. He's battling some awfully strong religious currents. We'll just have to hope the children will make a decision that we can all live with."

"Thank you. I pray for that daily. Speaking of the children, where did they get off to."

Ruth and David, with the infinite resilience of youth, could only see a future filled with each other. There were no thoughts of war and death in that future, only love, and happiness, and family, and the fulfillment of their dreams. In a few short weeks they would enroll in college and in four years they would graduate and get married. This last bit of news they had not shared with their families, but it would come as no surprise to either. They both knew that education came first. What they couldn't know was how fickle the future could be and how ephemeral all dreams are.

An ominous cloud hovered over the celebrants that day at *Oheb Shalom*. The headlines of the newspapers left lying on their breakfast tables when they left for the stadium foretold of dreadful times ahead. As dignitaries all across America presided over hundreds of graduations, a ragtag fleet of boats was attempting to rescue thousands of British, French and Belgian soldiers from the beaches of Dunquerque, France. They had been herded into that small enclave on the Norman coast abreast of Dover, England by a brutal German onslaught. They were threatened with capture or annihilation. In the course of a few days the British cobbled together a flotilla of 700 small boats along with several British Man-O-Wars to attempt a rescue of their army. In the space of ten days 340,000 men of the Allied Expeditionary Force were ferried across the English Channel to safety. Inexplicably, Hitler had ordered a temporary halt to his army's advance. The ensuing escape would later be called "The Miracle of Dunkirk." It was following their audacious escape from the Nazi's clutches that Winston Churchhill made one of his most famous speeches, in which he said...

*"We shall go to the end. We shall fight in France, we shall fight on the seas and oceans, we shall fight with growing confidence and growing strength in the air, we shall defend our island whatever the cost may be. We shall fight on the beaches, we shall fight on the landing grounds, we shall fight in the fields and the streets, we shall fight in the hills; we shall never surrender...*

This was Britain's darkest hour and the moment the die was firmly cast. It was only a matter of time until the United States would be drawn into its second worldwide conflict in just twenty short years. How many of these fresh-faced, innocent, young graduates would soon be swept up in the brewing madness, their lives interrupted, maybe even sacrificed, in order to preserve the very freedoms, they were enjoying this day.

David and Murray spent their last summer before college puttering around the Epstein and Weiss factories and enjoying a few carefree days in Tolchester. Ruth was able to get away for two short weekends at her uncle's cottage. These brief interludes with David were bittersweet. College was looming with even more separation. Jacob's steadfast refusal to compromise on his demands hung like a sword of Damocles over all they did.

September 1940 was unusually hot and humid in the Washington area. School for both David and Ruth began on the first Monday. He drove down to see Ruth for one last time before classes began. It was uncertain when they would be together again. Ruth was sitting on the porch swing when he drove up, reading literature from the GW nursing school. She was dressed and ready for their formal date — a last dinner before they both settled down to their studies. David had chosen a fancy French restaurant in Georgetown that he had checked out during one of his visits to the school. David loosened his tie as he sat down across from Ruth. The air inside was stifling. Their waiter came over.

"It is a little warm in here. We have a table on the patio if you'd like it. There's a little breeze out there."

"That's great," David said.

"Right this way, please," the waiter said as he escorted them outside.

"Thanks, this is much better "

"Here are your menus. I'll give you a few minutes to look them over. Anything to drink?"

"Ruth would you like some champagne to celebrate," David asked.

"Sure," she said. "it'll be a long time before we get the chance again."

"Are you both 18?" the waiter asked.

"Yep," David said "this is our going away to college dinner. We both start next Monday."

"Okay, here's a wine menu. Pick something out and I'll be right back."

They were finishing their first glass of the split of Veuve-Cliquot when the waiter came back for their dinner order. When he walked away, David cleared his throat.

"You know, I hadn't given a lot of thought to my future before I met you at the pool in Mount Airy, but suddenly I realized I had to think about more than football, clowning around with the gang and summers down shore. You probably think I still don't have a serious bone in my body, but I love you very much, and if we're going to have the life I want us to have, I know how important a good education is. Even though I'll be up in Baltimore and you'll be down here, I want you to know how seriously I take this responsibility. I want you to know that I listened to you, and I respect your opinion."

Ruth looked up with misty eyes, that wry little smile crinkling the corners of her mouth.

"I couldn't be happier, David. Sharing these times with you and looking forward to the next four years is a dream come true. But you're right. As we discussed the other day we have to remain disciplined. Our studies have to come first, and we'll just have to make time for the other stuff when we can. We'll still be able to carve out time for ourselves as long as we keep our eyes on the goal. Despite the times we feel like choking our parents we owe them a lot. All the things they have fought for and believe in, we inherit. Any sacrifices we might make are nothing compared to theirs. The pain your mother felt when Miss Szold told her no more children would make *aliyah* was devastating. In her own way she was there in Palestine when the boats stopped coming. She suffered such depression that I feared for her sanity. But she's such a strong person. She came through it because she knows so much remains to be done — for her family and the world. It's so good to see her moving on in support of the other efforts to help the Jews over there. Her struggle continues, and it becomes our struggle as well. Nothing is more important than carrying on her work and the work of all the Henriettas and Leahs of this world. I know you understand all of this as well as I do, and I know you take it just as seriously. We have to be sure we keep sight of our goals. By the way, I love you, too."

The last sop of *Coq au Vin* was gone. David took the last sip of his iced tea before they walked back up the street to his car. He opened the door and Ruth swung her legs in. He leaned down and kissed her. She reached up with both arms, taking his face in her hands and returned his kiss. She finally pulled away.

"It's been a wonderful evening, David. I wish it didn't have to end, but we both have busy days coming up tomorrow with freshman orientation and class scheduling. I don't want to be responsible for screwing up our first day of college. So, take me home young man and get started on the rest of your life."

It was just past eleven when David kissed Ruth goodnight on her front porch and pulled away from the Braddock home. He was still in starry-eyed awe of the impish little redhead, still standing there, framed in the glow of the porch light, waving goodbye.

~ 169 ~

# 19

# Wars and Rumors of War

One by one, like so many dominoes, the European democracies fell to Hitler's onslaught. By the end of April, no longer able to withstand the Nazi juggernaut, Denmark and Norway capitulated. By June the Netherlands and Belgium had fallen.

On June 22, France signed articles of surrender at Compiegne, France, a location chosen by Hitler to avenge the humiliating German surrender after WWI — on the exact same spot. He further rubbed salt in the Gallic wounds by retrieving the railroad car used for the German surrender, from a Paris museum, for the signing ceremony. While waiting for the French delegation to arrive he stood contemptuously atop the granite boulder on which a plaque commemorated the November 11, 1918 German surrender. Three days later SS troops destroyed the monument and all other remnants of the WWI armistice — with one conspicuous exception — a sculpture of a German eagle, pierced by a sword. It was removed and sent to Berlin as a memento for Hitler. Nazi storm troopers, their hobnailed boots goose-stepping down the Champs Elysee, celebrated the fall of Paris, draped in black, no longer the "young and gay" city celebrated in song. All Parisian hearts mourned the loss of their "city of light."

With the fall of France, England stood alone, spared only because millions of years ago an unpredictable continental drift saw fit to place the North Sea between Shakespeare's "sceptred isle" and the European continent. Neville Chamberlain's spineless attempts at appeasement with Hitler had cost him the confidence of his people and with the fall of France he resigned in disgrace. King George VII, casting about for someone who would give hope to his anxious subjects placed Britain's fate in the cigar-stained hands of Sir Winston Churchill who described his ascendancy to the Prime Minister's job as his *"walk with destiny."* His first speech to parliament was one of three major war addresses for which he is remembered. He said that he had nothing to offer the people of England but *"blood, toil, sweat and tears."* After five long and bloody years, and the shedding of many tears, Churchill would successfully complete his *"walk with destiny."*

The North Sea provided a natural barrier to any German land assault on England, but it was no obstacle to the German Luftwaffe. Hitler declared a complete blockade of England and ordered Hermann Goering to unleash the full might of the German Luftwaffe on the British Isles. He sought to destroy

England's factories and its air force. Once Goering's planes achieved mastery of the skies over England, Operation Sea Lion, a massive land invasion of England, would commence. The ensuing air battle raged on for six weeks, a seeming eternity for the British subjects on the ground. Wave after wave of German heavy bombers, escorted by their fearsome Messerschmitt fighters, pounded England's centers of commerce and manufacturing.

Initially, the Germans held a huge advantage. Many of their pilots had cut their "air teeth" in Spain when Germany went to the aid of Generalissimo Franco during the Spanish Civil War. The Brits suffered terrible losses in the early stages of the battle; however, they had an ace of their own up their sleeve. A new weapon, under development in top-secret British laboratories for years, was rushed into service. It was not a weapon in the conventional sense of the word, but it would spell the difference between defeat and victory for the Royal Air Force. Radio Detection and Ranging equipment was deployed all along the North Sea coast. RADAR, as the acronym was quickly adopted, allowed the RAF to detect and intercept the incoming German planes over the North Sea where they could neutralize the fighter escorts thereby leaving the lumbering bombers at the mercy of anti-aircraft fire. The Germans were unaware of this newest innovation in air warfare. The Hurricanes and Spitfires launched from English airbases when the German planes were detected over the English Channel, were matches for the Messerschmitt fighters. Hundreds of German planes were shot down over the North Sea, their pilots killed in battle or quickly succumbing to a watery grave in the frigid Channel. Meanwhile, injured RAF pilots were able to limp back to base or were able to bailout over friendly territory. Hitler's mammoth war machine could quickly replace the downed planes but the 1700 pilots he lost were a devastating blow. Their loss proved crucial as the war wore on. Unlike war machines, flesh and blood did not lend themselves to assembly lines.

England lost 900 of her own pilots, a horrific number, but far less damaging to her ability to carry on than that of the Germans. Two days after suffering the single worst day of the campaign, Hitler called off the Battle of Britain. In a message to parliament Churchill immortalized those brave RAF pilots when he declared, *"Never in the history of human conflict has so much been owed by so many to so few."*

The blitz of England continued sporadically for another nine months. Over 36,000 tons of bombs rained down on her population centers. Her people, heeding the wail of air raid sirens gathered in their shelters, singing, praying and awaiting the all clear signal. Then they would climb out of those holes in the ground, shake their fists at the sky, and continue the fight. Hitler succeeded in destroying much of England's manufacturing capacity, public buildings and military installations, but he could not destroy the one thing that would ultimately defeat him — the indomitable spirit of the English people.

A major factor in Hitler's decision to de-escalate the Battle of Britain was his growing and deep-seated fear of the *"Great Bear"* to his east — Russia. He, like Napoleon before him, always saw that hibernating beast as the ultimate threat to his quest for European domination. He quickly recognized that he could not continue to sustain the devastating losses of pilots over the English Channel while he was preparing for an invasion of Russia. When he called off the air war with England in June 1941, the ink was barely dry on the German-Russian mutual defense treaty he had signed with Joseph Stalin following their partitioning of Poland. Hitler's war planners were already putting the finishing touches to an operation he had dubbed *"Barbarossa"* or "Red Beard" in Italian.  Hitler admired the ruthlessness of his Teutonic predecessor, Frederick Barbarossa, who ruled the Holy

Roman Empire in the twelfth century and was known for his barbarism in battle, including two crusades into Palestine to reclaim the Holy Land from the Muslim infidels.

Hitler chose June 22, 1941 to launch *"Barbarossa."* Whether coincidental or by design, that was the exact same day that Napoleon had invaded Russia – 129 years earlier. Hitler believed that a quick thrust into Russia along a 900-mile front from the Baltic to the Black Sea, with an Axis force of 3,500,000 troops, would bring Russia to its knees. Early on, the *blitzkrieg* was so successful that Panzer tanks were gobbling up as much as 50 miles of territory per day. By the end of October, Moscow was only 65 miles away and over 500,000 square miles of Russian territory was under Nazi control. Of the 5,000,000 Russian soldiers captured, 3.5 million died of malnutrition, disease and Nazi brutality. The siege of Leningrad lasted for 900 days. Over one-million of its inhabitants died. That was one third of the pre-war population. Another 250,000 German troops laid siege to Stalingrad. Only 7,000 of them returned home after their capture, and imprisonment in Siberian labor camps. Maintaining that Eastern Front for three long years consumed much of Hitler's resources and ultimately led to Germany's defeat.

The first of Hitler's core goals was the extermination of the Jewish race — second was his ambition to enslave all the "inferior" Slavic peoples of Eastern Europe. He wished to convert the entire region into a German "breadbasket." When *"Operation Barbarossa"* reached its final conclusion three years later, five million Axis soldiers, nine million Russian soldiers and 20 million civilians lay buried under the frozen tundra and windswept steppes of *"Mother Russia."* Like Napoleon before him, Hitler learned the awful truth about the iron will and dogged tenacity of the Russian people — and the unspeakable brutality of Russian winters. The little Austrian corporal tasted the same bitter defeat on the banks of the Volga as the little French Emperor

132 years earlier. If Hitler had honored his pact with Stalin, it is entirely possible that Germany would have prevailed over the Allies in the West.

Unknown to the Nazis, Sandy Braddock and his superiors at the State Department had convinced Roosevelt to sign the Lend-Lease act passed by Congress. It was this pipeline of food, clothing, munitions and other war materiel that sustained the Red Army during that long and bitter siege. Congress voted to change the Neutrality Act, permitting the sale or lease of armaments to the democratic countries of Europe. In signing the act Roosevelt proclaimed that it would make the United States the *"arsenal of democracy."*

With the German push into Russia came other atrocities that impacted the Weiss family directly and in a personal way. In the Belarus capital of Minsk the Gestapo walled off the entire Jewish section of the city creating a ghetto of 80,000 Jews. In the city of Iasi, Romania Ion Antonescu's Iron Guard slaughtered 1500 Jews. Echoes of distant drums of war sounded across the Atlantic. They grew louder by the day.

****

"Hi," David said.

"Hi, yourself," Ruth countered as she picked up the phone.

They were well into their first semester of college and mired in the countless details of college life. They had seen each other only once during that first month, when David drove down to Silver Spring. Now it was late September and the pain of separation was becoming excruciating.

"I miss you so much," Ruth said. "Dad's still away and we don't know when he'll get back home. Mom and the boys are busy with school and their own problems. It seems like all the world is conspiring against us."

"I know how you feel, but Thanksgiving is coming up soon and we both get a week off. I've promised Mom that I'll help out some at the JRA. Maybe you and your mother can come up for a couple of days. Dad's going to be on a trip to Cincinnati. With all the rumors of war, the government is gearing up to produce all kinds of things. I think he'll be asked to make uniforms and clothing for our soldiers. It's getting pretty serious. Anyway, I spoke to my mother and she would love to have you stay with us. What do you say?"

"I'll ask Mom. If Dad's not here she may agree."

"Great. Let me know. I've gotta run. I have a chemistry test tomorrow. I never realized how hard college would be. Murray and I kinda skated through high school. We are both having to buckle down now. There's another reason we need to make good grades. My ROTC instructor says that if there's war, and a draft, the best students may get deferments. It's something I hadn't thought about before but with war staring us in the face. I do now."

The war in Europe required Sandy Braddock to travel often to England and Russia. He and his colleagues braved the icy North Atlantic in fast navy cutters or took circuitous air routes to avoid the war zones. They met with their allied counterparts, in nondescript buildings, on back streets, in out-of-the-way little villages. Any U.S. state department employee discovered in such a meeting would immediately contradict America's claim of neutrality and add more grist for Joseph Goebbel's propaganda mill. Such an event would drag the U.S. into war with ominous repercussions for Roosevelt. He continued to walk that fine line between vows of neutrality and covert aid to the Allies. The isolationists, particularly Charles Lindbergh, would be in full cry demanding FDR's resignation or impeachment.

Each time Sandy returned, his face more deeply etched, he could tell them little of what he was doing or where he had been. The obvious strain on his face was just one more stark manifestation that America was being drawn closer to the rumbling volcano that the war in Europe had become. The only question remaining was whether she would be pushed into the cauldron or be caught in its eruption. That question was answered on December 7, 1941 when the Empire of Japan sent 353 fighter bombers to sink the unsuspecting American fleet at anchor in Pearl Harbor.

War worries were no less prevalent in the Weiss home in Baltimore. Dinner table discussions inevitably veered into news of the war and the plight of the Jews caught up in its fury. Almost all of Europe was now under the Nazi heel. From the Bay of Biscay to Odessa and from Athens to Oslo, regime after regime had fallen victim to the German juggernaut. In that fall of 1941, only England and her colonial empire in the West and Russia in the East were left to confront Hitler and his Axis allies.

\*\*\*\*

Snippets of news continued to escape from under the curtain the Germans had drawn on continental Europe. Partisans and spies reported the construction of sprawling labor camps all over Germany and Poland. Prominently displayed above the iron entrance gates were these words in German "*Arbeit Macht Frei*" — Work Makes you Free. Most prisoners entering those forbidden gates never found work; they were lined up in rows and slaughtered with machine guns and rifles — after digging their own graves. The fortunate few, the strong, were given jobs from which few survived. They worked long hours, with meager rations and little water, until they fell in place. They were hauled away to the ovens.

The process of executing so many people by firing squads became both onerous and expensive. The ammunition used was badly needed on the front lines. The thousands of prisoners arriving on cattle cars, suffering from malnutrition, disease and dysentery, were overwhelming the capacity of the camps to deal with them. Some other method of extermination was required.

The initial answer to *"faster and cheaper"* mass murder came in the form of mobile vans equipped as portable gas chambers. The vans too proved to be cumbersome and presented a logistical nightmare. Disposing of so many bodies became an insoluble problem.

The ultimate answer to Hitler's *"final solution,"* as his campaign to exterminate the Jews was called, took the form of a grotesque charade acted out by the camp guards and their unsuspecting prisoners. As the prisoners walked through the gates, Gestapo officers herded them into two groups, the young and the strong in one and the old, the ill and the children in the other. The first group was marched off to the laborer's barracks while the other group was sent to the "delousing" showers. There they suffered further indignation as they were required to strip naked for the showers, in full view of the guards and other prisoners. They were then instructed to place their clothes in neat piles, along with their shoes and eyeglasses, to be reclaimed after they exited the showers. Each prisoner was handed a bar of soap and led into the showers. The massive steel doors through which they entered clanged shut ominously behind them. The deadly hiss of the Zyklon-B gas pouring from the fake shower heads was the first indication that these were not ordinary showers.  The prisoners were struck with the deadly realization, as the cyanide gas seared their lungs, that all those rumors they had refused to believe were really true. Sealed into the airtight chambers, bloody fingers clawed at the doors. Mothers clung in desperation to their small children, their anguished screams heard only by a God whose eyes remained averted from the indescribable horror, as his chosen people perished.

In the release of death, they were spared the final indignity. Gold teeth were yanked out and flowing hair was cut off – – the gold for the Fuehrer's coffers and the hair for his soldiers' mattresses. The still warm corpses, blood trickling from their gaping mouths, the terror frozen on their faces for all eternity, were stacked like so much cordwood to be hauled away to the crematoria by fellow Jewish laborers — saved from the same fate—as long as their usefulness lasted. **This** was Hitler's "**final solution**."

Ominous, low-flying clouds, driven by winds off the wintry Baltic blew across the camp at Oswiecim, Poland (Auschwitz in German). Carrion birds circling overhead looked down on a scene so monstrously grotesque that only the writer Dante could possibly do justice to its sheer inhumanity. His seventh circle of hell, reserved for those whose sin was violence, never envisioned such acts of sadism as Hitler's henchmen inflicted on their fellow man. The acrid stench of burning flesh wafted southward on those Baltic winds toward the nearby Czech border. Far off thunder proclaimed the rain that was approaching to carry the blood and ashes into the gutters of Auschwitz. But, no amount of wind or rain could purge the agonizing screams, screams that would hang in the air for eternity over Hitler's charnel house as silent witness to this latest incarnation of man's inhumanity to man. Screams that would proclaim to the civilized world, *Never Again, Never Again.*

# 20

# Armageddon

General George Catlett Marshall was appointed chief of staff for all American armed forces in 1939. He faced a military in major decline. The drawdown of men and machinery following the 1918 Armistice ending WWI had turned a formidable war machine into a hollowed-out shell. The onset of the Great Depression, following the collapse of Wall Street in 1929, had only served to hasten the decline. By the time Hitler began rattling his sword in 1933, America's military had become an aging, toothless, paper tiger. The isolationist view had prevailed. Some even hailed Hitler as the new "*savior*" of Germany, following hyperinflation and the collapse of the Weimar Republic under President von Hindenburg. Hitler was seen as a strong and bold leader who could conquer the rampant inflation, reunite the country and lead Europe out of its WWI hangover.

Marshall was hard-pressed to carry out even his basic mission of protecting the continental United States: defense of its far-flung territories was an impossible task. Sensing the inevitability of U.S. involvement in the war, he reinstituted the draft and ordered the formulation of a contingency war plan. The army, the navy, the marines and the nascent air force were beefed up to confront the escalating international threat to America. He began to shift away from the old paradigm of continental defense to a new focus on hemispherical defense. The U.S. could not allow a foreign power to establish a foothold in the Americas from which it could launch aerial attacks on the homeland. Of paramount importance was securing the Panama Canal, the sole nexus between the Atlantic and Pacific fleets. The canal also provided a vital passage for the transshipment of war materiel. Keeping the canal open for both military and commercial shipping became a major priority for the re-constituted U.S. military.

Reacting to the menace of the spreading war in Europe, President Roosevelt declared a limited national emergency in the U.S., authorizing increases in the Army Reserve and the National Guard. He also ordered the retooling of American factories to begin rolling out the munitions and machinery promised under the Lend-Lease act. Fortunately, this also allowed Marshall to begin the long process of re-equipping his troops with the latest weapons of modern warfare. World War I vintage tanks and planes were re-designed and updated to meet the challenges posed by Germany's modern arsenal. By 1940 these re-tooled armaments were flowing to Europe and to American military posts at home and abroad.

Meanwhile, half-way around the world, Japan was flexing its military muscle. Korea and Taiwan had already fallen victim to Japan's territorial ambitions. She invaded Manchuria and began a campaign against China proper in 1937, seeking to consolidate her hold on the Asian continent. The initial successes led Japanese leaders to believe that the conquest of China would be a walk-in-the-park. It was anything but.

The Japanese Imperial Army command in Tokyo, growing impatient with the slowing conquest of China proper, ordered an invasion of the Nationalist Chinese capital of Nanking. In the fading days of 1937 one of the most horrific chapters in human history unfolded. Japanese soldiers, whipped into frenzy by their commanders, slaughtered 300,000 men women and children in that city. The *"Rape of Nanking"* stands with the *"Holocaust"* as seminal events of WWII that remind us of just how brutal man can become. When Germany occupied France and established the Vichy government there, Japan immediately allied herself with Hitler and Mussolini. Hirohito joined his infamous partners as a signatory to the *"Tripartite Pact,"* officially establishing the Axis powers. He also signed a non-aggression pact with Russia which freed Japan to pursue its interests in Asia without the threat of a Russian invasion. It also freed "Mother *Russia*" to concentrate its efforts against Hitler on the Eastern Front.

Having concluded these alliances, Japan was free to annex French-Indochina (Vietnam) and to begin an assault on the colonial outposts of Old Europe: Borneo, Java, New Guinea, Hong Kong, Singapore, Sumatra, Malaysia and the Dutch East Indies. She also was casting her eyes covetously southwestward toward Burma and India as well as to the south and Australia. Japan sought hegemony over what she called a *"Greater Asia Co-Prosperity Sphere"* and the vast natural resources of the entire Pacific region.

Tojo and his generals realized early on that Japan could not realize its goals without access to those resources since the Japanese islands had none. They needed the oil, rubber, tin and iron to turn Japan into *the* industrial power of Asia. They also knew that ultimately, that would mean neutralizing American influence in the region, and that meant destroying the American positions in Hawaii, the Philippines, Wake Island and Guam. The common wisdom among the Japanese military was that the United States, which was becoming heavily embroiled in Europe, could not possibly protest the Japanese offensives on so many fronts. America would be forced to sue for peace in the Pacific and seek accommodation with *"The Land of the Rising Sun."*

This was the first of many miscalculations by the Japanese Supreme Command. It turned out to be their worst. Autumn came early in 1941. The cherry trees around the tidal basin were ablaze in gold and scarlet, responding to a surprise October frost. The Japanese delegation to Washington showed up each day in their formal cutaways to negotiate a settlement of the American embargo of fuel to Japan. The negotiations seemed at an impasse. Fruitless meetings dragged on for weeks. Winter was fast approaching. Unknown to the American delegation, the Japanese High Command had already authorized Admiral Yamamoto to draft plans for a surprise air strike on Pearl Harbor, Hawaii.

The Lend-Lease program had kicked into high gear. Tanks and artillery were rolling onto freighters up and down the Atlantic Seaboard. German U-boats patrolled off the coast, exacting a terrible toll on shipping in the North Atlantic sea lanes. However, life in academia proceeded as if the entire world was not on the verge of a major cataclysm.

David and Ruth were certainly well aware of the turmoil across the Atlantic. Their work with *Aliyah* and information gleaned from Sandy Braddock's clandestine activities had them more involved than most. David in Baltimore and Ruth in Washington paid closer attention to the newspaper reports and radio announcements than their contemporaries, but even they were unprepared for the tremulous voice crackling through Sandy Braddock's old Philco radio the Sunday morning of December 7, 1941. David had sneaked away for a few brief hours to see Ruth before his semester finals began on Monday.

*"Radio relays from our affiliate in Honolulu, Hawaii report that the naval base at Pearl Harbor is under attack by planes from the Empire of Japan. Large plumes of black smoke can be seen rising over the harbor. Eyewitness reports say that several large warships have been damaged with some of them sunk or sinking. Other reports claim that several waves of planes also struck Hickham Field, Schofield Barracks and Wheeler Field. Casualty numbers are not yet available, but it is safe to say they will be in the hundreds if not thousands. No official reports have been received from either Japan or the United States confirming this attack."*

The disembodied voice, reporting from a studio several miles away in Honolulu, was distraught, verging on hysteria. His voice, soaring octaves higher than normal, cracked and faltered as he described the unfolding horror. Spotters from the radio antenna site high above the city could discern the small black specks as they climbed out of their bombing runs, closely followed by explosions and fresh billows of thick, black smoke. Sailors on liberty in the bars and brothels along Waikiki began streaming back toward Pearl, their faces contorted with grim looks of disbelief.

*"Efforts to contact army and navy commanders have been unsuccessful. We don't yet know to what extent our forces are able to respond to this surprise attack. Nor do we know if this attack is coordinated with others in the Pacific or on the mainland.*

*"A check with the local newspapers indicates that almost all the Pacific Fleet battleships are tied up alongside each other in Pearl Harbor. If so, they are sitting ducks for an attack like this. We were unable to substantiate whether the Pacific carrier fleet is also in Pearl. Earlier reports said they were at sea. Pray to God that's true. Otherwise we have no Pacific Fleet left."*

"My God," said Sandy Braddock as he crossed the room to turn up the volume. "This was what I was afraid of. I warned General Marshall and his staff months ago that a sneak attack by the Japanese was a distinct possibility given the corrosive relations with them the past few months. I knew they felt backed into a corner with their fuel supplies and raw materials cut off. They have lived in feudal isolation on those few little islands for centuries. Now, with the industrialized world closing in on them, they feel mortally threatened. They have practically no resources of their own and they've been shut out from Southeast Asia's riches by the colonial empires of Europe. I knew when they invaded China it was just the tip of the iceberg. Manchuria was just an appetizer for them. Well, there'll be hell to pay now. We have no choice but to declare war on them. And that means war with Germany and Italy because of their mutual defense pact. The U.S. is not prepared for this type of global engagement. We don't have enough troops under arms and we don't have the munitions to fight a two-front war. Thank God for the Lend-Lease program and the build-up in the reserves and National Guard over the past two years."

Sandy turned to see stark terror in the eyes of Ruth and Elaine. David sat silently, ashen faced. His rant had only served to magnify the fears already brewing in the room. He quickly sought to tamp it down.

"Well, we were less prepared in 1917 for the First World War and we were able to mobilize for that one. Obviously, Hitler, Mussolini and Tojo didn't learn from Kaiser Wilhelm's mistake — you just don't mess with Uncle Sam. They've awakened a sleeping tiger. When we get our industry and our military up to speed they had better watch out."

"Daddy does this really mean war? Will David and Murray be drafted? What about college, won't they be allowed to continue? They're going to need doctors worse than ever. Won't they exempt David? "

Fear and disbelief mingled with Ruth's tears. Surely this event, half-way around the world, won't be allowed to ruin their plans. What of their dreams; college, graduation, marriage, career, children. What's to become of them? Sandy took his trembling daughter in his arms as if to shield her from the stark reality he knew they were facing.

"Now, now," he said, "nothing's going to happen tomorrow. Any action we take won't affect you for a while. Both of you will go back to school tomorrow and go to your classes as if nothing has changed. I'm sure President Roosevelt will meet with his advisors and then address the nation. There is no reason to panic. Life will go on; it'll just be with a little more uncertainty as the nation gears up for war. In the meantime, the best thing we can do to help is to stay calm and just go about our daily lives. In all due time events will sort themselves out and we'll each know what part we must play. Our country has been here for us when we needed her and now we will be here for our country.

"David, you'd better call your folks. They're going to be worried. Let's all take a deep breath and calm down. In the immortal words of Scarlett O'Hara, 'tomorrow's another day.' "

Classes reconvened at George Washington and Johns Hopkins on Monday morning. No one could concentrate on their studies. The hallways were overflowing with small clusters of students. Their animated conversations were about the attack on Pearl Harbor and what meaning that event held for their own lives. The girls cried and the boys stared with dazed, faraway looks in their eyes as they imagined themselves on some foreign battlefield. Everyone had questions. No one had answers.

David wandered from class to class in a fog, unable to replace the images of burning ships with the chemical equations his professor was scribbling on the board. Monday, December 8, 1941 found an entire nation suspended in limbo, knowing what was to come, yet dreading the finality of the words that would confirm it. Banner headlines in the *Washington Post* and the *Baltimore Sun* read:


JAPS BOMB PEARL HARBOR


The wire reports said the casualties were staggering. More than 2,000 were believed dead or trapped in the capsized hulls of the great gray ships, their black underbellies now exposed to the tropical sun. Rescuers worked feverishly to reach the trapped men knowing any air pockets would soon be used up. Tapping noises from inside the *USS Arizona* became fainter as the hours slipped by. A wounded nation sat by its radios afraid to leave, afraid to miss a bit of news, or a late breaking story, and asking themselves the question on everyone's lips, *"how could this have happened?"*

As the casualty reports mounted, the War Department geared up to notify the families, a grisly task to be learned anew by a generation of the military that had not experienced war. It was a grim duty, once made routine by the obscene casualties of WWI at places like Belleau Wood, Chateau Thierry and Verdun. The olive drab Ford sedans with the large white star on the door, driven by army officers in spotless uniforms, became chillingly frequent sights in quiet neighborhoods all across America. The officers would stand quietly at the door with their caps held tightly under their arm out of respect, waiting for a response to their knock. The mothers and fathers who answered knew instantly what the message would be. The tell-tale yellow Western Union telegram always began with:

"We     regret     to     inform     you     that     your son.............................."

And always ended with:

........................."A grateful nation thanks you for his brave sacrifice."

Then the officer walks away to the mother's soft sobs behind the closed door and the father seeking to console her, the pride on his face melting into tears of grief for the son he will never hold again.


The Supreme Court justices, the cabinet officers and the Joint Chiefs of Staff filed silently into the chamber of the US House of Representatives and took their privileged seats in the front row. Senators and congressmen filled the ascending rows behind them while invited foreign dignitaries and other guests filled the upper reaches of the chamber. The Speaker of the House, Sam Rayburn and Vice-President Henry Wallace occupied their seats of honor on the dais above the speakers platform. The Sergeant-at-Arms led the Chaplain of the House, Ms. Cheryl Montgomery to the podium to offer the invocation.

"Eternal Father, strong to save," she began, reciting the familiar opening stanza to the seaman's hymn and going on to beseech God's blessing on America for her coming trial.

Speaker Rayburn of Texas stepped down to the podium. He called the joint session of congress to order to consider the joint resolution before them. It was the enabling legislation that would formally declare war on The Empire of Japan. Only one member of congress voted against the resolution, Congresswoman Jeanette Rankin of Montana. Ironically, she was the only member of congress to vote against the resolution which took the country to war with Germany in 1917.

At high noon the caravan bringing the president to the capitol started up Pennsylvania Avenue. The normally empty Sunday morning streets were lined with uniformed members of the armed services and legions of DC police. The president was driven around to the east steps of the capitol and taken in his wheelchair down to the anteroom of the house chamber. He doggedly rose from the chair and snapped his leg braces into place. With a grimly set jaw he struggled down the aisle, his ever-present son Elliot on his arm. He passed in front of the dignitaries who stood in respect of the man and the office. He thrust one lifeless leg in front of the other, willing himself to walk. Most of the nation was unaware that the president was an invalid. He had been crippled by polio after serving as Secretary of the Navy in WWI. He never allowed himself to be photographed in his wheelchair. All public appearances were orchestrated so that he was either standing or seated in a regular chair.

There, flanked on one side by the mace symbol of the house and on the other by the stars and stripes, he addressed the assembled leaders. The rest of the nation, indeed the rest of the world, sat by their radios, awaiting his words of reassurance, hope and inspiration.

"Mr. Vice-President, Mr. Speaker, members of the Senate and the House of Representatives:

Yesterday, December 7, 1941 — a date that shall live in infamy — the United States of America was suddenly and deliberately attacked by the naval and air forces of the Empire of Japan."

FDR went on to say, that an hour after the attack began, the Japanese ambassador to the United States, in reply to a formal request concerning the ongoing negotiations, stated that it appeared fruitless to continue those negotiations, while making no mention of the attack on Pearl Harbor which was already underway. Furthermore, Roosevelt said, the vast distances the carrier fleet traveled to reach Hawaii proved that the attack had been planned for weeks if not months, further compounding the treachery.  The president continued,

"No matter how long it may take to overcome this premeditated invasion, the American people, in their righteous might, will win through to absolute victory. I believe that I interpret the will of the Congress and the people when I assert that we will not only defend ourselves to the utmost but will make it very certain that this form of treachery will never endanger us again.

"Hostilities exist, there is no blinking at the fact that our people, our territory and our interests are in grave danger.

"With confidence in our armed forces — with the unbounding determination of our people — we will gain the inevitable triumph — so help us God."


So that was it. The nation expelled its collective breath, leaned back from their radios, and uncupped their ears. It then began to roll up its sleeves. The angry voices of its people rose up to say:

"Okay, if those dirty little yellow bastards think they can bomb our ships on our own soil and get away with it, they have another think coming. Nobody sneaks into our backyard, gives us a sucker punch and gets away with it. Tojo, you don't know what a big mistake you just made."

*December 11, 1941*

*To the Congress of the United States*

*On the morning of December 11, the government of Germany, pursuing its course of world conquest, declared war on the United States. The long known and the long expected has taken place. The forces endeavoring to enslave the entire world now are moving toward this hemisphere. Never before has there been a greater challenge to life, liberty and civilization. Delay invites great danger. Rapid and united efforts by all of the peoples of the world who are determined to remain free will insure a world victory of the forces of justice and righteousness over the forces of savagery and barbarism. Italy also declared war on the United States.*

*I therefore request the Congress to recognize a state of war between the United States and Germany, and between the United States and Italy.*

*Franklin D. Roosevelt*

With a heavy heart the president sent this message to Congress. He knew that war with the Germans and Italians had been inevitable. The mutual defense pacts between the three Axis powers stated that Germany only had to weigh-in if America was the aggressor. It did not require him to go to war with the US. He chose to ignore that fine political nuance. Mussolini, the pompous, strutting, megalomaniacal dictator of Italy had no choice but to follow Hitler's lead. Italy, seemingly an afterthought in the president's letter to Congress, was held in low regard by most western nations and was the butt of numerous jokes. Italy's prominence as a warrior nation died with the last Caesar.

Following Roosevelt's declaration, Hitler made an incendiary speech to the Reichstag. He called Roosevelt "*the main culprit of the war.*" Now, every player who would "*strut and fret his hour upon the stage*" had made his entrance and the stage was set for the second worldwide conflagration in twenty-three years, and none of the "*players*" knew how the final act would end.

# 21

# The Long Good-Bye

David managed to get through the tumultuous week. He had remained on campus for the finals. When the last bell rang on Friday afternoon, he pointed the nose of his little Ford coupe toward Linden Avenue. He saw Bernie's and Murray's cars in the driveway and parked along the curb. Good! He wanted desperately to talk to both of them, and his parents, about the events of the week. An overwhelming feeling of home and all the emotions that word conjured washed over him. He sat behind the wheel composing himself for what he knew would be a difficult evening. He saw his mother silhouetted against the light of the kitchen. She would be the most distressed of all as they gathered for the *Shabbat* meal that Friday, December 12, 1941. He burst into the room and swept her off her feet, ignoring the tears.

"Oh, David I'm so glad you're home. I've been so worried about you. All this talk of war has everyone so upset. Bernie and Murray are home. This is the first time we've all been together in a while. Everyone seems to want to be with their loved ones in the face of all the terrible news. The Sternberg boys across the street are home, and the Tomlinson's next door.

"Have you heard anything from Ruth? What does her father have to say about all this? We keep the radio on all the time.

We listen to every H.V. Kaltenborn and Gabriel Heatter broadcast during the week and Walter Winchell on Sundays. I don't think any of them are getting the full story of what's going on. We read the *Sun* editorials every morning; Walter Lippman, H.L. Mencken, Westbrook Pegler, but I don't know if they're allowed to tell the full truth. It's all so frightening. There are pictures of all the young men lined up to join the army. I understand Sid and Isaac have already enlisted; and, two of the Sarofsky boys. I hope you boys don't get any wild ideas about signing up. I can't stand the thought of you being shot at in some foreign land."

Leah poured out her doubts and fears in a gush of anguish, and all in one breath.

"Mama I haven't thought much about volunteering, but I know the draft boards are kicking into high gear. Murray and I may not have a choice. I don't think they'll draft Bernie because he's past thirty, but if it gets really bad, you never know what may happen. I know at least five guys at school who have received telegrams from their draft boards back home telling them to report for induction. We all thought because we were in college and going to medical school that we would be exempt from the draft, but that doesn't seem to be the case. All the ROTC guys are already on notice to report and the reserves are being called up. I'll bet you that by the end of next semester the student population at Hopkins will be cut in half."

These were not the encouraging words Leah was looking for from David. She began to cry anew. She picked up the tail of her apron to wipe away her tears.

"David, I don't want you to have to go to war, but if you do I know you'll make a fine soldier and will make us all proud of you. Both you and Murray are fine young men and a credit to our country. You are in the prime of your lives with brilliant futures ahead of you. I just don't understand why these madmen have to stir up so much trouble. I've known that since you and Ruth and I worked on the *Aliyah* project to save those poor children in Europe that it would come to this. I prayed that it wouldn't, but here we are. I just hope we'll be able to save the rest of those children who were left behind. I still hear from Henrietta. She continues to get reports from inside Germany and the Nazi territories. She says the atrocities are continuing and on an even larger scale. Maybe our entering the war is God's way of stopping Hitler from killing all the Jews. I just hope it doesn't cost the lives of my boys." Leah took one final, fruitless dab at her eyes. "Let's go into the living room. The family needs to talk."

Jacob, Bernie and Murray were gathered around the radio, straining to hear the announcer "...as the Japanese forces continue to overrun the islands of the Dutch East Indies. The Dutch nationals who were unable to flee before the invasion have been interned in Japanese prison camps or put aboard ships for transport to the home islands. There seems to be no military force capable of stopping the Japanese juggernaut as it presses ever further southward. Australian forces are massed around the northern port of Darwin anticipating an invasion in the next few weeks by the Japanese from their forward base at Rabaul, New Guinea."

Both boys jumped to their feet as David entered the room. Bernie was first to reach him with his bear hug.

"Damn, it's good to see you. It's been too long. I know it's a long way out US-50 to the Eastern Shore," he said sarcastically, "but you could make the effort once in a while. After all, I'm out there trying to save those farmer's and crabber's children from pellagra, conjunctivitis, impetigo and a host of other ills caused by inadequate hygiene and sanitation. The least you could do is come out there and support me."

Bernie was grinning from ear-to-ear.

"Bernie you know how hard Hopkins is. Especially in medicine. Besides I haven't seen your old yellow jalopy over this way in a while. You too busy with those corn-fed cuties over there in Easton?" David shot back.

He knew full well that Bernie was still seeing Marie Belzer, the nursing student he had met at Hopkins. He planned to return to Hopkins for post-graduate work in pediatrics when he finished his stint in Easton. They all expected him to pop the question when he did. Murray came over and gave his twin a big hug, even though it had only been a week since they saw each other.

Jacob sat there beaming. The whole family hadn't been together like this in a while and he was savoring every moment of it. He realized that future get-togethers like this may be few and far between. The looming hostilities across both oceans would surely make that so. He got up and walked over to Leah, brushing her tears away and kissing her gently on the forehead.

"It's great to have everyone home isn't it Mama? Don't worry. God in his infinite wisdom will not visit more on us than we can handle. I hope the boys will be spared military service, but if they must serve we have to give them our full support. I know they'll give a good account of themselves if they have to face the Nazis or the Japs. So, let's not borrow the future. Let's just wait and see what happens."

The boys had finished their "hail fellow, well met" routine when they recognized that Leah had entered the room, her face wreathed in sadness.

"Mama, I know you're worried about us," Bernie said, "but with war in both the Pacific and the Atlantic we're going to need every able bodied man in the country to fight. I expect all young, single doctors will be called up right away. Driving the

Japs out of all those islands will not be easy and if we send troops into Europe there'll be thousands of casualties. When I'm called I'll ask to be assigned to a field hospital unit. It's where doctors will be needed most and it's also where I can get the greatest experience. One of the senior doctors at Easton served with that group in 1918. He's one of the best surgeons I've ever met."

Bernie's words were of little consolation to Leah. She couldn't get used to the fact that her sons were going to war.

"Bernie, won't that be the most dangerous place for you to be, so close to the front lines. Why can't you ask to be stationed to a stateside hospital?"

The tears began to roll again. She wiped her eyes once more with her apron which by now was a sodden mass. She was ashamed of her normal mother's instincts to protect her child yet more afraid of losing him.

"Mama I want to go where I can be most useful and I think that's treating the wounded on the battlefields. Historically, there weren't many casualties associated with the WWI field hospitals. They were pretty far removed from the fighting. Don't worry. I'll be careful. I've got you and Marie to come home to," he added while giving Leah a playful squeeze of reassurance. "It's these galoots you'd better worry about," he said, pointing to the twins. "They don't have any initials behind their names yet so they may be handed a rifle and a backpack."

"Not me," David said. "If I get a draft notice I'm heading down to the recruiting station to enlist in the Army Air Force. I spoke to the head of the ROTC at Hopkins and he said if you have some college, good grades and can pass the physical you can apply for Officer's Candidate School. Then if you pass all their requirements and rank high in the class you can apply for pilot training. If you make it to pilot training and wash out, worse case you can become a navigator or a bombardier. That's a lot more appealing than slogging around the jungle on some South Pacific island. I would love to get a crack at those Nazi bastards who are persecuting our people in Germany."

"Watch your language young man," Jacob scolded. "What are they teaching you in school. We may not like what's going on in Europe but that's no excuse for language like that, Now apologize to your mother."

"Sorry, Ma, but I really get steamed when I think about what they're doing. It almost makes me want to go ahead and enlist so I can get into the fight. Hitler has to be stopped and it's going to be up to us to do it."

Murray, who had been taking this all in from across the room jumped into the conversation.

"I feel the same way David does. If we've got to go sooner or later it might as well be sooner. I agree I'd like to be able to choose how I fight rather than accept whatever comes along. I tell you what. If either of us gets a draft notice let's both go down and sign up together. That way maybe we'll be assigned to the same unit and can serve together. Hey, it'd be neat to be flying along side-by-side and dropping bombs on the Nazis. I can see the headlines in the *Sun* now, '*Baltimore Boys Bomb Berlin*.' Wouldn't that make you proud of us Mama?"

Leah leaped from her chair and rushed from the room, her face buried in her apron. She could stand no more of her son's bravado. They reacted like all young men down through the ages. They had never seen the halt and lame return from battle, shattered and lost. They had never stood on that stoop when the olive-green car drove up and the young officer stepped out. It was all romance and adventure to them. That is until that moment when the saber descends or the lance pierces. Then war becomes what it has always been – HELL!

"You boys need to understand how much this upsets your mother," Jacob said. "She had to live through too much bloodshed in the old country. We lost a lot of relatives to the sword. Bernie, your namesake, your great-grandfather Bernard, was cut down by a Cossack sword while trying to protect his family. War is never a pretty sight, but sometimes it's the only answer to evil. And that's what we face now, unspeakable evil –– on both sides of the world. Leah understands that, but it doesn't make it any easier for her when she thinks of you lying wounded or dying on some foreign shore. She is a strong woman or else we wouldn't have got this far, and she'll come to terms with this in her own way and in her own time. You just need to be a little more sensitive to her feelings. She loves the three of you so much that she can't bear the thought of some-thing happening to you. It would be overwhelming to her — as it would be for me. We will all do what we have to do, just be a little more considerate around your mother."

The boys looked sheepish, recognizing the unintentional pain they had caused their mother.

"I'm sorry, Pop," David said. "I knew Mama was upset but as usual we acted like the goofs we always become when we get together. I'll apologize to her later. I know it's going to be a hard time for her and for all of us. We shouldn't make it harder by shooting our mouths off.

"If we're called up it's going to throw a monkey wrench into all of our plans. Bernie's medical career, his and Marie's wedding plans, your plans for Murray in the business, my plans to become a doctor."

"And, what about you and Ruth?" Jacob said. "Have you two made any decisions?"

The question came out of left field and it caught David off guard. He hadn't discussed their relationship with his father very much over the past few months. Just letting those sleeping dogs lie as he and Ruth had discussed. Now it was back out in the open, and he had to come up with an answer for his father's question.

"No sir. We've kinda put everything on hold until we finish school. We've talked about getting married then and in the meantime, we don't want to make any decisions that might upset either family. I don't know what the war will change as far as we're concerned. Obviously, if I get called up, that will change everything."

"And you Murray?" Jacob asked. "Do you feel a little left out since you don't have a girlfriend like these two?"

"Nah Pop, it's probably good that I don't. That's one less thing to have to worry about in the middle of all this war talk. I'll just sit back and watch these two sweat it out. It's going to be an interesting few weeks."

"I didn't tell you boys, since I just found out this week, that the government wants to contract for the manufacture of army uniforms from Epstein and Weiss. We'll start after New Year and their requirements will take up most of our capacity."

Jacob's words were tinged with a hint of resignation. It was clear by his tone that this was not something he wanted to do.

"Seth and I both agreed it was our patriotic duty to support our country, but I've seen too much war in my lifetime. I wish we didn't have to do this."

"I know Pop," Bernie said, "but if we do get involved, maybe it will be over soon, and we can all go back to our normal lives."

"I sure hope so, Bernie, I sure hope so."

"Are we going to get anything to eat tonight or what?" Murray asked. "I'll go up and check on Ma and see if Deborah can put out some food for us."

All five members of the Weiss household were in the pews at Chizuk Amuno on Sabbath Morning. It was their first worship together as a complete family in months. They were surrounded by other families with anxious faces and drawn looks. It seemed that the entire congregation felt a need for community and shared purpose; a time for divine guidance. The rabbi's sermon was eloquent, patriotic and reassuring. It struck most of the chords that were already resonating in the minds and hearts of everyone seated before him; duty, honor, sacrifice, righteousness, patriotism. After the service many families gathered in the social hall to share their latest news: the departure of a son, the disappearance of a relative, sad news from the camps.

The rest of the day was spent trying to evade the subject uppermost in everyone's mind. When Sunday morning rolled around the boys had packed to go their separate ways. Leah stood on the front porch as they drove away, her arm raised in a sad farewell. She felt as desolate as any mother can feel, not knowing what was going to happen to her children and helpless to do anything about it.

David took a slight detour on the way back to school. He had a deep-seated need to see Ruth. She heard his car drive up and met him on the front porch. She was still wearing her heavy coat from morning Mass.

"Let's go for a walk David," she said even before he got out of the car. "I know it's a bit chilly out but the sun's warm and we need to talk."

As they walked along the leaf-strewn sidewalk Ruth described the past two days in her life. The scenarios she had observed could have been mimeographed and handed out in most homes, churches and synagogues in the area. No other subject, and few other concerns, could drive thoughts of the war from the minds of the people; it overshadowed everything. Last Sunday a switch had been thrown and it caught the entire nation in the glare of its single, searing light. The winds of war blew into every crevice of the American conscience, displacing completely the peaceful world of seven short days ago. This was no less true in the lives of Ruth Braddock and David Weiss.

"Mom and Dad and I and the boys had a long conversation at lunch today," Ruth said. "We were trying to figure out what war meant to us as a family and individually. Dad says its going to mean even more travel for him. For Mom things will rock along as usual at school but she's worried about Brian. He'll be seventeen soon and eligible for the draft next year. If the war lasts more than a year or two he'll be called up. Dad says you and Murray will be going for sure and that Bernie will be called up faster than a heartbeat because he's a doctor. He says they're going to need medical personnel by the thousands.

"And that brings us to me and you David. I know we have said we'll wait until we both graduate before we even think about marriage, but the war changes everything. Should we rethink that now?"

"I've been thinking about that, too. If I go off and get killed, is it better to leave a widow or a fiancée? Those are pretty mind-boggling thoughts. I know we have to decide, but there are so many things going on it's hard to know what to do. If we decide to marry, then we've got to decide the children's religion thing, and that's such a large burden to place on our parents right now. Ma is a nervous wreck already, and a rushed wedding might push her over the edge. I know Pop will require an answer and I'm not sure we're ready to give him one. So, while I'd like nothing better than to get married right now, I believe it's best that we wait. I left Ma in tears this morning after we spent the last couple of days talking about the changes war will bring. When I left we were all pretty well reconciled to the fact that a year from now all three of us will be in uniform somewhere in the world. Murray and I have both agreed that when the first gets called up the other will go with him. We'll try to enlist in the Army Air Force. Neither of us wants to slog across Europe with a rifle on our shoulder. I'm sorry if you're disappointed Ruth"

"That's okay David. If we got married now, that would be thinking with our hearts and not our heads. I think you're right. As hard as it will be here without you I know you'll come back to me and that's what really matters. Putting a ring on my finger won't change that. Besides, that'll give me a lot of time to plan a proper wedding — one with a gazillion guests."

Large clumps of wet snow cascaded down as they trudged back toward Ruth's house oblivious to the cold and lost in their thoughts of a very uncertain future.

# 22

# Uncle Sam Wants You

· A somber Christmas and New Years passed with little fanfare in either the Weiss or the Braddock households. Their perfunctory celebrations, like those in most homes, did little to mask the gloomy pall that hung over the entire nation. People went about their daily tasks in a state of suspended animation, afraid to wake to the reality that would face them. January's snows became April's rains and still they waited. Each day that the letter carrier came and went with no draft summons in the mailbox was but a tiny reprieve from the inevitable.

May 15, 1942, a Friday, was the fateful day so long dreaded at the Weiss home. Leah Weiss was sitting on the front porch in the chill evening air when David drove into the driveway. He saw her there, clutching an envelope to her breast. He knew immediately what it meant.

"Hi, Mama," David said with a touch of bravado, "what are you doing out here in the cold? You'll catch your death of pneumonia."

"In truth, I did die a little when I opened the mailbox today. There were two letters from the Baltimore Selective Service office; one for you and one for Murray. I didn't open them but we both know what they say. I've been dreading this day for five months and now that it's finally here I'm kind of relieved. I no longer have to live in dread of opening that box each day. I know that's a strange thing to say but I keep remembering an old saying from the past — death by a thousand cuts. I think it meant that it's better to get something over with than to have it linger and torture you forever. I went through this before Bernie got his call and now I've had to go through it all again."

She held out one envelope to David. He opened it gingerly and began to read:

*"Order to report for induction" the form notice began:*

*The President of the United States,*

*To: David Benjamin Weiss*

*Order No. 1304*

*Having submitted yourself to a local board composed of your neighbors........*

The remainder of the boilerplate information on DSS form 130 instructed David to report to the induction office on St. Charles Street in downtown Baltimore for processing into the military service on Thursday June 1, 1942.

There it was. Short and sweet. No pussyfooting. No beating around the bush. Just "get your butt down here and get ready to serve your country." The finality of it began to sink in. David now knew what he and Murray must do. Come Monday morning they would show up on the doorstep of the recruiting office on Pratt Street. David folded the letter and put it in his pocket just as Murray drove up.

"What's going on," Murray said as he bounded up the steps, "you look like your best friend just died?"

Wordlessly, David handed the second envelope to Murray. He ripped it opens and began to read.

"Well, I'll be damned. Both of us. On the same day. I guess that clinches it then."

"Yeah," David said, "we'll be heading downtown Monday morning."

Leah burst into tears and ran inside. Murray started to run after her when David grabbed his arm.

"No, Murray, this is something she'll have to work out on her own. You know Ma. She'll cry it out and then hop right back on the horse. Deep inside she's stronger than all of us combined. She'll be all right."

"I guess you're right. It just hurts to see her in so much pain."

"I know," David said. "Changing the subject; it looks like we'll both get to finish our first year of college. That should help when we apply for aviation training. Man, I do not want to be a dogface soldier."

"You got that right," Murray said. "Slogging through mud and snow doesn't appeal to me either. Do you think they'll let us volunteer for the Air Force?"

"That's the feeling I got from the ROTC officer at school. He'd transferred to Hopkins from a recruiting assignment, so he should know. Let's go inside. My stomach doesn't recognize this news. I'm hungry."

Jacob had just arrived home from work and joined the boys in the dining room.

"Why such glum faces?" he asked.

"We got the official word today," Murray said, reaching into his pocket for the draft notice. "David and I both have to report for evaluations on the fifteenth."

Jacob slumped into his chair. Suddenly the weight of the world seemed to settle on his shoulders. His features aged perceptibly. The long-awaited day was here and still he was not prepared. He reached unconsciously for his pipe. It was a habit born of many past trials and a sign of suppressed emotions. Outwardly he displayed the calm façade that he always maintained. Inside he was in turmoil. He tamped the tobacco and struck a kitchen match to it. He took a long drag on the pipe and released a fragrant cloud of smoke into the room. When he had finished his routine, he had decided on his response.

"You boys know how opposed I am to war and violence, however, in this instance war has been brought to our doorstep whether we wanted it or not. It was probably inevitable that we would be dragged into it anyway. I hate to see you go, but I think it's a good idea to try to get into the Army Air Force. You're both intelligent, have a year's college under your belt, and should make fine pilots. Your chances of survival are probably a little better in a plane."

"Mom's taking this pretty hard," David said. "She went upstairs crying."

"That's to be expected, boys, but she's a tough customer. She'll be all right after she's had a good cry. Women are like that you know, a bit more emotional than men, but they get it all out and then deal with it. They move on and don't let it all stay bottled up inside like we men do."

The men sat down to dinner as H.V. Kaltenborn's apprehensive voice announced the latest news. Things were not going well on either front. The Japanese were extending their gains in the South Pacific while the U.S. was trying to mount a response to Pearl Harbor. The carriers that had narrowly avoided the fate of the battleships were assembled into battle groups and steaming westward in pursuit of Admiral Yamamoto's fleet. Hitler continued his assault to the east and south, overrunning the fragmented Balkan nations and threatening Greece and Turkey.

The early morning sun was burnishing the penthouses atop the majestic apartment buildings lining Eutaw Place as David steered his little Ford down Linden Avenue. It was 7:30 and they wanted to be at the recruiting office when it opened at eight. Jacob wanted to go with them, but they said no. His influence did not extend to the army. They were on their own now.

The gold wings on Captain James Edward's chest sparkled in the sunlight bouncing off the Pratt Street sidewalk. He was placing the open sign on the door as the twins walked up.

"Good morning fellows, you must be the Weiss twins. Which of you is Murray? I spoke to you yesterday."

"I'm Murray and this is my brother David. You must be Captain Edwards."

"Right you are young man, come inside and have a seat. Here are some forms you need to fill out. You can get started on them while I put on a pot of coffee. I don't function very well in the morning until I get some caffeine in my system. There are some pencils on the table over there."

The clatter of pots and pans came from the small kitchenette behind the office as they sat down at the table. The forms required names, addresses, ages, birthdays, parent's names, education — all the accumulated data that defined two young men about to go off to war.  Captain Edwards came back with a steaming pot of coffee and sat down at the table next to the cups, spoons and sugar.

"Either of you take cream? If so I'll run next door to Ish's deli and get some."

"No thank you sir," David said. "This'll be just fine."

The tall airman lifted the coffee mug to his lips, gingerly testing the scalding liquid.

"So, you boys want to fly. What makes you think you'd be good pilots?"

Both boys were taken aback at the abruptness of the question. David stammered an answer after a few seconds of hesitation.

"Well, sir our dad let us go up in a plane at one of those barnstorming fairs at a little airport in Gaithersburg. I said then that if I ever had the chance I wanted to be a pilot. When that

~ 210 ~

little bi-plane broke loose from the ground I never felt so free. It made me feel like anything was possible from up in the air. I felt like I could do anything with such freedom. I can't explain it, but that experience has stayed with me ever since."

"How about you, Murray, you feel the same way?"

"Yes sir, it was a great experience. It was an open cockpit plane and the rush of cold air was exciting. The pilot did a loop that scared the dickens out of me, but I was ready to go up again as soon as we landed."

"Did you guys bring your birth certificates? I think I said you'd need them."

"Yes sir, I have them right here," Murray said.

"Good. Give me a few minutes to look these forms over. There are some magazines if you want something to read."

David nervously turned the pages of a year-old *Life* magazine while Murray scanned an old issue of the *Saturday Evening Post.* Neither would recall anything they read that day. They kept glancing nervously over at Captain Edwards, trying to divine what conclusions he might be reaching from the information they had submitted. After a seeming eternity—actually only ten minutes—he motioned them to take a seat in front of his desk.

"Well boys everything seems to be in order. I'll have to check a few things at the courthouse, but barring anything negative I'd say you're in. Both of you will have to sign these induction papers."

He slid more forms across the desk. Each had five carbons attached. Welcome to the army bureaucracy. They read through the forms quickly. Terms like "own free will" and "swear allegiance" were liberally sprinkled throughout the document.

David pulled an ink pen from its holder and signed his name with a flourish, handing the pen to Murray. When Murray finished signing the Captain rose to his feet and extended his hand.

"Welcome to the army, gentlemen. You need to show up here Monday morning, June 1, at ten a.m. for a physical. If you pass, you'll be sworn in immediately and you'll be taken over to the B & O terminal with the other recruits for transport to the Southeast Air Corps Training Center at Maxwell Field in Montgomery, Alabama. So, bring at least one change of clothes. If you want to ship your things home from camp you can do so, otherwise they'll be donated to the Salvation Army."

"Yes sir, we'll be here," they said in unison.

They walked out of the recruiting station and back to the car in a daze.

"What just happened?" Murray asked rhetorically. "Two hours ago, we walked in there as happy-go-lucky civilians and now we're in the army."

"Yeah," David said "that was pretty fast. In a couple of weeks, we'll be in basic training in Alabama. I guess Pop will have to drive us to the recruiting center. I don't know what he's going to do with two extra cars. Maybe I'll leave mine with Ruth. She can use it to go to school."

"Where'd you come up with that cockamamie story about flying with barnstormers?" Murray asked.

"It was obvious that he wanted us to have some tie to flying. I figured if we had some experience he wouldn't reject us on the spot. We did go to that show, remember. Just because Mama wouldn't let us go up doesn't mean we wouldn't have enjoyed it. Besides you seemed to go along with it all right."

"I didn't have much choice after you started it. I just played along."

David dropped Murray off at home and headed to Silver Spring. He had promised Ruth he would let her know the outcome right away. She was on the porch awaiting him. She could tell from his actions that he had been accepted.

"How long do we have?" she asked.

"We report on Monday, June first. We'll take a physical and if everything is okay we'll ship out that day."

"Where are they sending you?"

"Basic training is at Maxwell Field in Montgomery, Alabama. The recruiter said that would last for eleven weeks. That's where they turn you into ninety-day wonders as the regulars call them. We'll get into some basic flight training there and you graduate as a second lieutenant. From there you move on to advanced flight training in fighters or bombers. I hope I can get a shot at fighter training."

"Oh David, I'm going to miss you so. Promise me you'll write every day. I'm going to continue on at nursing school. At least that will keep be busy. If I had to sit at home with you gone, I'd go crazy."

"I promise I'll write every day. We've got a few days before we leave. Let's pretend there's no tomorrow and go out and enjoy the weekend. We'll go to a movie with Murray and maybe have dinner out together. If Bernie is home maybe he and Marie will join us."

The days flew by. It was time to go. Ruth insisted on going to the induction center with Jacob and the boys. Leah invited her to spend the night. The boys said their tearful good-byes to

Leah, threw their duffels into Jacob's Packard, and headed downtown at nine o'clock on Monday morning. Ten or twelve other inductees were milling around outside the center when Jacob drove up to the curb. The boys insisted that Jacob and Ruth not stay until the induction was over — the process could take three hours.

David stood on the sidewalk with the tearful Ruth while Jacob embraced Murray then turned to embrace David. It was one of the few times in his life that he had seen his father cry or say the words "I love you." David gave Ruth one last peck on the cheek and escorted her and Jacob back to the car.

"Goodbye, Pop. I'm going to miss you. You take good care of our girls while I'm gone. Me and Murray'll be back before you know it. It won't take long for us to lick those Krauts."

The twins picked up their duffels and strode into the induction center and into another world. David turned to see the large black car turn the corner onto Charles Street, heading north. The lump in his throat would not go away. He turned away so that Murray wouldn't see the tears. The other men had gathered into small knots and were introducing themselves. Murray saw an old friend from Cardozo and headed his way.

By eleven-thirty, the fifteen recruits had completed their physicals. Thirteen lined up to raise their right hands and take the oath that would usher them into this new phase of their life. Two recruits failed the physical. One was Murray's high school friend.

It might have been David's imagination, but he thought he detected a sharper tone to the commands of the recruiting staff. They were irrevocably in the army now and civilian niceties could be dispensed with. The raw recruits were herded into two ranks and marched over to the bus waiting to take them to the train station. Robert Ambrose, a strapping junior fullback at the University of Maryland, was placed in charge of the scraggly contingent. The large manila envelope he carried contained their train and meal tickets and their orders to report to Maxwell Field.

# Book Two

-

# WAR

# 1

# So, You Boys Want to Fly

The massive, black locomotive, its boiler belching steam and its enormous drive wheels spewing sparks, roared into the station at two o'clock, right on schedule. The eighth and ninth cars were already filled with recruits from New York and Phila-delphia. More recruits were to be boarded in Washington, Char-lotte and Atlanta. Two cars filled with Marine recruits were to be diverted to Parris Island, South Carolina when the train reached Augusta. The Weiss twins and the Baltimore contingent piled into the tenth car, already half filled. Twenty minutes later the train pulled out for the brief run to Union Station in Washington. Many in the New York and Philly contingents had never been to their nation's capital. They strolled over to the capitol building and from the western steps looked out over the reflecting pools to the Washington and Lincoln monuments in the distance. The buildings of the Smithsonian Museums ranged along both sides of the mall and the dome of Mr. Jefferson's memorial was visible above the cherry trees ringing the tidal basin. Few among them were aware that the 3000 trees there were a gift in 1912 from the people of Japan as a token of friendship between the two countries. Now, exactly thirty years later, the Nation of Japan had laid waste to Pearl Harbor — and that friendship. Their actions had forced the United States into the Second World War. Only cruel fate knew how many of those innocent and naïve young men gazing out at the symbols of America's history would fall victim to the treachery of Japan. A light rain began to fall from the leaden skies as a stiff wind whipped the flags wildly. The lights atop the capitol came on, illuminating the statue of "*Armed Freedom*" atop its dome.

Darkness enveloped the train as it rumbled across the trestle bridging the Potomac River into Virginia on its renewed journey southward. The two hundred recruits aboard required three separate dinner seatings. It was well past eight as the twins made their way back to their Pullman cars. Porters had already converted the seats into upper and lower bunks. As the enormity of what had transpired that day settled over the men their earlier boisterous mood ebbed. Each recruit crawled into his bunk under the weight of his own individual thoughts. What lay ahead? Will I succeed in flight school? What will happen to me if I don't? Will I ever see my family again? Will my girlfriend be waiting for me when I return? These along with a thousand other thoughts fought for attention in the turbulent moments before sleep came.

David was jarred awake by the blast of a northbound freight. He pulled back the curtains to reveal the marshalling yards in Charlotte. They were waiting for the freight train to clear before they could continue.

"Murray. You awake?" David whispered to his brother in the bunk above.

"Yeah," came back a sleep laden reply.

"Let's head to the bathroom before everyone else gets up. There's going to be a real rush soon."

"Okay. I'm rolling out."

They were in the first seating for breakfast and were back in their seats when the train pulled out of Charlotte with twenty-five more recruits: fifteen for Parris Island and ten for Maxwell. Three hours later they crossed over the Savannah River into Augusta, Georgia. The two cars carrying the marine recruits were uncoupled and shunted onto a siding. Another Pullman was attached for the new men awaiting them in Atlanta. Within a half-hour they were underway again with a two hour run down the Piedmont plain into Atlanta's Union Station. They gazed out at the verdant countryside, passing through dusty farming hamlets where men clad in denim overalls were tending their crops of cotton, corn and peanuts. The rumors of war and the war itself had put more money into the empty pockets of these hardscrabble farmers than they had seen in years. The war, with all its evils, had the effect of dragging the country out of its decade long depression. FDR's "*happy days are here again*" finally became a reality for many.

David and Murray were seated in the dining car for lunch when they slowed to transit the marshalling yards northwest of downtown Atlanta. A tall brick tower rose above the trees to the east. Large, yellow, block letters around the top spelled out "TECH." It was the administration building of the Georgia Institute of Technology where many students were undergoing accelerated courses in engineering to prepare them as *"ninety-day wonders"* for the army and navy. The train rolled into downtown Atlanta on tracks that had been first laid before the Civil War. They were below street level. The advent of the automobile and street car had necessitated raising the streets to avoid traffic nightmares and creating an eerie underground city. The twenty-seven Atlanta recruits descended the stairs and boarded quietly. Meanwhile a carload of recruits from the Midwest was attached to the train for its final two-hour run to Montgomery.

The train was underway again by two in the afternoon. An hour later they crossed the Chattahoochee River into Alabama at Columbus, Georgia. They stopped long enough to offload soldiers and baggage bound for Fort Benning, the large infantry training center just south of the city. The train pulled into Montgomery's downtown terminal just before five. An armada of gray buses was lined up outside the terminal, prepared to whisk the new troops away to Maxwell Field. Four khaki clad soldiers with MP armbands barked orders directing the recruits to their buses as they stepped down from the train.

Maxwell Field began its life as the nation's first flight instruction school. The forward-thinking burghers of Montgomery offered to donate the old Kohn cotton plantation to Orville and Wilbur Wright if they would locate their flight school there. They agreed, but the school was short lived. After just three months of operation, the Wright brothers packed up and moved back to Ohio. The Kohn field lay fallow for eight years until the army bought it in 1922 as a location for its budding air wing. They re-named it Maxwell Field in honor of William C. Maxwell, an army lieutenant who was killed in the Philippines in 1920. Maxwell had crashed his disabled plane in a cane field while avoiding a schoolyard full of young children. Over the years, the army added other functions to the site and in 1928 classified Maxwell as the Air Force Tactical School. In 1940, General Hap Arnold designated Maxwell Field as the air force's central command center for the eastern United States.

The long gray line of buses came to a stop in front of building 836. This was the first permanent structure erected at Maxwell Field. It was the enlisted men's barracks. The buildings architectural design became the standard for all future con-struction on the base. The long, rectangular edifice had walls of hollow blocks and was capped by a red tile roof in the Spanish Mission style.

The recruits were quickly hustled off the bus and into the barracks at double-time. Each was assigned a bunk and a locker then ordered to form up for the march over to the supply of-fices. The ranks and files were sloppy and disorderly with cries of pain as feet were stepped on and sides elbowed. Each man was fitted with two work uniforms and one dress uniform as well as two pairs of shoes: one dress, one work. They also received seven sets of underwear, six pairs of socks, two mattress covers, sheets and towels. This was followed by a quick march back to the barracks loaded down with their newly issued wardrobes and a lesson in how to pack one's foot locker.

"This is how I expect to find your lockers every day during inspection," boomed Staff Sergeant Jim Axelrod, who would be their drill instructor for the next eleven weeks. "I will not toler-ate sloppiness or dirt. Each of you will be assigned cleaning duties in the barracks. Any discrepancies I find during the daily inspections will earn one demerit. Two demerits and you'll find yourself marching around the grinder with rifle and full pack at four in the morning. Assignments will be posted outside the latrine when you return from the shearing. Now fall out to the grinder and form up again."

The 60 men in Recruit Company 407/42 scrambled out of the barracks to line up as six squads of ten men each. Sergeant Axelrod marched them over to the base barber shop. David entered the shop just as Murray exited. He did a double take before recognizing his own brother. Murray's clean-shaven head glistened in the last rays of sunset. The military barbers made certain that vanity would not distinguish one recruit from another.

"Man, do you look different," he said.

"Yeah, I feel like a sheep after shearing season. See you back in line."

When all the company had been shorn they marched back to the barracks rubbing the fuzz where their hair used to be. No one had prepared them for these harsh conditions.

Darkness was falling as the bewildered recruits trudged over to the mess hall for their first official army meal. They shuffled through the lines holding out the segmented metal trays while the mess cooks plopped huge servings of meat loaf, mashed potatoes and green beans onto them, all to be washed down by that uniquely southern beverage, iced sweet tea. The mess hall was eerily silent. Everyone had retreated into their own shell as they tried to absorb the shock of the day's events.

The march back to the barracks was followed by a demonstration on bed making. Sergeant Axelrod picked a bunk and proceeded to make it up per army regulations. When he had finished he pulled a half-dollar coin from his pocket and tossed it onto the bed catching it as it bounced.

"That, gentlemen is how I expect to find your bunks made whenever you are not in them. There will be an inspection at 6:00 each morning. I expect you to be up, shaved, showered, dressed and bunks made, and standing at attention, when I arrive. You don't want to know what happens if you aren't standing there. Am I understood?"

A chorus of "yes sirs" answered him.

"You have forty-five minutes until lights out I suggest you attend to all your personal affairs right away. That includes your first letter home. I'll be collecting them for posting when we return to barracks tomorrow. Am I understood?"

Another chorus of "yes sirs" followed.

"Good night, soldiers. Welcome to the United States Army Air Force. Get a good night's sleep. You're going to need it."

David lay on his bunk staring up at the bottom of Murray's, in the dim light cast by the street lamps outside. Even when he closed his eyes the strident images of the past few days didn't go away. He heard Murray's snores and other harsh sounds from the bunks around him. It was a re-experiencing of Mount Airy, but to an exponential power. The racket finally subsided into a discordant concerto as he succumbed to the arms of a beckoning Morpheus.

The clock on the administration building campanile struck five just as the bugler stepped up to his microphone. The bone-tired recruits sat bolt upright in their bunks as the blaring notes of reveille surged through the loudspeakers at each end of the barrack. Those in the lower bunks were rudely awakened to the fact that there was a bunk above them. David's head bounced off the springs under Murray's mattress. Cries of pain came from several others. It was four in the morning back east. This was a cruel hour to be blasted awake by a disembodied bugler. Most of the men were still wiping the sleep from their eyes as Sergeant Axelrod stormed into the barracks. He strode down the corridor between the bunks, raking his baton across the uprights like a picket fence.

"Drop your cocks and grab your socks. This ain't no country club we're running here. Get your mangy asses out of bed. I'll be back through in an hour. You'll be showered, shaved — those of you who need to shave — dressed, bunks made, barracks cleaned and standing at attention. Your uniforms better look like those pictures posted on the wall. Future latrine duty will be assigned to the cadets with the sloppiest dress and the worst made bunks. Do you hear me?"

He marched out as fast as he had entered, to another sleepy chorus of "yes sirs."

Sixty pairs of bare feet hit the floor in unison, footlockers flew open and there was a mad dash for the latrines at each end of the long room. A long row of metal sinks ran along the end wall with a six-inch metal tray above. Mirrors filled the wall above the trays. Five commodes, exposed to the world, lined one side wall and a row of urinals the other. The front wall contained eight shower heads above a long concrete trough — no curtains and no dividers. Timidity and bashfulness were lost on this man's army.

Miraculously, the sixty cadets under Sergeant Axelrod's charge were in place, shoes shined, clean shaven, properly attired, and with their bunks made at the stroke of six when he once again charged into the barrack. This would be the first of the interminable inspections they must endure before they could pin on their pilot's wings — for those who made it that far.

"ATTENTION!" he commanded. "I don't want to see so much as a muscle twitch. As I pass in front of you look straight ahead and hold your hands out, palms down."

"Matthews," he said to the first man in line, "your name tag is too low and it's crooked. Your fingernails are dirty, and your tie is knotted wrong. I want to see more shine on those boots. Your cap is all wrong."

He reached up and straightened the cap on the quivering cadet. One by one he passed down the two lines of cadets, liberally dispensing demerits as he went along with a healthy dose of raunchy language, thereby burning a few innocent ears in the process.

"Listen up," he said as he came to the last cadet, "Like I told you this ain't no picnic you're going on. My job is to turn you mama's boys into soldiers and by God I'll do that or die trying. Some of you won't make it but I don't ever want to see any of you not giving it your best. I don't want anyone flunking out for lack of effort. Believe me, I'll know, and you can expect my size 12 brogan up your ass. If you get past me it'll be up to those guys over there to make pilots out of you," he said gesturing across to the flight training school. "Look at the two men on each side of you. One of them will not make it through the next eleven weeks of hell. Those who don't will be transferred to the regular army. The guy on the other side will not make it through flight training. he'll get a crack at navigator or bombardier training. The twenty of you who make it through basic will be selected to go to advanced pilot training at another base. Those who don't cut the mustard there will wind up as crew members or ground maintenance. Of the sixty men standing here today maybe fifteen will see duty as a combat pilot. Everyone who successfully completes pilot, navigator or bombardier training will be commissioned a second lieutenant. So, if it's your desire to be a pilot you can assess the odds. The rest is up to your efforts and your natural abilities.

"The next few days will be critical to your army career. You'll be undergoing a lot of tests, both physical and mental. You're going to have every orifice in your body poked. You're going to take a bunch of shots. And don't believe all those rumors about a shot in the left testicle with a square needle. They don't do that much anymore. You're going to take a lot of aptitude tests. Do not take them lightly. Your future assignments may depend on how well you score. Now, I know most of you are college boys, so listen up. I don't care how smart you think you are or what you have studied, I can't stress enough the importance of these tests. The scores can come back to haunt you throughout your service career. They'll affect positions, assignments, promotions: you name it.

"Now, Berry, Matthews, Garner, Bolton, Sternberg, Rice, Connors and Weiss you have latrine duty when you get back from the mess hall. That's both of you Weiss guys, in case you were wondering," he said with a chuckle at his own pun.

"Now, everyone fall out and line up on the grinder in six squads of ten men each. I want the tallest men at the head of each squad. We're going to march over to the mess hall for chow. I want to see how many of you clowns have two left feet. MOVE!" he shouted. The terrified cadets stampeded through the back door of the barracks, causing a huge traffic jam. Once they were finally untangled they rushed onto the parade quadrangle and began forming ranks under the glaring spotlights. The twins wound up halfway back in squads one and two. Axelrod barked for attention.

"Okay, let's see how you respond to marching orders. When I say "forward march" I want you to step out on your left foot. I'll count cadence with 'hup, two, three, four' and you just follow along. When I say 'left turn' or 'right turn' I'll follow that with 'harch,' and the left squad leader or the right squad leader will pivot ninety degrees and the other ranks will swing around in that direction until every one is realigned. You got that?" he demanded. "FORWARD, HARCH."

The company headed out across the compound toward the mess hall. They resembled a Chinese New Year's dragon dance more than a military body. Sergeant Axelrod shook his head in disgust as he circled the amorphous mass of struggling cadets, trying to force them into some semblance of order. When they reached the mess hall and he shouted, "Company Halt," only a few were still out of step — that is until the rear ranks banged into the forward ones.

Sergeant Axelrod smiled. "I may be able to make soldiers out of this pile of crap after all."

The next week was a succession of tests, both mental and physical. In between the shots and examinations, the cadets were subjected to a rigorous physical training routine. They climbed over, ran through, or burrowed under every single obstacle the sadistic DI could devise. Their arms already tender and aching from the battery of shots, were screaming in pain. Their legs felt like dead weights and their feet were a mass of blisters from the new, ill-fitting brogans and the ceaseless marching. They became intimately familiar with every crack in the asphalt and each rock on the parade ground. Murray fell into bed each night after a grueling day only to be aroused at some ungodly hour and sent on a work detail. He continued to amass more demerits than anyone else in the company.

"David how did I ever let you talk me into this? I don't know if I can make it through eleven weeks of this torture. Old hardass Axelrod seems to have it in for me for some unknown reason. Why? What did I ever do to him?"

"It's not just you Murray, it's all of us. You're just one of teacher's pets," David laughed. "Look, it's his job to either turn us into soldiers or wash us out. If he doesn't think we will be reliable buddies in the field when things get rough, it's his responsibility to weed us out now. If we can't take this now, then how will we react in the heat of battle? Just hang in there; it'll ease up after a few weeks. I hear most of the dropouts come in the first two or three weeks."

"I sure hope so. I've never been so sore in my life. Not even after we went up to Carlisle for football camp."

Between bouts of K.P., running obstacle courses, and marching off demerits, there were classes covering every aspect of the knowledge needed to enter pilot training. They learned to read graphs, charts, photos and maps. They studied the principles of mechanics. They were tested on their speed and perception, technical understanding and reaction to external stimuli. Manual dexterity and response time were tested. Their blood pressure and heart rates were measured after each exercise. These were followed by batteries of psychological tests. The army left no stone unturned in qualifying their future combat pilots.

Ruth's and Leah's letters arrived with clock-like regularity. David's replies were not quite as prompt. At the end of hellish eighteen-hour days, the bone-tired men collapsed into their bunks, exhausted. Personal chores and letter writing filled most of the Sunday hours which were not so rigorous.

His mother's letters kept him up to date with the family and matters back in Baltimore. The tinge of worry was still there but seemed to abate after a few weeks. Ruth's letters were also homey and full of happenings around the Braddock household; her mother's teaching, Sandy's ever-increasing absence, the boy's school activities, etc. It was around the third or fourth paragraph that she began to touch on their personal matters.

"David, I miss you so," she would say. "I can't wait until you finish basic training. Maybe you'll get leave then — or I can come for a visit."

This was a new and exciting development. He couldn't imagine the Braddocks allowing her to visit him in Montgomery, unaccompanied.

"I've been spending more time with your mother at the Jewish Relief Agency. She is devastated by the inability to aid the Jews trapped behind the enemy lines. She gets word occasionally from some of your relatives but the conditions they describe send her into even darker places. I fear sometimes for her sanity. There's so much she wants to do and so little she can.

"Your dad comes around occasionally. He seems warmer and more accepting since you went off, but he still won't discuss the prospect of our marriage. Oh well, one thing at a time. I love you. Write soon."

The most recent letter from Leah confirmed that Epstein and Weiss had been selected to make uniforms for all the armed services. Their entire production capacity had been commandeered by Uncle Sam.

"My dearest David, I received your letter of the 15th and was so happy to hear from you. Tell Murray to write more often. In my last letter I mentioned that your father might be selected to make uniforms. Well, that has come to pass. He says to check inside the neckband of your jacket to see if there's an E & W stamped there. All the shops are working around the clock to keep up with the demand. I seldom see Jacob anymore.

"I've seen Ruth at the JRA a couple of times. She seems well but misses you just as I do. We're still trying to get Jews out of Europe but it's now almost impossible. I get dribs and drabs of news from Belarus. So far, all the family is safe. Jacob is working to get papers for them to go to Romania. So far, no luck.

"I hear from Henrietta occasionally. She is so upset. They have sent many Palestinian Jews into Eastern Europe to try to rescue people. The organization is called the *B'richa* network. They are having some success, but nothing like before the war. She is pleading for money to sustain their effort. She's also asking for volunteers to come and help. Sometimes I am tempted to go. With all of my boys off to the war and Jacob working such long hours I really don't have a lot to do. Take care my son and write when you can.

Love, Mama"

At the end of week nine a list of platoon standings was posted on the bulletin board. The standings were determined by the induction test results, physical conditioning and overall class standing. David and Murray found both their names in the top ten, which assured them of advancement to basic flight training — assuming no major screw-ups in the final two weeks of basic. Each cadet was asked to submit his first and second choices for assignment at the end of basic. To a man, everyone asked to be assigned to fighter pilot training. That was the glamour assignment, even though the most critical need was for crews to man the thousands of bombers that were rolling off the assembly lines all across America.

September 25, 1942 was unusually cool for a fall day in Montgomery, Alabama. It was bright and clear with a crisp hint of impending autumn in the air. Ten companies of cadets, almost 600 men, were arrayed across the parade ground for their graduation ceremony. Fifty-six members of Company 407/42 stood at attention as the Maxwell army band played the *"Star Spangled Banner."* Only four of the original sixty had washed out, an unusually high graduation rate.

The ten companies of graduates stepped out smartly to the strains of John Phillip Sousa's *"Stars and Stripes Forever."* As they passed the reviewing stand their spirited march and the snappy salutes bore no resemblance to the rag-tag group that stumbled to the mess hall on that first day, eleven weeks ago. The chests of the soldiers swelled with visible pride, the banners on the guidon's staff snapping sharply in the breeze, including the one for top company in this graduating class. They circled the parade ground and reformed with Company 407 front and center before the reviewing stand with Sergeant Axelrod and his company officers in front. He saluted the commanding officer as he proudly accepted the top company award.

"Yes indeed, I did make soldiers out of those miserable recruits."

Colonel Elmer J. Bowling, Commanding Officer at Maxwell delivered the address.

"Ladies and Gentlemen, parents, members of the press and distinguished guests, it is indeed a pleasure and privilege to address this cadet graduating class, not only to recognize their outstanding accomplishments while here at Maxwell field, but to send them off to do great things for their country. With men like these it's only a matter of time until Hitler, Mussolini and Tojo will be defeated...

… and in conclusion, I challenge all of you cadets to continue in your hard work as you progress to flying status and are deployed to help this nation to ultimate victory over the forces of evil."

David and Murray marched back to the barracks, proud of their own accomplishments and that of the company. They would enjoy a long weekend on the town in Montgomery before reassembling at Maxwell to receive their next assignments.

Following breakfast on Monday, the ten companies assembled on the grinder for the last time. Ten drill instructors, each armed with a basketful of envelopes, stood at the front of their respective companies. Sergeant Axelrod stepped onto a small wooden box and began to read out the names and assignments for 407/42.

"Abbot, Aldrich, Barbutti…, Weber, Weiss," he read off the names alphabetically. David and Murray were last to receive their envelopes, and they eagerly ripped them open. David was ordered to report to Gunter Field, just across town, to begin basic flight training.

"Murray, I'm going to Gunter," David shouted, "what's your assignment?

Murray 's crestfallen face told it all.

"They're sending me to San Antonio for further assignment."

Both twins were stunned. They had just assumed the army would keep them together. They had not been separated for more than a few days in their entire life. Now they would be apart for an indefinite period of time. The shock was palpable. Sagging shoulders and quickly squelched tears told the whole story as the realization of a future apart swept over them. When the assembly was dismissed, the two trekked back to their barracks in stunned silence, not certain of what they should say to each other — or how they should feel.

Murray was to catch a train to San Antonio on Tuesday morning. David was to transfer to Gunter on Wednesday. Sergeant Axelrod wangled a pass for David so that he could go to the station to see Murray off. The parting was hard on both men. Their stoicism finally crumbled as Murray stepped onto the railcar steps with his duffel slung over his shoulder. He turned back, dropped the duffel, and hugged David fiercely. This time there was no holding back the tears.

"You take care of yourself," Murray said.

"You too, Murray. Remember we have a date in Germany. We'll rendezvous over Berlin and blow the Hell out of Hitler and his Third Reich. The Baltimore Boys, remember," trying to make himself heard over the hiss of steam and the clanging bell.

Murray picked up his duffel and boarded. David stood on the platform waving until the blinking red light of the caboose disappeared around a curve. The bus ride back to Maxwell was the loneliest journey of his young life. Suddenly, he felt very alone in the world.

# 2

# The Wild Blue Yonder

That night David packed his duffel and cleared out his footlocker as he tried to put thoughts of Murray's departure out of his mind. The bus to Gunter was scheduled for eight the next morning. It arrived on time, and the busload of cadets passed through the gates of Gunter Field a half-hour later. Gunter's appearance was a major disappointment when compared to the relative opulence of Maxwell. Old textile factory buildings had been pressed into service as makeshift barracks for the mushrooming corps of cadets.  The newly constructed barracks weren't much better as they resembled a cluster of tarpaper shacks. There were signs of rats and other vermin everywhere.

David was assigned to a building that had been constructed for a tuberculosis hospital but had never been occupied. Five men from the Baltimore/Philly area were assigned to the same building.

In a previous life, Gunter Field had been the Montgomery Municipal airport. It was commandeered for military purposes. Seven satellite airfields had been built in a ring around Montgomery to be used for pilot training. Primary pilot training for this contingent of budding shavetails would begin bright and early on Thursday morning.

Six were from Company 407/42. The six of them laid claim to three double-decker bunks at the far end of their barracks. The six all came from the Baltimore or Philly area and there was an instant bonding among them. They hurriedly unpacked, stuffed their belongings into their footlockers and headed out to explore the base. Gunter had three runways ranging from 3500 to 4800 feet in length. Two were parallel and located several hundred feet from the hangars. Student pilots didn't always land exactly where and how they were supposed to. The third runway ran at an angle to the others to accommodate different prevailing winds. A row of hangars lined the taxiway nearest the base. There were wide aprons separating the taxiways from the hangars where row upon row of Vultee Valiant trainers with their electric blue fuselages and their bright yellow wings were parked in the bright, early morning sun. The young cadets couldn't resist walking out onto the apron to inspect the vibrantly colored planes. They were intercepted by a burly MP with a .45 strapped to his side. He persuaded them they should not go any further.

"This area is off limits to you guys. You're only allowed here if you're actually flying. Don't worry. By the time you get out of here you'll have your fill of these blue and yellow birds.

Now skedaddle," he said, resting his beefy hand ominously on the butt of his .45.

The boys wasted little time getting back to the barracks and getting ready for evening mess.

David was sure the bugler from Maxwell must have transferred with him to Gunter. The same shrill blast reverberated through the barracks at six a.m., the same time that First Lieutenant Cory Tower from Teaneck, New Jersey burst through the door.

"All right you guys, you've finished the easy part of your training. Now we get down to the serious business, so gather 'round," he shouted.

The bleary-eyed cadets groaned and scrambled out of their bunks in their skivvies to scurry across to where the lieutenant was standing, looking for all the world like a bunch of kids at summer camp.

"I've got your assignments and schedules. You'll be in a classroom for two entire weeks. You won't get to even smell a plane until you show that you can comprehend the science and mechanics of flying. What you learn in class is critical to your understanding of how a plane performs once you are at the controls so pay attention. There's a comprehensive test at the end of the two weeks and any score below 75 will wash you out of pilot training, so it behooves you to concentrate and work hard. You all are aware, I'm sure, that there's an enlisted men's club on base. I suggest you avoid it at all costs for the next two weeks. Spend that time in the evening studying. There'll be plenty of time later to let your hair down and cut loose.

"My name is Lieutenant Corey Tower. I'm the officer in charge of the trainee barracks. Staff Sergeant Albert Poindexter will be your barracks supervisor while you are here and he'll' be posting duty rosters and schedules as well as conducting inspections. Keep your nose clean and show him respect and life will go a lot easier for you. Screw up, and you'll find yourself cleaning out the grease traps in the scullery. You do not want to do that. Do you understand?"

Twenty four clean shaven heads bobbed up and down in joint affirmation.

"You'll have duty every third weekend. Sergeant Poindexter will post your duty assignments. You're not allowed off the base from six p.m. on Sundays until eight a.m. on Saturdays. If you choose to have your wives or girlfriends visit you here, you need to know you're on your on. There is no official army position on that, but you need to know that off-base housing is vey scarce in the Montgomery area — and very expensive. Besides you'll be shipping out in the next ten or twelve weeks and God knows where you'll be going. So, my advice is to wait until you know where you're going before you make any of those decisions.

"Classes begin in the morning at eight sharp. Be late once and you'll be introduced to the grease traps. Twice and you'll be on your way to staring at a scorpion in a North African foxhole. Now get yourself ready and get over to the chow hall. I'll see you back here at five after the first day's classes are over. Dismissed."

The next two weeks were a total immersion in the art and physics of flying. The physics explained why the plane flew, the art explained what made it a weapon. Everything from Bernoulli's Principle to zero-gravity was crammed into the swimming heads of the nascent flyers. The arcane language of the aviator unfolded on page after page of the student's flying manual. Airfoils, lift, pitch, yaw, roll, altitude, stall, thrust, velocity, acceleration, mass, wind speed — these were among a thousand terms each man had to commit to memory and regurgitate upon demand if he hoped to move on to actual flying.

When David returned to the barracks after evening mess he joined in *"skull sessions"* with the *"Yankee Six"* as his group had been dubbed. Taps sounded at eleven, giving them one hour more than they had at Maxwell. Even that was insufficient time for some to absorb the mountain of information thrown at them. Four empty bunks greeted him on Saturday evening when he came back from the mess hall. The harsh reality of flight training had claimed its first victims in Barracks 409.

Each flight instructor at Gunter was assigned three trainees when they successfully passed the classroom gauntlet. First Lieutenant Larry Armbruster was chosen to instruct based on his innate skills as a pilot. He had requested deployment as a fighter pilot upon graduation for fighter training. He had been denied. His superiors felt it was more important to pass those skills on to the new recruits. He bristled at the decision but held his tongue. His ambition since he was twelve was to be a barnstorming stunt pilot. He learned to fly his father's Stearman Model 75 biplane at the age of fourteen. Their cattle ranch in Wyoming was remote and the plane was converted for agricultural use and to ferry supplies from Laramie, fifty miles away. Babysitting these wet-behind-the-ears college boys was not his idea of participating in the war.

"First of all I want you boys to know I don't want to be here. I want to be in Europe or Africa where I can shoot me some Nazis. As a compromise with my superior officers, I have been promised that if I graduate thirty, fully qualified pilots, they'll let me name my next assignment. You'd better listen to me and listen well. You are my eighth class and represent ten percent of my dream, so don't screw up. If you pay attention and work hard I promise to make pilots out of you in the next eight weeks. Then you can move on to advanced flight training. If you screw up I'm not going to waste my time with you. There are a hundred more "shave tails" coming through that gate every week and they want to fly just as much as you do. Do we understand each other?" He paused to let his words sink in. "Okay, let's get you assigned to a plane and show you what this flying stuff is all about."

For the next four days, Lieutenant Armbruster was true to his word. He spent two hours per day in the air with each of his three students. The two on the ground had to pore over the Vultee manuals to discover what they were doing wrong. They sat in the trainee's seat in front of the instructor watching and absorbing how the plane responded to the different maneuvers he made. They saw how the plane stalled at low speeds and steep climbs and what was needed to pull out of a stall. They learned how the wind affected the planes course and speed. They also learned what a "barf bag" was for after several Immelmans and Hammerheads left the plane's occupants temporarily weightless. By the end of the week all three were "handling the plane."

In the second week, Armbruster toured the seven outlying fields that were used for training. These were fields that would be used to practice "touch-and-go's" the repetitive take-offs and landings that would hone their skills for the two most dangerous moments in flying. They were also used as rendezvous points when all three pilots were in the air. He also put the men through coordination exercises to familiarize them with the handling of the plane in all situations. Finally, on the last day of the first week, all three pilots were allowed to exercise a take-off and landing in the Valiant BT-13.

When it was David's turn he taxied the small trainer to the end of the runway, revved the engine, and released the brake. The plane lurched forward, straining to maintain its course down the centerline of the runway. As it gathered speed the tail lifted, giving him greater control of the plane. Within seconds the front wheels cleared the ground and David rose into the air for the first time under his own control. It was a moment of sheer exhilaration — and stark terror. The plane began to slip from side to side as he sought the proper rudder pressure, and realized that less was more. He allowed the plane to seek its own equilibrium. He pulled back gently on the yoke until the altimeter registered 200 feet before leveling out and maintaining his course, speed and altitude until Lt. Armbruster instructed him to take her around for a landing.

David began to replicate all the moves he had seen his instructor perform for the past five days. He applied left rudder pressure and dropped the left wing slightly, beginning a smooth bank for the crosswind leg. He repeated the maneuver twice more before making his approach to the runway. The Valiant was aligned perfectly with the runway as David lowered the airspeed and descended, allowing the trainer to settle slowly to earth. He felt the sweat seeping from under his leather helmet. The combination of speed and glide angle were key to a good landing. David struggled to keep the proper balance.

The Valiant skimmed across the runway threshold, hanging suspended for what seemed an eternity before reaching stall speed and dropping the final two feet to the ground, producing a sharp jolt to both pilots. David taxied onto the access ramp and delivered Lt. Armbruster back to the hangar apron. David climbed down from the wing, his knees almost buckling as he hit the tarmac. Lt. Armbruster was grinning as David righted himself.

"That's not the worst thing I've seen happen after a first take-off and landing," Armbruster said. "You'll get used to it soon. You did pretty good for your first attempt. You were a little shaky on the run-up and your speed control needs a little work but otherwise, well done. Now go over to the EM club with the other guys and have a beer. You all deserve it."

Clyde Nagle from Bluefield, West Virginia and Harmon Page from Narragansett, Rhode Island were the two other students under Lieutenant Armbruster's charge. Knowing this was David's first control flight the two waited at the hangar apron for his return. They both had broad grins and tried to refrain from laughing as he walked up.

"Boy, you sure did look a little piqued when you climbed down from that little ol' airplane." Clyde said in his best hillbilly twang.

"I thought you wuz gonna puke on old Armbruster's shiny boots. You were as white as the sheets on the Klan Wizard back in Bluefield."

Clyde Nagle was as far from a bigoted redneck as one could find in all of West Virginia. He had completed two years at the Virginia Military Institute and was slated to follow in the footsteps of his father and grandfather, both having risen to flag rank in the army. As soon as the smoke cleared over Pearl Harbor he was in the adjutant's office asking to be transferred to active duty.

The three had gotten well acquainted at the enlisted men's club over the preceding weekends. With a few inhibition-lowering beers their conversations ranged over many subjects – – among them religion. Clyde was a Presbyterian and Harmon Episcopalian. When David hesitantly divulged that he was

Jewish, neither man batted an eye. Both men had been reared in households that taught and practiced tolerance.

Harmon traced his ancestry back to Roger Williams of the Plymouth Colony. Williams had been banished to Rhode Island for protesting the Crown's confiscation of Native Indian lands. There he negotiated purchases of land from the Narragansett tribes, thereby winning their friendship. That spirit of fair play lived on in Harmon Page. He was an undergraduate at the Brown University Divinity School in Providence before leaving to enlist. His plans for a life in the ministry as an Episcopal missionary to Africa had to be put on hold.

The three sat down at a table with several other trainees, most of whom were celebrating the passing of their initial flight tests. David recognized a couple of guys from Company 409 at Maxwell but didn't know the others. One beefy, disheveled student was introduced as Waco from the town in Texas. He appeared surly and wore a perpetual scowl. Waco was holding court when the trio arrived.

"I don't understand how I got stuck with this asshole, Parminter. He's giving me a hard time for no reason. I think he's a kike from New York and you know how they are. I don't know why they let these "Jew boys" into the army; much less make them officers and instructors."

Clyde tensed and glanced at David. This was the first act of anti-semitism David had experienced since leaving Baltimore. His first reaction was to just let the insult pass. Clyde had other ideas.

"Listen to me you anti-Semitic bastard, he has just as much right to be here as you, maybe more. Where do you get off criticizing anyone? Thousands of Jews have died in America's wars and their blood runs just as red as yours. Now I expect you to apologize to my friend David Weiss here," Clyde said as he put a hand on David's shoulder. "He's a Jew and just as patriotic as anyone at this table."

"Hey, man," Waco slurred, "I ain't apologizing to nobody, especially no Hebe like him, and if you don't like it that's too fucking bad."

Clyde bounded across the table faster than the bully could react, grabbed him around the neck and dragged him outside. The room emptied as everyone sensed a fight.

"Okay, bigmouth, you have one more chance to apologize or I'm going to beat the living shit out of you," Clyde snarled.

The boozy Texan lunged at Clyde who sidestepped the charge like a matador teasing a bull. Waco stumbled and went down in a heap. He popped up and took a swipe at Clyde, missing wildly. As he turned Clyde's fist smashed into Waco's nose. The big man crumpled to the ground like a rag doll. He lay there dazed, blood gushing from a broken nose. Finally, a couple of his buddies dragged him to his feet and guided him toward the barracks, one under each arm, struggling to keep him upright.

"Well, gentlemen, shall we resume our celebration," Clyde said as he picked up his cap and slapped it against his leg to get the dust off. As soon as they were seated, and another round ordered David spoke.

"Clyde, I appreciate you coming to my defense like that, but I can take care of myself."

"I know that David, but it will make a more lasting impression on the big galoot coming from a non-Jew. Besides, I expect you to defend my honor the next time someone makes a crack about hillbillies."

Clyde went back to his drink as if nothing had happened.

"Do you think he'll file charges against you Clyde?" Harmon asked. "That was a pretty mean shot to the nose."

"Nah," Clyde said. "These types are all wind. If he files charges he'll have to admit that he was beaten, and he'd rather die than admit that. We just have to be on the lookout. He's the kind that'll sucker-punch you when you're not looking. Look out for him if you're out alone. He'll be eaten up with this and looking for revenge — but not in an honest fight. Just be careful."


David continued to progress in his flight training. Armbruster essentially turned the craft over to him once they were airborne. He repeated all the maneuvers of the past three weeks and passed with flying colors.

"Okay Weiss, show up here Monday morning ready for your first solo flight. It's about time you began to earn your keep. If you pass solo, I'll pretty much turn you loose to practice all the maneuvers you've learned. If that all goes well, I'll take you back up for a few new maneuvers that will prepare you for advanced flight training. Meantime I'm going over to welcome the next ten-percent of my ticket to England."

"Yes, sir! I'll be here bright and early, sir," David said as his instructor walked away.

David muttered to himself as he walked back to the barracks. The late afternoon shadows were lengthening as he walked past the hangar.

"Is it really true? Am I really going to solo on Monday? Am I ready? If the lieutenant thinks so then it must be true."

He saw the shadow out of the corner of his eye, before the blow came. He ducked reflexively, the fist missing his head and glancing off his shoulder. A sharp stab of pain ran down his arm. He threw up his left arm to ward off the second blow and swung wildly at the form in the shadows.

"Dirty kike. I'll teach you to sic your buddies on me," the disembodied voice came from the dark.

David saw the figure re-emerge from the shadows, this time clutching a length of pipe. It swung the pipe at his head and David parried it with his left arm while swinging from his toes with his right. He caught the attacker square under the chin, sending him reeling back into the dark. The man came at him again and David ducked under the arc of the pipe. He grabbed the weapon and swung his attacker around, pulling the pipe into his neck. He grabbed the other end and pressed the choke-hold.

"You son-of-a-bitch! Not only are you a bigot but a coward as well," David said as he tightened the pipe against Waco's neck.

He held it there until he felt the man go limp and the he let him fall to the ground. Two MPs came running up just as Waco stirred in the dust.

"We were coming down from the tower when we saw him swing at you. What in the world made him do that?"

David related the story from the EM club, being careful not to implicate Clyde in the process.

"Well, you won't have to worry about this badass again. We'll take him to the stockade and press charges for assault with a weapon. You'll be contacted to make a statement and you'll have to testify at the court-martial. He'll do a few months in Leavenworth before he's booted out of the army. We don't need people like him. We've got a war to fight. Are you all right? He took quite a swing at you with that pipe."

"Yes, sir, I'm fine. My shoulder's a little sore but I'll be okay. Thanks for coming to my rescue."

"Don't mention it. It looks like you had things pretty well in hand."

"Is it okay if I go now?" David asked. "I need to get back to the barracks."

"Sure kid. If that arm starts to bother you get over to the infirmary and let the docs look at it. They'll take care of it for you."

The MPs slapped handcuffs onto the groggy Texan and hauled him off to the stockade. David arrived back at the barracks just as the KP detail was heading off to the mess hall.

"What happened to you?" Harmon asked. There was a welt on David's neck and a tear in his blouse.

"Waco jumped me on the way back. I'm okay. He's on his way to the stockade. A couple of MPs witnessed the attack from the tower. He won't be causing any more trouble. Good riddance to bad rubbish as my mother would say."

"You'd better get cleaned up and changed into your work clothes. We've got KP in twenty minutes. Beating or not, you know those cooks won't let you off. Clyde said he'd meet us over there. Do you need any help?"

"No, I'll be okay as soon as I shower. I feel dirty just knowing I touched that creep. I hope I don't meet any more like him. I hate to think this country still breeds people like that."

"Sadly, it does, but his kind represents a very small slice of society. Their lack of self-esteem makes them look for other people to take out their frustrations on. They pick on Jews, Negroes, immigrants; you name it, just to make themselves feel superior. We're fighting a war to get rid of people like that. People named Hitler, Mussolini and Tojo. It's the same thing, just on a grander scale. When we're done with them maybe we can come back and clean up around our own back door," Harmon concluded with a bit of missionary zeal.

# 3

# Life—and—Death

       The weather in mid-Alabama was unusually warm for late September. Shimmering mirages rose in waves from the hot asphalt runways as David rolled his vibrantly colored Valiant down the long taxiway. When his turn to take-off came he pulled onto the run-up strip, spun the tail around and faced the plane into the wind. He waited for the green flash from the tower before pushing the throttle forward and releasing the brakes. The plane shuddered before picking up enough speed to lift the tail. David passed the normal lift-off point, still struggling to get his craft airborne. He remembered that warmer air expands, decreasing lift pressure. He slammed the throttles to the wall. With only 500 feet to spare the yellow and blue bird lifted into the air, scattering a herd of frightened cattle grazing below.

His orders for the day were to execute a single touch-and-go to assure the tower that his aircraft was airworthy for a solo flight, then he was to climb to an altitude of 2000 feet and fly a triangular course around two of the auxiliary fields. He completed the touch-and-go with a minimum of bounces and rose to the required 2000 feet before banking the plane and setting a heading for Danelly Auxiliary Airfield. He covered the seven miles to Danelly in just a few minutes at the rated speed of 120 miles per hour. He rounded the field and set a course for Mount Meigs Field five miles southwest of Gunter. Five minutes later he swung the plane around Mount Meigs and set his heading for Gunter. The Valiant streaked down the opposite side of the field and turned on a crosswind leg before banking for the landing. David slowed the engine as he crossed the threshold of the runway and let the small bird settle to the tarmac. He completed the roll-out and turned onto the taxiway back to the hangars. He parked next to Clyde Nagle's plane near the tower. Clyde and Lt. Armbruster were leaning against the wing as David taxied up. David hopped down and ran over to the two with his parachute pack bouncing off his backside.

"Well done Weiss," Armbruster offered. How does it feel to get that first solo flight under you belt?"

"Great, sir. I was a little shook up when I began to run out of runway on the takeoff. I gunned it and made it over the fence. Getting over to Danelly and Meigs was a piece-of-cake after that. Gunter sure looked good on my way back in. I'm sure glad to have that behind me."

A small blue and yellow dot appeared on the horizon as Harmon Page's plane made its way back to base. Armbruster pushed himself away from the plane and grabbed for the binoculars around his neck.

"Son-of-a-bitch," he spat between clinched teeth. "Page's engine is on fire." By then they could see dense, black smoke pouring from the engine and enveloping the cockpit.

"Come on," Armbruster commanded, as he rushed over to a jeep parked near the tower.

He jumped in and gunned the engine as Nagle and Weiss scrambled to climb aboard. Sirens from the fire and rescue trucks wailed as they emerged from their firehouse beyond the tower.

Page's plane was turning upwind toward the main runway as the jeep approached the apron. They could see him struggling with the controls as he urged the plane toward a landing. The swirling smoke obscured his view and the Valiant slewed left, fifty feet off the centerline. Harmon cut the power as he drifted over the threshold and the stricken plane dropped rapidly, bouncing several times before burrowing its nose into the dirt median. The left wing sliced into a mound of dirt erected to divert water from the runway, flipping the plane up and over. It came to rest on its canopy, trapping Page inside. The jeep tore along the runway, watching as the catastrophe unfolded before them. Armbruster whipped the steering wheel to the right and screamed up to the crash site.

"Weiss grab that fire-extinguisher and try to knock down those flames. Nagle, help me try to get him out of there. Page hung upside down by his safety harness, blood dripping from his helmet. The windshield had been ripped off and it was apparent that Harmon's head had taken the brunt of the crash. The small extinguisher was no match for the flames being fed by ruptured fuel lines.

"It's no use," Armbruster said. "We can't get him out with that fire raging."

The emergency vehicles came roaring up and began training their fire suppressant chemicals onto the flaming wreck.

"Lieutenant, you'd better get back from there!" the fire chief said. "She's about to blow."

The firefighters began to back off just as the small plane erupted into a fireball. The three rescuers were blown off their feet and wound up by the jeep.

"Are you guys all right?" Armbruster asked as he got to his feet.

His hair was scorched, and his eyebrows were gone. David's face was burned, and Clyde's jacket was afire. David grabbed a blanket from the jeep to beat out the flames. The entire area was a sea of small fires and the stench of oil and burning flesh filled the air. David leaned against the jeep and threw up. He had never seen anyone die before.

"Come on fellas," Armbruster said, "the medics and rescue team will take care of this. There's nothing more we can do for Page. Poor guy didn't stand a chance. I don't know if we'll ever figure out what went wrong with his engine."

The burning wreckage of Harmon Page's plane joined the mounting inventory of Valiants lying in the fields and forests around Montgomery, many the result of mechanical failure, many the result of pilot error. Whatever the cause, too many of America's brave young men were dying in the nation's haste to battle. Shaken, Armbruster, Nagle and Weiss made their way back to the tower and reported to the duty officer. After giving their statements, Armbruster took them to the officer's club for a drink. The look he gave to the officer in charge said, "Don't question the presence of these two men with me." It took three stiff rounds of Jack Daniel whisky before the raw nerves began to subside.

"Okay men, I know I can't expect you to forget what you just saw out there. I can only tell you that it sometimes happens to the best of us. It's obvious that Page did everything in his power to bring his plane in safely, but it was not to be. I expect to see both of you early in the morning. You'll have to suck it up and climb back on that horse. If Page were here now he would tell you the same thing. Now go home and get a good night's sleep. I'll see you tomorrow."

David lay staring at the ceiling until midnight when he heard the footsteps of the roving patrol outside his window. Try as he might he could not dispel the images and the smells of Harmon's fatal crash. Apart from the occasional family trauma associated with the fate of his relatives in Europe, David had been spared personal tragedy. The stark reality of Harmon's death touched a part of him that didn't consciously exist before today. Sure, he was aware of the pain and suffering in the world, but it had not intruded directly into his life. Today it had. The sheer unpredictability of life was brought home in the cruelest of ways. He slipped from his bunk and padded down the hall to the barrack's meeting room. He sat down at the battered desk and pulled a sheet of stationery from a pigeonhole.

*Dear Mr. and Mrs. Page,*

*I can't begin to describe how terribly sorry I am for your loss. I only knew Harmon for a short time but long enough to recognize his remarkable character and his great love for his fellow man. We talked often of our plans for the future, after the war, and he was so excited about becoming a missionary to Africa. I can only imagine what wonderful parents you were to instill such dedication in your son, and I can only mourn for all those lost souls who will never benefit from his passion for life.*

*I will gather Harmon's belongings and send them to you. I hope that when this is all over I'll have a chance to meet you someday.*

*Kindest regards,*

*David Weiss*

The naked hardwood trees scattered among the pine barrens around Gunter stood in stark contrast to their red and gold plumage of a few weeks earlier. David was nearing the end of his basic flight training and had passed all the tests needed to graduate. His lone major obstacle now was to complete a cross-country, solo flight. The triangular route would take him south into the Florida panhandle then northeast back over South Georgia before returning to Gunter. The distance of nearly 300 miles was well within the Valiant's maximum range of 500 miles.

The flight altitude of 8,000 feet meant the early January temperature outside was well below zero. David had dressed as warmly as possible, but he still shivered in the unheated cockpit. His departure time was nine a.m. He had been aloft almost an hour when he crossed the Alabama-Florida line and executed a left turn over Marianna, Florida. He set his compass heading for Albany, Georgia where he would listen for the vertical radio homing beacon at Turner Army Air Field before heading back toward Gunter.

The control tower operators at Turner Field gave David an all clear signal as he passed overhead and began the last leg home to Gunter. The runway below was lined with twin-engine B-25 bombers. He could see them taking off and landing beneath him. He wondered if this base might be in his future. He still wanted to be a fighter pilot but the B-25 would be a good alternative.

As David crossed back into Alabama near Columbus, Georgia his thoughts turned to Ruth. The time of his graduation was fast approaching, and he began to question their decision not to marry. He had wanted to honor his father's wishes but at the same time he knew that ultimately, he and Ruth must determine their own future. He decided he would invite her and his mother to come to Gunter for his graduation and the pinning on of his wings and lieutenant's bars. The thought of seeing Ruth again lifted his spirits and in some small way lessened his sadness over Harmon's death.

The blasts of steam rose into the frigid air. The train was the same one David had arrived on months earlier. He waited anxiously for the porter to place the steps, so the passengers could alight. Several soldiers and businessmen in suits and ties stepped down. He looked about anxiously, wondering if Leah and Ruth had missed the train. He was relieved finally to see the glint of sunlight from a heap of copper colored hair on the platform. He waved excitedly, shouting.

"Ruth! Mama! Over here."

Both women caught sight of David at the same time and waved furiously as they hurried down the steps, precariously juggling their hand luggage. David ran to the platform as Clyde Nagle followed him at a more sedate pace. David swept Ruth into his arms and kissed her firmly then turned to his mother with a big hug.

"Gosh it's good to see you two," he said. "It seems like an eternity since I left Baltimore. You both look wonderful."

He stepped back to take them in, stepping on Clyde's foot as he did.

"Oh! I'm terribly sorry. I forgot to introduce Clyde Nagle. He's from West Virginia and he and I have gone through this whole ordeal together."

"Why howdy, Miss Leah and Miss Ruth," Clyde said in his best drawl with an elegant bow. "It's a great pleasure for me to welcome such beautiful daughters of the old South to our humble city. You do us great honor to venture into this remote outpost. Welcome."

"Mr. Nagle, thank you for such a warm and gallant welcome," Ruth said. "It's been so long since I've been in the company of such a true and gallant southern gentleman. I'll be sure to inform my girl friends back home of this divine representative of the Old South. I'm sure they'd be delighted to make your acquaintance."

"I warned you Clyde," David said. "You shouldn't cross swords with this young lady. She can give as good as she gets. I learned long ago not to joust with her."

"Mrs. Weiss," Clyde said.  "If you'll come with me we'll collect your luggage while these two get re-acquainted."

"Why, certainly Mr. Nagle, I can see we've got a lot to catch up on," Leah said with a wink.

Alone at last David kissed Ruth again, this time a bit more passionately.

"I can't believe you're really here. It's a dream come true. We have to make the most of these few days. I don't know where they'll send me after this."

"Me too," she said. "I was surprised when your dad said it was okay and my parents agreed. This has been the longest time of my life."

"Come on; let's catch up with Clyde and Mom. We have a taxi waiting to take us to the hotel."

The cab dropped David, Ruth and Leah at the Capitol Hotel in downtown Montgomery then waited while Clyde said his goodbyes to the women.

"I sure hope I get to see you all again before you head back north," Clyde said. "Besides, I need to get some of Ruth's egg off my face. David was right about you Ruth. You are something special. If those girls back home are anything like you I might just take you up on that invitation. Hey, I've got an idea. Why don't I take Miss Leah to dinner tomorrow evening and give you two a chance to be alone?"

"Clyde, you're a prince. I was wondering how I was going to shake Mom for a while. There's the perfect answer. Thanks. Not that I don't want to spend time with you Mom, but, you know, first things first."

"David you don't have to remind me that I'm a fifth wheel on this trip, but I'll remind you that Ruth wouldn't be here but for me," Leah said with an impish grin.

"All right then," Clyde said as he headed for the door, "I'll pick my date up here at six tomorrow evening, and we're going to paint the town."

"He's as great as you said he was," Ruth said. "What a charmer. I'm glad you had each other to get through Harmon's death. That must have been very painful for both of you, losing one of your three musketeers like that."

"I don't know how I would have survived without Clyde. He's a rock. He comes from a long line of military men. They certainly passed their genes along to him. I just hope we are assigned to the same training command."

"Me too," Leah said. "I'll feel a lot better knowing he's around to look out for you."

"Aw, come on, Mom," David teased. "I really can take care of myself you know."

"Okay, let's get you two registered. I'll give you a few minutes to freshen up and then we're going out on the town. I've got several months of army pay burning a hole in my pocket and I intend on spending a chunk of it on you two tonight."

The yellow Desoto carrying Clyde back to camp disappeared around the corner as David herded his fiancée and his mother out of the cold and into the lobby of the Capitol Hotel. It was full of politicians and men doing business with the state government. The legislature was in session and getting two rooms had been like pulling teeth. David had appealed to the patriotism of the reservations clerk and surprisingly it worked.

Men in uniform, many with brides and girlfriends in tow, were scattered around the ornate lobby. David picked up the two room keys from the desk clerk and ushered the women to the elevator. The aging attendant was a dignified looking Negro with graying hair. His eyes told of a hard life. He was dressed in the gold and garnet livery of the hotel. He slid the safety fence back while welcoming the three to the hotel. He delivered them to the sixth floor and wished them a good evening.

"You know," he said before closing the door, "I've got a son about your age. He's just up the road in Tuskegee. He's training to be a pilot too. Maybe y'all will run into each other somewhere along the way."

The man's voice was strong and full of pride.

"That would truly be an honor, sir. What's your son's name?"

"His name's James Patterson, Jr., but we just call him Pat," the old man said.

No white man had ever called him sir before.

"I'll surely keep that in mind," David said. "You have a good evening too."

David sat the bags down in front of room 622 and fished the key from his pocket. He opened the door, waved them in, and picked up their bags.

"Welcome to Montgomery Mrs. Weiss and Miss Braddock. It's my great pleasure to offer you the keys to the city," he said as he handed the room key to Leah. "Your wishes are my command. Now if you'll put those flowers I ordered into a vase I'll order up some champagne to celebrate this auspicious occasion."

"Oh David," Leah said. "Don't be so extravagant."

"I told you I had a pocketful of money and I intend to spend a big chunk on you two this weekend."

Leah took the roses into the bathroom and placed them in the cut crystal vase provided while David arranged the small table to receive the champagne bucket. A soft knock at the door announced its arrival. The attendant placed the tray with its bucket and glasses on the table.

"Will that be all sir?"

David took the cue and handed the young man a half-dollar tip as he bowed appreciatively and backed from the room, closing the door behind him.

The loud pop of the cork from the bottle of Veuve Cliquot was followed by a gush of foaming champagne. David hurriedly directed the stream at the three flutes, then handed one to Leah and one to Ruth.

"Here's to the two most important women in my life. Thank you for coming down. It'll make my graduation all the more meaningful. With such an uncertain future we have to grab every moment that we can. Murray's off somewhere in Texas and God knows where Bernie is now. This war is upsetting everyone and everything and who knows how long it will last. Based on reports from Europe, Africa and the Pacific we could be in for a long siege.

"Enough of that gloom and doom. What would you like for dinner tonight?"

"Why don't you surprise us," Ruth suggested. "You know the area. I'm sure you've had some good recommendations from some of your buddies."

"Okay, I'll surprise you," he said, downing the last of his champagne. "I'll go and get cleaned up and pick you up in about forty-five minutes."

Promptly at seven David rapped on their door and Ruth let him in.

"All set?" he asked. "I've got a reservation at Luigi's, reputedly the best Italian food in town."

"I think so," Ruth said. "I believe your mother is just finishing up in the bathroom."

"Great. I'm famished after all this running around today. I completely forgot to eat lunch although you don't miss much when you skip army chow."

"I've heard that it's not all that bad," Leah said as she emerged from, the bathroom. "Bernie seems to like it."

"Yeah, but Bernie's an officer. They get all that white linen and napkin ring stiff. We lowly grunts get bologna and navy beans."

"I'm sure it's not all that bad," Ruth added. "You don't appear to be any thinner."

"It's all muscle now. You won't believe how hard they work us. Come on, dinner's awaiting us. Luigi's was a ten-minute cab ride from the hotel. The taxi dropped them at the door where a line was waiting.

"That's a good sign," Leah said. "At least it is in Baltimore."

"I hope they held our reservation," David said. "I'd hate to disappoint my girls on their first night."

The maître d' took David's name and advised him there would be a fifteen-minute wait for their table.

"You are welcome to wait at the bar," he said. "I'll call you when it's ready."

"We might as well get started with a little wine," David said. "We can take the bottle to the table."

"What'll it be?" the bartender asked.

"How about a bottle of your best Chianti?" David said.

"Coming right up, sir."

David's previous experience in wines was limited to the Manischewitz his mother served during Jewish holidays. The 1939 bottle of Castello Gabbiano bore little resemblance to the bland, fruity taste of kosher wines. He raised his glass.

"Another toast to you, and a prayer for a speedy end to this war so we can all get back to normal lives," he said.

"Hear! Hear! I'll drink to that," Ruth said as she took a small sip. She wasn't used to drinking and the champagne had already produced a slight buzz.

"I just want all my boys to come home in one piece," Leah said. "I'm wearing out the carpet by my bed with my nightly prayers. Promise me you'll be careful, David."

"I promise, Ma. I've got too much waiting for me to screw it up by getting killed."

The last of the lasagna and spaghetti disappeared from their plates as the clock over the bar registered ten.

"I'd better get you two back to the hotel. You've had a long day and you must be worn out."

"Yeah, with the champagne and the wine I'm feeling very mellow," Ruth said. "I won't have any trouble getting to sleep tonight."

"Neither will I." Leah chimed in. "That's a long train ride and I didn't sleep very well in the Pullman berth last night."

David called for the check, paid the waiter, and asked the maître d' to call a taxi for them. They were back at the hotel by ten-thirty and asleep by eleven. The graduation ceremonies were scheduled for Monday at ten a.m. That meant a full weekend for David and Ruth to catch up on their separate lives.

David tapped on the door of Ruth and Leah's room at 7:30. They were dressed and ready for breakfast. Following their eggs and corned beef and hash browns — they declined the ubiquitous grits — David invited the pair to a tour of Montgomery's historic Capitol Hill.

The walk up the hill to the old capitol building was steep and the early morning sun was in their eyes. On the way they passed the house used by Jefferson Davis during the brief interval that the Confederate capital was in Montgomery. Just across the wide boulevard was the headquarters of the United Daughters of the Confederacy where the struggle to keep the precious memories of their ancestors alive took place. Everywhere one looked there were reminders of Montgomery's role in the "War Between the States." No one down here dared refer to it as "The Civil War."

They mounted the wide marble steps to the columned capitol building and wandered through the corridors. Statues and plaques honoring the fallen of that *glorious cause* filled the alcoves and lined the walls. Seventy-five years had failed to dim the memories or diminish the passions. They exited the building through a side door and strolled along the tree lined streets, admiring the magnificent antebellum mansions which now housed the wealthy and prominent citizens of Montgomery.

David had received permission to take Leah and Ruth onto the base at Gunter. After a quick lunch at the hotel they boarded a shuttle bus that took them to the main gate. Ruth was amazed at how accurately David had painted the base surroundings in words; its bustling core of administrative buildings, its field side hangars and the runways busy with the constant drone of aircraft engines — and the relative quiet of the barracks areas. This was the women's first up-close and personal interaction with the military world and they were fascinated.

Clyde joined them for snacks at the enlisted men's club. They sat and talked for hours about home, family, the army, religion, philosophy and almost any other subject that entered their stream of consciousness. Finally, Leah posed the question that was on all their minds.

"Clyde, do you think you and David will be assigned to the same advanced training base?"

"I don't know, Mrs. Weiss. I certainly hope so. We've both let it be known to Lieutenant Armbruster that we would like to, but I don't know how much sway he has over the assignments. We've got our fingers crossed."

"Both of us have scored well on all the exams and the flight tests, so maybe that will count for something," David added.

It was approaching five before they headed back to town. Clyde took the bus with them and waited in the lobby until the dinner appointment with Leah. David and Ruth came down first and had a Coke with Clyde. Leah was a few minutes late. She had ordered an iron to get the wrinkles out of the linen dress she brought. When she arrived a few minutes later every hair was in place and the dress looked impeccable.

"David you might have second thoughts about letting your mother go out with me. She looks more like your sister than your mother."

"Oh, tosh Clyde. You really are the charmer. Come on and take my arm so these young ones can get on with their courting."

"I promise to have her back before midnight, David — but don't wait up."

"I'm going to hold you to that Clyde. It's been a long time since Mom has been out on a real date so you be careful. I don't want to see any lipstick on your shirt when you get back."

Clyde gave a halfhearted wave and took Leah's arm. He led her to the door with a big grin on his face.

"Okay little lady," David said when they were alone, "what's your preference tonight, a fine French dinner at Emile's or a return engagement at Luigi's?

"I kinda like Luigi's. Maybe we can get one of the tables in the back corner. I want to get you alone."

"Well we could just go up to the room and order in," David said.

"Now you're really trying to get us in trouble young man. All we need is for your mother to come back early and find us in an embarrassing moment."

"Well it was worth a try," David sheepishly replied. "Luigi's it is. I'll call from the desk."

Ruth watched him walk away, admiring how nine months in the army had whipped David's already lithe body into such a strong physical specimen. She really wished they could just go upstairs, but mores being what they were they couldn't risk it.

It was ten-thirty when David drained the last of the Chianti from his glass and looked at his watch. The evening had flown by as they rekindled the affair that Tojo and Hitler had so cruelly interrupted. They sat on the same side of the banquette. David couldn't get his fill of Ruth's kisses. Sidewise glances from some of the other diners suggested that they should get a room. If they only knew. The evening had only confirmed what *they* already knew. That they were deeply in love and nothing that had transpired since he left home had changed that.

"David, I love you so. I wish we had just gone ahead and got married before you left. At least I could go with you to your next duty station."

"I know. So do I. But, it's probably for the best. I heard last week that they are speeding up the training sessions in order to get the crews over to England faster. The increase in bombing runs is outpacing the available crews."

He didn't want to frighten her with how many crews were being lost to enemy fire.

"If I get into fighter training, it'll probably be no more than four or five months long. Bomber training will be even shorter, maybe only three months."

"I guess you're right, but it's so hard. Anyway, my nursing studies are keeping me busy. I'll probably graduate before the war's over and at least we'll have an income so you can go back to med school. Still... By the way, has your mother spoken to you about her work with the JRA?"

"No. What about it?"

"She's heard from Henrietta Szold in Palestine. They've been in contact with some of your relatives from Russia. A sister and brother with their families were able to flee ahead of the German invasion last June but they are trapped in Moldova, wherever that is. A Polish diplomat arranged papers for them. The *Bricha* organization is trying to recruit people to help them escape to Palestine. I know your parents have sent money, but the *Bricha* is also asking for Yiddish speaking American volunteers to come to Palestine. I don't think Leah or Jacob would do that, but you might want to speak to her about it."

"Oh my God!" David said. "That's all we need, members of our family in harm's way. I'll talk to her."

"I didn't mean to put a damper on the evening."

"No, that's all right. I'm glad you told me. Come on, we need to head back to the hotel."

David was morose during the cab ride back to the hotel. He knew how involved and desperate his mother was to help her family but surely, he thought, she wouldn't do anything so foolish. Clyde and Leah were seated on a sofa in the lobby nursing their nightcaps when David and Ruth entered the hotel.

"Well, I'm glad to see you got my mother back without anything untoward happening," David joked.

"How do you know it didn't, sir?" Clyde retorted.

"He was a model of decorum," Leah interjected. "We had a wonderful time and Clyde introduced me to some Southern cuisine I was not even aware of. He said it was venison, but I really think it was squirrel."

"Yuck!" Ruth exclaimed. "Remind me not to let Clyde order any meals for me."

"Well, I've got to get back to base before curfew," Clyde said. "I'll see all of you Monday morning at the graduation ceremonies. I had a great time Mrs. Weiss and I assure you it was not squirrel, although I've eaten my share of squirrel in those West Virginia *hollers*. Good night."

"Do you think he was serious," Ruth asked as Clyde disappeared through the front door.

"I believe he was," David said.

The streets of Montgomery were quiet on Sunday morning and the trio managed to wander around to visit several other historic sites. By noon they were footsore and headed back to the hotel for lunch. When they finished, Ruth excused herself and said she was going to take a short nap.

"Don't come up on my account," she said. "There are things you two might want to catch up on in private. I'll be back down in an hour."

David watched her disappear into the elevator knowing full well she wanted him to talk to Leah about Palestine.

"Well Ma, how is Papa doing? We haven't talked much about him."

"Oh, you know Jacob. He's always got his nose to the grindstone. He and Seth are hard pressed to keep up with the demand for uniforms. They bought out two more manufacturers in South Carolina late last year. He's spending a lot of time down there getting them converted over to uniform manufacture. I believe he said they were called The Horse Creek Manufacturing Company or something like that. Anyway, he's busy and he leaves me alone to worry about you boys."

"Ruth says you're spending a lot of time at the JRA."

"Yes, the need is greater than ever. Even though a curtain has fallen across Nazi Europe, information still manages to escape."

"Ruth said that Henrietta has been in touch with you."

"Yes," Leah said hesitantly. "They've found one of my sisters and a brother in lower Moldova. They're being hidden by Eastern Orthodox families in Palanca, a little commune near the Black Sea. The area is controlled by Romania and hasn't seen the mass deportation of Jews that northern Moldova has. Reports say that over 100,000 from that area have been shipped to the death camps. Henrietta and the *Bricha* organization have been trying to get a ship into a nearby port to rescue as many as possible. Money and people — that's always the problem. Jacob has sent as much as he can, but they still need more."

"Ruth said she thought you and some others at the JRA might even be considering going to Palestine."

"I'll admit that Henrietta makes a good case for our help, but I'm 48 now and I don't know what skills I could bring to them."

"Mama, I beg of you. Don't even think about it. That part of the world is in such turmoil. You'd be putting yourself in grave danger. So, don't! Please!"

# 4

# Wings

Ruth and Leah were seated near the top of the bleachers overlooking the Gunter Field parade ground. There were a few other families of graduates huddled together, shivering in the January cold. Promptly at ten o'clock a bugle sounded and a contingent of officers marched onto the field and mounted the reviewing stand. Minutes later two companies of fifty men each marched onto the field to the band's martial music. They halted in front of the stand and, on command, executed a right face.

Unlike the pomp and circumstance accompanying the graduation from basic training, this ceremony was brief and to the point. It was as if the urgency to get these pilots into battle precluded the necessity of an elaborate commencement. The commanding officer at Gunter rose, pulled his prepared notes from his jacket pocket, and began.

"Ladies and gentlemen, parents and friends, we are here today to recognize the accomplishments of these men. They have passed through an ordeal by fire. In the past few weeks they have gone from raw cadets to gifted pilots. Now, as we congratulate them on this great achievement, we also wish them Godspeed as they move on to their next assignments. At the conclusion of these brief remarks, mothers, wives, fiancées and friends will be invited to pin the wings on the chests of these young men. Following that, the pilot instructors will pass out the envelopes detailing their next assignments. I wish all of you the very best and I know your country thanks you for your sacrifice.

"In view of the very cold conditions this morning I'm going to cut my comments short. I know you all are anxious to learn where your loved ones will be going from here and also you would like to get inside out of the cold. I am going to ask that the cadet graduates be dismissed and reassemble in the gymnasium across the parade ground. Thank you for coming and best wishes to you as you return home and to your cadets as they go forward in the service of our country. Major Evans, dismiss the troops."

The women arrived before David and Clyde and were standing in a corner near a heat outlet trying to thaw their hands. Suddenly the double doors burst open and all the graduates came pouring in.

"Okay you guys," said the officer in charge, "settle down and we'll try to get through this as fast as possible. I would like for all the cadets to group up around their instructors. I will have the envelopes delivered to them momentarily."

There was a mad scramble as the men raced to find their instructors. David and Clyde stumbled over a row of chairs before finally landing next to Lt. Armbruster.

"Here's hoping," David said. "Fighter school - and together."

He held up both hands with crossed fingers.

"Right on old buddy," Clyde responded. "I've got mine crossed too."

Five NCO's were stepping down from the podium and headed toward the little knots of students. Within minutes Lt. Armbruster held several small, manila envelopes in his hand.

"Carson."

"Here, Lieutenant."

He grabbed the envelope and tore it open. It was hard to tell whether he was happy or not.

"Nagle."

Clyde stepped forward and took his envelope. He stood there awaiting Dave to open his.

"Weiss."

David grabbed the envelope and ran over to Clyde.

"You ready?" Clyde asked.

"Go!" David said as he tore into his envelope. Both men stared at the assignment papers.

"What'd you get Clyde?" David asked.

"Victorville, California Multi-Engine Bomber Training. Where the hell is Victorville, California? How 'bout you? What did you get?"

David stared down at the paper in his hand and broke into a big smile.

"Same-o, same-o," he said. "I'd really rather get into fighters but going with you is more important. Come on, let's tell Ruth and Mom."

They hurried over to where the women were standing.

"I'm almost scared to ask," Leah said.

Ruth was shaking like a leaf.

"It's okay Mama. Clyde and I are both going to a base in California. It's in a town called Victorville. I've never heard of it. Clyde and I both got assigned there. They'll teach us to fly multi-engine airplanes there, then I guess we'll go somewhere else for bomber pilot training. We both wanted to get into fighter pilot school, but as long as we can stay together, that doesn't really matter so much."

"Oh, David," Ruth said, "I'm so glad you two will be together. I was hoping you'd be closer to home. How long will you be there?"

"The multi-engine school lasts about eight weeks. If we make the grade there we'll be sent to one of the bomber training schools. They last about eight to ten weeks. Together they're about four months long. That means we'll be finishing up sometime in April or early May."

The gaggle was interrupted by Lt. Armbruster.

"In all the confusion I forgot these," he said, holding up two small jewelry cases. "These are your new wings and second lieutenant's bars boys. I thought you might want them."

"Thank you, sir," Clyde said. "I know David will want Ruth to pin his on, and I'd consider it a great honor if Miss Leah would do mine."

The two women smilingly obliged.

The ceremonies were over, and the crowd drifted out of the gymnasium. Clyde bid his farewell and headed back to the barracks to begin packing. They were to fly out on a C-4 army transport the next day. No grass would grow under the feet of these budding bomber pilots. They were desperately needed in Europe.

"Good-bye Mrs. Weiss. It's been a great pleasure meeting you. I'll always remember our "date" and the venison dinner. I promise you I'll take care of your son for you.

"Ruth, what can I say? You've latched onto a great guy here. And, he's got an equally great gal in you. I'll make sure he gets back to you in one piece 'cause I want to be there for a piece of the wedding cake. Bye now, ya'll take care."

David saw Ruth and his mother back to the hotel. He had to be back on base by six. They had a quick lunch and Leah excused herself. She left the two young lovers at the table. She knew their parting would be bittersweet. She wanted them to store-up as many memories as possible in the few hours they had left. Despite all of Clyde's assurances, the future held no guarantees. At five there was a knock on the door of room 622 of the Capitol Hotel. The hour had arrived. There was no forestalling it.

"Well, Ma, I guess this is it."

David crossed the room and embraced Leah. She seemed so small and vulnerable at that moment. He fought back his tears. He thought, 'This is going to be difficult enough without my blubbering.' He released his hold on his mother and turned to Ruth. She too was in tears.

"Well my love, what can I say? I hope I'll get some leave after Victorville, but I don't know. Word is the new pilots are being shipped off to Europe as soon as they finish their training. We'll just have to wait and see."

"Oh, David. We've had such a short time. But, I wouldn't take the world for it. I so appreciate your mother and father making it possible. Now, I want you to go off and make us proud. Don't worry about your mother. I'll look out for her. You just concentrate on staying safe and getting back to us when this is all over."

"You have my promise. I told Murray we'd meet up somewhere over Berlin and bomb the hell out of Hitler. Then we'll head back home."

He took Ruth in his arms and kissed her gently. Fearing he could no longer hold back the flood, he slipped quickly out the door and headed back to Gunter. The women had a nine o'clock train back to Baltimore the next morning.

# 5

# High Desert

The Victorville, California US Army Air Corps training field occupied 2200 acres northeast of the town. The land had been donated to the federal government by the people of Victorville in the desperate hope that a military base would be established there. The hordes of Okies and Arkies that had descended on the area during the *"dust bowl"* had long since migrated northward, seeking better jobs in the more fertile fields of the San Joaquin Valley.

Wedged between an inhospitable Mojave Desert and the rain-denying San Gabriel Mountains, the desperately poor high desert town, had never recovered from the depression. A few struggling ranches and scraggly vineyards were the only remaining visible means of support for its dwindling population.

Cactus, yucca, agave and a multitude of vividly colored wildflowers stretched to the horizon as the C-4 air transport carrying the newly minted pilots lowered its landing gear and began its slow descent. The setting sun reflected off the hills to the east producing kaleidoscopic colors of ochre, red, purple, yellow; every hue of the rainbow. Looking down on this magical landscape David decided that even the sunsets across the Chesapeake from Tolchester paled in comparison.

The lumbering plane circled the hastily constructed, tarpaper buildings that constituted most of the base structures and struggled to a bumpy landing as the capricious desert crosswinds pushed the yellow tetrahedron wind indicator in several directions at once. Runway 45L was nearest to the base and as soon as the pilot had the plane under control they were at the hangar complex.

David and Clyde were last down the ladder to the tarmac. They and the ten other cadets posted to Victorville gathered their duffels from the baggage cart and lugged them over to the reception shack by the hangar. On the way they walked past several Curtiss AT-9 Fledgling twin engine trainers. The planes were bulbous looking, the two large engines overpowering the smallish fuselage. Like their avian namesake they didn't look ready to fly, as if they needed a nudge from their parents to propel them over the edge of the nest. However, as the trainees quickly learned, once airborne the ugly duckling transformed itself into a graceful swan. Its engines, so ungainly on the ground, blended with the whole to produce an amazingly adept flying machine.

Learning to fly the twin engine planes came naturally to the neophyte flyers. That would have been unsurprising to the US Army Bomber Command. Unbeknownst to all twelve of them, they had been singled out to train together in Victorville. Clandestinely, all their records and test results, as well as their instructor reviews, had been forwarded to General "Hap" Arnold's command headquarters in Washington. Arnold himself had assembled a hand-picked team of experienced bomber pilots to review those records and make recommendations to him. He wanted men with the highest possible aptitudes for a very special mission. These 12 men and 108 others, now scattered among nine other training commands, would form a pool of candidates for a top-secret mission. After graduation from multi-engine training the pilot's records would be scrutinized anew by the team and the unequivocal top 60 candidates would be sent to other bases for heavy-bomber pilot training. The plans were so well guarded that not even the ten base commanders had any inkling of it.

After the first week, David was so comfortable and proficient he was allowed to fly "first seat." First seat — the left seat — is universally recognized as the command pilot seat, the right being the co-pilot's seat.

"Hey, Clyde," David said as he greeted his buddy.

They were both enjoying a beer in the officer's club. Neither was yet fully comfortable with this newly earned perk. Rubbing elbows with captains, majors and colonels was a tad disconcerting. It was a reticence they quickly shed after a few beers.

"Hey, David, how was your day?"

"My instructor let me fly first seat today. It was a lark. I thought these multi-engine planes would be much more difficult to fly, but so far they're a piece of cake."

"Mine, too. Why do you think they did that?"

"I dunno, but it's a lot of fun. Still, it smells a little fishy."

"I guess we'll find out Monday," Clyde said. "But, for now I'm just going to enjoy it."

It didn't take long on Monday for the new guys to unearth the source of the fish smell.

The first week had been an innocent prelude to the devilish intricacies of flying a twin-engine plane. The second week rudely introduced them to its perils and they quickly learned that much sweat, time, concentration and sheer terror would be experienced before they mastered the beast.

The instructors delighted in surprising their students by cutting power to one or both engines in the middle of a loop. Initially, panic ensued, and the instructor would be obliged to take the wheel from the green-gilled student. Gradually, the recovery moves became second nature, and by the fourth week most of the men were able to recover from almost any instructor provoked situation. The few who did not were quietly offered transfers to navigator or bombardier schools.

The final four weeks were devoted to honing their navigational skills on long cross-country flights. David was blindfolded and flown to a desolate spot north of Death Valley. Upon arriving at the pre-planned location, the blindfold was removed.

"Okay, Weiss. Take her home."

David had memorized the plane's moves and the duration between changes in direction. He had a vague idea where he was. He noted the position of the sun and the lengths and angles of the shadows cast by the giant Joshua trees below. He activated the planes radio direction finder and twisted its dials until he heard the faint sounds from a transmitter. He recognized the frequency and direction of the signal and noted it on his knee-pad notebook. He repeated the maneuver for two more beacons and noted them as well. He found the three beacons on his map and drew a line from each in the reverse direction. He knew that where the three lines crossed would be his location. He was ten miles west of the Naval Ordinance Test Station at China Lake. He banked the plane to give himself a view to the east. There, spread out across the desert floor was the Navy's largest and most significant weapons proving grounds. David judged his position to be about a hundred miles almost due north of Victorville. He checked the coordinates on his map and using the plane's compass set a heading for home. Forty-five minutes later he sat the Fledgling down on 45L and taxied to the hangar.

"Well done Weiss. I'll have to give you an 'A' for that," Captain Gerald Cowan said. "Don't get too cocky though. Wait'll you get dropped in a desert valley on a cold, dark night where the radio beacons don't reach. Then we'll see how good you really are."

The days were so hectic and full of exercises that David had little time to think of Ruth and home. But at night when lights out came and taps played on the loudspeakers his thoughts turned to her. What is she doing right now? How are Sandy and Elaine doing? Is he still gone most of the time? What about her brothers? There were so many questions. Her letters were newsy and comforting and they kept him up-to-date on most things, but they were no substitute for her presence. He hoped and prayed that he would get leave when he left Victorville.

Clyde and David, having passed the dreaded cross-country flying test, were totally out of gas. Tomorrow was Saturday, and they had been promised a day off if they passed. They were both more than ready for a little R & R.

The Green Spot Café was located on Adelanto Road, just off US-395, only a couple of miles from the main gate. It was a popular hangout for airmen. Midge and Tom Folsom ran the Green Spot. Well, Midge really ran it because Tom drove a truck for the Gallo Brothers who had started their eponymous winery in Modesto in 1933. Tom was on the road most of the week delivering wines and hauling grapes all over southern California. He made it home most weekends, when the café was at its busiest.

The Green Spot wasn't like most other juke joints surrounding the air base. Several were thinly disguised fronts for prostitution. Midge ran a tight ship, not that she was a prude by any means. Many of the local girls came to the Green Spot to dance with the men in uniform. There was a big Wurlitzer juke box in the back and Tom had carved out a good-size dance floor. If the occasional couple hit it off and decided to pair up that was okay with Midge — just don't do it in her establishment. She was also a stickler for courtesy and sobriety. You could have a few drinks, but you could not become obnoxious or start cursing. If you did you'd find yourself face down in the parking lot. She made it a point to have at least one six-foot two, 225-pound waiter on staff.

"Hi Dave. Hi Clyde," Midge yelled as the two entered.

They had become regulars during the past few weekends. Three weeks ago, after a few beers, David had poured his heart out to Midge. He needed to unburden himself. Midge was a good listener with a sympathetic ear and a big heart.

"David," she said at the conclusion of his confessional, "there are a million more young men just like you who have left home and hearth, and their girlfriends, to answer the call to service. Every one of them, like you, would rather be curled up by a warm fire with that girl right now than be out here flying airplanes or shooting rifles. It seems like in every generation one of these quarrels comes along. Then the old men declare war and the young men go off to die.

"This time there's a difference. Don't get me wrong, the old men still declare war and the young men still die, but this time the stakes are so much higher. If Hitler and Mussolini have their way, we'll be living in a world that none of us will recognize. They must be stopped, and it's fallen to young men like you and Clyde over there to stop them. I'm not saying you shouldn't feel bad about missing Ruth or your mom. I'm just saying that the stakes are so high that we all have to play our part and make our own sacrifice to defeat this evil.

"Now, have a cup of strong coffee and go call your girl. You can use the phone by the kitchen. Consider it my gift for your sacrifice."

The phone rang seven times and David was certain Ruth must be out. Finally, a hoarse voice, heavy with sleep, answered.

"Hello."

"Oh, hello Mrs. Braddock, I'm terribly sorry. I forgot about the time difference. I hope I didn't wake you. It's David. Is Ruth there?"

"Just a minute, I'll call her," Elaine said. Her tone told him that she had been sound asleep.

"David, oh I'm so glad you called. It got so late and I was afraid you wouldn't."

"Hi, darling, I miss you so. I just had to call. Mrs. Folsom told me it was all right to call you on her phone. She's a peach. Apologize to your mom for me. I forgot about the time zone difference. I'm sure the three beers didn't help my memory."

"She'll get over it. It's so good to hear your voice. Is everything all right? Is there any word on when you'll leave there or where you'll go?"

"No, not yet, but something peculiar happened this week. They moved up one of our flight tests. I don't know what it means but I think they may shorten the twin-engine school. We were originally set for twelve weeks. It looks like they may cut it to ten for a few of us. I'll probably find out next week. I heard through the grapevine that they're sending us out on our final test run on Friday. That normally doesn't come this early. If there's a change, I'll come in to the Green Spot next Saturday and let you know."

"Oh David, I'm so worried for you. I saw your mother this week. She's still trying to find out about your aunt in Moldova. She's really worried. And, she's a wreck from worrying about you, and Murray and Bernie. It's almost too much to bear."

"Thanks for keeping in touch with her. Please call her tomorrow and let her know what I told you tonight."

"I will my darling. Say hi to Clyde for me and take care. I love you."

"I love you too. I'll talk to you next week. Bye."

He set the phone back in its cradle and heaved a big sigh. It was always so good to hear Ruth's voice, but saying good-bye was like a dagger to the heart.

"I'm sending you and Nagle on your final orientation flight tomorrow," Capt. Cowan told David and Clyde on Thursday, "you as pilot and Nagle as co-pilot. You will fly the entire triangular route under IFR conditions — takeoff, outbound leg, return leg and approach to base. You will only go VFR when you are five miles out, inbound, at 5,000 feet. The IFR blackout covers are rigged to record the position and altitude at which they are removed — so no cheating."

IFR, instrument flight rules, meant that the entire cockpit was covered, and the pilots were flying blind. VFR, visual flight rules, means just that, the pilots are using visual landmarks to determine their flight path. IFR capability allows planes to fly in inclement weather through the use of ground based, directional radio beacons. Some locations were experimenting with the recently installed RADAR systems (radio detection and ranging) which used electronic echoes to determine altitude and position. Both pilots had only flown IFR with an instructor. This would be an acid test of their skills and their nerves. What Cowan did not tell them was that their training schedule was being accelerated at the behest of U.S. Bomber Command. The secret mission's launch date had been moved up due to changing conditions half-way around the world.

To compound the problem the flight was scheduled for midnight and the dark of the moon. David and Clyde tried to get a few hours sleep before the appointed time. They both tossed and turned. Sleep wouldn't come. They finally got up, showered and donned their flight suits. They arrived at the hangar at eleven, downed numerous cups of black coffee, ate several doughnuts, and declared themselves ready to fly.

"Okay, fellas," Captain Cowan said, "it's time to get this show on the road. The tug operator will tow you to the 45R take-off threshold. From there you're on your own. When you're all set, radio the tower for permission to takeoff and then get the hell out of here. Good luck and good flying. I'll see you in a couple of hours. "

David inspected the Fledgling's underbelly, its landing gear, and the engines before hoisting himself up into the belly of the beast.  Clyde was already in his seat.

"Okay, Charlie," David said to the tug driver, "we're ready to go. Button us up."

The tug operator swung the fuselage door into position and turned the handle. David and Clyde were plunged into total darkness but for the lights on the instrument panels. They could feel the jostling of the bumpy taxiway as the plane was maneuvered into position. The loud clank as the tow bar was released and the rap on the side of the cockpit told them they were in position.

Clyde had gone through the preflight checklist while David inspected the plane so there was nothing left but to fly. David gave the thumbs-up signal and Clyde pressed the starter button for engine number one. The powerful Lycoming engine coughed and sputtered before catching and roaring to life, spewing clouds of black smoke across the desert. When Clyde was content that number one was performing properly he pressed the starter for number two. Like its twin on the other side, it hesitated before catching. It emitted the characteristic whine these engines were noted for.

"She's a go," Clyde yelled.

"Weiss to tower, we're beginning our roll. Wish us luck."

"God speed men. You're cleared to the outer beacon. We'll keep the coffee hot for you."

David rechecked all his instruments: altitude, temperature, engine rpms, engine temperature, oil pressure, radio frequency settings. When he was satisfied that all conditions were proper he pushed the throttles forward and released the brakes. Clyde monitored the heading to be sure they stayed in the middle of the runway. The gangly looking plane lurched forward, gaining speed rapidly. David felt the tail gear lift. He pushed the *"balls-to-the-wall"* and the little bird leapt forward. Seconds later he felt the forward gear break loose and the plane tilted skyward. They were safely off the ground. He retracted the wheels. Now it was Clyde's job to navigate their course by reading the radio beacons and triangulating their positions. Their instructions were to fly north on a 010 heading until they crossed the radio beacon at the Inyokern marker. They were then to fly east on an 090 heading for 20 minutes before turning for home. There were multiple beacons strung along the foothills of the Sierra Nevada range, as well as throughout Death Valley and the China Basin bombing range. As navigator, Clyde had to determine the three strongest signals, tune them in, set the direction finder to maximum for each and triangulate their position. He determined their position on his chart and toggled the intercom button.

"Okay, Dave, put her nose on 185 degrees and take this baby home."

"Roger, Clyde, here we go."

David dropped his right wing and swung the plane around to the heading Clyde gave him then headed south at 200 knots with an altitude of 12,000 feet. An hour later Clyde picked up the unmistakable signal of the Victorville beacon, recali-brated their location and gave David a corrected heading.

"We're 20 miles out, drop the airspeed to 150 and re-duce altitude to 5000 feet."

David complied and fifteen minutes later they crossed over the field. Clyde pulled down the blinders while David com-pleted their downwind leg and swung around to land on 45R. The bright lights of Victorville sparkled in the crisp desert air. Both men breathed a sigh of relief. The worst was over. Ten minutes later the Fledgling pulled up to the hangar. Captain Cowan was there to meet them.

"Good morning, Captain," David said. "Isn't it a little early for you to be up?"

"I don't know what's going on, but there's been a lot of heat coming down to get you guys ready for the big birds. I just wanted to be sure you got back safely. Come on in to the hangar office and we'll have some coffee."

David and Clyde followed their instructor, with their bulky parachutes banging off their butts as they walked. Once inside they unstrapped the clumsy chutes and dropped them on a bench before heading for the coffee urn.

"Great job guys!" Cowan said. "I couldn't tell you any-thing before, but this was your final test. You two and six others who came with you are shipping out in two days. You'll be flown over to Davis-Monthan Air Base in Tucson, Arizona. A week from now you'll be training in B-24s. You're on some hush-hush, fast track program to get you ready for a secret mission. No one knows what it is, only that it's being directed from the highest levels of the army. I understand "Hap" Arnold is personally in-volved. I'm really proud of you guys. I just wish I could go with you, but Uncle Sam says I need to keep turning more of you guys out so we can go whip Hitler's scrawny ass. Good luck to you. I'll be by before you go to see you off."

"Thanks, Captain," Clyde said. "We couldn't have done it without you. Wherever we're going we'll paint your name on some of the bombs. Then you can say you were there."

"Yeah, Captain Cowan," David said. "It's been a real honor to serve under you even though you did bust our butts a bit. All for the good of the cause I'm sure. Thanks."

Clyde and David finished their coffees and headed for the barracks. The sack was going to feel awfully good after the night they'd just spent.

# 6

# Tucson

Tucson, Arizona was the quintessential, sleepy, south-western town. It was surrounded by the Sonora Desert in a valley rimmed by mile-high mountains and sitting just 50 miles north of the Mexican border town of Nogales. The lingering influence of the Spanish colonial rulers was evident in its adobe architecture, its baroque Catholic churches, and its somnolent pace of life. Spanish was as likely to be heard on its streets as was English.

Davis-Monthan was located just a few blocks southwest of the city center. Forward looking city fathers had built a commercial airport in 1927 but were farsighted enough to acquire sufficient land for expansion. After Pearl Harbor the Army Air force requisitioned the field and began a major construction effort. Within months they had created a sprawling base capable of handling the largest bombers. Davis-Monthan became one of the army's major strategic pilot training facilities.

David quickly adapted to the larger twin-engine aircraft that were used for the next level of training. The B-25 was twice as large as the AT-9 Fledgling he had flown in Victorville. The handling characteristics were similar, but the latency in their response characteristics took getting used to. The tricycle landing gear helped in avoiding the dreaded ground-loops and made the takeoffs and landings much easier. The B-25, stripped of all its excess weight, was the plane flown off the USS Hornet by Jimmy Doolittle and his valiant crews for their daring bomb run on Tokyo in April, 1942.

On his first flight in the B-25 David gripped the yoke, bowed his head, and said a little prayer for those who didn't make it safely to China. Of the eighteen planes launched from the Hornet, fifteen made it to China and one to Russia. All but three crewmen survived and were ultimately returned. Three were captured and summarily executed by the Japanese army in a fit of national rage. Sitting in the darkened cockpit of his B-25, David felt a profound kinship with those brave warriors who were launched off the deck of a heaving ship to an uncertain fate.

Clyde Nagle was assigned to the same training squadron as David. The two made frequent cross-country navigational runs together in sorties of three to six planes. Flying wing-to-wing was a nerve jangling experience for the novice pilots, especially at night with their running lights off. After several such runs achieving and maintaining formation became second nature to the brash young airmen.

Four weeks into this phase of their training they were introduced to the lumbering, cold, four-engine B-24s — the Liberator. The B-24 was first produced by Consolidated Aircraft in 1941. When the war ended in 1945 Consolidated and four other manufacturers had completed an astounding 18,000 of the heavy bombers, more than any other aircraft ever produced. Two of the gangly Fledglings could fit comfortably under the Liberator's wings with room left over for a Vultee. The Four Pratt and Whitney engines produced a combined 4800 horsepower and could propel the massive plane to an altitude of 30,000 feet with a bomb load in excess of 8,000 pounds.

She carried a crew of ten: pilot, co-pilot, navigator, bombardier, engineer, radioman and four gunners. The engineer and radio operator also served as waist gunners when the ship was under attack. The other gunners manned twin-mount turrets in the nose, the tail, on top and beneath the ponderous plane. The belly gunner had to be helped into his Plexiglas ball which was then lowered into position hydraulically. Many of these brave souls died in their little bubbles when the crew was unable to extricate them as their plane was going down. The navigator and bombardier shared cramped quarters in the Plexiglas *"greenhouse"* located below and in front of the flight deck and the nose gunner.

David spent the first week riding right seat with a seasoned instructor at the controls. He had to re-learn all the procedures that had come so easily to him in the smaller aircraft but became awkward and clumsy in this 65,000-pound leviathan. Handling the four engine levers, while trying to control the plane with the flaps and the two giant rudders in the two vertical tail fins, took almost superhuman concentration and exceptional leg strength – not to mention monitoring the multitude of gauges: altitude, airspeed, hydraulic pressure, oil pressure, manifold pressure, fuel levels, engine temperature, etc., etc. For the first time since he arrived at Maxwell Field, David began to question his ability to master the intricacies of this enormous flying machine.

Gradually, after a week of coaxing, pleading, cajoling and shouting from his instructor, David began to regain confidence in his ability to fly. His mastery of the B-24's idiosyncrasies grew each time he went aloft. After the second week his instructor climbed into the right seat.

"It's all yours, Dave. Take her up," Captain Lofgren said. "I think I've taught you everything I know about this old bird. Now, let's see what you can do with it."

David gulped as he settled into the left seat and buckled himself in. The chief of the ground crew gave the okay to start the engines and David punched the first starter button. The 1200 horsepower engine roared to life. Sequentially, the other three engines coughed and sputtered as each joined in the chorus. Satisfied that everything was in order, he took the checklist that dangled from the yoke and began calling out a list of readings critical for takeoff. Captain Lofgren checked off each one, then gave the thumbs up. David nodded to the crew chief who motioned him onto the taxiway. Five minutes later David's plane was first in line for takeoff on runway 160-left with three others waiting behind him. Clyde Nagle was sitting left seat in the fourth plane.

Beads of sweat were popping out on his forehead as David received the green light to takeoff. He pushed the four balls forward to three-quarter power and took his foot off the brakes. The plane shuddered then began rolling rapidly down the runway. At the half-mile marker Dave shoved the balls to the wall and felt a burst of acceleration as the plane gathered speed. The nose wheel lifted at the mile marker and seconds later David felt the main wheels break free. He was airborne in a B-24 for the first time under his own control. He felt exhilaration and terror simultaneously and recognized the effects of the adrenaline rush he always got at takeoff.

David made a slow left turn and headed downwind as he awaited the other three planes to join the formation. The Sonora desert stretched to the northeast horizon. The orders of the day would take the formation on a 500 mile, triangular route that included Albuquerque and Las Cruces, New Mexico, before turning westward for home. During this last leg the greenhorns got to experience flying these juggernauts on three engines, then two engines and finally a single engine. It was possible to keep the 65,000 pounds of steel and aluminum aloft on a single engine, but it took a superhuman effort to do so. David had to almost stand on the rudder control for the last fifty miles while on the single engine. His calves cramped, and it was all he could do not to cry out in pain. He heaved a huge sigh of relief when Lofgren gave the go ahead to fire up the other engines in preparation for landing. The four Liberators followed each other in to Davis-Monthan as the sun began to set behind Kitt Peak to the west.

"I've never felt such pain in my legs," Clyde said as they hobbled back to the barracks. "I didn't think I was going to make it. I hope I never have to fly one of these beasts on one engine for real. My instructor just smiled as I struggled with the rudders. He finally took pity and took some of the pressure off."

"You'd better be glad you didn't have Lofgren. He didn't touch a pedal until we had landed. I still can't feel my left leg. I'm heading straight to a hot shower. I won't be able to walk upright for a week. On the positive side, it's good to know the bird will fly on one engine, but I'm like you, I hope I never have to prove it in battle."

The Chocolate Mountains and the Cabeza Prieta bombing ranges occupied the desolate southwest corner of Arizona. The vast Sonora Desert filled the arid expanse between. Instructors often took their charges in the opposite direction and their students had to navigate their way back. It was here that the B-24 student pilots honed their navigation and bombing skills while decimating huge tracts of saguaro and organ pipe cactuses. The distant roar of the Pratt and Whitney engines, the exploding bombs, and the starkly white contrails were swallowed up in the vastness of such a wilderness, the only witnesses being the coyotes, kangaroo rats, gila monsters and other denizens of the desert.

David took his crew on missions of high and low altitude bombing and in mock air battles to sharpen the gunner's skills. On one such mission, Oscar Page, who had gone to Victorville with Clyde and David was flying left wing in a three-plane formation, with David leading and Clyde on the other wing. As they approached the range below Cabeza Prieta there was an urgent radio message from Oscar.

"Lieutenant Weiss, I'm losing my hydraulic pressure and having difficulty maintaining altitude. I'm heading back to Tucson."

"Roger, Oscar. Good luck. We'll see you back at the base."

David watched as the stricken plane banked to the left, struggling to maintain altitude. As it tried to clear the last ridge of Cabeza Prieta the plane shuddered and pitched forward in a death spiral. The ensuing fireball lit up the black Arizona night. David radioed base to send out a rescue mission knowing full well that no one could have survived such a horrific crash. The other pilots straggled back to base that evening with lumps in their throats and the sinking feeling that there, but for the grace of God, go I.


Following their fourth full week of training, David, Clyde and four other trainees were summoned to HQ for what was called a top-secret meeting. They were not to discuss it with anyone.

"Gentlemen," Colonel Oliver Pless said as they gathered in the HQ briefing room, "your mission here is being accelerated and in two weeks you will receive orders to proceed to a top-secret location for further instructions. Even I do not know what the instructions are or where you will be going. Your orders will be unsealed when you are airborne from here. This comes directly from Army Air command in Washington. I can only imagine something akin to Doolittle's raid on Tokyo is afoot. But that's pure speculation on my part.

"I am justifiably proud of what you six men have accomplished here at Davis-Monthan while under my command. I understand that your records were requested by Washington along with those of many other pilots at several other bases and that you are among those selected for this mission.

"I wish you the best as you leave here and can only add that I am envious of you. Every pilot in this man's army wants nothing more than to taste action in the field. Godspeed and good hunting."

The pilots walked back to quarters in stunned silence. No one dared utter the words on everyone's lips.

"Where are we going and what will await us there."

Clyde pulled David aside as they walked into their room.

"Come on Dave. Let's go over to the officer's club. We'll decide whether we should celebrate or commiserate after we have a couple of brews."

"Holy shit!" Clyde said as they settled onto their bar stools. "Did you know anything about this?"

"Hell, no! I was just as blindsided as you."

"What do you think it means?"

"Like the Colonel said, it must be some secret mission to bomb the Germans or the Japs somewhere they don't expect it."

"I know we've done well here," Clyde said, "but they're cutting three or four weeks off the normal training schedule. I hope we're ready for whatever it is ol' Hap has planned for us."

The news of the day fought valiantly with the four beers each had consumed, but finally at midnight the tired warriors drifted off to sleep with visions of aerial warfare dancing in their heads.

At the end of the next week the pilots were again assembled in the ops room at HQ. The base adjutant, Major Heath Slovinski entered the room carrying several large manila envelopes.

"Gentlemen," he started, "you must know by now that you are the highest rated pilots in our program. Each of you has demonstrated a mastery of the B-24 under the most adverse of flying conditions. As a a consequence, all six of you are hereby promoted to first-lieutenant. These twelve envelopes contain the names of all the pilots who finished just below your rankings. They also contain the proficiency ratings of all the crews here at Davis. Each of you will select one pilot from among the twelve

~ 296 ~

to be your co-pilot. You will also select a navigator, a bombardier, an engineer and a radioman. Then from these other envelopes you will select the four men who will make up your gunnery crew. I will need these lists by Monday morning. You will fly your final week with these men. You will get to know one another on a personal basis and decide if you can rely on every one of them to carry out your mission. Good luck."

He dropped the envelopes on the table and exited the room.

"Well, so much for a relaxed weekend," Sandy Osborn said. "I guess there's no time like the present to get the job done."

He picked up one of the pilot envelopes and began to read through the dossiers. The others gathered around and followed suit.

Monday morning found the group of six, red-eyed and frazzled, back in Major Slovinski's office with their lists in hand. There had been some wrangling over a few of the crew selections, but most had been amicably assigned.

"Good morning, gentlemen," the major said. "I see you have completed the task at hand. I am at liberty to say that you will be rendezvousing with select groups from other bases around the country. I don't know how many or where. You will assemble here on Saturday after your last day of training with your new crew. Lieutenant Weiss has been selected to command your team when you leave here. He will have sealed orders. They will be opened thirty minutes after takeoff, and he will direct your flight plan from there. You are to discuss this mission with no one. Not even your families. Those of you who have wives or girlfriends here in Tucson must make arrangements to send them home. I repeat, do not discuss these plans with anyone.

"I don't need to tell you how proud we are to be a part of this mission. I know that whatever it is, you will bring great honor and glory to the army, your family and your country. Good luck and God bless you."

In addition to Clyde and David the other four pilots were: Ed "Stumpy" McGraw, Tom "Dutch" Van de Venter, Terry Mulholland and James "Red" Powell. Like David and Clyde, all four had volunteered for the air service and all four had interrupted their schooling to enlist.

"Stumpy" McGraw was only five feet eight inches tall and weighed 180 pounds. He had earned the nickname while earning all-state honors as the fullback on the El Reno, Oklahoma football team. His football scholarship was a ticket to a career in medicine. Now that dream was on hold.

Tom Van de Venter was descended from Dutch immigrants. He hailed from Ossining, a town on the banks of the Hudson north of New York City. His ruddy cheeks, fair skin and sandy hair confirmed his ancestry. He planned to support his family's dairy farms with his Veterinarian degree from Cornell University in nearby Ithaca.

Terry Mulholland's family settled in Iowa in the late 1800's. His plans to return to the family farm after finishing a degree in agriculture at Iowa State, in Ames, were put on hold by the war. He would have been the first in his family to complete college.

"Red" Powell had watched as the sheriff tacked an eviction notice to the front door of his family's farm in Stillwater, Oklahoma in 1934. Howling dust storms and drought had ruined three successive crops. He helped his parents load their meager belongings onto a rickety Model-A truck and like thousands of others set out for a better life in California. His father ultimately found work at the Gallo Winery near Fresno. The promising and industrious young redhead caught the eye of Julio Gallo who sponsored young Red to attend the newly minted course in oenology at the University of California at Davis.

The sixty men sat expectantly on Saturday morning as Colonel Pless entered the auditorium. They had spent a busy five days getting acquainted with each other and forming the bond that would be necessary to carry them through future ordeals. There was an anticipatory hum in the room. They had no idea what great adventure lay before them, but they were now anxious to get on with it. They had flown together as a team now for sixty hours, flying cross-country courses and making bomb runs on Cabeza Prieta. They flew at 30,000 feet and at cactus-top levels, sending jackrabbits and kit foxes scurrying for their burrows. At the end of the week they were all exhausted but rated fit for combat.

That evening David slipped off to the club to make a last call to Ruth. He had hinted earlier that he might be leaving Tucson earlier than planned. Now he must break the news that the time was imminent — and the hard part was that he could not tell her where he was going, indeed did not know himself. He slipped into the booth farthest from the noisy bar. He listened to the far-off Silver Spring ring and dreaded the moment when she picked up the handset. He longed to talk to her but hated the message he must give.

"Hi," Ruth said, "I was waiting for your call. I was afraid you had gotten tied up."

"No, I'm here," he said cheerlessly. "I'm afraid I've got some bad news. We're shipping out tomorrow morning. I don't know yet where we're going, but it doesn't look like there'll be any chance of seeing you. I'm so sorry, but this all came up suddenly and I didn't want to worry you until I knew something more definite. Well I still don't know anything definite.

"I miss you so and want to see you so badly, but it looks like Uncle Sam has other ideas."

"Oh, David, I'm so sorry. I know how much you were looking forward to a few days at home. You know I was too. I guess we just have to accept that we can't do much planning until this whole mess is over. And who know how long that will be.

"On the positive side, I saw your mother last weekend and she's doing much better. She's still in contact with Henrietta Szold in Palestine but things seem to have slowed down there. She hasn't had any recent news about her sister's family. We're just hoping that no news is good news. She had a letter from Murray and he's still in training somewhere in Montana. He doesn't know yet where he'll be going when he finishes. Bernie is expecting to be sent to North Africa soon. It appears that we'll be fighting the Germans there. Your dad is doing well — still awfully busy. Mom is struggling because of dad's frequent travels. We just hope he doesn't wind up in any of the danger zones."

She kept talking to hide her tears and disappointment at David's news.

"Look Ruth, I don't know when we will see each other again, but I want you to know how much I love you. Sooner or later this nightmare will come to an end and when it does the first thing I'm going to do is marry you. I don't care what anyone else says. I wish now we had gone ahead before I left but that's water under the bridge."

"Me too, David. I didn't know a heart could break so many times. Take care of yourself and be careful. I hope you'll be able to tell me soon where you are. I worry so about you. So many of my classmates have been sent over to England. I just know there's going to be a big invasion soon and so many of them will be injured or killed. I pray every day for your safe return to me. I love you. Good night."

She hung up the receiver as the tears began to cascade down her cheeks. She didn't want David to see her like this.

"He has enough to worry about without worrying about me," she said to the silent black instrument in her hand.

# 7

# Halpro

Twenty-four mighty engines roared to life in the early morning mist hanging over Davis-Monthan. One–by-one the giant aircraft lifted off the runway and cleared the low hanging clouds. The blazing Arizona dawn seared their eyes as the sun cleared the eastern hills. David circled the field until the second group of three planes could form up on his lead then he headed into the sun. As soon as he crossed over into New Mexico he pulled the envelope stamped top-secret from his flight jacket and eagerly ripped it open.

"Brad, take the wheel while I figure out where we are going."


Brad Mathews was the pilot David had chosen to be his first officer and co-pilot. Brad was from Moultrie, Georgia, the son of a tobacco farmer. His father Tom owned and operated the Matthews tobacco warehouse in downtown Moultrie. Brad told stories of walking the long rows of tobacco pallets each fall as the auctioneer moved among them with his sing-song chant echoing through the cavernous warehouse. His was an arcane language, understood only by the buyers for the tobacco companies; Reynolds, American, Lorillard and a dozen others. A raised finger or slight nod by any of them indicated a sale.

The farmers in their bibbed overalls and faded denim work shirts rushed to read the tags affixed to their bundles. How much had their nine months of backbreaking labor yielded. Anxiously, they wondered if it would be enough to pay off their bank loans and give them a start on the next year. Farming in the depression era for most was a matter of surviving from one harvest to the next. Each winter, sharecroppers and their families loaded up their ramshackle trucks with their meager belongings and crisscrossed the countryside, shuttling from farm to farm, seeking a better opportunity. Small children, barefoot and in rags, rode atop the nondescript piles and shivered in the cold.

Brad Matthews was more privileged. He lived a relatively affluent life compared to his classmates at Moultrie High School. Tom Matthews was able to produce sufficient tobacco and row crops to support a modest living. The extra money made from the warehouse afforded his family a few of the luxuries that were denied most of the people around Moultrie. Many of Brad's classmates had dropped out of school to work and help their families make ends meet. Still others enlisted in the military and sent stipends home to their parents just to get them by. Brad entered the University of Georgia School of Agriculture in the fall of 1938.

Following Pearl Harbor, Brad felt a duty to enlist in the military. One of his high school classmates was on the Arizona when it went down. He had always wanted to fly. After School he would go to Spence Field and pester the pilots at Pitts Aviation to take him up for a spin. Those flights left him yearning for more. The Army Air Force presented an opportunity to fulfill that desire. Completing his senior year at Georgia would have to wait.

Operating Order 1942-120 DMAB
September 25, 1942

Lieutenant David Weiss is hereby ordered to take his flight of six (6) B-24 aircraft from Davis-Monthan Field, Tucson, Arizona to Fort Myers Air Base, Fort Myers, Florida. He will route the flight to Kelly Field in San Antonio, Texas for refueling. He will then enter the Gulf of Mexico airspace at Lavaca, Texas proceeding southeast to Page Field at Fort Myers, Florida where he will report to Colonel Harold A Halverson, commanding officer of the First Provisional Bomb Group.

By order of Colonel Frank Adams,

Commanding Officer, Davis-Monthan Field.

Brad Matthews had the wheel. He circled the field at Kelly and aimed the Plexiglas nose of *Baltimore Babe* at the east-west runway. He thought to himself that this was a long way from the little Pitts crop-dusters he flew at Spence Field. He listened as David checked off all the critical gauge readings and then he set his glide slope. The screech of the tires and the puffs of blue smoke as they met the runway attested to another good landing. He taxied the plane to the apron by the control tower to watch the other five planes make their landings and join his.

The crew unbuckled their harnesses and wriggled out of their parachutes. David toggled the switch that opened the bomb bay doors and then dropped to the tarmac. The other nine crew members followed in short order. There was all manner of bending and stretching to relieve their cramped muscles. When all six crews had assembled, two gray army buses arrived to transport them to the base mess hall. They devoured a meal of pork chops, mashed potatoes, green beans and biscuits, all washed down with that ubiquitous southern beverage, sweet iced tea.

The flight had covered the 800 miles from Tucson in less than four hours, cruising at 215 miles-per-hour. They had another 1100 miles to Fort Myers. It was after noon local time when the crews climbed back into their refueled planes and took off for the second leg of their five-hour, 1100 mile journey to Fort Myers. With the time difference they would arrive in Fort Myers around six.

"Okay guys, listen up."

David used the secret frequency assigned to the mission.

"Now that we've left Kelly I can tell you where we are going. Our orders are to fly to Fort Myers, Florida where we'll rendezvous with several other B-24 groups. Where we go after that, I don't know. We are to report to a Colonel Harry Halverson for further instructions. You can be sure they haven't flown us all the way to Florida for our health. I remind you that we are still under top secret orders and you are not to contact anyone when we get to Fort Myers."

Spurred by the success of Jimmy Doolittle's raid on Japan from the decks of the USS Hornet, General Hap Arnold was looking for other ways to stick a finger in the eye Japan while simultaneously boosting the sagging morale on the home front. Following the failure of two earlier attempts to move heavy bombers to the Chinese theater, Arnold authorized Halpro early in 1942 and placed Colonel Harry Halverson in charge. Harry Halverson enlisted in the army during WWI and rose through the ranks. He was commissioned a 2nd Lieutenant and assigned to flight training. In 1924 he participated in the first globe-circling flight.

The Kuomintang forces of Chiang Kai-shek controlled several major airfields in southeast China. Arnold thought that if he could get his heavy bombers to those fields, they would have the range to reach the Japanese Islands. He needed a seasoned, veteran commander to lead such an ambitious and daring undertaking. Colonel Harry "Hurry-Up" Halverson, at times considered by many of his peers to be too impulsive and brooding, was nevertheless considered to be a good field commander by Arnold; one who could get the job done and motivate the men under him. That strong, can-do attitude was the primary quality that drew Arnold to choose him for this quixotic mission.

Order #63 which became known as Halpro for *The Halverson Project* gave the mercurial colonel the daunting task of assembling 24 B-24 bombers and flying them half-way around the world. They would not take the normal, direct, great-circle route across the Atlantic, but rather a tortuous path from Florida to Brazil, then a hazardous crossing of the south Atlantic to the bulge of Africa. From there they would traverse the vast African continent before crossing the Arabian Peninsula, Iran, Afghanistan, India and Burma, with the final push being the death-defying climb over the Himalayas to China. It was not an expedition for the faint-of-heart.

B-24s had been arriving in Fort Myers for several days. The Davis-Monthan contingent arrived last. No sooner had the crews checked into their quarters than Colonel Halverson summoned the 24 command pilots to his headquarters for their first briefing. David sat down next to Clyde Nagle as Halverson burst into the room.

"Attention!" shouted the adjutant.

Everyone jumped to attention as Halverson strode across to the raised platform. He rolled a large map down from the ceiling.

"At ease, gentlemen," he said. "You twenty-four men have been chosen to lead one of the most daring missions the United States has ever attempted. I have been ordered by General Arnold to take this force half-way around the world. When we get to our final destination in eastern China, we are going to bomb the shit out of Imperial Japan."

Every jaw in the room went slack. There had been hundreds of wild guesses as to the purpose of this mission. Not one of them had envisioned an attack on Japan. Most thought they were opening a second air-front in Egypt to go after Erwin Rommel and his *"Afrika Korps"* in northern Egypt. The buzz in the room grew to a crescendo before Halverson raised his hand for quiet.

"I know this must come as a great shock to you. General Arnold wants to build on the positive effects of Jimmy Doolittle's raid on Tokyo. The feeling is that if we can launch attacks on the Japanese Islands from the air bases in eastern China, we can damage their morale, disrupt their manufacturing, and perhaps draw some of their forces back from the south where our boys are taking a shellacking. As most of you are aware, General Mac-Arthur had to abandon the Philippines and has moved his command to Australia. Now there is a good chance the Japs are going to invade there as well. We need to do everything possible to prevent that. Halpro is one of the tactics we're using. We need to take the pressure off MacArthur until the army can get reinforcements to him. Needless to say, this would be a great shot-in-the-arm for the Chinese who are trying to hold out against the Japanese army."

"Now for the details; in addition to the full complement of ten men on each plane, there will be two mechanics. These men will be the nucleus of the ground crew we must set up when we arrive. In addition we will have Dr. Lachlan Currie on board. He is President Roosevelt's adviser to the Chinese government. General P.H. Chang of the Chinese Air Force will also be joining us, following his consultations in Washington. There will also be a contingent of intelligence officers who are tasked with establishing a network in eastern China to assess the Japanese strategy for the entire region.

"We will carry sufficient supplies for three months in China. After that we'll be relying on General Claire Chenault's Flying Tigers to ferry supplies to us over the Himalayan Hump from Burma. Conditions over those supply lines will be tenuous at best. We can rely on our Chinese hosts for some help but I'm afraid not much. They are constrained as it is. That means we will need to conserve our supplies to the utmost when we get there.

"We leave at dawn three days hence. Make sure your aircraft are in tip-top mechanical condition. Repair facilities are few and far between once we take off from Brazil. We'll be flying over a lot of uncharted water and across equatorial Africa. Do not divulge any of this information to your crews until we are in the air. The fewer who know, the fewer who can blab.

"Now make sure you, your crews and your planes are ready and rested. It's going to be a tough trip and everyone needs to be at the top of their game. That's why you all were chosen. You and your crews comprise the finest air contingent the US Army Air Force has ever assembled. There'll be a final briefing at three p.m. the day before we leave. Go see to your crews and planes and get some rest. You're going to need fully charged batteries for this adventure. Dismissed."

David and the other Tucson pilots shook their heads in disbelief as they trudged over to the officer's club in stunned silence. Stumpy McGraw was first to speak.

"How the hell do we get from here to China? That's got to be at least 10,000 miles, and as far as I know there are no reliable charts covering most of that route. And, where the fuck do we get fuel. Those gas sucking bastards don't run on water or air. I don't recall Esso or Texaco having any service stations along the equator. This sounds like a suicide mission to me."

"Well we know Chenault got his planes over there somehow and is still flying them," Clyde said. "We have to assume that Arnold's logistics people have worked the details."

"You know what assume means don't you," McGraw said. "It makes an <u>ass</u> out of <u>u</u> and <u>me</u>."

"Think about it this way, Stumpy," David jumped in. "You're getting a chance to do something that's never been done before. If we pull this off we'll go down in history with Doolittle."

"Or we'll just go down," Stumpy harrumphed.

"Keep your hat on until we get all the details," Clyde said.

"I agree with that," David said. "Let's go have a beer and get ready for this little jaunt."

# 8

# Leap of Faith

"We'll lift off at dawn tomorrow," Halverson advised the gathering in the staff conference room. Our route takes us over Cuba and several Caribbean islands. We'll land in Trinidad just off the coast of Venezuela to refuel. We'll overnight there and resume our mission at dawn the next day. It's 1800 miles to Trinidad. We'll get there about six in the evening, their time, cruising at about 180 knots. That'll save fuel and reduce wear on the engines. Remember they have to carry us all the way to China."

"After Trinidad our next stop is Natal, Brazil, another 1800 miles. Natal is located on the part of Brazil that juts out into the Atlantic, making it the closest point to West Africa. We'll skirt along the Guiana coast, passing abeam of the Amazon delta and arriving in Natal at the end of the second day. We plan a two-day layover in Natal to ensure that our planes are in tip-top shape for the hop across to Accra on the Gold Coast. From there we proceed to Khartoum in Sudan where we'll pick up our orders for the flight to China.

"Colonel McGuire and I will be flying with Major Kalberer in "Babe *the Blue Ox*." Colonel McGuire will now brief you on the flight formations and your positions. Any other questions you can take up with him. See you in the morning."

The bleary-eyed crews loaded aboard their planes at dawn. "*The Blue Ox*" took off as scheduled but immediately experienced trouble with its landing gear. The right wheel would not fully retract. Halverson contemplated turning back but decided instead to plow ahead with the crippled plane. His maximum speed was 135 knots, which was slow and extremely inefficient. Stall speed for the B-24 was 110 knots. He ordered the other planes to proceed in formation to Trinidad. The command plane would straggle along behind and get the wheel corrected there.

Halverson and his command crew arrived well after dark, tired and bedraggled after so many hours aloft. The ground crews attacked the gimpy wheel with a vengeance but gave up in utter frustration after several hours. Halverson stewed all night over the impasse then decided to proceed to Natal in hopes that the mechanics there could solve the problem.

The B-24 armada lifted off from Port-au-Spain at dawn with full tanks and a furious commander, tagging along behind. The broad expanse of the Orinoco River delta spread out like a gigantic green fan before them. It melded into the impenetrable jungles of the Guianas. By noontime, they gazed down in awe at the mighty Amazon as it emptied 2,000 miles of silt-filled water into the Atlantic. Radio operators strained to pick up the signals from the navigation beacons at Natal as the formation skimmed along the virginal coastlines of Brazil's northeastern provinces. Weary pilots lowered their landing gear just as the sun began to disappear beyond the interminable horizon of jungle. Three hours later *"Blue Ox"* limped into Natal dragging its right wheel like a wounded albatross.

"Halverson ordered everyone to stand down until *"The Blue Ox"* was repaired. The air base at Natal was slowly getting up to speed as the Air Corp's jumping off point to Africa, but it was still woefully understaffed. The newly formed Ferrying Command was beefing up its capabilities there as rapidly as possible, despite the Brazilian government's resistance. Many in high military and political positions resisted stationing of foreign troops on Brazilian soil — despite the increasing threats to Brazil from German U-boats off their shores. It was also an excuse to extort maximum military aid from Uncle Sam.

The crews were granted passes to go into sleepy Natal on the second day. Major Dumphey called the crews together for a lecture on the dangers lurking outside the gates.

"I know that some of you guys have engaged in sexual intercourse and some of you haven't," he began. "I'm here to tell you that if you get involved with any of the local prostitutes, there's a good chance of contracting a venereal disease. Now, you've all seen the movies where this guy's dick swells up the size of an oilcan. I can't tell you that will happen to you, but I can tell you, that if you don't use a condom, chances are twenty times greater that it will. So, if you don't want to pay a visit to the *chancre clanker* in a week or so you'd better help yourself to some of these condoms."

Natal lies on the eastern edge of an arid plain that is plagued with periodic droughts. Dust wells up around one's boots and swirls in the air. It reminded David of his days at Davis-Monthan in Tucson. The populace was extremely poor, and they latched onto the influx of rich American GIs as a new and ready source of income. Native artisans hawked their local merchandise from rickety stalls lining the street into the base. Closer to the center of town, ladies-of-the-night displayed their wares from red draped windows overlooking the sidewalks.

*Clube Praia de Natal* fronted the most beautiful beach many of the airmen had ever seen. Clyde picked up a bar menu and scanned the limited drink offering. He spoke no Portuguese and attempted to ask the bartender what a *cayparinna* was as he pointed to the drink on the menu.

"Senhor, una Caipirinha es una bebida com cachaca, azucar y limon," the bartender tried to explain.

Sergeant Sandoval Ruiz from El Paso overheard the conversation and interjected.

"Pardon me sir, I don't speak the local lingo but it's pretty close to Spanish. I think he said it's made with rum, sugar and lemon."

"Thanks, Sarge, I think I'll have one of those. How about you Dave?

"Sure," he said.

Cachaca is a rum made from pure cane juice, not from molasses, as in Cuba. It is two to three times more potent than regular rum. The bartender spooned some sugar into a glass and dropped in several slices of lime. He muddled the mixture with a pestle then added ice and two ounces of cachaca. He handed the caiparinha drink to Clyde.

Three caiparinhas and a plate of greasy, linguica sausage later, both Clyde and David made a beeline for the head – from which loud retching noises arose. Minutes later both officers slinked back into the bar with sheepish grins on their faces.

"What the hell was that?" Clyde asked. "I feel like something the cat dragged in."

"Welcome to 150 proof rum fellows," Brad Mathews said. "These folks may call this stuff cachaca but back home in Moultrie we call it *cane buck*. Folks around home make their own molasses from sugar cane. We call it syrup. The cane juice is boiled in a large vat. While it's condensing the foam on top is scooped off and poured into a cloth-covered barrel. You let that stuff sit for a couple of weeks then run it through a pot still and you get some mighty fine white lightning. We always gave it to the sharecroppers who work the mill. Come Saturday night there was some real celebrating going on down on the other side of the tracks. I tried some once. Nearly burnt my throat out. I ain't touched it since."

"You mean you sat there and let us drink this stuff and didn't say a word," Clyde said. "Why, I ought to punch you in the nose."

"Hey, I reckon both of you are big boys. It ain't my place to tell you what to drink or not drink. Besides, you seemed to be enjoying it."

"Well it tasted a hell of a lot better going down than it did coming up I'll tell you." Clyde said. "I don't know about the rest of you but I think I've had enough of this Brazilian high-life. I'm going to head back to base and hit the sack."

The temperature was already approaching 80 degrees when the crews were rousted out at dawn. A cooling breeze was rustling through the palm trees, and the plop of an occasional falling coconut added color to the tropical scene. Hardy stragglers from a night on the town in Natal checked through the gate. They were disheveled, groggy, and bleary-eyed. Several would have lasting memories of their night with the *mestizas*. Latrine visits suddenly became very painful for those who ignored Dr. Dumphey's advice.

The efforts of the mechanics in Natal were as infuriating as they had been in Port-au-Prince. Despite the higher level of skill among the Natal crew, they still could not get the recalcitrant wheel to retract properly. Halverson decided to send the rest of the squadron on to Accra while Kalberer called in reinforcements to work on "*The Blue Ox*."

Twenty-Three B-24s lifted off from Natal, forming the inaugural flight of American aviators across the South Atlantic to Africa. The expanse of ocean between Natal and Accra was uncharted territory. The flight route maps were sketchy at best. The flight leader set his dead-reckoning for Accra and trusted that his navigator could factor in the winds for the necessary course corrections along the way. Amazingly, after a debilitating twelve-hour flight, the headlands above San Pedro, Cote-de-Ivoire, welcomed them to Africa. San Pedro was near the Liberia-Ivory Coast border. Four-hundred miles later the runway lights at the Pan American Airway's passenger terminal in Accra came into view. There were no military airfields in the area.

Plans called for a two-day layover in Accra to rest the crews and to attend the planes while awaiting Halverson. However, the Pan Am station agent was adamant that they refuel and leave immediately. He was concerned that if the Germans in the area discovered the American contingent they would bomb the base. After only a few hours rest and rudimentary care for their planes the pilots lifted off at dawn for another 2400-mile leg to Khartoum in Anglo-Egyptian Sudan. Halverson would have to catch them there.

As luck would have it, a tropical cyclone was forming over central Africa and the expedition was headed right for it. The planes became scattered as they passed over the jungles of central Nigeria. The weather prevented the navigators from getting good star sightings and there were no radio-navigation beacons in that region. Each pilot was on his own to claw his way blindly across the inhospitable skies of Equatorial Africa. Meantime, Kalberer took off from Natal with an unrepaired landing gear, to limp across the Atlantic. It was an extremely gutsy move on Halverson's part – or else he was insane.

The first planes to clear the cyclone gazed down on the trackless wastes of jungle, with no landmarks to guide them. The geographical survey maps they brought were useless. The navigators were left to their own devices in plotting a dead-reckoning course to Khartoum.

"Hey McNally, where the hell are we?" David shouted down to his navigator, who was feverishly trying to get a fix on his sextant. He passed his chart up to Matthews with a vaguely circled area within which he thought they were.

"I can't make out where we are from this," Matthews said.

David took the chart and said, "I think I've got it!"

"Okay then," McNally chimed in, "Be sure to mark the chart correctly."

Clyde was a few miles ahead when he began to notice dark patches in the jungle below his wings.

"Hey navigator, what's the highest mountain around here?"

"Mount Marra at 3,070."

"Holy shit," he said, "this is a damn French chart. Those altitudes are in meters."

Clyde yanked the stick back into his lap and pushed the balls to the wall. The plane just barely cleared the peak.

"Get on the radio to the rest of the guys and make sure they realize those dimensions are in meters," he said to the radio operator. "We don't want anybody making a hole in the jungle down there."

Slowly, the vast green expanse transitioned into broad savannahs on the eastern side of the mountains. Great herds of wildebeests darted in all directions at the sound of the engines. Zebras, giraffes, elephants and an entire African menagerie that they had only read about, cavorted below them. The unfolding spectacle was something none of them had ever dreamed of in their mundane civilian pursuits.

Most of the planes resumed a hap-hazard formation as they approached the Pan-Am base at Wadi Seidna, on the west bank of the Nile, just north of Khartoum. An RAF officer asked the first navigator in how close they had come to their ETA.

"Two miles off the heading and one minute early," he replied, fudging his calculations by 75 minutes, prompting the Brit to twist his mustache in admiration.

Halpro had navigated 8000 miles over hostile seas, uncharted jungles and trackless deserts, through storms and starless nights, carrying a warehouse of food and a maintenance depot in their bellies, to find this small outpost in east Africa.

Meanwhile, Major Kalberer struggled as he coaxed his crippled plane into Abidjan on the Ivory Coast with his fuel gauges reading zero. Still dragging his right wheel, he refueled and struck out for Khartoum. Once again, running low on fuel, he landed at El Fasher, an RAF base in the Sudanese desert. He implored the base commander to give him 500 gallons of fuel to get the plane to his destination.

"Major, you must understand, every pint of petrol coming into this godforsaken base is ferried on camel's backs, 800 miles across the desert.

Finally, after much cajoling from Halverson, and acknowledging the strategic importance of the mission, he relented and gave Kalberer the fuel. The base commander had mistakenly assumed they were on their way to Egypt to help disrupt Rommel before he could destroy Viscount Montgomery's tank forces.

# 9

# Khartoum

Once again Kalberer clawed his way aloft with his stricken plane for the final leg to Khartoum. He lumbered into Wadi Saiad to rousing cheers. When Halverson finally rejoined his happy band of warriors he was greeted with a great outpouring of hospitality by his British hosts. He took advantage of the lavish welcome to requisition as many supplies for the trip on to China, as the British could afford. Each man drew a full outfit of the standard British desert regalia, right down to the green cashmere knee stockings and the ivory cigarette holder. They were a sight to behold in the Khartoum nightclub which was run by three expatriate Vietnamese women. The men danced the night away, stopping only long enough to pull up their sagging, cashmere hose.

The Liberators were forced to stay in Khartoum longer than planned because the Germans were raiding the airfields in Egypt where they needed to land for refueling. The Axis powers were ascendant on all fronts.

The Bataan peninsula in the Philippines had fallen to the Japanese. Its defenders were now isolated on the island of Corregidor. Their surrender was only a matter of time. Hundreds would die on the infamous death march to Manila.

General Vinegar Joe Stilwell was in retreat in Burma.

Sevastopol in Ukraine was under siege and the Baku oil fields, needed by Hitler for his war machine, were in dire peril.

The lone bright spot during that dismal period was that U.S. Admiral Fletcher had defeated Japan's Admiral Shigiyoshi Inoue at the Battle of the Coral Sea, marking a turning point in the battle for the South Pacific.

"Damn it," General Halverson spat, "we can't just sit here on our asses waiting for the situation to clear. We need to train and keep morale up."

He ordered all the planes to fly practice missions. Captain Ulysses Nero, who had flown with Billy Mitchell in WWI, was in charge of maintenance. The heavy mission schedule, the scouring dust, and the lack of maintenance spares, made his life a living hell. Even his magic touch wasn't sufficient to keep all the birds in the air. Ultimately, only 12 of the original 24 were airworthy.

"General," the orderly said, "there's a cable from head-quarters, **<u>for your eyes only</u>**."

*"General Halverson*

*It is with deep regret that I must cancel Operation 63. I have received word that the airfields in Chekiang that were to be your base in China have been overrun by the Japanese army. Have your crews stand down until you receive further orders.*

*General Arnold*

When word got to the men, they were totally disheartened, having geared themselves up to redeem Pearl Harbor with strikes on Tokyo.

Meanwhile, the United States declared war on Bulgaria, Hungary and Romania, after their fall to Hitler. Their capitulation gave the Axis powers access to the abundant oil flowing from Romania's oil fields in Ploesti. Hitler needed the fuel for his insatiable war machine as it expanded all across Europe. With war declared on Romania, the U.S. was now free to attack those fields.

The directive from Air Force headquarters in Washington was brief and to the point.

*General Halverson,*

*You are hereby instructed to plan and execute an attack on the Astro-Romano oil fields in Ploesti, Romania.*

*General Arnold*

He immediately called his command staff together to relay the new directive.

"Gentlemen," he began "we have been handed a new assignment. It is to fly our fleet of B-24s across Egypt, across the Mediterranean, across Asia Minor and attack the oilfields located in Ploesti, Romania."

He waited for their reaction. Most of them didn't know where Romania was, much less Ploesti. This was self-evident on their puzzled faces.

"General, where the hell is Ploesti, Romania?"

"I thought you might ask that," he said.

He pulled down a map of the eastern Mediterranean region.

"Ploesti is on the southern Caucasus plateau, northwest of the capital of Romania, Bucharest. The oil fields around Ploesti supply nearly one-third of Hitler's fuel. Cut off the flow of oil out of Ploesti and we can deal a crippling blow to the Third Reich. It would deprive Rommel of fuel for his tanks and give Ike and Montgomery a chance to drive the Germans out of Africa.

"But sir, by my calculation that's well over a 3,000-mile round trip. There's no way we could ever do that with a full bomb load."

"Headquarters recognizes that. They've arranged for us to move our planes up to a base on the Great Bitter Lake east of Cairo. From there it's only 2300 miles round trip."

"Big Deal," Lieutenant Rang said. "It's still at the ragged edge of our range."

"Bear with me Lieutenant. We will be equipping each plane with several extra barrels of fuel, which should allow us to make it there and back. The top brass is negotiating with the Russians to allow us to go on to Tiflis, Georgia, to refuel before heading back home. I haven't heard yet what they've decided.

"Success at Ploesti would also stop their advance on Azerbaijan and the Baku oilfields on the Caspian Sea. In other words, a successful raid on Ploesti would kill several birds with the same stone. Washington thinks it's worth the gamble."

"Yeah, it's not their ass that's on the line," grumbled an anonymous voice in the back.

Harry Hopkins, an aide to FDR, as well as high ranking officials in England had been lobbying for a strike against Ploesti for months. The strategic nature of the city was the subject of intense study at the U.S. war colleges and in top secret meetings in world capitals. Many said it was impossible. No allied bomber had the fuel and weapons capacity to reach Ploesti and return to base. Regardless, that opinion was disregarded, and Halverson was ordered to proceed with the mission.

Sam Nero painted fake ingignia on the thirteen planes that would undertake the mission. They were then flown to the RAF base at Fayid on the Great Bitter Lake. Luftwaffe planes had raided the base four times in the preceding two weeks. Halverson was taking a calculated gamble that he could get in and out of Fayid before the next attack.

Rommel's forces were rolling across the deserts of western Egypt. The fall of Cairo seemed eminent. The free French force at Bir Hacheim had fallen. Hitler was so certain of the fall of Cairo that he had reserved two floors of the Shepheard Hotel for the surrender of North Africa to his onslaught.

Washington pleaded with the Russians to allow Halverson's planes to fly on to Georgia. All they got from the Kremlin was silence. The pilots were being asked to fly the longest combat mission in history, over blacked out territories, at night, and in direct contradiction of the U.S. daylight bombing policy. None had ever dropped a bomb or engaged an enemy aircraft or flown through antiaircraft flak. The thirteen pilots were using antiquated charts and being asked to avoid flying over certain neutral territories. It was a recipe for disaster.

The British had received the first contingent of B-24s and had a longer history with their idiosyncrasies. Kalberer asked one of their mechanics to take a look at his landing gear. The mechanic emerged after a few minutes, grease smeared across his forehead.

"Sir, it's no wonder she won't retract all the way. She's got the wrong bloody strut. I'll have a look in the stores to see if we have one."

He was back in a flash and helped Nero's boys change the faulty strut.

"Sergeant, I can't tell you how grateful I am for your help. We've been chasing this problem all across Africa and the Atlantic. Thank God we ran into you."

That afternoon at three, an RAF officer briefed the pilots for the mission. He warned them that the Germans had erected a fake village resembling Ploesti about ten miles east of the target. The course he had plotted for them took them across the Mediterranean to a lighthouse in the Aegean Sea off Turkey. A neutral country.

"Gentlemen," he continued, "you are not – I repeat – not to enter Turkish neutral territory."

Everyone in the room was stunned. A quick check of the map clearly demonstrated that the most direct route to the target was over the heart of Turkey. This detour would add hundreds of miles to an already dicey adventure.

"You will swing out to the west and skirt Turkey in this fashion," he gestured, "then turn east to the Romanian port of Constanta on the Black Sea. Head west following the pipeline from there to the Danube. Then follow the river inland until you see a fork and a diamond shaped island in the river. From there it's a northern heading to the Astro-Romana refinery."

The pilots were flabbergasted. Not only were they being asked to fly an impossible mission but they were tying one hand behind their backs. An American officer took the podium to conclude the briefing.

"This will be a momentous mission," he said, "and can have a tremendous effect on the outcome of the war. You are to bomb from 30,000 feet and then land in Ramadi, Iraq."

"This briefing is straight out of *The* Wonderful *Wizard of Oz*," one participant remarked. "Many of our ships can never make thirty thousand feet, especially with an extra bomb bay tank and six five-hundred pounders in the belly. And range? The calculated round trip is 2600 miles. Even if we stripped the bombs and put two tanks in the bomb bay we'd never make it back over the route we've been given."

Bernard Rang, the mission navigator, and a civil air transport veteran, called a meeting of all the navigators without the knowledge of General Halverson. He pinned a National Geographic Society map of the Middle East on the wall.

"It can't be done. If we have to veer around Turkey, nobody will make it to Iraq. But for God's sake don't land in Turkey or you'll be interned for the duration of the war. If your pilot insists, because of your fuel situation, try to make it to Aleppo,

Syria, just south of the Turkish border. Or try to hit the Euphrates River and take it to Ramadi."

Colonel Halverson suddenly interrupted the unsanctioned meeting. Everyone leaped to attention. The colonel walked over to the National Geographic map and drew his finger down a well-worn crease running from north to south. The line was at 30 degrees east longitude running from Egypt through Turkey to the Black Sea.

"Can we help it if the National Geographic put this line through Turkey. Furthermore, I suggest that we bomb at fourteen-thousand feet."

The colonel wheeled about and left the room with a big smirk on his face. There was a collective sigh of relief.

"A penny for your thoughts, Dave," Clyde said. You've been in your own world now for the last couple of days. What's bothering your old boy? Thinking about Ruth?'

"Nothing like that Clyde. Ever since I learned that we'd be bombing Ploesti, I've been sick to my stomach. I never told you this, but I have relatives there. When Hitler began to round up Jews in Germany, several of my father's family fled Belarus and moved to Ploesti. My Uncle Levi, who is the oldest, is a high-level manager at one of the refineries and my Aunt Rebecca is a nurse at the hospital. I know I have a duty to follow orders, but I also have a duty to God and family. If I knew that I might kill my own flesh and blood I don't know if I can do it."

"I'm sorry Dave. I didn't mean to be so flip. I had no idea."

"No way you could've known. Don't worry about it."

"What are you going to do? You can't just back out of the mission. Why don't you go to see the chaplain? Maybe he can help."

"I thought about that, but he's Catholic and I don't know how he feels about counseling a Jewish kid."

"Hey, all chaplains are first and foremost God's representatives. They know there are many religions in the military, but it's their job to represent them all. Besides, maybe he'll have a different slant on the problem than a rabbi. Give it a shot. You don't have anything to lose."

"Okay. I guess I will. Thanks Clyde."

David entered the small room that had been secured for a chapel. Father McNamee was busily reviewing the sermon he was preparing for Sunday.  He looked up as David entered the tent.

"Good morning Lieutenant. Come in and have a seat. What can I do for you?"

David twisted his cap and hesitated. This was proving very difficult for him.

"Don't fret son, I'm not going to bite you."

"I know Father, but I have a rather unusual situation and I'm not sure it's appropriate to ask you to help."

"Let's start by getting acquainted. My name is Robert McNamee, Captain, chaplain and priest, in that order. My first responsibility is to the men in this command regardless of faith or creed. And you?"

"I am Lieutenant David Weiss, a pilot, a plane commander and a Jew with a moral dilemma."

"Tell me about it and let's see what we can do."

David re-told the same story he had related to Clyde. When he finished he looked into the chaplain's eyes hoping to find relief from his torment. Captain McNamee leaned back and closed his eyes in contemplation. After a few seconds he responded.

"Son, these questions have confronted man since the beginning of time. When is it right to knowingly sacrifice a life in exchange for a greater good? And who decides that greater good? When can the end really justify the means used to achieve that end? When does one life become more valuable than any other?

"I don't know that anyone has ever received a completely satisfactory answer to those questions. I can only offer this counsel. Whenever I see the terrible decisions that war forces upon us, I turn to the bible for answers. There are two particular passages that give me solace. One comes from the Old Testament, your bible, and one from the New Testament, the Christian bible. Being Jewish, the first passage may carry more meaning for you. As a Catholic, the second gives me strength.

"In Genesis God instructed Abraham to take his family out of Chaldea and to go down to Canaan where he would be the leader of God's chosen people. One day God told Abraham to take his son Isaac and to go up to Mount Moriah, where he was to build an altar.

"When Abraham arrived at the appointed spot he erected the altar. God told him that he was to sacrifice his beloved son Isaac as testament to his faith in Jehovah. If he truly loved God, he would not hesitate to follow God's command, no matter how difficult it may be. Abraham left his servants and took Isaac up to the altar.

"Where is the sacrificial lamb, father?" Isaac asked.

"God will provide the offering in due time." Abraham said.

"Abraham turned to his beloved son in agony and tears and told him of God's choice for the sacrifice. In obedience to his father and God, Isaac submitted himself for the sacrifice. Having placed his son on the altar, and with his knife raised, Abraham beseeched God once more to spare his son.

"Before the knife could descend an angel of the Lord appeared and stayed Abraham's hand, telling him to not harm Isaac, that he had proved his love and allegiance to God.

"Simultaneously, there was a noisy thrashing about in a nearby bush where a ram had become entangled. Abraham took the ram and placed it on the sacrificial altar in the stead of his son. He had passed God's test and been spared the most horrible agony any father could endure. God had provided the sacrifice.

"The second source of comfort comes from the story of the Passion. In this instance God replicated the Abraham and Isaac story by choosing his own son, Jesus Christ, as the sacrifice. He was chosen to die a horrible death by crucifixion, so that all mankind could be freed from the death of sin. Christ was offered up so that man could have everlasting life.

"You see, Jesus knew from the beginning that he was to be the ultimate sacrifice. He spoke at the Passover meal in the Upper Room, our Last Supper, of going to prepare a place for us. In the Sermon on the Mount he had told us what we needed to do in order to join him. We know there are many references in the Old Testament of a Messiah who would come to free us. Therefore, from the foundation of the world, we know He was part of God's plan.

~ 330 ~

"For me, Jesus' sacrifice defines my life. Knowing he was going to die on that cross, he went into the wilderness for forty days and forty nights and wrestled with the temptation to save himself, to exercise the free will God gives to all men. In the end, like Abraham, he surrendered to God's will. He returned to his disciples one last time, as they waited in Gethsemane, having prayed for God to remove this bitter cup from him, but in the end he submitted to God the Father's will and went to the cross in order to fulfill his destiny, and to grant us the opportunity for everlasting life. He became God's sacrificial lamb.

"Both Abraham and Jesus could have said no to God. They could have turned their backs on Him in order to spare themselves great agony. Yet they both chose to obey God. They chose to fulfill God's plan for them.

"For his reward, Abraham became the Father of God's Chosen People, ancestor to Jesus. Jesus' reward was to set his people free from the death of sin, and to sit on the right hand of God.

"So, you see David, by following God's will, both men were simply fulfilling His plan for the world. If either had faltered, the world as we know it would not exist. The lesson I draw from that is, if we do the right thing, as God leads us to see the right, then we too are fulfilling our part of His plan and however it turns out, we can accept it with a clean conscience.

"I don't know if this helps you any but as I said, I take solace in knowing that throughout the ages, men mightier than I have faced hard decisions and ultimately God's will was done."

David sat with his head bowed, tearful. After a few seconds he looked up at Father McNamee.

"Thank you sir, you've helped more than you know. At least I can now face this knowing there is someone else who understands."

Father McNamee stood and placed his hand on David's shoulder.

"May God go with you my son, and may He give you His peace, Amen."

"Well, did he help?" Clyde asked when David returned.

"I can tell you that I feel much better about it. He helped me to see my predicament in the overall scheme of things, and I think I can live with that."

"I heard that Father McNamee is holding an interfaith service at seven this evening. What say we see what he has to say? Can't hurt to have the man upstairs in our corner."


The first U.S. Air Force mission to bomb continental Europe took off at 22:30 that evening. The last plane in the formation was *Babe the Blue Ox.* Formation flying was impossible at night. Each crew was on its own as they streaked across a moonless, starlit, Mediterranean sky. The lead plane hit the coast on the mark and the pilot took her up to the sub-stratosphere for the transit over Turkey. The unbelievably cold air at that altitude was forty below zero. David asked his co-pilot to go back and check on his crew. The tail-gunner, Henry Gibson, was slumped over his gun, unconscious. His oxygen mask had frozen with the moisture from his breath. Brad swapped out his tank and revived him. For the next four hours, either the pilot or the co-pilot made regular sweeps of the plane.

A last-minute communiqué came through to the Great Bitter Lake headquarters advising that the planes could re-fuel in Georgia. It was too late. The planes were maintaining radio silence. They never received the message.

Kalberer could see the lights of Constanta reflecting off the Black Sea. No other planes were in sight as he completed a left bank and headed up the Danube. Heavy rains had turned the placid blue river into a sea of roiling red mud. It bore little resemblance to the thin blue line on the charts. The fork and the island were lost in the turgid waters. They would have to use dead reckoning for their northerly run.

One-by-one the other planes fell in behind the *Blue Ox* and began searching for landmarks. The navigators handed up their hastily marked-up charts from their greenhouses and prepared to open the bomb bay doors. The bombardiers had been left behind as a weight saving maneuver.

Bright flashes from below confirmed they were near the target. Anti-aircraft bursts filled the air. Puffy black clouds preceded sprays of flak hitting the fuselages. Each plane took its turn over the target, unburdening their load of five-hundred pounders before banking sharply and high-tailing it for home.

*Little Eva's* fuel system had frozen over Constanta. Three engines went silent and were feathered. The pilot dropped his payload over the harbor, trying to take out as much shipping as possible. He turned and headed back toward Turkey.

*The Blue Ox* landed in Aleppo, Syria. Kalberer drafted Clyde Nagel's *Blue Tick Hound* squeezing every last drop from his empty fuel tanks. Both planes were immediately surrounded by French troops with sub-machine guns. They identified the B-24s as American despite Nero's clumsy attempts at disguise.

A German Messerschmitt chased *Little Eva* to a new field in Turkey, her single engine breathing fumes. Ironically, the German was out of fuel and had to land also. Both crews were interned, as well as the two that landed in Ankara. Most of the remaining planes, including *Baltimore Girl* piloted by David Weiss, made it to Ramadi, Iraq. Twelve of the thirteen planes made it to the Astro-Romano refinery target.

Four crews were interned in Turkey. The rest, after refueling, trickled back to their base on the Great Bitter Lake. Halverson's plane was the last to return.

When compared to Doolittle's foray into Japan, the Ploesti raid was a stunning success. Doolittle had lost all his B-25s and five men. Yet Halverson's raid received none of the publicity back home that had accompanied Doolittle's mission. In fact, the army did not even release a communiqué. In an attempt to cover up the attack, the Vichy radio attributed the planes to a flight of lend-lease aircraft being ferried to Russia. A brief article in an Ankara newspaper alluded to some unidentified planes landing in Turkish territory. In the absence of any denial from Washington, Germany's Joseph Goebbels cranked up his propaganda machine claiming the planes had been forced down by the Turks after dropping propaganda leaflets over their territory.

One intrepid reporter for *The New York Times* unearthed the story and ran it as a six-column feature on the front page of the paper. The banner headline read,

**U.S. BOMBERS STRIKE BLACK SEA AREA. BASE IS A MYSTERY.**

Washington maintained its silence.

Few Romanians were aware of the raid. Bucharest adopted the Vichy line that the planes were lend-lease and that on their way to Russia they took the opportunity to strike Ploesti. However, there was one man on the ground who understood all too well the ramifications of the raid.

Luftwaffe Colonel Alfred Gerstenberg, military attaché to the German embassy in Bucharest, had just witnessed his worst nightmare come true. His pleas to the German high command for re-enforcements to defend Ploesti had fallen on deaf ears. Now they would be forced to listen. He immediately called a meeting of his "Nazi Military Assistance" staff to announce that,

"About fifteen American heavy bombers of the newest long-range type, penetrated sectors Sixty-five, Seventy-five and Eighty-five of defense zone Twenty-Four East. This is the beginning."

His solemn proclamation heralded a long and bitter campaign to destroy Hitler's Romanian oil fields.


The Ploesti raid coincided with an alarming uptick in hostilities all around the Mediterranean basin. The battle for Tobruk in Egypt, which would ultimately decide the fate of North Africa, was raging. Erwin Rommel, *The Desert Fox,* was holed up in his seaside den at Mersa Matruh, sending out orders to his field commanders. Both the Allied and the German supply lines were stretched to their limits.

Two convoys of Allied ships, one from Gibraltar and one from Alexandria, were converging on the island of Malta. Their cargoes were critical to the survival of the garrison stationed there. Malta's continuing harassment of Axis ships and planes was vital in preventing Rommel's re-supply. Without Malta, the Axis could focus all its efforts on North Africa. Mussolini reluctantly agreed to send his fleet to intercept and destroy the two convoys.

Halverson was absent from his command, leaving Kalberer in charge of the remnants of Halpro. The RAF requested Kalberer's help with the Italian fleet. Could the Americans launch an attack with their long-range *Liberators?* This was precisely the sort of mission for which they had been developed. Sam Nero was there with Billy Mitchell when he proved the bomber's worth against battleships in WWI. He patched together seven American B-24s and one British Liberando. A young British officer was sent along with each plane as a spotter to distinguish friend from foe. Beleaguered Tobruk added their few battered *Beauforts* to the force.

David flew left wing to Clyde as they passed over Mersa Matruh. Great billows of sand spiraled skyward from the ferocious tank battle unfolding below. Montgomery and Rommel were locked in mortal combat. The vast Egyptian desert wasteland became the final resting place for thousands of combatants and machines on both sides.

A black smudge on the horizon signaled the location of the Alexandria convoy as it steamed westward. Kalberer ordered the flight to descend and identify the ships. They were Admiral Vian's warships steaming back to base for fuel. The convoy was running naked. The merchantmen aboard the freighters had no idea who these menancing planes were and opened fire. Kalberer took his planes back up to an altitude beyond the gunner's range but not before the British plane was hit. It turned back to Egypt.

When the B24s found the Italian armada, the *Junkers* flying cover were flying at a much lower altitude, expecting the aging *Beauforts* out of Tobruk. They never knew what hit them. The first five-hundred pounders pierced the decks of the battleship *Littorio*. Others took out the heavy cruiser, *Conte di Cavour*. The *Junkers*, recognizing their error, climbed to engage the Americans. Kalberer took his charges down to white cap level and streaked for home. The only damage his planes suffered was the friendly fire from the merchant men. A British submarine gave the *coup de grace* to the cruiser. The rest of the Italian fleet turned tail for Taranto, where they remained for the duration of the war.

As a trophy for the stunning victory, Nero awarded Kalberer a precious can of Spam. It was more welcome than a Silver Star. The RAF officer who had pleaded for Kalberer's help dashed off a communiqué to London. It was quickly forwarded to Washington. The War Department finally broke its silence and acknowledged the heroics of the Halpro group.

Kalberer continued to command the remnants of Halpro. Exercising old-fashioned Yankee ingenuity, the crews that were interned in Turkey wangled their release and made their way back to the unit. They immediately joined their *confreres* in hassling the Germans. They flew a total of 63 missions against Rommel as he continued his advance toward Cairo and the Allied bases east of there.

Remnants of General Brereton's command in the Far East re-deployed to Egypt and joined forces with Halpro. His B-17s were driven out of Indonesia and Burma by the advancing Japanese forces. No sooner had he taken command at Great Bitter Lake than he was forced by Rommel's advance to flee again. This time he took his command to Lydda, Palestine to avoid destruction.

# 10

## The Build-Up

In the months following the daring raid on Ploesti, Alfred Gerstenberg had to contend with three sporadic raids by Russian planes. They caused only minor damage but served as impetus to Gerstenberg's incessant pleas for reinforcements. Prior requests to build his *Festung Ploesti* continued to be ignored or rebuffed at Luftwaffe headquarters.

Reports of the raids, and Gerstenberg's requests. ironically landed on Field Marshall Herman Goering's desk simultaneously. Gerstenberg's fondest dreams were soon to be realized. Goering ordered 50,000 additional troops and 250 planes to Ploesti. He also conscripted 70,000 Slavic prisoners to construct new fortifications. Along with the reinforcements came a promotion for Gerstenberg to Generalmajor. The promotion moved him ever closer to his dream of an autonomous theater of war under his singular command with lessened interference from Berlin.

The diameter of Ploesti proper was five miles. The refineries encircling the town were interconnected with a ring of pipelines designed to minimize the effect of losing a single unit. Beyond the refineries, Gerstenberg ordered the construction of a virtual wall of mobile anti-aircraft emplacements. Many were concealed in large haystacks. Others were mounted on railcars whose sides could be jettisoned to reveal the guns within. Rail lines circled the entire complex. Gerstenberger was now prepared for the long-range bombers massing across North Africa. Those distant rumblings portended a return of the enemy – only this time in much larger numbers with much greater firepower.

Viscount General Bernard Law Montgomery arrived in Egypt to take command of British forces in August of 1942. While waiting to be re-supplied, he put the demoralized forces through rigorous re-training exercises. Whitehall was furious that he didn't immediately engage the enemy. Morale building could wait. Montgomery would not be hurried. He would engage when he felt his troops were ready to engage and he felt there was opportunity for success.

In late October, while Rommel lay ill in Germany, Montgomery confronted the vaunted *Afrika Corps*. General Somme, whom Rommel had left in charge, died of a heart attack. Hitler ordered the still gravely ill Rommel back into service. The British victory at El Alamein in November was the turning point in the war for Africa. Churchill went so far as to claim it was the tipping point of the entire war.

"Prior to El Alamein," he said, "we didn't have a single victory. After El Alamein we didn't have a single defeat."

Just as Montgomery made his push at El Alamein, American forces were landing in Morocco and Algeria to initiate a pincer movement that would ultimately ensnare Rommel in Tunisia. Germany responded by pouring even more troops into Tunisia in a futile effort to halt the Allied advances and thus stem their own losses.

The fall of Tobruk to the British came as the untested Americans were suffering a devastating defeat at Tunisia's Kaserine Pass. However, Eisenhower, with George Patton's reinforcements, was able to regroup and push northward toward Tunis. A wounded Rommel retreated to the peninsula and began the inevitable withdrawal of his forces to Italy. He was forced to leave behind 250,000 German and Italian prisoners. Montgomery and Patton met on the tip of the peninsula from whence they could see the volcanic peaks of their next military objective – Sicily – the gateway to Hitler's *Fortress Europa*.


Finally, Brereton could relinquish his role as the hunted and become the hunter. His bombers ran interference for Monty at Tobruk and El Alamein, playing a vital role in Rommel's defeat. The successful defense of Malta and the unrelenting attacks on German supply ships had spelled the end for Germany's African campaign. Mussolini's hegemony over the region was at an end.

Now the long-awaited invasion of Europe was at hand. Eisenhower ordered General Spaatz to launch "Operation Corkscrew" to capture the island of Pantellera between Tunisia and

Sicily, sitting astride the sea lanes from the eastern Mediterranean to the Atlantic. The island was heavily fortified with 10,000 German troops and hundreds of anti-aircraft emplacements. The rocky shoreline, dotted with pillboxes, presented a formidable deterrent to any attempted amphibious invasion. It became critically important to destroy them. The Ninth Air Force initiated continuous runs at the island fortress. On June 10 alone, 1,640 sorties blasted the island.

David Weiss, Clyde Nagle and their remaining cohort from Tucson took part in the campaign. They were approaching the Marghana airfield at an altitude of 15,000 feet when a flight of 40 Messerschmitt 109s came at them from the cloud cover above. Within seconds three of the lumbering bombers were hit. *Baltimore Girl* sustained major damage to her starboard rudder. Ten feet of her port wingtip dangled like a broken arm. The tail gunner was severely wounded when the rudder was hit. David and Brad fought to control the plane with its remaining surfaces. There was a struggle to keep the plane in the sir. Having lost half of the plane's control surfaces, engine speeds had to be varied to correct for the roll and the yaw.

No sooner were these corrections made, and the plane's stability restored, than they were hit by a fresh wave of 109s. To the puzzlement of the crew, as suddenly as they had arrived they fled, pulling up and shooting skyward. The explanation came within seconds when a squadron of red tailed P51s streaked across the horizon in hot pursuit of the Messerschmitts. The pursuers were the feared flyers from the 99th Pursuit Squadron. Like the cavalry in an old fashioned western thriller, the Tuskegee Airmen of the 99th had arrived in the nick of time.

David managed to maintain altitude. He sent the navigator back to check on the injured tail gunner. The dangling wingtip finally fell away, decreasing some of the drag on the plane and making it easier to maintain level flight. Everyone had their eyes peeled for more German planes, but thankfully, no more materialized.

"You guys keep a sharp lookout," David said. "I don't think those Me's are through with us yet. They like nothing better than to sit back and pick off cripples."

The words were barely out of his mouth when an Me streaked by with a *"Red Tail"* in hot pursuit. A short burst of fire from the P-51 and the Me burst into flame before beginning a downward spiral. The P-51 wheeled around and took up position off *Baltimore Girl's* damaged wing. The large white A in the center of the red tail identified the 99th. Imprinted under the cockpit window David could make out the name of the pilot – Captain James Patterson.

"I'll escort you back to Bitter Lake," a distinctly southern voice said over the crackling radio. "You're not in much shape to defend yourself. Should have you back there in less than an hour. Just hang on."

David toggled his mike.

"You're not going to believe this Captain, but I met your father at the Capitol Hotel in Montgomery when I was stationed at Gunter. I remember him saying how proud of you he was, and he said, 'maybe you two will run into each other.' I never dreamed it would be under these circumstances. You guys saved our asses today. I'll look you up after this is all over and buy you a drink. Give my best to your dad. I'm David Weiss." David heaved a big sigh of relief and settled in for the bumpy trip home.

Brereton moved his 9th Bomber Command to Benghazi, Libya, a city in ruins. As the war surged back and forth it had been the command center for Italians, Germans, French, English and Americans. A hotel complex south of the city center had served for most of their headquarters. It had survived relatively unscathed. Thumbing through the hotel's guest book one could find the names of Vittorio Mussolini, Erwin Rommel, Marshal Graziani, Sir Arthur Teddy and many others. A recent German entry scrawled in a German hand warned,

"Keep this book in order. We'll be back."

That was a boast that never materialized.

The bombers were now based 200 miles closer to Romania. Axis Intelligence memos kept Gerstenberg abreast of events unfolding in North Africa. Newer versions of the B-24 were arriving in Benghazi daily. The 98th Bomb Wing, a new group known as the Pyramiders, began appearing in the battle summaries. They were commanded by a swaggering Texan named John Riley 'Killer' Kane.

A second new group arrived, painted in green and loam colors rather than the standard desert camouflage. Colonel Ted Timberlake's "Traveling Circus" was on loan from the Eighth Air Force in England.

Observing the steady buildup, Gerstenberg once again petitioned Goering for more men, guns and planes. What he got instead was Colonel Bernard Wohldenga, the new Romanian air force controller. Wohldenga came directly from the Africa campaign where he had encountered both Kane and Timberlake. He was the ideal candidate to prepare Ploesti for the coming invasion by General Brereton's burgeoning Ninth Air Force in Benghazi. During January 1943, as the beleaguered American forces battled hunger, thirst, snakes, scorpions, and the unrelenting dust of the Libyan desert, events were unfolding that would alter their lives forever.

Fifteen hundred miles east of Benghazi, in Casablanca, Morocco, Franklin Roosevelt and Winston Churchill met to settle on a strategy for the invasion of Europe, once the Axis was expelled from Africa. The Russians continued to occupy a huge number of Hitler's troops on the Eastern Front. The Americans wanted to launch an amphibious invasion across the English Channel. Churchill was adamant that the Allies were not yet prepared for such an undertaking. The disaster at Dunquerque was still fresh in his mind. Instead, Churchill wanted to launch an invasion into the under belly of Europe, through Italy. After much wrangling among the two staffs, FDR acquiesced to Churchill and authorized Eisenhower to begin planning for such an effort.

Churchill also harbored a long-held desire to launch a Balkan campaign as well. His critics say it was due to the humiliating defeat he suffered at Gallipoli, in WWI, when he was Lord of the Admiralty. They felt that the ill-fated venture failed because of Sir Winston's overreaching ambition to capture the Straits of Dardanelle and seal off ship traffic to the Black Sea. For 25 years, Churchill was haunted by that ignominious defeat. Losing the battle of Gallipoli was Churchill's darkest moment.

When it became apparent that the Americans held no brief for a Balkan campaign, the Brits backed off – but not completely. They dropped the call for an all-out Balkan offensive. Instead they hauled out their Ploesti portfolio calling for a massive bombing raid on the Romanian oil fields. Relieved that Churchill had dropped his demand for the Balkan drive, the Americans enthusiastically got behind the Ploesti scheme. Common wisdom was, that destruction of those oil fields would deprive Hitler of one-third of his petroleum resources and would deal a crippling blow to his entire war effort. It could shorten the war by as much as six months. The Ninth Air Force was given the green light to begin planning for "Operation Tidal Wave" the code name given to the mission. Plans called for the mission to take place between the fall of Africa and "Operation Husky," the planned invasion of Sicily. Bomber support for that major offensive could not afford to be jeopardized.

Colonel Jacob Smart was "Hap" Arnold's choice to plan "Tidal Wave." Smart flew directly to London where he enlisted the British Intelligence community and the RAF in his plans. Their knowledge of the goings on in Eastern Europe was far superior to that of the U.S. In one of those unbelievable coincidences, Lieutenant Colonel Lesley Forster, for eight years a manager at Astro-Romano, was available to assist Smart's team.

Smart and Forster assessed their options.

First, they were unlikely to amass an air armada of more than 200 planes, a number deemed insufficient to completely destroy all the widely dispersed refineries. They chose instead to concentrate the raid on the five most critical units.

Second, due to the previous Halpro raid and the Russian incursions, it was unlikely that the Ninth could launch a surprise attack. Also, knowledge of Gerstenberg's massive buildup of Ploesti's fortifications was widespread. German radar and scout planes would certainly intercept the air fleet long before they entered Romanian territory.

Third, the Germans would expect a high-level raid in concert with those out of England. Because of that, Smart envisioned a tactic totally unexpected by Gerstenberg – low-level bombing. He met stiff resistance from many on the planning staff. They argued that the lumbering, low-speed bombers would be sitting ducks for ground fire. Smart heard everyone out before he finally green-lighted the ground level bombing tactic

Roosevelt and Churchill met again at the Trident conference in Washington in May of 1943. Colonel Smart was given a brief opportunity to present his "Operation Tidal Wave" plans.

The Allied planners were so embroiled in their competing strategies for "Operation Husky" that little time was allotted to review the *quixotic* scheme put forward for Ploesti. Several of the low-level British and American staffers thought Smart was, to use a common British adjective, *daft*. They turned thumbs down on his proposal. However, they had not reckoned with General Arnold. His view of the strategic and psychological benefits of the raid far outweighed the very real possibilities of failure. He authorized Smart to proceed with the planning and to take it to Benghazi.

The summit adjourned and moved to North Africa – without Roosevelt. This offered Smart an opportunity to present his plan for "Tidal Wave" to Churchill personally and Winnie was enthusiastic for the opportunity to neutralize Ploesti. So enthusiastic that he volunteered a large number of Lancaster bombers for the occasion. He was later persuaded that the operational characteristics of the Lancasters were inconsistent with the larger bombers. That decision also avoided revealing the *sub rosa* interpretation of the offer – that American pilots would be unable to find their way to Ploesti without British leadership. Despite their leader's enthusiasm, many RAF veterans were less sanguine about the plan. Twelve Lancasters had been sent against the U-boat engine manufactory at Augsburg, Germany – five returned. In another low-level raid on hydroelectric dams in the Ruhr Valley, only eight of sixteen planes returned.

Colonel Ted Timberlake ferried his "Traveling Circus" force of B-24s back from North Africa to England following the German capitulation at Tunis. Shortly after arrival he received a visit from Colonel Jacob Smart. Smart knew that Timberlake was the most experienced B-24 leader in Europe. He wanted "The Traveling Circus" to lead his raid on Ploesti. Ironically, Timberlake had just been given command of the 201st Combat Wing and was in the process of turning the "Circus" over to Colonel Addison Baker.

Timberlake considered an opportunity to take out Hitler's petroleum source as a once-in-a-lifetime opportunity for him to have a major impact on the course of history. He also did not relish his new assignment, which was a non-combat, desk jockey, training position. Edward Timberlake was a warrior, drawn to the 'smell' of battle. He began assembling his team immediately and promoted Colonel K.K. Compton to Group Commander to lead "Tidal Wave."

For operations officer, Timberlake chose the youngest kid on his staff, Major John "Jerk" Jerstad. Jerstad had long since completed the qualifying missions to send him home, but his dedication to Timberlake and his comrades kept him flying. He had survived a running gun battle with Goering's "Yellow Noses," the most elite fighter group in all the Luftwaffe.

Timberlake chose Captain Leander Schmid for Mission Navigation Officer. Schmid had retired from active flying but jumped at the chance to find the target for the "Tidal Wave" pilots.

Two Britons were asked to join the team, Group Captain D.G. Lewis, an expert on enemy fighters and also a former manager at the Ploesti refinery complex, as well as Wing Commander D.C. Smythe, an ardent proponent of low-level bombing who begged to come along.

Gerstenberg placed his strongest defenses in the northern, western and southern salients, expecting future Russian attacks to fly down one of those corridors. With this intelligence, and for other tactical reasons, the planners chose to approach the targets from the Carpathian Mountain foothills to the northwest. In addition to the possibility of surprising the defense, this route followed the shiny silver rails from the oil fields to the soaring refinery smokestacks.

Floresti, Romania, thirteen miles northwest of Ploesti, was chosen for the Final Initial Point of the attack. The three-minute run from Floresti would allow the winged armada to spread out across the five-mile swath that bracketed the chosen targets. To avoid confusion with the tongue twisting Romanian names the five refineries were given numerical designations – 1 to 5 reading from left to right approaching the target.

Colonel K.K. Compton was given the lead group which drew Target White One, the Romano Americana plant farthest to the left. Section One of Addison Baker's "Traveling Circus" drew White Two, the Concordia Vega refinery. Section two drew White Three, led by Ramsay Potts. White Four was assigned to Colonel "Killer" Kane's Pyramiders in an attempt to complete Halpro's mission of taking out Astro-Romano. Leon Johnson's "Eightballs," flying just to the right of the rails, got the Colombia Aquila complex, White Five. Five miles south of the main Ploesti complex was the Blue target, Creditul Minier, assigned to James Posey. The seventh and final target, Steau Romana, was located in Campina, eighteen miles north of town, the only site removed from the city proper. Jack Wood's "Sky Scorpions" were to execute a left turn at Floresti as the other groups veered right.

Two larger towns to the southwest of Floresti were designated Initial Point One (Pitesti) and Initial Point Two (Targoviste}. The two towns were perfectly aligned to lead the formation to Floresti. Targoviste had the added advantage of a large medieval monastery sitting on top of the highest hill in town as an unmistakable landmark. Timberlake, Jerstad and Schmid would lead the pack.

General Gerstenberg had a few tricks up his sleeve to counter the careful planning and the 'northwest' surprise of Colonel Smart. The constant flow of intelligence from Italy and North Africa convinced him that Halpro Redux was coming. On a hunch, he began beefing up the western and northwestern approaches to Ploesti. He was determined that he would not be taken by surprise again.

"Johnson come over to my staff quarters when you get back from your run," the note on Leander Johnson's desk from Ted Timberlake read.

"What's up, Ted," he greeted Timberlake.

"I want you and Compton to begin low-level bombing run practices over rural England. The pilots need to get used to the reflexes they'll need in the heat of battle."

This order came on the heels of two disastrous low-level runs that had lost several planes. The pilots were jumpy about practicing such maneuvers with their old instruments.

Timberlake brought in a specialist who introduced them to a new low-level bomb sight that was designed to remove some of the danger. Still there was much mumbling and grumbling.

"If Timberlake wants us to fly low-level practice missions, we will fly low-level practice missions," Colonel Johnson said, "and I'll be in the first plane."

The grumbling stopped and everyone fell into line.

The Traveling Circus and the Eightballs terrified the livestock for miles around their bases. Complaints poured in from all points of the compass. They complained of traumatized horses, suddenly dry dairy cows, and eggless chickens.

As cover, Timberlake planted rumors that the German submarine *Tirpitz* was lurking in the fjords off Norway, beyond the range of British planes. He borrowed several Norwegian navy officers and paraded them around the B-24 bases and the operations rooms, much to the consternation of the officers. They had no idea the purpose of their visit, but it seemed to quell the native uprising and deflect the true purpose of the mission.

Timberlake knew that the current flight aids would be of little use in low-level runs. He needed something better. He was introduced to an unemployed intelligence officer who had a better idea.

"Mr. Geerlings," Timberlake began, "I understand you have developed a new scheme for target identification on low-level flights."

"Yes, Colonel. The idea of converting two-dimensional charts into actual ground features is impossible. I have developed a process that shows the objects as they will look when you approach them – oblique drawings."

Gerald Geerlings was sworn to secrecy and put to work immediately. No reliable aerial maps of the Ploesti area were available and any attempt to fly aerial reconnaissance would alert Gerstenberg immediately. Geerlings combed the libraries at Cambridge. Huge repositories of pictures had been volunteered at the behest of the military. Geerlings copied hundreds of photographs of widely disparate locales so as not to tip his hand. The small folder of prints he took back to base would prove crucial in developing realistic target information.

Geerlings went to the Admiralty Library in London. He took a job as a night watchman as cover. He spent 14 solitary nights combing the archives for information on Romania. When he was finished he resigned his position, saying he had found a better one.

Geerlings haul of photographs from both libraries were sufficient for him to reproduce the target approaches.

"Colonel this folder displays eleven key landmarks en route to Ploesti." Geerlings explained to Timberlake. "I have added no identification for security purposes. As you unfold the 'accordion' you expose the next 'oblique landmark' view."

Timberlake studied the pictures closely.

"Great work Geerlings. I have a top secret British printer lined up to reproduce these. We can add the defining nomenclature just before we depart."

The miniatures of Ploesti were so detailed that Group Captain Lewis recognized his former house.

Additional training aids were developed by Lord Forbes and "Tex" McCrary, chief of the Eighth Air Force Photo and Newsreel section. They produced a forty-five-minute sound film to give the flyers the most realistic view possible of the approach to Ploesti. It was the first use of film to prepare men for battle. They used a child's tricycle to move the cameras through Geerlings landmarks. They then added eight-millimeter films of each refinery target so that each of the seven attack groups could practice their runs individually.

The plans and aids for the low-level mission were completed a month before the scheduled "Operation Tidal Wave." In fact, General Brereton had not even decided for the Low-level technique. He was so totally absorbed in preparations for

"Project Husky" that he turned over the major decision making to his bomber chief, General Uzal Ent. Ent scurried about to find the men and planes he needed to staff the blitzkrieg of Ploesti.

Uzwal Ent had compiled a distinguished military portfolio following his graduation from West Point. He was qualified in many military fields. He was awarded the Distinguished Flying Cross, the air force's highest honor, for safely landing his racing balloon after the pilot was killed by lightning. But General Ent counted as his greatest accomplishment the wooing and winning of a Ziegfield Girl.

"Norman," Ent told K.K. Compton, "I'm still not sold on this low-level bombing approach. Every instance that's been reported to me seems to have ended in disaster. What do you think?"

"I would have agreed with you General, but one of my squadrons just came back from Messina, Italy where they took out the underground rail yards with just that tactic."

"Why haven't I heard about that?" Ent demanded

"It was authorized by General Brereton's staff during the run up to "Husky." It has been kept under wraps for intelligence purposes."

"Tell me about it."

"We had been trying everything to knock out the rail landings at Messina. First, to stop supplies coming in to Sicily, but secondly to trap the Germans on the island when they tried to escape. The flak above the harbor has been so intense that high-level bomb runs are suicidal. You'll remember Bernard Rang who was the navigator for Halpro. He died when his plane was shot down and his chute didn't open. They were trying to take out the ferries before they got to the underground rail terminals.

"I gave Norman Appold permission to put together a mission to do a low-level run and try to skip time-fused bombs into the terminals. At the time he was unaware of our plans for Ploesti. It presented a readymade, real life, test laboratory for Ploesti."

"And?"

"Appold seconded three Liberando B-24s and flew them to Malta. While they were being refueled, Appold laid out the mission for the other pilots. They were to fly up the west coast of Sicily, skirt the north coast and swing around the Lipari Islands to the northeast.

"It was a moonless night and two of the "Liberandos" got lost and flew back to Benghazi in disgust. Appold took his one remaining plane into the straits and pointed his nose toward Messina. As soon as he approached the coast, impenetrable fog developed, and he aborted the mission. However, on the way home they passed over a huge chemical complex at Crotone. Appold unloaded on the unsuspecting complex and then made a low-level strafing run before the ack-acks could uncover their guns."

"That doesn't sound like a very successful low-level raid, Norman. What's your point?"

"A single plane, flying at low-level, and from a direction not used before did to that complex what nine, high-level, strike forces had been unable to achieve.

"The excitement generated by Appold's exploits inspired another young man named Flavelle to volunteer for the Messina operation. And get this, Uzal, he is a forestry student out of

Oregon. I asked him why he volunteered, and he explained that his hatred for the fascism represented by Hitler and Mussolini was all the motivation he needed.

"Flavelle took the same route as Appold, but he brought his flight in at dusk to avoid the fog. The three planes delivered 24, five-hundred pounders, right down the throat of the concrete reinforced ferry terminal. Those terminals will never host another train.

As they pulled up they plowed right through a flight of unarmed *"Junker,s"* shooting one of them down.

"Thanks K.K. that gives me something to chew on."

General Ent authorized the unorthodox strategy the next day.

David and the few remaining crews from Halpro continued to operate out of Benghazi. They watched the almost daily buildup of a powerful force of B-24s, while they continued to harass the Germans in Southern Europe by day and battle the Libyan Desert by night.

# 11

# The Homefront

David had received a long letter from Ruth the previous day.  The news was both exhilarating and disturbing. Ruth explained that after long and prayerful consideration she was in the process of converting to Judaism. She quickly reassured David that it had much less to do with their relationship than it did with the horrors she saw unfolding in Europe. She had watched with morbid fascination the implementation of Hitler's 'final solution' – the complete eradication of all Jews, as well as the other Nazi proclaimed undesirables, and it sickened her. She drew parallels between Nazi fascism and the Spanish Inquisition, which had been imposed on the Jews in Iberia in 1492. It became an ethnic cleansing witch-hunt—and it had been decreed by her Catholic forebears. She repudiated the idea of a 'collective guilt,' a stigma that the Nazis ascribed to the Jewish race for the death of Jesus. Instead she felt a 'collective guilt' among the so-called Christian nations for their continuing persecution of God's 'chosen people.' She went on to explain her decision.

"I have been working more and more with your mother in the Aliyah movement. While the Germans have closed off the former pathways available to smuggling children out of Europe, they have not shut them down completely. We continue to work closely with Henrietta Szold and the Hadassah in Israel. We send them as much money and as many supplies as we can, but it's not enough. They desperately need people to help them, both in Israel and in Europe. I watch your mother grieve for those that can't be freed from Hitler's grip. We have had lengthy discussions. She wants to do more. She sees the sacrifices being made by her sons and those on the front lines and she feels a need to do more.

I fear that she is thinking of going to Palestine. She has broached the subject with others in the Jewish Relief Agency and has found support. If she goes, I will go with her. We can't just sit here and do nothing when so much needs to be done. Of course, your father is adamant that she can't go. But Leah is a strong person as you know. She will do what her heart leads her to do. My family is close to disowning me over the Jewish decision. They've sought help from our priest for an intervention. He says my decision is a matter of my personal relationship with God and he will not intervene. I haven't dared discuss going to Palestine with them. I'm sure that would be the end. I must simply follow my heart and trust in God that I make the right decision. I love you my darling and I pray for you daily. Please take care of yourself.

Ruth

# 12

## The Final Push

The barbaric conditions that had plagued competing armies for millennia continued to beleaguer the ever-increasing numbers of airmen arriving in Benghazi. Even the officers had to pitch their own tents, scrounge for uniforms, fight the kangaroo rats and check their boots each morning for scorpions and snakes. The jerboas could leap six feet in the air and lay waste to food hanging in burlap sacks. Boiled water and coffee were the only beverages available. Hygiene and sanitary conditions were abysmal. Generals sat alongside privates on makeshift, oil-can privies. And they bathed alongside them in the

Mediterranean. The primitive conditions enforced an unantici-pated democracy on everyone.

The Halpro pilots had to scrounge for planes. Mickey McGuire's "Blue Ox" was lost in a runway accident and he asked Colonel Kane for a new plane. Kane took him outside and pointed across the field at the patched-up, pink hulk of "Jersey Jackass", a veteran of fifty missions. McGuire and his crew pitched in and helped the mechanics whip the old tub into shape: then he took it up for a test spin. On the landing approach his crew chief alerted him that there were no brakes. "Jersey Jackass" stopped when she hit the sand piles at the end of the runway. McGuire and the other pilots needed to fly as many practice missions at ground level as possible in preparation for Ploesti, so they dragged the old heap out of the sand, cleaned her up, and proceeded.

Such flights were fraught with danger. In one incident the wingtip of one plane slipped over another, forcing the sec-ond plane to hit the deck – literally. The pilot, Howard Freese, kicked up a monstrous dust storm but managed to get his craft back in the air with little more damage than a bent keel.

Despite the dreary conditions and grimy work, there were moments of levity. Peter Keeble was leading an Aussie sal-vage crew trying to clear the harbor of derelict ships. In the pro-cess he recovered much valuable cargo. He dropped in to report on his progress. The base commander apologized for not having anything to offer him in the way of adult beverages.

"Matter of fact I have a flask in my lorry if you'll have them pass it through the gate," Keeble said.

"By all means!"

The lorry trundled up to headquarters and off-loaded a hundred cases of Scotch.

"My God, man! Where did that come from?"

"Bottom of the harbor," he replied. "We found a thousand cases of Scotch and 200,000 quarts of beer, intact."

Lacking any ice or refrigeration, good old Yankee ingenuity kicked in. Several B-24s went up on training missions that afternoon with simulated bombs – cases of scotch and beer. At forty degrees below zero, with open bomb bay doors, the 'bombs' came back well chilled. Needless to say, there was a 'hot time in the old town' of Benghazi that night.


The planes of "The Traveling Circus," "The Eight Balls" and the "Sky Scorpions" continued to trickle in from East Anglia, slowly filling out the five proposed air groups. They were thrown into battle over Italy as soon as they arrived, but the desert conditions took a far greater toll on the planes than did the Germans. Sam Nero was placed in charge of all aircraft maintenance and preparation. General Ent asked him for 100 planes when only sixty or seventy were airworthy. Nero drove his crews mercilessly through the night. Come dawn, he rolled the 100th plane onto the flight line. He and his crews rested only when the hot Khamseen winds shut down air operations.

Rumors became rife throughout the North African theater that a new raid on Ploesti was being planned.

"General Arnold," Brereton told "Hap" Arnold in a memo, "security is almost non-existent in Benghazi. All the typists and clerks are local hires and I don't trust a one of them. The city is full of intelligence operatives gathering and selling information."

Airmen wandering the streets were stopped and queried about plans for Ploesti. None of this was lost on General Gerstenberg. He was asking the same questions.

On July 9, 1943, Gerald Geerlings sat on a mound of unmarked containers in the belly of Captain Hugh Roper's B-24 en route to Benghazi. Roper and his precious cargo were accompanied by four other B-24s. The contents of those canisters were so secret and so vital that nothing could be allowed to stop their delivery. The only person on any of those five planes who knew the contents was Gerald Geerlings. If any piece of the puzzle fell into enemy hands the entire operation would have to be scrapped. That is why the cargo was laced with cordite in the event of an attack. Only Geerlings and Roper knew of the incendiaries. They saw no need to unduly alarm the crews with that information. A flight of *Junkers* over the Bay of Biscay was too occupied with a British ship to see the five planes slip by at high altitude. They were in the same general area that Leslie Howard of *Gone with the Wind* fame had been shot down. Once out of range of the *Junkers* the squadron breezed into Benghazi unmolested. Geerlings and a corporal off-loaded the containers into a green hut in the HQ compound and took turns sleeping against the door with a loaded .45 in hand.

Alfred Kalberer, hero of the Halpro mission, when apprised of "Tidal Wave" plans, railed against its foolhardiness. He predicted that at least 32 planes would be lost. He was summarily relieved of duty and sent home. Tragically, his predictions proved horrifically low.

This was only one of many predictions General Ent received that the mission would fail. He forwarded the comments to Brereton and Ent himself predicted the loss of 75 planes, while achieving only fifty-percent destruction of the refineries.

He begged Brereton to reconsider his approval of the low-level bombing strategy.

"I must turn down your request for a change to high altitude bombing," he told Ent. "I have already briefed Ike and he has given the order to proceed as planned. Any problems now are in the hands of the Ninth Bomb Group. Ploesti is a go as originally envisioned."

On July 19, Eisenhower ordered a bomb run on Rome comprised of 150 B-24s. There were three categories of exempt airmen – Catholics, Catholic haters and anyone with knowledge of the upcoming raid on Ploesti. However, Ramsey Potts was one of the pilots. Ted Timberlake agonized over the assignment even though Jerstad said that Potts had not been briefed on Ploesti.

"Jerk, anybody with one eye and half-sense around here has figured out where we're going."

Luckily Potts returned unscathed.

"Ramsey, do you have any idea what our plans are?" Timberlake asked him when Potts returned.

Potts walked over to a wall map and placed his finger on Ploesti.

General Ent was furious that his planes had been dragooned into the Rome raid, thereby jeopardizing "Tidal Wave." He responded by taking the Ninth off operational status and initiated intensive training exercises for the coming raid. Mock targets were erected across the Libyan Desert and the B-24s turned the countryside into a cyclonic dust storm.

Colonel Woods of the "Scorpions" was so concerned about the ability of the disparate flights to re-assemble after the long flight into Romania, that he sent Major Jack Brooks off on a six-hundred mile journey into North Africa. He wanted to see if Brooks could bring his contingent in to bomb the Ploesti mockups at a predetermined time and bearing. Brooks did his calculations and told Wood he would be back over the target at exactly 16:03. To further compound the errand, Wood ordered smoke pots deployed to obscure the target. With the ETA just minutes away, one of Wood's aides said,

"Colonel it's almost 16:00 hours, don't you think we should clear the area?"

"Don't worry," Wood replied, "they'll never make it on time."

At exactly 16:03, Brooks led his charges across the target at 100 feet and began blasting the mock Ploesti. Wood and his staff bailed out in all directions to escape the bombardment.

"Well, Colonel," Brooks said to a chagrinned Wood at dinner that night, "you knew the ETA."


While the Ninth was making its bomb runs on desert Ploestis, Colonel Wohldenga was preparing countermeasures around the refineries. Thousands of laborers were dispersed all across the Carpathian plain.

Meanwhile, specialized teams began arriving at the Benghazi desert camps to begin equipping the planes with auxiliary fuel tanks for their unprecedented run. They also beefed up the undercarriages with armor for protection against ground fire.

Colonel Smart was anxious about the morale of those men who had already completed their missions and were eligible for rotation back home. He asked Colonel Kane if he thought they would follow him.

"Look," Kane exploded, "if you have any doubt about it, you have the authority to remove me here and now!"

Smart backed down. Ent came by to soothe Kanes's ruffled feathers.

"Even if nobody comes back, the results will be worth the cost." Ent said.

Just at the worst possible time, a wave of dysentery struck the base, hospitalizing scores of GIs, including Colonel Smart. Days later Smart emerged from the hospital, ashen and weak, to resume command of the operation.

Two days before the mission's scheduled departure, Sam Nero finally received the shipment of three-hundred new Pratt and Whitney engines for the mission aircraft. The desert conditions had reduced the normal longevity of the engines from 300 hours to 60. Without these new engines the whole mission was doomed. In a forty-eight-hour frenzy, Nero's crews replaced every single engine.

General Brereton, Lord Forbes and a *Colliers* magazine reporter named Frank Gervasi were flying from Cairo to Benghazi.

"Well Frank," Brereton said, "this is it. This is where the Ninth Air Force makes history or wishes it had never been born. Hap Arnold has handed us a tough one."

Gervasi hadn't a clue what he would be covering until he stepped into the little green tent for a top-secret briefing. The only other correspondent included in the briefing, and covering the Ploesti story, was Ivan Dimitri of the *Saturday Evening Post*.

He happened to have landed in Benghazi while on a round-the-world assignment at exactly the right moment to witness history in the making.

In their final dress rehearsal, 175 B-24s, spread wing tip to wing tip, roared across the Libyan Desert, unloading hundreds of 100-pound bombs, obliterating the Ploesti mockups and relegating their debris to history. The successful rehearsal bred a sort of euphoria amongst the crews. They were totally primed and psyched for the mission: nothing could hold them back now. When the dust had settled, Brereton called the entire complement of warriors together for one last campaign address.

*"Gentlemen, I am the only person I know who has held a commission in both the army and the navy. I have seen the fleet steam up the Hudson. I have seen the corps of cadets pass in review in full dress. Those sights were soul-stirring, but today, as I saw 175 four-engine bombers come roaring across the African desert at fifty feet, bringing dust from the ground with your mighty roar; I enjoyed the greatest thrill of my life.*

*"Tomorrow when you advance across that captured country you will tear the hearts out of them. You are going in at low-level to hit the oil refineries, not the houses, and to leave your impression on a great nation. The roar of your engines in the heart of the enemy's conquest will sound in the ears of the Romanians – and yes the whole world – long after the blasts of your bombs and fires have died away."*

The general concluded with special instructions to the bombardiers. He wanted precision, precision, precision on the targets.

"When you get on the bomb runs bombardiers, I want you to go in like…"

Before he could end the sentence a wayward dust-devil whipped through and blew Brereton off the speaker's stand and into the crowd below. The general got to his feet, dusted himself off, climbed back up to the stand, and concluded his remarks.

"I want you to go in just like that."

Later that day there was another rousing pep talk delivered by a legendary WWI hero, Eddie Rickenbacker.

A steady stream of anxious airmen poured through the chaplain's tents that night. Letters to loved ones, last wills and testaments, poker winnings, you name it and it was committed to the safe keeping of the padres.

John Jerstad, who would co-pilot *Hells Wrench* with Addison Baker at the controls and leading the "Traveling Circus," gave money to Chaplain Burris to fulfill a pledge made years earlier to a Wisconsin church.

Red Franks wrote to his father, pastor of the First Baptist Church of Columbus, Mississippi.

*Dearest Dad,*

*I want to write you a little note before our big raid tomorrow. It will be the biggest and toughest we've had yet. Our target will be the refineries that supply Hitler with three-fourths of his oil. We will get the target at any cost. We are going in at fifty-feet so there will be no second run to finish the job. We will destroy the refineries in one blow. Dad, if anything happens, don't feel bitter at all. Please stay the same. Take care of yourself, little Sis, and don't let this get you down, because I would never want it that way. Hope you don't get this letter, but one never knows what tomorrow may bring. My favorite chapter is the 91st Psalm.*

August 1, 1943, Sunday, was market day in Ploesti. The rich harvest was displayed in white tiled stalls along the streets of town. Delicacies unheard of across most of war-torn Europe were there for the taking; corn, peas, beans, tomatoes, apples, chickens, pigs, cheeses, salamis. Women in colorfully embroidered skirts and old men in white tunics with hard black hats hawked their wares to an unsuspecting populace, while their young men were dying all across Europe, either for the Germans or the Russians.

Armaments bristled all around *Festung Ploesti*. Four wings of Messerschmitt 109s, fifty-two aircraft in all, waited on the aprons at Mizil, twenty miles east of Ploesti. A few miles further east, at Zilestea, seventeen twin-engine Messerschmitt 110-night fighters sat at the ready. Numerous Romanian built fighters were stationed around Bucharest. 124 Czechoslovakian fighters, captured in the 1939 putsch, were stationed around Sofia and Karlovo, Bulgaria. The outer bands of Gerstenberg's air defenses were deployed in Greece and on the island of Crete. Any incursion from Benghazi would likely be interdicted there. Gerstenberg's main problem was that these forces were being constantly siphoned off to defend the Italian peninsula. However, he was confident that he could withstand any air attack from any quarter.

An ominous quiet fell over Gerstenberg's HQ. The Ninth Air Force had not been seen over southern Europe for two weeks. It was at that oddly unpropitious moment that the General decided to take a holiday from his offices in Bucharest. He retreated to the mountain resort of Timisul, to escape the smothering summer heat.

Back in Benghazi, General Brereton had received the staggering news that neither he, Smart nor Timberlake were permitted to take part in "Tidal Wave." The news, decimating the leadership of the mission, prompted anger and outrage at HQ. The mission had just lost its three top leaders.

"God, my men will think I am chicken," Timberlake moaned.

General Ent would helm the lead ship, replacing Brereton in command. Killer Kane now had to replace Ent, who was to be his co-pilot. Captain Ralph Thompson found himself flying with Ent and Compton. Timberlake pulled Leander Schmid from the mission and tried to persuade Jerstad to stay behind. "Jerk" protested and said that he and Baker would be okay. Musical chairs went on with the crews into the night as unease spread over all the changes.

General Ent issued Battle Order 58 containing the final mission objective and the latest intelligence assessments of the Ploesti defenses. It projected less than 100 anti-aircraft guns, most manned by poorly trained Romanians. In truth, Gerstenberg's final report listed 237 batteries with 80% German crews. These were augmented by hundreds of machine gun emplacements.

Colonel Kane wandered about his encampment at Lete, Libya, listening for any indication of the mood of his crews.

*"There was quietness, quite unlike the usual buzz. Some crews were quietly giving away their belongings. I sat on my favorite perch, on an old engine, and stared for a long time at the stars. In my short lifetime the stars have stayed in their places as they have for countless lifetimes before mine. They would remain unaffected whether I and the men with me lived or died. Whether we died in the near future or years later from senility mattered not in the great scheme of things. Yet the manner of our dying could have far reaching effects. I have a young son I may never see again, yet I shall be content if I feel that his*

*freedom is assured, and he is never forced to be humbled in spirit and body before another man who proclaims himself master."*

Veterans and first timers alike wandered the desert that night, unable to sleep, their thoughts turned to loved ones far away, wondering if they would ever see them again.

David Weiss sat atop a large boulder above a dry ravine. He could see Ruth's soft face and flowing red hair as he gazed at that same canopy of stars. In the dry, crisp, desert air they seemed close enough to touch. He thought of Mama and Papa and the difficulties they had faced for the past two years. Bernie, even though he was far from the front lines, had been badly burned in a fuel tank explosion near their field hospital. And Murray, who had finally gotten permission to fly, was facing death daily over the industrial centers of Germany. In a world gone mad he suddenly felt an inexplicable peace. Somehow, at that moment he was touched by something he could not explain. He calmly walked back to his tent and slept as he hadn't for weeks.

# 13

# Black Sunday

At two in the morning of August 1, 1943, horns and sirens blared all along the strip of Benghazi desert camps of the Ninth Air Force. Men rolled out of their sacks, dressed in their flight suits, had a quick breakfast, and gathered for their last briefings before "Tidal Wave" commenced. They clambered aboard their B-24s and queued up for takeoff. The lead plane circled for almost an hour before the 175th plane cleared the runway.

The co-pilots on each plane circulated escape kits to each crew member containing a map of the Balkans, a British gold sovereign, an American twenty-dollar gold piece, ten one-dollar bills, ten dollars in drachma and lire, dried dates, water purification tablets, biscuits, sugar cubes and chocolate. The crew also received tiny compasses that could be hidden on their bodies as well as mimeographed vocabularies in Romanian, Bulgarian, Serbo-Croat, Turk, and Greek.

Sam Nero performed the herculean task of providing 17 more planes than had been called for. Bomb loaders had struggled through the night to load 311 tons of munitions into the yawning maws of the giant beasts and securing their shackles. Each plane was also supplied two boxes of British incendiaries to toss into the volatile gas diffusion stacks as they buzzed by at fifty feet.

The Khamseens, normally a late afternoon occurrence, chose this particular day to bring their wind driven sands to Benghazi at four in the morning. Mechanics fought to keep the eroding sands from the engines. Each plane needed all of its power to lift the 3100 pounds of fuel and 4300 pounds of bombs, far more weight than any B-24 had ever carried into battle. There were also the 1,250,000 rounds of armor piercing .50 caliber machine gun rounds to contend with.

Precisely at 04:00, the first flares screamed aloft at the Berka Two base. *Wongo-Wongo* released her brakes and roared down the runway, spearheading the greatest air armada in history. Woody Flavelle and his mission route navigator Robert Wilson were tasked with getting this great crusade to its target. Flavelle, who had led the history making raid on the Messina rail yards, was fortunate to be on the mission at all. Four days earlier, he had crash landed into a sodden pasture on Sicily. The peasants who rescued him and the fishing boat crew that ferried him to Malta made it possible for Flavelle to get back to Benghazi and keep his rendezvous with destiny.

After circling for an hour, Thompson set *Wongo-Wongo's* compass for the 500-mile first leg, the island of Corfu off the eastern coast of Greece. Ominously, *Kickapoo,* on loan to the "Travelling Circus" from "The Pyramiders," lost an engine on takeoff. The stricken plane circled the field and attempted a landing into the fierce sandstorm. It struck a utility pole and burst into flames. Only two of ten crew members survived, the first of many casualties suffered by the Ninth Air Force on that fateful day.

Twenty-nine pink-hued "Liberandos" trailed Flavelle and Thompson into the frigid, moonless sky. The thirty-nine planes of the "Traveling Circus" under the command of Addison Baker formed the third flight, followed closely by "Killer" Kane's forty-seven tawny "Pyramiders." Leon Johnson led his thirty-seven "Eight Ballers" aloft next while the "Sky Scorpions" flew in tail-gunner Charlie's position – dead last – with Colonel Jack Wood in the lead plane.

The planes flew under radio silence hoping to avoid discovery until they were close to the target. It proved to be a futile and costly decision. Allied intelligence was unaware of the German Signal Intelligence Battalion's recent posting to Athens. The planes appeared as 175 blips on their radar shortly after they cleared the Italian boot. Radio communications between the flight elements could have avoided the impending catastrophe. Germany had broken the American radio codes and was reading the Ninth Air Force's transmissions out of Benghazi. Curt messages to alert friendlys along the route were intercepted by the Germans and decoded immediately. The enemy knew that Ploesti was the target as soon as *Wongo-Wongo* breached Sector 00 of Zone 24 over Corfu.

Young Douglas Pitcairn of Perthshire, England, whose Prussian heritage was traced back to the HMS Bounty, was in charge of the air control bunker that morning. Pitcairn's ancestors had immigrated from Perthshire to Prussia in 1830. Bernard Wohldenga foresaw the importance of monitoring the Italian and Greek peninsulas and the waterways surrounding them.

Young German specialists sat deep in the bowels of the bunker facing a large Plexiglas map of the Balkans. Female operators relayed information from far-flung sites across the area. Each sighting was flashed on the screen with a flashlight and marked. This morning young Pitcairn observed abnormal activity in the southwestern quadrant. Large numbers of bombers were approaching from the direction of Benghazi. The Luftwaffe base at Salonika, Greece reported that the flight was approaching at altitudes of 2,000 to 3,000 feet. This was definitely more than a normal training mission. Pitcairn ordered a first level alert, requiring all personnel to remain on station throughout the entire air defense zone. He admonished everyone to have a big breakfast. It was going to be an extremely long day.

The Khamseen had wreaked havoc with the new Pratt and Whitneys. Ten aircraft had to turn back with feathered engines, seven of them "Pyramiders." Fog and haze en route required widening the separation between planes beyond the normal 500 yards. The units began to drift perilously apart. The formation disintegrated. Kane's group lost sight entirely of Addison Baker's "Traveling Circus."

Norman Appold's flight was scheduled to pass over Cape Asprokavos on Corfu three hours after departing Benghazi. As they approached the Greek landmass he watched incredulously as *Wongo-Wongo* began to *'noseup'* and gyrate wildly. She assumed a vertical position then began slipping backward, finally plowing nose first into the sea. Without warning the lead plane and the mission navigator were gone. Flavelle's wingman broke formation to drop life rafts and vests but to no avail. There were no survivors. David Weiss and the other "Liberandos" watched in horror as their sister ship went into its death spiral. Captain Iovine, in *Desert Lily*, too heavy and too far behind, turned back to Africa, taking the deputy route navigator with him.

Back in the 98th, *Lil Joe* discovered a bad fuel connection which had already siphoned off 800 gallons of fuel. A quick calculation by the navigator confirmed that they could not get to Ploesti and still make it back to Benghazi. A poll of the crew determined that they wished to fulfill the mission and then look for a friendly place to land on the way back.

*Brewery Wagon* now became the lead plane by default, saddling a very young Lieutenant William Wright with the awesome responsibility of leading the remaining 164 B-24s to the target. Over Corfu he dialed in a thirty-degree tack to the northeast, a direct route to Ploesti.

Douglas Pitcairn, deep in his bunker north of Bucharest, ordered all defenses to Alert Level Two, all the way down to squadron and anti-aircraft battery levels. When radars all over the lower Balkans picked up the mass of planes, he ordered Alert Level Three. Major Ernest Kuchenbacker got on the phone to Gerstenberger at his mountain retreat to inform him of the developments.

"I"m on my way!" the area commander said.

The drive from Tumelin to Ploesti was three hours, the approximate flight time between Corfu and Ploesti for a B-24 cruising at 200 MPH.

Lieutenant Wright checked the navigational aids developed by Geerlings and took the armada to 11,000 feet in order to clear the Pindus Mountains of Albania.

K.K. Compton, flying left seat in *Teggie Ann,* ran into a bank of cumulus clouds, towering to 17,000 feet. He was command pilot and it was his decision as to whether he should attempt to climb over them or plow through. Taking the planes to that altitude would drain valuable fuel needed to complete the mission. He turned to General Ent.

"I'm going to take us over the top General, anything else will jeopardize our ability to return."

Colonel Baker, in the formation behind, recognized Compton's wing-waggle signal and fired off a flare alerting the planes behind to follow Compton's lead. The first three flights rose to the new altitude, donned their oxygen masks, and surfed across the cumulus tops. The "Eight Balls," "The Sky Scorpions" and the "Pyramiders", opted for a frontal penetration of the cloud bank – Killer Kane was aware that many of the planes straggling behind him were not equipped with oxygen. The already widening gap became even larger as the headwinds slowed their advance.

An isolated radar site high above Sofia, Bulgaria had not spotted a plane in months. Mules and men had hauled the equipment to the top of Mt. Cherin to construct the site. Their radar screens suddenly became a beehive of activity. Green echoes of countless targets lit up their screens. They relayed their observations to soft-voiced airwomen in control rooms from Salonika to Vienna.

"Many wings! Zone 24 east, sector 11. Bearing 30 degrees."

Compton passed over Yugoslavia, and past Mt. Cherin. The radar operators below confirmed the earlier sightings of a huge force of planes. At 17,000 feet his element began to experience a phenomenon unknown to meteorologists of the day – the jet stream. They were being carried along at a much greater speed than their compatriots below, in the clouds. The two flight segments were now irretrievably separated. Compton eased back on the throttles and began his descent into the Danube Valley, hoping against hope that Kane's command would catch up.

Colonel Vukov scrambled two squadrons of Czech *Avias* from bases near Sofia. Simultaneously he ordered 16 *Avias* and nine *Messerschmitt 109s* from Karlova, east of Sofia to launch. He was convinced by the compass headings that the raid was to be on Sofia, the Bulgarian capital.

The B-24s disappeared from Pitcairn's radar as they descended into the Wallachian Plain, blocked by the intervening mountains. They were too far away to be picked up by the Ploesti radars. The immigrant Prussian was momentarily blind.

Compton led his command across the fertile crescent of the Danube where the crops were at full harvest. This verdant valley with its cornucopia of riches presented a stark contrast to the sprawling brown of the Libyan Desert. Every man watched as the fields slipped beneath their wings, devoutly praying that they didn't have to crash land into those same fields on their way home.

Kane's odyssey through the clouds was filled with tense situations. Planes would disappear from view and reappear in entirely different positions. There were two near collisions that skillful piloting narrowly averted. As he cleared the clouds, Kane searched frantically for any sign of the lead element. All he saw before him was an empty sky. His charges were spread out below and behind him at 11,000 to 13,000 feet.

William Cameron, in *Buzzin Bear,* was first to spot the enemy fighters. They were Vulkov's Bulgarians out of Sofia. The old *Avias* could not operate effectively at bomber altitudes. They gave up in frustration and returned to their bases, hoping to intercept the invaders at lower altitudes on their return to base. Fortune intervened to give the first flights a few minutes of added obscurity. The old Czech planes had no radios with which to alert the ground crews of the invader' heading.

*Teggie Ann* looked down on a wide, brown ribbon of muddy water. The beautiful Blue Danube of song and verse had been transformed into an unsightly brown welt on the bright green flesh of Romania, just one more childhood illusion shattered. A farmer, spreading manure from his wagon, looked up in fright and then scurried for the cover of nearby woods. His horse, spooked by the fury of a hundred roaring engines, bolted, dragging his wrecked wagon across the field. Peasant women in colorful dress looked up in amazement at the lumbering bombers. Some crewmen swore they could detect smiles on their upturned faces. Several were waving handkerchiefs.

Captain Harold Wicklund sat in the greenhouse of *Teggie Ann* with his charts arrayed before him. Pitesti, Initial Point One, appeared right on schedule. Minutes later, Targoviste with its unmistakable hilltop fortress, sped by at 200 miles per hour, a speed that was accentuated by the low altitude. The next landmark was Floresti where the planes would initiate a sharp right turn and barrel down the railroad line to Ploesti. Wicklund was set to declare the 58 degree turn in ten minutes when he felt the plane veer right.

"What the hell is happening?" he yelled into his intercom.

Above Wicklund, in the pilot seat, Compton had mistaken a railroad, a bridge and a power plant as the Floresti landmarks. The following planes were confused by the turn but followed their commander's lead to avoid confusion and avert potential mid-air collisions. The airwaves crackled with pilots breaking radio silence to voice their alarm.

"Mistake, mistake, we're turning twenty miles too soon!" they protested.

Their transmissions fell on deaf ears. *Teggie Ann's* radios were turned off.

John Palm, bringing up the rear of his contingent in *Brewery Wagon,* continued on to the Floresti IP.

"Little Willie Wright always knows where he is," Palm declared.

Willie Wright reset his course for Floresti and *Brewery Wagon* flew on alone, into a rain squall which obscured the other planes now streaming off toward the eastern horizon. *Brewery Wagon* was the first plane to spot Ploesti when she burst out of the clouds into blinding sunlight. There she sat, framed by an incredible rainbow. Anti- aircraft fire from the ring of outer defenses began to explode all around the plane. One shell struck the greenhouse, instantly killing Willie Wright and the bombardier.

"Tramping on the pedals was like fighting a bucking horse," Palm remembered later. It was an apt metaphor for a young man who grew up in El Paso, Texas.

"Although my bombardier was dead, we were obsessed with doing good with our bombs. I noticed I was not getting much pressure on the right pedal. I reached down. My right leg below the knee was hanging by a shred of flesh."

He jettisoned the bomb load.

Willie Steinmann in one of the Mizil *Messerschmitts* saw the crippled bomber spewing smoke from two engines and went into a steep dive. He had developed his own theory of how to attack the B-24 while studying models of the aircraft. He approached *Brewery Wagon* from above and behind on an oblique angle, aiming for the wing/fuselage nexus and the cockpit. The plane's vital signs vanished with the impact and Palm was forced to take her down immediately. Co-Pilot Love avoided an explosion by flooding the interior of the fuselage with flame-retardant foam. The doomed plane pancaked across an empty field. Palm clawed at the cockpit window with his good hand, forcing it out.

"That was something I could not do with both hands in a week under normal conditions."

He dived head first out the opening and rolled on his shoulder. Love and engineer Robinson carried Palm away in a firemen's sling, hiding with five other survivors in a nearby corn-field. They were soon surrounded by German soldiers with menacing rifles. Palm drew his .45 and pointed it at the German soldiers. Robinson, who was applying a tourniquet to Palm's leg, pushed his arm down.

"Don't do that sir."

It was the first time the engineer had ever called Palm sir.

Their captors hauled the dazed and wounded survivors into the open. Palm carried his mangled leg in his arms. One of the Germans sliced Palm's watch from his wrist, before he was confronted by a large Romanian soldier who took control of the group of prisoners. *Brewery Wagon's* eight survivors spent the remainder of the war in Romanian prisons.


David and Clyde's planes were stuck in the middle of the "Liberandos" and had no choice but to follow Baker's lead. Clyde was first to break radio silence.

"*Hells Wench, Hells Wench* we're not over the IP yet. There's been a mistake."

There was no response from *Teggie Ann.* Baker knew that he had to get the entire flight turned if he was going to avoid mid-air collisions. Then he could take corrective action. At the same time *Utah Man* saw the smoke, flames and towers of Ploesti off his left wing. Baker saw the same thing and ordered a 90-degree left turn. Everyone behind saw what was coming and executed on cue. It took fully five minutes for that many planes to execute the turn, spreading them all across the sky.

Ploesti's defenders had been on full alert for twenty minutes when the first plane came into view. Fortuitously, the aborted turn to the east had confused the ground commanders. They were fully convinced now that the attack was aimed at Bucharest. They shifted their focus to the capital city.

Pitcairn paced back and forth in his windowless room at Otopenni, just north of Bucharest. He was confused by the fact that the flight had disappeared from the Mt. Chernin radar but had not yet appeared on his. He was now left to puzzle out which was the target – Sofia, Bucharest or Ploesti. He chose to release the Romanians to defend Bucharest. It was an easy decision. He didn't want their sluggish planes mucking around over Ploesti if he had to unleash the speedy *Messerschmitts.*

At Mizil, the most experienced fighters in Wohldenga's command sat at the ready in their Me-109 cockpits. The Full Alert signal came from Pitcairn and the ground crews manned their cranks to start the Me's engines. Only two swift turns were needed to bring the killing machines to life. Five minutes later, fifty-two fighters had cleared the runway to meet the enemy.

Dr. Hans Arthur Wagner entered his surgery to begin laying out his instruments when he heard the roar of the planes taking off. When he had finished, the Me's were already patrolling at 6,500 feet over the initial IP, Floresti. In Gerstenberger's absence, Major Kuchkenbaker ordered the Me-110 night fighters at Zilistea into the fray.

Paul Baetz, a pianist and entertainer from Germany was at HQ in Ploesti arranging his next performance to entertain the troops. Usually his performance included two women, an accordionist and a coloratura singer. Baetz's refusal to discontinue playing Jewish music in Berlin had gotten him exiled to Romania. Irony was lost on his audiences, who often requested "White Christmas" and "Tea for Two," both written by Jews – and Americans to boot.

The duty officer called Baetz aside to tell him that enemy bombers had been tracked across the Mediterranean that morning and things might get a little heated around Ploesti. Baetz thanked him and quickly hustled his little troupe out of town.

People on the streets of Ploesti paid little heed to the air raid sirens, which blared at 1:30 on a warm, summer Sunday afternoon. Surely it was just another in a long series of drills. Many could not be bothered as they headed out of town with heavily laden picnic baskets. Others simply strolled through the city's many parks past its fountains and lakes. Others gathered to admire the towering abstract sculpture by Ploesti native Konstantin Brancusi, prominently lionized in the toniest of salons in Paris.

When *Hell's Wench* veered left, "The Traveling Circus" faced a naked fifteen mile run through Gerstenberg's heaviest defenses in order to reach the refineries.

White Three, the 93rd Bomb Group with twenty-four planes, was in the lead with Addison Baker's flight on the left and George Brown's group on the right. White Two under Potts and Roche was in formation just behind.

Almost instantly, word spread among the defenders that the invaders were coming in at extremely low altitudes.

"Change all fuze settings to point blank," the gunners were ordered.

Russian prisoners went to work furiously re-setting the proximity fuzes on thousands of ammunition rounds. The "Liberandos" were heading directly into a massive fusillade of anti-aircraft fire. The first salvo of blue-white 88mm shells streaked skyward, lighting up the sky.

Major Norman Appold was flying at fifty feet off the ground in *G.I. Ginnie* at two hundred miles per hour in the wake of *Teggie Ann,* barreling toward Bucharest when he ran into the unthinkable defenses constructed by Alfred Gerstenberg. Squadron Leader Barwell, the unlisted British gunnery ace aimed his .50 caliber guns at the personnel scrambling for cover in their emplacements. Dirt, men and body parts flew in all directions. A battery of six 88s lay dead ahead, spewing shells at an incredible rate, laying down a withering screen of flak. As Appold brought the plane into range, Barwell loosed several five-second .50 caliber bursts, leveling three of the AA emplacement, permitting those coming behind to power through. Many of the 40 planes took hits, but none went down.

Leycester Havens, tail-gunner on *Jersey Bounce* spotted enemy fighters. He called up front to Pilot Worthy Long.

"Enemy fighters at six o'clock."

The announcement was followed by a loud 'whump.' Havens came back on the intercom and in a weak and surprised voice noted a hit.

"Direct hit on the tail-turret, Lieutenant Long. I've had it."

Laycester Havens was the first battle casualty of the great Ploesti air raid.

Meanwhile, General Gerstenberg was speeding through Ploesti trying to get back to his HQ at Bucharest. Seeing the attack, he ordered his driver to turn off and proceed to the local command center. He observed the remainder of the Battle of Ploesti from there.

"Where are the fighters?" Barwell asked. "The flak was ready for us, why not the fighters? "

He was unaware that the MEs had been dispatched to Floresti to interdict the projected path of the expected onslaught which would have occurred but for Compton's error, proving to be a small blessing. The obverse of that coin was that the initial units were delivered into Gerstenberg's fortified 'mouth of hell' in eastern and southern Ploesti.

"All of a sudden, out about 10 or 11 o'clock there were these haystacks," reported Walt Stewart, pilot of *Utah Man*. "One of them tipped over and there was an 88mm gun. It fired, and the shell went right through the tail assembly of my ship. My tail gunner called and said, 'Don't do that! Don't do that! I said 'I didn't, they're shooting at us."

Addison Baker aimed *Hell's Wench* at the refinery complex on the southwest corner of Ploesti, two minutes away. An immediate hit to the greenhouse killed the two men there. Baker and Jerstad struggled to keep their ship on course despite the damage. They took another hit to the fuel cell in the right wing, puncturing it. A third shell struck just below the flight deck. The plane shuddered, wavered momentarily and then proceeded toward its target. Walt Stewart watched in horror from his wingman position.

"Look at the Colonel! Look at the Colonel! His number three and number four engines are on fire."

Flames streamed back past the horizontal stabilizer.

"We pulled up on the Colonel and waved at him, trying to get him to belly-land or pull up so his crew could bail out."

Someone aboard was able to release the bomb load and with the decreased weight the plane shot skyward. A figure fell from the open bay and a chute tried to open. Too late. Another direct hit smashed into the plane and the left wing began to fall away. Several men were seen tumbling from the craft as it catapulted into the rail marshalling yards.

Colonel Addison Baker and Major John Jerstad were true to their word. They had brought their men to Ploesti. They refused to crash land and save their own lives. They led the "Tidal Wave" force to the target – and they died in the process.

Planes were being ripped apart on all sides. A few struggled to an altitude where jumping was possible. Others plowed into cornfields and swamps with their crews aboard where they died. *Utah Man* was the only plane in Baker's contingent to reach the target intact and release its lethal payload. Her crew had witnessed Baker's exploits and later described them as the greatest act of heroism they had ever seen. Their plane had a gaping hole in the vertical stabilizer. They witnessed small 'chicken coops' begin to fall over revealing 20mm pom-pom guns which riddled the left side of the plane. Stewart was able to hold his 40-degree heading despite the damage and while avoiding the cables of barrage balloons. Gunner John Conolly exacted a measure of revenge by exploding a locomotive with his 50mm guns.

Dozens of other planes passed through the inferno that was Ploesti, suffering unimaginable damage and still managing to stay aloft. Wheat stacks, chicken coops and rail cars morphed into roaring fountains of death, still they kept coming.

*Jose Carioca* came barreling into town with flaming gasoline pouring through the fuselage. The pilot, Nicholas Stampoli, struggled valiantly to reach his target. He released his bombs, barely climbing over the looming stacks. The damage was too much. The plane plunged earthward spewing flames and tearing through a refinery, finally embedding itself in the third floor of a brick building beyond. It was the Ploesti Women's Prison. Forty inmates were hauled to safety while sixty more perished in the inferno, among them Rebecca Weiss, aunt to David Weiss. She was a visiting nurse at the prison that fateful day.

Route changes and smoky environs had reduced the target area to a jumble of mass confusion. B-24s were flying in all directions barely avoiding mid-air collisions.

The original target for David Weiss' flight of "Liberandos" was the Romano Americana refinery, White One. However, from this heading Astro Romano made a more logical target. Although it was assigned to Kane's group, there was no way of knowing his whereabouts. Compton headed for Astro Romano. On approach, the "Liberandos" saw the same inferno that several German bomb experts were driving their jeep into, hoping to defuse the large bombs with their delayed timers that were scattered all about like ticking vessels of death.

David Weiss in *Baltimore Girl* looked down and saw the railroad tracks snaking from Bucharest to Ploesti. Through the smoke and haze he watched as a B-24 crashed into a cornfield on the other side of the tracks. How could that be if all the other planes were behind them. He rubbed his eyes and credited the illusion to battle jitters. He had no way of knowing John Palm was lying in that cornfield with his leg shot off. Or, that the defenders of Ploesti knew he was coming. Nor did he know that Colonel Addison Baker had taken his "Traveling Circus" off course and was already attacking Ploesti from the east. As the convoy neared the target it was faced with unremitting chaos as Norman Appold recalled in his memoirs.

*"Flights of three or four or single planes were going in different directions, streaking smoke and flames, striking the ground, wings, tails, fuselages breaking up, big balls of smoke rolling out of the wrecks before they stopped skidding."*

Appold was approaching White Four while on his left Compton was closing on White Five. The resistance was so massive that General Ent went on the radio to anounce a change in the mission orders.

"We have missed out target, you are cleared to strike targets of your choice."

Pandemonium reigned. Planes were coming from all directions, passing above, beneath and alongside their sister ships.

Now Appold climbed and Pott's stragglers crossed underneath. Kane's "Pyramiders" were layered a few feet higher as they swept by on their target run. In one of fates more bitter ironies, *Baltimore Girl* caught the full blast of an exploding tank on the roof of the prison as she passed over. David struggled to keep his ship from sliding left and downward with the shock wave. The tail gunner reported that part of the vertical stabilizer was shredded and that the right rudder was hanging in tatters. The pilots struggled to keep the wounded beast from sliding left and down with the blast. They hauled back on the yokes for all they were worth and kicked the good rudder far right, trying to skew the plane through the towers and cables to get her skyward. Foot by grudging foot she rose, gaining traction on the sky as she went. Dave kept Appold's plane in sight and aimed the nose of *Baltimore Girl* in that direction. His crippled ship was losing ground. He asked his engineer for a damage assessment. Could they make it home?

Clyde Nagle in *Blue Tick Hound* hung on David's right wing, catching much of the blast as well. The exploding tank bounced the plane 250 feet into the air. It skewed sideways with its wing clipping a cable and swinging the plane around. Four feet of the wing stayed with the cable as wires and control leads flapped in the wind. Clyde regained control and took his ship to the ground in an attempt to avoid the solid sheet of flak at that altitude. He saw B*altimore Girl* dead ahead and tucked in behind the mortally wounded ship to give cover. Both planes looked for a path through the Black Death. That path led them toward the mountains of Macedonia in Southern Yugoslavia.

*Baltimore Girl* had taken several 20mm rounds through her Tokyo tank and just forward of the bomb bay. Despite the best efforts of the crew to stem the flow, most of the fuel was lost. The bomb bay doors remained open to siphon off the gas lest it explode. The slightest spark could ignite the fumes still swirling around. The crew was told to don their parachutes and prepare to abandon ship if conditions worsened. David headed west-southwest praying to clear hostile airspace before it became necessary to abandon ship. Belly gunner, Sergeant James

Ripley, watched as blood pooled in the bottom of his Plexiglas bubble. A 20mm shell had exploded into his gun mount leaving shrapnel embedded in his shoulder and thigh. The mount had shielded him from the worst of the blast but now lay useless in a twisted mass of iron. The two waist gunners had suffered non-life-threatening injuries as well. Ripley reached for his intercom button.

"Hey guys, I'm hit and I can't get the turret to rise. Can someone come back here and help me to get out."

The blast had disabled the lift mechanism.

"Tyler, Pearson, you two guys are closest, see if you can get Rip out of there. If we crash land he'll be crushed, and if we have to bail he'll never make it."

The two wiggled their way aft past the open bomb bay. Tyler pressed the elevator button and got a high-pitched whine.

"She's disengaged and free-wheeling," he said. "One of us has to get down in there to drag him out."

"I'm smaller than you Ty," Pearson said. "Let me have a go at it."

Doug Pearson stuck his head and shoulders down into the opening and grabbed Ripley under the arms. The cry of pain stopped him dead.

"Sorry Rip."

He wriggled back from the turret and took a first aid kit from the bulkhead.

"I'm gonna give him some morphine before I try again."

Pearson grabbed two ampules of morphine and dived back in. He administered the drug into Rip's good arm and waited for Morpheus to work his magic.

"Ty I can't get much leverage in this position. I'm going to snake a rope under his arms so we can both pull him up."

Doug passed the rope under Rip's arms and scurried out once more.

"Okay, on the count of three let's try to hoist Rip out of there."

The two stood on either side and braced their feet against the plane's spars.

"One, two, three," Doug said. "Pull!"

Rip's limp form slowly rose through the narrow opening. They dragged him over to a flat surface and covered him with a blanket.

"We've got to stanch that bleeding, "Ty said.

He slipped off his belt and wrapped it around Rip's thigh above the wound and tightened it. Slowly the spurting blood stopped. Meanwhile, Pearson was applying gauze bandages to the shoulder wound.  They uttered a quiet prayer as they stepped back. They were confident they had stanched the flow but didn't know if Rip could survive the loss of blood.

Chaos still reined behind them as the last formations pasted the refineries before pulling out. *Vagabond King* loosed the last payload on the powerhouse and boilers of Red Target. They linked up with four others and headed toward Cyprus.

From Walter Stewart's first bomb on White Five to John McCormick's last on Red Target, the entire mission had lasted for 27 minutes, much longer than predicted by their practices in Libya. The chaos and confusion had cost valuable time—and even more importantly—lives.

# 14

# Heading for Home

The wounded and bleeding survivors of "Black Sunday" were spread out across a 100 mile swath of southwestern Romania. They struggled to get to safe havens in Turkey, Cyprus, Syria, Malta — anyplace that had a friendly face and a landing strip. Some only made it as far as partisan territory in Yugoslavia or Albania. Many were so badly damaged they couldn't make it even that far and bailed out over enemy held lands. The prison camps of Romania, Bulgaria and Greece continued to swell with a steady stream of battered survivors. The fallout from "Black Sunday" continued long after the final bomb fell.

The safest route back was over Corfu and then to Benghazi. They knew the enemy would be lying in wait. Half the planes were damaged, and half had no ammunition left. They would have to depend on their companions for protection. Many of the wounded couldn't survive the seven-hour flight. Their commanders sought other, closer fields, where medical help was available.

The "Liberandos" and the "Sky Scorpions" were the least damaged of all and formed up together on the route to Corfu. They were spread out over a 70-mile path. Most of the surviving Pyramiders formed up on Julian Bleyer's *Nightmare,* as did many of the "Eight Balls." George Brown gathered up as many of his "Traveling Circus" as he could find and led them home.

The tales of heroism on the terrifying journey home would fill volumes. Death defying acts of courage to save their friends; superhuman efforts to keep their stricken planes aloft; sacrifices to save others. It can safely be said that their exploits marked a high point in the annals of self-sacrifice among America's finest gladiators.

One by one the planes that made it back descended on Benghazi. Gerald Geerlings was tossing horseshoes with Colonel Smart, Ted Timberlake and Leander Schmid when he detected the first drone of engines. General Brereton was sitting inside anguishing over the dreadful radio reports he was receiving from the raid. It was not good. His phone rang. The general's aide looked up,

"Sir, General Ent's plane has just landed at Berka Two."

Brereton hopped into a jeep and rushed across to Berka Two to welcome his mission commander home.

Norman Appold came in right behind Ent, with no flaps and no brakes. After a long roll-out he rushed to join the other survivors for debriefing.

"Norm I am really quite sorry for General Ent," British Gunnery Officer Barwell said. "He's one of the best of your chaps I've met, a nice man."

When later his unauthorized task was discovered, Barwell was returned to England and reprimanded for participating in the raid without permission. He was the only member of the mission to not receive a unit citation.

The flow of returning planes dwindled. Walter Stewart, the first man over the target was among the last three in – after 14 grueling hours aboard *Utah Man.* Ted Timberlake ran bellowing and sobbing across the sands to embrace the crew. Stewart discovered how fortunate he was to have made it home. A ground crew mechanic pointed out that a shell through his wing tank had plugged itself at the entry and the only fuel lost was what siphoned out of the exit hole. The engines were running on fumes.

Addison Baker returned with only 11 of the B-24s he led into battle. *Liberty Lad* was the last plane into Benghazi. She approached at 2000 feet. Sergeant Hayes lowered the gear manually to preserve hydraulic fluid. The instrument panel lights had been blown out and John Brown held a flashlight so the pilot, McFarland, could read the instruments. He needed to maintain exactly 120 knots to avoid a stall or an overshoot – the plane had no brakes. He went into an uncontrolled roll of a mile and a half, finally stopping after a record shattering 18-hour flight. Neither pilot could stand. Their legs were completely paralyzed from standing on the rudder pedals after the hydraulics went out. They were suffering from total exhaustion and spent several days in the hospital recuperating.

The last plane was down.

Ben Kuroki on *Tupelo Lass* walked past the anxious ground crews still staring into the distance, searching the skies for their planes to return. With tears streaming down his face he just shook his head and walked past them.

"The fools. Don't they know they'll never come back?"

Two weeks later the Ninth Air Force closed the books on "Tidal Wave." President Roosevelt gave a final report on the mission to Congress.

"The losses may seem disastrously high, but I am certain that the German or Japanese high commands would cheerfully sacrifice thousands of men to do the same amount of damage to us, if they could."

"Fifty-Three Liberators were lost, including eight interned in Turkey. Twenty-three reached allied bases in other countries. Eighty-eight made it back to Benghazi and of those, 55 had major battle damage.

Four hundred forty-six airmen were killed or missing. Seventy-nine were interned, and officially, fifty-four were wounded. Counting the wounded languishing in Romanian or Bulgarian prisons, one hundred and thirty were injured.

After the losses and damage, the Ninth Air Force was but a shell of its former self. With the return of the "Circus," "Scorpion," and "Eight Ball," survivors to England, there was precious little for Brereton to command. The remnants of the 9th were absorbed into the 15th Air Force to prepare for the invasion of Italy.

# 15

# Yugoslavia

*Blue Tick Hound* hung just beneath *Baltimore Girl's* right wing. Clyde did a visual check of the damage to David's tail assembly and fuselage. Smoke streamed from number four engine. Number one was already feathered. Manifold pressure on number two was falling, a result of cylinder damage.

"Dave, it doesn't look good." Clyde radioed. "If you lose another engine I don't see how you can make it back to Benghazi. Your best chance of surviving capture would be to land in Yugoslavia. Most of Macedonia is under the control of guerilla partisans. The topography there presents a real problem. The land is mostly mountains. If you get to the Vardar River Valley you can follow it all the way to Greece. It essentially divides Macedonia into two before it flows into the Aegean Sea. That whole area is a partisan stronghold."

"Thanks Clyde. Rather than risk going down over Albania or Greece, or plowing into a mountain, I'm going to look for a clear valley and try to set her down in one piece. If we lose another engine, I'm going to hit the gong. I don't relish trying to crash this bird on one engine."

"Okay, Dave. I'll stay with you until you decide. I'll note your coordinates and get them to the rescue teams. Hang in there buddy. We'll be back for you guys. Good luck and God-speed."

Two cosmic travelers, alone in the trackless Balkan skies, crossed from Bulgaria into Yugoslavian airspace. Macedonia, legendary home to Alexander the Great, lay like a capstone separating Serbia from Greece. Its forested peaks and valleys, like corrugations on a washboard, stretched toward the horizon where they melded into the Pindus Mountains of Albania – and beyond them, the Adriatic Sea.

Twenty miles into Macedonia Number four engine gave up the ghost. With two engines gone and devastated wing surfaces *Baltimore Girl* began to lose altitude. The peaks ahead presented an impossible task for the battered old girl.

"Brad we'll never clear those mountains," David said. "There's a river valley off to starboard on the chart. The Bregalnitsa."

David steered the steadily falling ship through the twists and turns of the valley looking for a decent flat, clear, strip of land. Like the Danube, this river too was running at flood stage, the ochre currents surging far out of its banks. The gunners worked furiously to transfer fuel between wing tanks. The electric pumps had failed and the mechanism of the clunky manual one was jammed. Five minutes later, fuel starved number two engine sputtered and died, its un-feathered prop spinning freely. David feathered it and ordered Brad to hit the gong. No promising flat areas were apparent. Trying to bring her down in the river was not an option, and besides, with a single engine it was an impossibility. The navigator stepped back into the fuselage, strapped on his parachute, and toggled the bomb bay doors open. The gunners had managed to strap a chute on Ripley who was still in excruciating pain even though the bleeding had stopped. Tyler and Douglas took one arm each and dropped through the doors with Ripley. Tyler held Ripley's ripcord and pulled it as soon as the threesome cleared the plane. He and Pearson fell another 200 feet before they could yank their chutes open. They floated to earth silently with a dazed Ripley just above them. Garret and Hughes, the other gunners, followed the trio through the yawning doors with the engineer and radio operator on their heels.

""Get the hell out!" Dave told the navigator as he set the plane on auto-pilot.

"Let's go Brad," he yelled to Matthews, "get out of here!"

Dave made his way back to the gaping abyss, took one last look around, grabbed his 'D' ring, and dropped through the floor. He could see Brad's chute deploy below.

*Blue Tick Hound* circled the area. Clyde looked down with a sigh of relief to see the tenth chute deploy. He knew Dave wouldn't jump until he was sure everybody else was out.

"Note the co-ordinates," he told his co-pilot, "We'll be coming back here for these guys."

Dave hung suspended between earth and sky, the panic and noise aboard the plane replaced by stillness and a serene quiet. The delicate whisper of the wind was all he could hear. A sense of overwhelming loneliness passed over him, heightened by the receding drone of *Blue Tick Hound's* engines as she disappeared over the horizon. Thoughts of Ruth and Murray and of his parents flitted through his consciousness. Would they know he was alive, or would they receive the ominous 'missing in action' letter and assume the worst? At least Clyde had witnessed their safe evacuation from the plane. He could attest that they were down over enemy territory. A thunderous explosion roused Dave from his thoughts. Smoke and fire rose from a blackened patch half-way up the side of the mountain across the river. *Baltimore Girl* had completed her last mission.

David looked down to see several parachutes unfurling in the field along the river. Others were spread further away like rumpled covers from an unmade bed. Brad unhitched his harness. He heard a distinct 'whumpf' nearby. Dave's chute had caught a gust of wind and he was being dragged helplessly across the rain slicked ground toward the rushing waters. Brad ran after him. He was able to grab the shrouds and spill the air from the billowing silk before Dave was washed away by the surging waters of the Bregalnitsa River.

"Boy, that was close," Brad said. "It'd be hell to survive what we just went through only to be drowned in some muddy river half way around the world."

"Grab that chute Brad. We've got to dispose of these things before the German's come nosing around. That explosion was an open invitation."

The two pilots headed back upriver, walking in the surf to cover their tracks. Dipaolo, Stepanovic and Proffit watched as their leaders approached from downstream. They had found a small cave in a cliff above the river where they dragged their chutes.

"Hey Brad, Skipper, up here."

They scrambled up the steep incline to join the trio, away from the prying eyes of the inevitable scouting parties.

"Where are your chutes?" David asked. "We don't want to give the Krauts any more help than necessary."

Cliff Proffit pointed toward a fresh mound toward the back of the cave. They had covered the area with brush.

"Did you see the other guys?" asked Brad. "They jumped ahead of you. They're probably further upstream. Dave, should we send out a search party?"

"No! We should stay put until it's dark in an hour or so. Then we can check out the area."

David rustled through his escape kit for charts of Macedonia.

"There's a village about five miles downstream. Stip. We're probably forty miles from Greece to the south and the same to Serbia in the north. The German forces are headquartered in the capital of Skopje, about fifty miles northwest. I'm sure they have a contingent in Stip who've heard about the crash by now. After we find the other guys we'll just hole up here and see what happens. If we can convince the Krauts that we all died in the crash maybe they'll go away. We need to cover our tracks as much as possible. They probably have blood hounds. Hopefully they won't cross the river to our side.

"Most Macedonians hate the Germans and there's a considerable group of partisans operating throughout the country. A Colonel Mihailovich from Serbia is in overall charge, but due to the mountainous territory most bands operate on their own. Britain and Yugoslavia have officially recognized Mihailovich as the legitimate leader of the rebel forces. London has been ferrying supplies to them. They're known localy as 'Chetniks.' I'm not sure what that means."

"It comes from the word 'ceta', which is Macedonian for a military group of 100 warriors."

Radioman George Stepanovic suddenly found himself the center of attention.

"How the hell do you know that?" Brad Matthews asked.

"My folks emigrated from Belgrade to Chicago in the twenties. I was born there and grew up speaking Serb. A Chetnik is one of the 100."

"Well I'll be damned," David said. "We had a secret weapon all along and didn't know it."

Dave walked to the front of the cave and looked out through the tree branches.

"It's too dangerous to go out looking for the other guys," Dave said as first light flooded the front of the cave. "Let's just pray they found some place to hole up."

"Skipper, since I speak the language, maybe I should go out and get the lay of the land," George Stepanovic said. "I can grab a peasant outfit off a clothesline and blend in with the crowd. If I can get into Stip, I'll be able to find out where the Germans are, as well as any local Chetniks."

"It never occurred to me that Stepanovic is a Serbian name," Dave said. "How's that for a stroke of luck? But, I can't let you risk being captured. I think we should go as a group."

"Dave, far be it for me to countermand my superior officer's orders, but I think George is right. One man in local dress who speaks the lingo can blend in a lot easier than five yokels in military uniforms. I think you should take George up on his offer."

"What do the rest of you guys think?"

"I think Brad and George are right," DiPaolo said. "But remember George, if you are captured by the Germans out of uniform you will be treated as a spy. That means they can execute you on the spot. So, you might want to think about that."

"I know, but I'll be careful. I think it's the only choice we have to hook up with the Chetniks and have a chance of getting out of here."

"Okay," Dave relented, "but you promise me you won't take any unnecessary chances. If things start to smell fishy skedaddle pronto. We need your talents."

"You got it Skipper. I don't relish the idea of spending the rest of the war in some German stalag. I want to find us a way home."

Dusk was settling in at the end of the first day and shadows crept across the mouth of the cave. George Stepanovich took a deep breath and skittered down the cliff face toward Stip, and a pathway home. It was agreed that if he didn't return in 48 hours they would assume his capture and strike out on their own. He took his and Proffit's local currency, forty dollars. He had dehydrated food for two days.

The river wound its way through a pass then broadened as it encountered flat farmland on the other side. He followed the river until it came to a bridge. The dirt road ran north and south. He listened intently for sounds of life. The distant lowing of a cow, heavy with milk was all he heard. Some farmer late with his chores he guessed. He crossed the bridge to the shadows on the other end. He moved in the direction of the cow. Three hundred yards down the road there was a silhouette of a house with a barn behind. A lone figure emerged from the house, milk pail in hand. He watched as a woman crossed the barnyard and pushed open the barn door. He heard her soft voice comforting the cow as she pulled the milk stool up to the cow's right side. He heard the soft slap on the cow's flank urging her to move her leg back. Then came the sibilant sound of two streams of milk striking the sides of the pail.

Stepanovic crept closer to observe the milk maid through a crack in the barn wall. She held the pail between her legs, pulling rhythmically on one teat and then the other. The pail filled rapidly as she emptied all four udders. She rose slowly, pulling the stool away and sitting the pail on a shelf. She filled the empty manger with hay and oats. She retrieved the pail and turned toward the door.

George waited until she was safely inside. He saw no evidence of a man about the place. Her husband would have been conscripted by the Germans. The unkempt nature of the place attested to the absence of any other caretakers. Chancing that she was alone, he crossed to a window. He peered through a parted curtain as she strained the milk into a churn, in preparation to make butter. There was no one else around. He tapped on the door.

"Ko si ti?" came a startled voice from inside.

"Just a hungry traveler," George responded. "I'm just back from Skopje and I haven't had anything to eat all day."

The woman cracked the door slightly and could make out a dusty figure in what resembled a military uniform. She opened the door and George stepped inside.

"Where is your husband?"

"The German's came and took him away. How is it you are here and not in Skopje?"

"What are your sympathies Madam? I have served the Germans because I had no choice. I ran away to come back home and fight with the Chetniks. I need your help. Will you give me some of your husband's clothes? I can't appear in Stip in this uniform. I'm trying to find Ratko Pavic. I need to locate him. I have information that will be useful to the resistance."

"How do I know I can trust you? How do I know you're not a spy for the Germans? They've already taken my husband. All I have left is this little farm and my two children."

"I assure you I am not a spy. I just need to get this information to Colonel Pavic. I will pay you for the clothes. Help me to strike a blow for your husband."

"Wait here?"

She disappeared into a room off the kitchen and returned with a farmer's shirt, pants, shoes and hat.

"Here, this is the best I can do. You can change on the back porch. I'll burn your uniform. You can have a bite to eat before you head to Stip. It's about ten kilometers from here. If you leave by midnight you can be there before dawn. This old farm road is lightly traveled. I don't think you'll run into anyone out that late. I don't know a Colonel Pavic, but if you'll go into The Serbian Crown Bar and ask for Manja Vukovic, she may be able to help you. Tell her Lidija Avramov sent you."

The pants were two inches too short and the shirt was snug. The shoes were a size too large but would have to do. He stuffed paper into the toes. Lidija fed him a nondescript bowl of stew. He washed it down with a fiery glass of slivovitz, a potent local plum brandy that he'd enjoyed in his Chicago neighborhood bars. He thanked her profusely, slipped five denars into her hand and went out into the dark of the Macedonian night praying that she would not betray him.

Stepanovic stared down from the crenellated parapet of an abandoned fifth century monastery high on a hill overlooking Stip. Bats returning from their nocturnal prowls kept him company. Small furry creatures scurried across the floor trying to escape his disturbance.

Below, the first stirrings of the morning were farmers unloading their products on the periphery of the town square. Meats, cheeses and a variety of vegetables began to pile up in the stalls. Crowing roosters echoed each other across the red tiled roof tops. Sheep, cattle and pigs noised about near the auction barn. Bleats and squeals rose in the morning air as they were goaded into their pens. Several sleepy passengers stepped down from a blue and red bus stopped in front of the city hall. A flag pole prominently displayed a large red flag with a swastika emblazoned in a circle of white. Two gray staff cars were parked out front. The German garrison in Stip seemed rather meager.

By eight, the streets came alive. George summoned his courage and headed down the hill into town. In the hustle and bustle of the market place few paid attention to another poor farmer walking the streets. Hearing the language of his childhood on every tongue seemed strange. Although he hadn't spoken it in a long time he was encouraged that he understood most of the local dialect. A few local idioms escaped him. The conversations were typical of any small-town market place anywhere in the world; crops, weather, war, children, subjects that bound neighbor to neighbor everywhere. Most of the men were either very young or very old. A whole generation of able bodied young men had been shipped off to do the bidding of "Der Fuehrer." An occasional snippet about the war arose and was quickly suppressed in the furtive atmosphere created by the occupiers.

Stepanovic walked past the town square where the two gray staff cars were parked. The massive front door swung open. A German officer, rows of ribbons lining his chest, bounded down the stairs.

"You there. Come here."

George froze. His heart sank. The officer was pointing his riding crop straight at him.

"Why aren't you at the front?"

"Sir I was wounded in Hungary. I was sent home for recuperation.

"Show me your wound!"

George had been wounded earlier on a bombing run over Palermo, Sicily. His right side was pierced by a sliver of shrapnel from flak that bounced off his radio. He was offered repatriation home but elected to recover in Benghazi and stay with his crew. He returned to flying status just two weeks before Ploesti. He pulled up his shirt to reveal a nasty scar running from his hip up to his rib cage. It was red around the edges attesting to its recent origin. The laddered stitching was still evident.

"Very well young man. The Fuehrer appreciates your service to the Third Reich. I look forward to your reunion with your comrades in arms. Heil Hitler," the officer said as he snapped his right arm into the air.

"Heil Hitler," George responded forcefully.

The man walked past him and climbed into one of the cars. He spoke to the driver and sped off in a cloud of dust.

"Whew," George muttered. "That's the only good thing to come out of my visit to Palermo?"

He continued to circle around the square looking for the Serbian Crown. Streets radiated from the central square like the spokes in a wheel. The village had sprung up in Roman times at the intersection of trade routes along the rivers. He noticed a flurry of activity down one of the side streets. Moving toward the commotion he discovered a concentration of bars and restaurants around a small plaza with a large, black, granite obelisk rising from its center. He tried to read the fading Cyrillic inscription as he walked past. It appeared to be a tribute to the city's fallen in the Balkan War of 1912 that overthrew 400 years of Ottoman rule. Directly across the plaza from where he stood there was a two-story stone structure with a crumbling, wooden galleria clinging to its front façade. Rampant wisteria vines encircled its columns, their unkempt foliage covering the roof and cascading over the edges. Two old men in fading flannel work shirts sat on the porch, engrossed in a chess match. They paid no notice to the stranger entering the Serbian Crown.

George took a few seconds to allow his eyes to adjust to the dark interior of the bar. Several decrepit tables were scattered about, none of them occupied at this early hour. A massive bar, carved from imported mahogany, ran across the entire back wall, its mirrored backdrop faded and chipped. A lone patron absorbed in his morning eye-opener noted the stranger's entrance then returned to his drink. The burly bartender leaned against the bar absent mindedly polishing glasses. The only sound came from the kitchen where the clanging of pots and pans signaled preparations for lunch.

George took a seat at the far end of the bar, away from the tippler. The bartender held up a shot glass to the dim bulb overhead. Satisfied that the blemish was gone he replaced it on the bar and moved leisurely toward the new customer.

"What can I do for you, stranger?" he asked.

There was a hint of curiosity in the way he stretched out s-t-r-a-n-g-e-r.

"A cup of coffee – and some eggs and sausage if you're serving breakfast."

"The kitchen is getting prepared for lunch now. We don't normally serve any breakfast I'll see if Manja will fix something for you."

The bartender eased through the swinging doors into the kitchen. The shrill, high-pitched voice that followed told him that Manja wasn't too pleased with his request. The barkeep returned, frowning.

"That woman drives me crazy. She acts like she owns the place. It's not like she can't start serving early. She'll bitch about it, but she'll do it."

" Thanks, I'll sit at one of the tables if it's okay."

"Sure, go ahead. By the way, I haven't seen you around here before, have I?"

"No, I'm from Skopje. Came in on the early bus. I'm down here visiting my sister-in-law. She lives on a little farm about five miles up the river. My wife, her sister, is already here. Her husband was killed in Poland. By the way, is there a taxi service in town?"

"Yeah, it's behind the city hall, near the marketplace."

Satisfied with George's explanation he went back to his glass polishing. George took the table nearest the front window where he could see the chess players and have a view of the doorway. The bartender brought over his coffee, spilling some on the table.

"Sorry," He muttered, pulling a bar rag from his apron to wipe up the spill.

George sat in silence sipping the heavy, black coffee. He began to consider the scene and wonder what he would do if Manja couldn't, or worse, wouldn't, help him. His musings were interrupted by the approach of a starkly beautiful young woman with long black hair, braided and falling to her waist. Manja Vukovich resembled the glorious, cartoonish heroines portrayed in the books his parents brought to America. She sat the steaming plate of eggs and sausage on the table in front of him, not troubling to hide her disdain for the rude interruption of her morning routine. She turned to go back to the kitchen when he took her wrist. She recoiled in surprise, jerking her hand away. George put his finger to his lips. She stared at him curiously. What could this impudent troublemaker want? George pulled a scrap of paper and a stubby pencil from his pocket.

"I was sent here by Lidija Avramov," he wrote. "She said you might help me to contact Mihailovichs's men in the area. I come from Skopje and I have news from Draza."

He hoped the use of the familiar names would convince her of his authenticity. She hurried away into the kitchen without a word. George's adrenaline kicked into high gear fueling his 'fight' or 'flight' impulses. Should he run and trigger a panic, or should he wait to see if she sounded an alarm. He reasoned that she would have done the latter at the table. He decided to wait and see what developed – good or bad. Besides, he was ravenously hungry, and the eggs and sausage looked really good.

After an eternity, Manja Vukovic re-emerged from the kitchen carrying a pot of coffee.

"More coffee, sir," she asked loudly.

As she poured the coffee she leaned forward. There, peering out from her ample cleavage was a small rolled up paper. She shifted her eyes down in a signal that he was to take it. She made sure that her back was turned to the bar lest curious eyes observe the transaction. He plucked the note from her blouse and in one continuous motion placed it in his shirt pocket.

"Why yes, thank you very much, I must say this is a wonderful breakfast and I apologize if I put you out."

"Don't worry about it, it's all in a day's work for me. Enjoy the food. Pay the bartender on the way out."

She returned to the kitchen, her sinuous moves creating urges he had suppressed for a long time. The rush of blood caused the welt under his shirt to throb.

George finished his meal and fished a cigarette from his pocket. It had been a long time since he was able to enjoy a cigarette with his morning coffee. The brackish, tar-colored liquid they served at Benghazi hardly qualified as coffee. He stubbed out the cigarette butt in the ash tray, left a one denar note on the table, and walked back to the bar. He took the check, paid the bartender and left. He waited until he was well out of town before he slipped off the road into a clump of trees. He made certain there was no one around before he retrieved the note from his pocket and read it.

"Meet me at the old monastery on the hill just west of town at seven this evening. Come alone. Your approach will be observed from a distance. Do not carry any arms."

George breathed a sigh of relief. There was at least a chance that she could help him. If she was going to betray him she would have done it at the bar. On the other hand, it could be a trap to see if there were others involved. He had little choice. He would return to his early morning lookout to await the evening rendezvous with the comic book vixen. Who else might show up was open to conjecture. He circled around the town through the forest. He didn't want anyone to spot him who might contradict the stories he had given to the German officer and the Serbian Crown bartender.

He climbed back up to the ruins and began a survey of the area. The bowels of the ancient site contained row upon row of empty crypts, ransacked long ago by artifact seeking grave robbers. The monks and brothers of a thousand years were still not allowed to rest in peace. In the dim light of one crypt he stumbled over a pile of rocks, setting off a miniature avalanche. When the dust had settled, the corner of a small metal container lay exposed among the rubble. He dragged the box over to the light for further examination. Inside were a sheaf of bank notes and a list of names. Several of the names had been crossed off. He didn't know if they were martyred Chetniks or assassinated collaborators. In any event, the discovery had the calming effect of establishing the monastery as a Chetnik haven and thus increasing the likelihood that Manja was a legitimate partisan. Feeling somewhat relieved, he took a few of the bank notes then restored the cache to its former hiding place. Having more local currency had to be a good thing.

George used a tree branch to obliterate his presence in the ruins. He retreated to a nearby thicket of fallow olive trees to await the evening's developments. His hunger pangs returned in late afternoon and George began to scrounge around the area for something to eat. A small tree of the plums used to make slivovitz yielded some late season fruit. He passed near a small farm with a garden plot behind the barn. Taking a circuitous route that kept the barn between himself and the house, he sneaked into the garden. He quickly snatched a small melon and two tomatoes before scurrying back into the woods. The tomato entrée and the melon dessert satisfied his hunger. He scurried back to his hiding place in the trees to await the evening's developments. The weariness of the past two days settled over the stillness and he began to nod off. A noise on the road startled him awake. Through the bushes he saw a gray squad car trailed by a panel truck. The vehicles stopped on the road below Stepanovic. Six German soldiers piled out of the van with rifles at the ready. The officers in the staff car led them down a rutted path toward the farm whose garden he had burgled. They formed a ring around the house as one of the be-medaled officers kicked in the front door. In a mixed Serbo-Germanic rant the officer accused the farmer of harboring American pilots. His attempts to evade discovery had failed. How did they know there was an American pilot in Stip? Had Manja betrayed him? Had she arranged an elaborate hoax to entrap him? He crossed the road after checking for traffic. He wanted more distance between himself and the patrol. He checked his watch. It was 6:45. He'd need all of the remaining fifteen minutes to get back to the monastery by seven and wiggle into the hiding place he had chosen. The dense woods where he emerged onto the road slowed him so that it was almost rendezvous hour when he reached the ruins. He climbed the steep slope for the third time that day, warily checking for pursuers. He crossed under the great arch that had once welcomed Serbian Orthodox prelates. He paused, straining to hear any sound from within that would alert him to betrayal. He ducked under the drooping limbs of the trees that had overgrown the courtyard. A dark figure stepped out of the shadows of the bell tower, a pistol pointing at George's chest. George froze.

"Who are you and why have you come to Stip looking for Chetniks?"

"I am George Stepanovic," he began, assuming that truth was the better course in this situation. "I am an American airman. My plane was hit during a raid on Ploesti, Romania. I bailed out here, just up the river."

"Step forward with your hands over your head."

The gunman searched George for weapons.

"How do I know you're telling the truth? How do I know you're not a German spy? How is it you speak our language and know your way around Stip? If you're not a German spy you could just as easily be one of Marshal Tito's partisans, collaborating with the Germans. His regime is out to feather its own nests in case Germany is victorious. Do you have anything to identify yourself?"

"May I lower my hands? I have something in my pocket to identify myself."

"Go ahead, carefully. No sudden moves."

George handed the man his twenty-dollar American gold coin. He removed his dog tags and dangled the chain. The man held both objects up to the fading light and smiled.

"I had to be sure. We knew a plane had gone down. We picked up four of the crew several miles from here this morning. They were holed up in abandoned farmhouse ten miles up the river. A lookout spotted them. We got there just ahead of the Germans. They're in a safe house. We were pretty sure you were who you said you were. A spy for the Germans went to their headquarters as soon as you left the bar. You were careless. No one in Stip smokes Lucky Strike cigarettes."

"Damn!"

"They sent out patrols immediately. I'd be surprised if you didn't see them"

"I did. I stole some vegetables and ten minutes later they were all over that farm. I wondered how they got there so fast. Leaving that cigarette butt was stupid. I don't think I'd make a very good spy."

"You said there were four guys in that old house. What happened to the fifth?"

A war weary Anton Povalic stared off into space. He swallowed hard.

"The fifth man didn't make it. They buried him underneath the house. They said they wrapped him in his parachute after they took his dog tags and other personal items. I'm sorry."

"Ripley was a good man, a good crew mate, he . . ." Stepanovic couldn't finish.

"Where's the rest of the crew? We need to pick them up before the Germans find them."

"They're holed up in a cave above the river, about five miles upstream, just across from where the plane crashed."

"I know that place. My father used to take me fishing there when I was a kid."

Povalic led him down into the catacombs where Manja Vukovic and the bartender awaited.

Manja took his hand.

"You gave us a real scare. I couldn't tell you the sot at the bar was a spy. The Germans suspect we're Chetniks and they keep the old man in drinks to spy on us. He got to your table before I could empty the ash tray. As soon as he saw that cigarette he ran straight to the German HQ."

"We can't worry about that now," Anton said. "We have to get those other guys in from the cold. The Germans will be hot on their trail. They have spies all over."

Anton pulled another box from the ruins. He flipped the top and pulled out a small radio transmitter. He led the other three to a dilapidated car and drove two miles through the woods. He got out and set up the radio. He attached the battery and a code key then fired it up. And started tapping out his message.

"We only have a few minutes before their radio detection gear picks up this signal."

He broke the rig down and drove them back to the monastery via a different route.

"All right, let's clean this place up and get out of here," Anton said.

He drove them to a farmhouse east of Stip. There was a flat bed, farm delivery truck in the yard loaded with alfalfa hay. Anton climbed onto the truck and with a large hay fork moved the hay aside. Under the hay was a concealed trap door leading into a false bottom. The area underneath was two feet wide, eighteen inches deep and seven feet long. The box barely cleared the drive shaft. The drop sides of the truck concealed it from view – unless someone was very curious and crawled beneath the truck. Most guards at road stops didn't bother. They would simply prod the hay with their bayonets and pass the truck on. Anton motioned for George to crawl into the box. Anton dropped Manja and the barkeep on the outskirts of Stip then skirted the town.

~ 415 ~

He picked up the road to Titov Veles, paralleling the Vardar River, where he headed south. At the small village of Negotino he turned off the main highway. An hour later he was in the outskirts of Prilep where the Germans had erected a checkpoint into the town. There was a gate across the road forcing Anton to stop.

"What's in the truck?" one guard asked as he walked around and prodded the hay.

"Just a load of hay for a dairy farm on the other side of Prelip."

The other guard took Anton's papers and scanned them briefly.

"Raise the arm. There's nothing here but hay."

Anton drove through town and headed up into the mountains above the town.

An old hunting lodge balanced precariously on the side of a hill, overlooking a verdant plain. Anton drove past the lodge and turned into an obscure farm road just beyond. The road traversed a ravine that was overgrown with weeds and vines. He eased across the ravine, turned left, and rolled to a stop. He pulled a whistle from his shirt pocket and blew three short trills followed by one long one. An innocent looking mound of brush and debris began to pivot away from the cliff. The unorthodox gate opened ninety degrees revealing a massive cave in the mountainside under the lodge. Anton drove into the cave and silenced the engine. Two men ran out to brush over the truck's tracks and to close the gate behind him.

George heard scraping overhead. The coffin lid was lifted. In the dim light of the cave he saw several men scurrying about. He unfolded his lanky frame and crawled out of his hiding place. He was stiff and tired. Anton led him to the back of the cave and up three flights of stairs hewn from cedar logs. Anton rapped lightly on a trap door above the final landing. Three short taps followed seconds later by a fourth. The door lifted, revealing a small alcove with three stone walls and one made of polished mahogany – the back panel of a ten-foot bookcase. The book case swung open, they stepped through, and it closed behind them. There were several men lounging around the room, most in hunting attire. George was led through the room to another door in the back. He entered a large windowless room. There, seated around a long table, were the four crew members of *Baltimore Girl.* They jumped to their feet to greet their comrade.

"Sorry Ripley didn't make it, what happened?'

"He landed on his shoulder and reopened the wound," Pearson said. 'He just bled out. Nothing we could do."

The four had been transported to the lodge in similar conveyances with varying cargoes. Poor Tyler shared his with a load of pigs. It took him three baths to rid himself of the smell. Food was still on the table from their supper. George lit into the venison and potatoes. The tomatoes and melon were now a distant memory. He washed the meal down with a dark lager and finished it off with a fiery glass of *slivovitz.*

While Anton was transporting Stepanovic to the lodge a band of his Chetnik buddies was making their way up the Bregalnitsa. They were within sight of the cave and made little effort to conceal their movements. They didn't want a trigger happy American to take potshots at them. At the base of the cliff Dusan Bozinov hailed the cave.

"Hallo, my name is Dusan Bozinov. I am one of Draza Mihailovich's Chetniks. We have Stepanovic and four other members of your crew. They're in a safe house. Come on down. We need to get you out of here to safety. There are German patrols all over the place."

Four dirty, tired, scruffy survivors tumbled down the slope toward their rescuers.

"Thank God George was able to get through to you guys," David said. "We were starting to give up hope. I'm Dave Weiss, pilot."

"There's no time for introductions now. Come with me."

Dusan hustled them to four waiting trucks hidden in the trees. Each was assigned a truck and a driver and quickly loaded into their boxes. There were pig squeals, sheep bleats, the rank smell of manure and the odor of rancid fat in barrels. The lorries sped off in different directions. That many farm vehicles traveling together would arouse suspicion.

At the stroke of midnight, the last truck trundled into the hidden cave and the cave door swung shut. The happy reunion lasted into the night as the *slivovitz* flowed freely. The death of Ripley weighed on them all.There were a couple of half-hearted, drunken eulogies and more than a few tears.Finally, fatigue overtook the crew and they descended to the underground lair. To the casual visitor dropping in, the hunting lodge was exactly as it was advertised, right down to the wild game in the cooler and the massive display of shooting guns in the front hall. Two different squads of Waffen SS storm troopers had searched the premises and declared it to be a harmless haven for hunters.

The next few days were spent in isolation in the cave. At dusk, if there were no reported sightings of Germans, the men were allowed out into the yard behind for exercise and fresh air under the abundant tree cover. The guerillas couldn't risk the possibility of a lone scout plane observing a large group of military age men cavorting around. If there were no paying guests, the men were allowed upstairs to dine with their Chetnik rescuers in the evening, returning after midnight to the safe seclusion of their hideout.

"What's the chance of a rescue mission," Dave asked Anton at dinner the sixth night.

"Some downed crews have been flown out, mostly further up in Serbia where there are more landing fields. We were able to send a few up there. Nobody has been rescued here, even though we do have occasional radio contact with Italy."

Ten days after delivering George Stepanovic to Wolf Lair Lodge, Anton returned from a foray into Stip. His demeanor foretold bad tidings. He entered the dining hall and sat with the guerilla leader. Words passed in whispers. Anton buried his head in his hands. His shoulders heaved with sobs. The others in the room held back, giving their leader a moment of private grief. It took several minutes before he regained his composure. The leader embraced Anton and left the room.

Minutes later a waiter entered the room carrying a tray of sandwiches and beer. He placed it in front of Anton, who picked at the food absent mindedly. His eyes were fixed on a scene far away from Wolf Lair Lodge. He pushed the tray away and asked for a bottle of *slivovitz*. He downed two quick glasses and then descended to the cave.

"What is it old man?" one of his lieutenants asked.

"The Germans know we have the crew from the downed plane. Their scouts counted the ten parachutes. They didn't find any of them. They know we picked them up. They arrested Manja and Boris. They were tortured for hours. Neither one broke. They didn't even know where we have the air crews. It was too dangerous to tell them. This morning they were found hanging from that big tree in front of city hall. Manja had a note penned to her blouse.

*"Any citizen found harboring American pilots will be arrested and executed. Their families will be imprisoned, and their property confiscated. Every day that the Americans are not delivered to the German authorities will result in the arrest and execution of two Split citizens."*

"So far they have executed four old men. They have four teenage boys in jail." Anton said, his voice cracking with emotion. "They stood the old men up before a firing squad and shot them in cold blood. Now they have declared a moratorium on the killings if someone comes forward in the next week. They think someone will break. No one has. Better to die fighting the cowardly bastards. I think they realize if the killings resume there will be an armed uprising in town. I heard someone say that there were mortars and machine guns hidden on the monastery mountain. It's better to die fighting than to be slaughtered like sheep.

# 16

# Rescue

"I'm going back to Split tomorrow," Vladic said. It had been six weeks since the discovery of Manja and Boris hanging from a tree. "Draza got a radio message from the Americans in Egypt. They are aware of the airmen we have here. An officer who is a specialist in rescue operations will be parachuted in tomorrow night. His assignment is to help us plan a rescue mission. His plane is coming out of Bitter Lake. They'll come up across the Aegean and Albania, over the thinly populated mountains. The drop will take place in a large open field to the west in a mountain valley. Practically no one lives in the area. The farm has been abandoned since 1939. We are to set up a 100-meter circle of flambeaus. If all goes as planned, we'll have him back here at the lodge by dawn. Now I'm going to bed. It's been a very sad and tiring day, but there's hope for tomorrow."

The nine survivors gathered in a room off the dormitory. It buzzed with their animated excitement and speculation ran rampant. David called for quiet. He attempted to inject a dose of reality into the wild discussions. They had been cooped up in this lodge for over two months and tempers had begun to fray.

"Look, it's a long way from trying to get someone dropped in here to us actually getting out. Just tone it down a bit until he gets here, and we have some idea of what the plans are. Okay."

The others grudgingly agreed and returned to their low-stakes poker game. Everyone was keyed up and sleep was the last thing on their minds right now. Their edginess was compounded by fear that the lodge might be raided, and their lair discovered before a rescue could take place. The fact that the Germans knew they were in Macedonia and had been in Split heightened their concerns. It seemed unlikely that the commanders there knew they were so far away.

News had filtered in about the successes of "Operation Husky." Sicily was under Allied control. The Ninth Air Force was moving to bases on the Italian boot, closer to Wolf Lair, just across the Adriatic. Many in the room, now grizzled veterans, looked forward to completing their 35 missions and going home. Their years in active combat had aged them all. Battle scars and worry lines were etched into their twenty-something brows. Those young, smooth-faced boys, who had crossed the Danube a year ago on the Halpro mission, were now transformed into haggard, sunken eyed men—too young to have witnessed so much—too young to be so old.

Their vacant eyes stared blankly into an innocent past and saw scenes from a carefree life; running through green fields, kissing young girls in back seats at the drive-in, scoring a winning touchdown—the things young American boys did growing up. Macedonia and Romania were far-off splotches on a map that Mr. Tichenor pulled down from the ceiling in geography class. That innocence had died with the sight of the first mangled, smoking corpse they dragged from a burning plane.

Jovan Vladic, commander of the Chetnik brigade in Macedonia, waited at the edge of the field as his men deployed the flare pots in the proposed landing circle. The thirty pots were enough to frame the landing zone and yet be transported without raising suspicions. The flambeaus, normally used for roadside warnings, were a common sight along Macedonia's pock-marked highways.

At precisely midnight the drone of a twin-engine transport plane was heard clearing the last peak to the southwest. Two minutes later a green light flashed a code from 5,000 feet. Vladic sent his men out to light the flares, creating a large bull's eye for the jumper. The plane circled then began a slow, helical descent into the pastoral valley. The engine sound swelled as the pilot began his final approach over the circle of light. A dark, silk parachute billowed as it floated gently to earth and the sounds of the plane's engines retreated into the western night.

Major Thomas Lancover, 33, West Pointer, 1st Ranger Battalion, specialist in martial arts, clandestine operations and explosives, stuck his landing in the middle of the bull's-eye. Lancover reported directly to Colonel William Darby. Darby was the commander of all Ranger forces. Earlier, Darby had been chosen to establish and then command that elite group. He formed his operation at a remote training camp in Scotland.

Lancover had moved with Darby to his new HQ at Bari, Italy following the Ranger successes in North Africa and Sicily. He was in the office of Major General Terry de la Mesa Allen when Major Donohue came in excitedly waving a communiqué. Donohue was OSS station head. Allen read the message then summoned Colonel Darby.

"Bill, our folks in Egypt have received information that one of the B-24 crews from the Ploesti raid has been rescued in Macedonia. They're holed up in a hunting lodge with their rescuers, a band of Chetnik partisans. They want to know if we can help them. Any ideas?"

"General," Darby said, "from what I remember Macedonia is a very isolated country and sparsely populated. It's separated from the Med by Albania which is even more mountainous and remote. I think it might be possible to insert one of my Rangers into the area to coordinate a rescue mission. We can equip him with cryptographic radio equipment to communicate with one of our destroyers in the Adriatic. "

"I will defer to Colonel Darby's expertise in operations like this," Allen's aide Colonel Mullins said. "Why don't I get a map of the area and let's see what we're talking about."

He returned with a rolled-up map of the Balkan Peninsula. He spread it on the map table thereby obscuring the battle plans for Patton's push up the spine of Italy. Mullins sat ash trays on the curled-up corners.

"Here we are in Southern Italy," Darby said, placing his index finger on Bari. "It looks like a straight run to Macedonia, mostly over water. We'll enter Albanian air space well north of

~ 424 ~

Tirana, the capital, to avoid their population centers. The run is only 350 miles. We can be in and out in a few hours. We've got a Lockheed Lodestar that could make the round trip with plenty to spare. We've used it for a lot of jumps behind enemy lines. It runs pretty quiet. I think it's a perfect fit for this operation.

"Okay, Colonel, let me run this up to Patton. If he gives the go ahead you've got yourself a mission," the two-star said. "Be thinking about who you want to send on this little adventure, Colonel. I suspect you have several qualified candidates."

"You're looking at him, General," Darby said, pointing to Major Lancover. "He's been on so many of these clandestine operations behind enemy lines that this one will be a piece-of-cake. Right, Tom?"

"I don't know about the piece-of-cake part, but it should be a fairly routine extraction. Looking at the map, I expect the toughest part will be finding a suitable landing site. It looks pretty rugged around there."

Two days later General Allen received a curt reply from Patton.

*'Permission granted, Terry. Just don't let this interfere with your basic mission.*

*George'*

General Allen called Darby back to his HQ.

"Okay, Colonel, you have a go on Macedonia. Put together your plan and have it on my desk by tomorrow morning and bring Lancover with you."

Darby handed Allen the folder he was holding.

"Here General, we worked this all out yesterday."

"Now that's what I call efficiency," Allen smiled.

Darby found Lancover on the training field. He was leading a company of embryonic Rangers in hand-to-hand combat drills.

"Tom, put someone else in charge of the training. We have a go on Macedonia. I gave Allen the dossier we worked up yesterday. He's reviewing it. We'll go over it with him in the morning."

"Yes sir. Moore, take over. Run them for another half-hour and then break. I'll check with you later." Several of the new men were replacements for the valiant men lost at Gela, Sicily.

"What do you think, Lancover," General Allen asked as they gathered around his table, "do you think you can do this?"

"General Allen I finished my five-year tour after the Academy and then went to work for the United Fruit Company in Costa Rica. We had to spend days getting from the airport in San Jose to the plantations. The local manager asked me if I could build a dirt strip that could handle medium size transports. Well, I got together a hundred campesinos, fifty mules and dozens of dirt pan excavators. We spent two months clearing a spot in the jungle and then leveled it to make a 2500-foot runway. Three months after we felled that first tree I flew the president of the company into that field. A C-60 can take off in less than a thousand feet on a solid grass field, fifteen hundred to clear a 50-foot barrier at the end of the runway. I guess if we can find a 2,500-foot-long pasture we can get a C-60 up, then circle until we achieve an altitude to clear the peaks around it. The trick will be to set that up without tipping our hand to the Krauts flying over.

"Sir, I believe if I can get in there without being seen. Then I can extract those guys. We certainly have to try. It's the least we can do after the hell they saw in Ploesti. A lot will depend on the Yugoslavs and how much help they can give me."

"I'm glad to hear you say that," Allen said. "We can have that Lodestar C-60 here in three days. In the meantime, get together a list of the material you will need and have the quartermaster assemble it for you. I've given orders that whatever you need takes top priority. The OSS guys are providing a crypto radio. If anything goes haywire there's a self-destruct mechanism in the radio. Just push the button and stand back. If the ship can't raise you every six hours they're going to push the button for you. Don't let it out of your sight for a minute. Never transmit for more than two minutes. We don't know the Krauts RDF capabilities. Finally, as I'm sure you're aware; this whole caper is super hush-hush. Don't discuss it with anyone who's not on the mission."

"Mum's the word sir. I'll be back here by nine with my final plans and my list of equipment. Thank you for the confidence you and Colonel Darby have placed in me for this mission. I won't let you down."

"Okay Darby, it sounds like Lancover is your man for the job. You may proceed on your own. Just let me know when you plan to execute so we can alert all the other elements involved."

"Yes sir, General, it looks like Friday is the optimum date," Lancover said. "When the plane gets here we'll get it loaded up for a 22:00 takeoff. They're expecting me at midnight. Friday will be moonless. Hopefully we can sneak in without being spotted."

"We'll keep you briefed General," Darby said as the two rose to leave.

He invited Lancover to his quarters for a nightcap. He still had two bottles of Scotch from Benghazi.


"Get those lights out. Hurry," Jovan Vladic barked. "Can't have some German scout plane picking up our position."

Lancover was shucking his harness when Vladic got to him.

"Welcome to Macedonia Major," Vladic said. Stepanovich translated.

"Thanks, Colonel. I sure was glad to see that circle of light blossom under us. I don't want to get lost in Yugoslavia with all those Germans lurking around."

"I agree Major, but we prefer to be called Macedonians. We've never accepted that we're part of Yugoslavia. That merger of nations was a huge mistake. We hope to achieve our old autonomy when this is all over. All right, enough politics, let's get you back to Wolf Lair."

He ordered his men to load the flares on the truck and take them back to the cave.

"We'll follow in the car."

The upper halves of their headlights were painted over to limit visibility from above. The vehicles bounced across the rocky field, making their way back to the farm road. After a mile, the road inclined up to the paved main road. The little valley was virtually invisible to the outside world—except from the air. It was twenty minutes back to the Wolf Lair turn-off. At one in the morning, the gate creaked open to allow the car inside. Most of the Americans were still up, sitting around the poker table. No one thought of sleep while the means for their escape was imminent.

"Lieutenant Weiss, this is Major Thomas Lancover. "

"How do you do sir? How'd it go?"

"The drop went off like clockwork thanks to these fine gentlemen," Lancover said.

"As you can imagine we've been on pins and needles. We're all going stir-crazy here with nothing to do but wait."

"All his stuff is on the truck sir," George said. "It'll be here shortly. They had to clean up the drop zone first."

"I hope we can pull this off, Weiss. I know you all have cabin fever here. Doesn't look like a bad place to hole up. Probably better than one of those Stalags we hear about.

"I know you guys must be tuckered out. I know I am. Point me toward a bunk and I'll fill you in on the plans in the morning."

"Sure thing Major. There's an extra cot in my quarters. Why don't you bunk there? Someone will bring your gear in when the truck gets here. Okay everybody hit the sack. We've got a big day coming up tomorrow."

The sun was breaking over the eastern peaks when Major Lancover sat down to breakfast the next morning. He began to explain the plan to the officers and the Chetniks.

"Colonel Vladic, it was too dark last night for me to get a good look at the field. Is it large enough for a 2500-foot landing strip?"

"The valley is about 1000 meters long. The cleared farm-land is probably 800 meters. You might get a 750-meter strip in. The peaks around the valley are 1000 to 1500 meters above the valley floor. Clearing them on takeoff will be tricky."

"Is the field reasonably level and clear?"

"It slopes down about 20 meters end-to-end. There are several large boulders the farmer couldn't move."

"What can you arrange in the way of equipment to help clear them out?"

"We have a couple of two-horse wagons that we use to transport the hunters. There's an old tractor stored in a barn at the field. It was abandoned by the farmer. I don't know what condition it's in."

"We got any crack mechanics in this crowd?" Lancover asked, looking around.

"Pearson and Tyler were in aircraft maintenance before becoming gunners," Dave said. "They're pretty good."

"We have a motor mechanic here at the lodge," Pavic added. "He's good."

"Great, we'll go over there today and see what needs do-ing. Round up the mechanics and their tools. We'll take them over with us. We'd better dress the part of farmers. How will you get the horses over?"

"We have a large horse trailer. We can keep them in that barn," Pavic answered.

"We'll take ten men over," the major said, "including the mechanics. We'll work in shifts. No more than four men in the open at a time. Make sure there are at least two men in each work party that speaks the local language. We might attract visitors. Can we get the horses and machinery over tonight?"

"Yes, we'll start preparations right away. I think the job will take about five days, assuming we can get the tractor going," Anton said. "I regret that I have to go to Skopje today. I'll be back tomorrow night."

The flash of the sun's corona as it fell below the western mountains was the signal for the convoy to set out. Four trucks left Wolf Lair at ten-minute intervals. They delivered the "farm workers" and horses to the field and returned before ten. Bunks, cots and a steno stove were set up in the old corn crib. Three men began digging a latrine under the shelter of oak trees nearby. They equipped it with a couple of rusty barrels. Shades of Benghazi they thought.

The heavy lifting began at dawn. Most of the stones could be handled by two or three men together. The larger ones were skidded by teams of horses. The really large ones—there there were four—awaited the recalcitrant tractor. Just after noon on day two there came a sputtering cough from the tractor shed. The old, two-lung, Fordson tractor rumbled to life amid shouts of jubilation from the mechanics.

The "farmers" had rigged a sledge and ramp to accommodate the large boulders. The ribbed-steel wheels dug into the clay soil as the Fordson strained to roll the stones onto the sledge. The second day ended with half the field cleared and two of the boulders intact. Finishing the task in two more days would be tight.

Lancover returned to the field at dusk the next day to survey the progress.

"Can you guys finish by tomorrow night?" he asked.

"We'll have it done sir! We want to get out of here!"

"Okay, I'm going to fire up the radio on the way back to Wolf Lair and contact the USS Buck off the coast of Albania. I will ask them to have the Lodestar here at midnight Friday. It'll take a few hours to relay and decode the message. We should have an answer shortly after I get back to the lodge."

The black cryptographic box came to life at thirteen minutes past ten. It spewed out a half-inch wide, yellow, paper tape with a series of four-letter, undecipherable words—gibberish to anyone unfamiliar with the code. Lancover ran the tape through a special decoding template that translated it into plain English.

"Gentlemen, your chariot will arrive as scheduled."

Lancover read the message to the men who were eagerly watching. Their response was so boisterous that David had to admonish to keep it down. The reprimand in no way diminished their enthusiasm. Men were clapping each other on the back and raising their drinks in toast to their imminent freedom. In less than forty-eight hours they would be airborne and on their way to friendlier confines, assuming no slip-ups.


A German listening post on Corfu picked up the return message to Lancover. The duty signalman passed the series of dots and dashes on to the watch officer. Oberlieutnant Heinrich Mueller fired up his 1000-watt transmitter and forwarded the re-coded message to Berlin. Code breakers in an underground bunker began the daunting task of trying to decipher the meaningless jumble of letters. Well past midnight a red-eyed cryptologist ran into his commanding officer's office jubilantly waving a sheet of paper.

"Sir, we've broken the code. It says the Americans are sending a plane into Macedonia to rescue some downed airmen. It doesn't give co-ordinates, but the message was relayed from an American destroyer in the Adriatic Sea. Our guess is that they'll be flying over the destroyer. It's north of Corfu. The plane will probably come from Sicily or southern Italy. We should be able to pick it up and track it to Macedonia."

"Good work, Hauptman Werner. Get this distributed to all affected commands. I'll notify Field Marshal Goering. I'm sure he'll want to prepare a little surprise for them." This will be a real feather in Colonel Willie Hess' cap with the Luftwaffe high command, he mused. There might even be a generalship in the offing.

The C-60 Lodestar lifted off the tarmac at Bari with a crew of four – pilot, co-pilot, engineer/radioman and a Ranger. They set a staggered course, first southeast toward Corfu then northwest toward Dubrovnik, then southeast again toward Macedonia. If their transmissions had been intercepted this should add some confusion for the Germans. They passed over the Buck before turning northwest and entered Albanian airspace north of Tirana. They flew in radio silence. At midnight Lancover was to activate a homing beacon at the end of the new runway which emitted a conic signal skyward. When the Lodestar passed over the mouth of the cone, its receiver would respond to a coded signal from the beacon. The same green light signal used before would alert the Chetniks to light the flambeaus lining the hastily prepared strip. All was in readiness.


Four of the newest German *Messerschmitt* 109s circled over central Albania, the sliver of new moon their only illumination. They received the agreed upon signal from the radar station on Corfu.

"The lamb is ready for the slaughter."

This was followed by a series of numbers, the co-ordinates and the altitude of the intruder when it had entered Albanian airspace. The 109s were twenty-five miles north of the Lodestar, flying at 5,000 feet. The lead plane peeled off toward the target. Six minutes later he picked up the faint, blue glow from the C-60s exhaust gases.

"There she is! Let's go!"

Hauptman Gerhard Prosser was unaware that his was not the only fighter squadron aloft over western Albania this night. "Operation Haystack" had deployed four P-51s to ride shotgun for the Lodestar. Captain James Patterson, at 20,000 feet, intercepted the radio transmissions of the 109 below him. He waggled his wings and nosed his P-51 over into a steep dive. Charles Dryden, Clarence Jamison and Sidney Brooks, three fellow Tuskegee Airmen, followed their Red Tail leader.

Hauptman Prosser brought his plane around, lining up on the tail of the C-60. He toggled the switch that armed his twin machine guns. His crosshairs found the rear stabilizer of his prey. He lifted the cover and placed his thumb on the trigger. He began to press down slowly, savoring the kill. A stream of tracers lit up the night sky—from James Patterson's wing guns. The fiery snake of 50-millimeter shells raked Prosser's plane from cowl to aileron. One entered the pilot's left rib cage and exited through his right arm, spraying flesh and blood across the inside of the canopy. The 109 came apart in midair, crashing seconds later into an unnamed Albanian peak.

The other 109s broke off their attack to engage the Red Tails. Lieutenant Dryden passed under the Lodestar and leveled off. An oncoming 109 pulled up to avoid a collision, exposing its belly to the Yonker's ace. Two quick bursts to the belly tanks disintegrated the plane. It was a massive ball of flame when it plowed into an alpine lake below. The two remaining Germans, their leader and his wingman gone, wisely broke off the engagement and headed back to their base in northern Italy. The Red Tails formed a protective shield around the C-60 and escorted it to the landing zone.

The radioman listened intently for the Morse code series from the beacon. The ground was barely discernible from this altitude and topographical features were impossible to see. The altimeter was passing through ten-thousand feet when the red beacon light flashed. The radioman tapped the pilot, Fred Newlin, on the shoulder and pointed down.

"There it is Captain. We're over the strip."

Newlin began a slow turn to port while the signalman punched in the coded signal bursts of green light. Almost instantly thirty flares burst into flame, illuminating the rustic runway. Newlin began a helical spiral downward to avoid the surrounding peaks. When the altimeter read 4500 feet, Newlin ran a downwind leg and made a 180 degree turn, lining up with the field. He placed the nose on a path bifurcating the flares, lowered the landing gear and began to add flaps. The venerable craft slowed, almost reaching its stall speed as they passed through 4,000 feet. Major Lancover's altimeter measurements had been extremely precise. At 3,985 feet the wheels touched down and the plane began to bounce along the rough field, coming to a stop 250 feet short of the last flambeau. Newlin whipped the plane around and taxied back to the other end of the runway. He wheeled around once more to position the plane for takeoff into the wind. Two lorries rolled up to the plane. The crew jumped down and ran toward the plane, bounding aboard. David Weiss turned and embraced Anton Vladic.

"Colonel I don't know how to thank you for what you've done. I'll be back when this war's over and Macedonia is free again. God bless you and all your men."

George Stepanovich finished translating and the last two men scrambled aboard. Newlin rammed the throttle forward and the C-60 lurched down the runway to begin its reverse helix out of the valley. Two red-tailed P-51s roared across the valley as the rescue plane cleared the last hurdle, positioning themselves on either side for the run to Bari.

The Bari Air Force Base PA system hissed and crackled.

"Flght Offficer Murray Weiss you have a visitor."

# The End

# Epilogue

David folded the fragile, yellowed letter and replaced it in the envelope. He walked back into the house and crossed the hallway to the alcove where the phone rested. He lifted it from the cradle and dialed. A familiar voice came on the other end.

"Murray, you're not going to believe this."

\*\*\*\*

Alfred Von Gerstenberg was captured by the Russians. He died in a Siberian prison.


Draza Mihailovich was betrayed by the British. He was tried for treason by Josip Broz Tito, the communist dictator of Yugoslavia, and executed by a firing squad.

\*\*\*\*

# In Memoriam

Addison Baker received the Medal of Honor, posthumously.

John Jerstad received the Medal of Honor posthumously.

Lloyd Hughes received the Medal of Honor posthumously.

Leon Johnson received the Medal of Honor.

John "Killer" Kane received the Medal of Honor.

Every man on the Tidal Wave Mission received The Distinguished Flying Cross.

Four-hundred-and-thirty Purple Hearts were awarded.

2,500 decorations in all were awarded for this single mission.

## To the Fallen of Ploesti

To you who fly on forever I send that part of me which cannot be separated and is bound to you for all time. I send to you those of our hopes and dreams that never quite came true, the joyous laughter and showery tears of our boyhood, the marvelous mysteries of our adolescence, the glorious strength and tragic illusions of our young manhood, all these that were and perhaps would have been, I leave in your care, out there in the Blue.

John Riley Kane, Colonel, U.S.A.F. (Ret)

Made in the USA
Middletown, DE
19 June 2018